ESCAPE to the ISLANDS

ESCAPE to the ISLANDS

a novel

Russell Clark

Islandtude
Tropical Adventures

Escape to the Islands

Published by Gatekeeper Press
2167 Stringtown Rd, Suite 109
Columbus, OH 43123-2989
www.GatekeeperPress.com

The editorial work for this book is entirely the product of the author. Gatekeeper Press did not participate in and is not responsible for any aspect of this element.

Library of Congress Control Number: 2021901123

ISBN (hardcover): 9781662909139
ISBN (paperback): 9781662909146
eISBN: 9781662909153

Cover Photo by Michelle Bailey Webster

ONE

SYLVIE LAY IN bed, dreaming of great riches. She had created the perfect plan and was about to begin the riskiest segment. After pretending to pass out from too much alcohol, she waited for Harrington to fall asleep, giving her the opportunity to complete her mission. With him asleep, she could go to his safe, find the information she sought, and leave his villa a rich woman. She looked at the prone figure beside her, and was comforted by the sounds of steady, heavy breathing.

Sylvie wormed her way to the edge of the king-size bed, and summoning her courage, slipped her painted toes out from under the sheet. She hesitated, then stepped on the cool tile below. She surveyed the room before beginning her search.

A few stars and patchy clouds were visible through the large bedroom window. The nearly full moon shone brightly on her deeply tanned skin. She held her breath as she tiptoed to the foot of the bed, nervously combing her fingers through her thick auburn hair. It was two o'clock in the morning and she decided she could no longer delay.

She silently slipped to the doorway, intently watching the sleeping Harrington. Looking over her shoulder, she stepped into the hallway and hurried to the study.

The safe was in the study closet. She prayed that any noise she made would be masked by the steady rhythm of the sounds of the tropics.

The light from the hallway was sufficient for her to see. She reached the safe and her manicured fingers carefully worked the combination. She eased the safe door open and rifled through the piles of papers. Several files looked promising and she collected four of them to quickly scan. She sat naked on the floor of the walk-in closet, then shifted her weight to her knees and elbows and began reading through the first file. Although the file made for mildly interesting reading, there was nothing of use.

She peeked back into the bedroom before beginning the second file. With still no movement, she opened the file and began to read. It also contained nothing that she hoped to find. Her frustration crept up as the fear of failure and of being caught increased.

Sylvie lifted the third file to the hallway light. She could not understand the contents. Her native French was no help, as much of the document was in Dutch.

As she opened the final file, her breath caught in her throat. The night had become still and the steady sound of heavy breathing had stopped. She felt anxious and was too nervous to continue reviewing the contents of the safe. Leaving the files on the floor, she bolted back to the bedroom. Sylvie stood at the bedroom doorway praying for all to be well. Standing as still as possible, she heard rustling from the bed.

Her fear turned into panic. She quickly strode back into the study. The four files were deftly gathered and hurriedly returned to the safe. She went into the bathroom as planned and flushed the toilet. Walking back into the bedroom, she tried to simulate the grogginess of sleep. She slipped back under the sheet and laid her head heavily on the pillow. Harrington's voice alarmed her.

"Having trouble sleeping?"

"No. Just had to go to the bathroom."

"Are you feeling well?"

"Oh yes." She forced a yawn. "Just sleepy."

"You seem to be sweating. Do you think you have a fever?"

"No. Well maybe a slight one. I guess I do feel a little under the weather. I'll be fine though." She yawned again. "Probably be good as new in the morning."

"Well then, try to go back to sleep. It's possibly just too much alcohol. Let me know if you need anything."

He lay on his back looking at the cathedral ceiling. His disappointment of the uneventful night continued, with now a concern that it was more than just the alcohol. What was she up to? He began wondering if her visit had a hidden agenda. He considered the possibilities as he drifted back off to sleep.

TWO

AS THE AMERICAN Airlines 757 jumbo jet approached its island destination, the deep blue ocean below became an alluring turquoise. The flight from Miami to St. Maarten had been uneventful; no panicked seniors, no screaming children, and no elbow duels to determine armrest dominance. The packaged airline food was good, and the calm spring day had permitted an especially smooth flight. Life in the islands was about to begin.

Packed among the beautiful people of the near capacity flight, Ben Carlisle tucked his Randy Wayne White novel in his carry-on bag wedged under the seat in front of him and prepared to land. *Not long now* he thought. Visions of swaying palms on white sand beaches were about to become a reality. Ben's friend, Nico, originally from the Abacos in the Bahamas, had made arrangements for Ben to stay at the new resort l'Hotel Lubrique. Nico shared with its owner that Ben was a successful businessman and could possibly share some helpful business knowledge, adding to the financial success of the new resort.

The new resort was in Saint Martin, the French side of the smallest inhabited island claimed by two nations, France and the Netherlands. L'Hotel Lubrique emphasized personal attention to its guests, living into the island's "Friendly

Island" slogan. Ben was looking forward to learning more about the island and the start-up of the new resort.

Ben needed a break from the pressures of work after long hours studying his investment monitors over the past year. It had paid off in a big way, with him making more in several trades than he imagined his total pay could be for several decades. Although he could easily afford a deluxe hotel, Ben cherished the idea of being at the smaller l'Hotel Lubrique. He trusted Nico's selection for him, and was excited to be one of the early guests at the recently finished resort.

Ben sat on the port side of the plane and could see the island as the landing gear was deployed and locked for landing. It was a beautiful view of the island and bay, with a quick descent seemingly just over the outstretched hands of bikini-clad tourists waving to the pilot and passengers. The plane touched down on the short Princess Juliana Airport runway, slowing to a halt with about 30 yards to spare. Arrived!

The plane quickly unloaded, Ben with only the bag at his feet and a carry-on in the overhead storage. The steps were rolled to the door and all passengers were directed onto the waiting bus to shuttle them to the customs area, a distance that could have been covered more quickly by foot.

The customs line moved rapidly, with a cheerful "Welcome to St. Maarten" or "Welcome Home" greeting each new arrival. Ben walked through the sliding door into the passenger pickup area. There he saw Nico, his customary huge grin and happy shining eyes spotting Ben. "Welcome to my home!" Nico gave the slightly larger man his biggest bear hug.

"Thanks Nico, it's so good to be here! Thanks for meeting me and taking me to Lubrique. I'm eager to get settled in and can check on a rental car tomorrow."

The two friends rode the twenty-minute trip to the new resort in Nico's multi-dented white Toyota sedan. Needing to meet a client on the Dutch side of the island, Nico dropped off Ben at the resort with a goodbye hug and promises to return the next day. Ben walked into the small lobby, and the informal check-in went quickly. The owner/ manager was out on errands, but there was a message he would be back to meet with Ben later that evening.

The resort consisted of a series of chalets, all one-floor only. With its 50 rooms, Lubrique was more an intimate lodge than a traditional hotel. Ben found his room, painted a tropical yellow with pale green highlights, overlooking the beach. He set his toiletries on the bathroom sink counter and decided unpacking his clothes would come later, if at all. It was time to slip on a pair of plain solid blue swim trunks, no designer name visible, and walk the sand dotted with crotons and flowering plants to the inviting beach just ahead. With the late afternoon sun lower in the sky, there was no need to apply sunscreen.

The beach was a beautiful bright white, the fine sand smooth and soothing to the feet. Placing the oversized beach towel in the sand, it was time to relax and allow sand gravity to work its magic. Orient Beach, the beautiful white crescent, measured 1.3 miles along the eastern coast of the island. The traditionally clothing-optional beach had become topless only for the large majority of the beach, with nudity allowed only on the portion previously occupied by Club Orient. Following the devastation of Hurricane Irma, the beach was wiped clean of all structures, including great damage to the Club Orient Chalets, the Perch Bar where snacks and drinks were served to nude bathers, and the restaurant at the southern-most point, Papagayo, where nude diners were the norm. After the island struggled in its comeback, a nudist miracle occurred, with the entire stretch of Orient Beach welcoming nude bathers, fueling an economic recovery for the area. L'Hotel Lubrique now occupied the former Club Orient grounds. The structure was small and charming, but with more luxury than the prior chalets had provided for decades to its loyal following. Although nudity was allowed, many of the Lubrique guests now were seemingly more modest, with topless more common than nude with the tonier lodging. Ben settled in, and with the elastic of his swim trunks firmly in place, laid back in the sand, to let the late afternoon sun warm his body.

THREE

BEFORE DAYLIGHT, MR. Harrington was already up and in his office. An early riser, 5 a.m. had seen him dress in a long-sleeve orange linen shirt, gold chain around his neck, loose fitting slacks, docksider shoes and no socks. His computer was humming with an array of spreadsheets detailing past expenses and anticipated revenues of his working list of projects. It was to be a busy day, with much money to be made.

At 7 a.m., Sylvie's red-painted toes kicked back the sheet and again left the warmth of the bed. The St. Martin sun had risen just past six, and the day promised to be bright with only a prospect for scattered fluffy clouds. Sylvie padded into the shower of the large master bath, applying body gel as she adjusted warmer the flow from the oversized nozzle. Five minutes later the plush royal blue bath towel absorbed the water from her body and was placed back in the rack. Opening some toothpaste, Sylvie applied a small amount to her right index finger and moved it briskly over her teeth to refresh her mouth. She slipped into her clothes from the previous evening, the blue tropical print island dress of cotton and rayon with its halter top and plunging bare back to just above her waist, thong underwear, and flat sandals. It was time to give a good morning kiss to Mr. Harrington before excusing herself for the day.

Walking into his office, the 5'4" Sylvie leaned and kissed Mr. Harrington on his right cheek. "Good morning Gregorio. I see you're up early this morning."

"Aw, good morning Sylvie. You look as if you've made a full recovery. I trust the last hours of sleep are helping you feel much better this morning?"

"Oh yes, feeling good this morning. Whatever bug seems to have run its course. Certainly, it wasn't the alcohol." She gave a smile and shrug as if explaining the alcohol was responsible for her forward actions. "I'm glad my experience driving after one too many got me here safely last night." The previous evening, Sylvie had followed Harrington to his villa after saying she would love to see where he lived.

"I've promised a visit to spend the day with a girlfriend, so I'll be off with an early start. I need to go by my place before meeting her for breakfast. She arrived on island yesterday, and we have a lot of catching up to do."

"I am sorry your time here was so short. After such a wonderful coincidence of meeting up at the Red Piano last night, I was anticipating we would be seeing a lot more of each other today. The few minutes in my bed last night before you passed out, and then awoke sick, was definitely not what I expected. Especially after you came over and introduced yourself, and we thoroughly enjoyed each other's company at the club. I must say last night was disappointing, and a letdown that you now need to leave so early."

"I'm so sorry... I'll make it up to you. I promise. Give me some time with my dear friend, and then we can see about picking up where we were having such a good time on the dance floor." Sylvie again leaned and kissed her targeted Mr. Harrington on the cheek. "You have been such a gentleman and so understanding. I hope we can pick it back up and see how things develop." Sylvie reached into her tiny clutch, withdrew her car key, and headed out of the office for the safety of her car.

Watching now from the villa entryway as the white Hyundai compact car reversed to leave, Harrington made note of the car description and tag. As Sylvie left the villa, Harrington reached for his phone.

"I am suspicious of the girl. She must be followed. I expect you to perform quietly and efficiently, as always. If my suspicions are correct, take care of the business. If so, after you're done, enjoy yourselves if you like. Have whatever fun you want with our little prize. Just remember - when you've finished, I expect you to be professionals. No leftovers for later. I do not want to know the ending. And make sure no one else will either. The Caribbean Sea is deep blue and continues to cleanse the earth. If more trash must wash away, so be it. Understood? Good. Get to work."

Harrington walked back into his office, put down his phone, and re-entered his computer password. If her visit was part of an untoward plan, she would soon be of no concern.

FOUR

....

THE LATE AFTERNOON sun had now set. Ben picked his towel up off the sand, and after shaking it briskly, folded it and headed back to his room for a quick shower. The plan was for a light meal at the Lubrique restaurant, now affectionately called Papatwo after the rebuilding of the old Papagayo, and then turning in for an early start the next day.

Ben entered his room, stripped out of his still dry trunks from never entering the ocean, and let them drop on the floor beside his queen-size bed. He stepped into the spacious shower with its two shower heads on opposite walls, which provided a cleansing and massaging action on those who entered. The dispensable shampoo and body wash affixed in the shower were liberally applied; first the coconut-scented shampoo, followed by rinsing and then lathering with the melon body wash. Following the shower and a quick brushing of teeth, Ben went into the bedroom and looked through his clothes in his carry-on bag on the floor beside his swim trunks. Pulling on a pair of blue shorts, a red cotton pullover shirt and flip flops, he headed out to Papatwo.

Papatwo had a cathedral ceiling similar to that of its predecessor, but painted white with a hint of rose. There were individual tables with seating for four at the perimeter tables. In the center of the dining hall was a large round table, big enough to allow a dozen diners who would not mind being within elbow touching distance of one another. It was a great design, with the large colorful sign suspended above the table "*Welcome New Friends. Please enjoy meeting other great patrons while sharing a wonderful meal. This is where magical new friendships begin!*"

Taking note of the table and its five diners, Ben continued to the bar to meet the owner of the new resort, Arnaud Temple. Nico had accurately described him as fit, mid-forties, distinguished and with the perfect smile of a TV weatherman. "Good evening, you must be Arnaud. I'm Ben, friend of Nico's."

"It is a pleasure to meet you. Nico spoke highly of you. Please join me at the table over here and become acquainted."

Ben and Arnaud leisurely dined, with Ben sharing his guesses on global interest rates and the expectation of minimal inflation in the major economies. Leading analysts were forecasting improvement for the coming several years in the American and European economies. The importance of strength in the western world was fully understood as needed for the financial success of French St. Martin, Dutch St. Maarten and of particular interest to Arnaud and his new resort. A nice bottle of wine was shared between the new friends at Arnaud's insistence, although Ben was more of a Coors Light man.

"How long is your intended stay? Nico said twelve days, but maybe you think to extend?"

"Yes, I'm way past due for a total escape from work. Looking forward to the time here. Wanting to de-stress, it always takes me a few days to fully relax, and do some thinking on what's next. If my room is still available at the end of the twelve days, I might want to extend awhile if that would be okay."

"Yes, looking forward to see you here from time to time. Let me know what I can do to be of help."

Ben was wearing down from the fatigue of the long day of flying and starting before daylight. The late afternoon time on the beach, followed by the satisfying meal and a couple glasses of wine, helped him to relax sooner than expected. It was time to head back to the room and enjoy a little time with the TV on in the background before calling it a night.

Ben walked the short distance to his room. From his door, he could see the table where he and Arnaud had dined, and beyond to the "new friends" table. There were still a few people gathered there, appearing to enjoy each other's company, with occasional laughter that faintly carried in the sea breeze.

Ben went into his room and looked at the carry-on bag on the floor. The thought of unpacking the few articles of clothing was immediately dismissed. Maybe tomorrow. Ben kicked off his flip flops into a corner of the room so he would not trip on them in the night, and where he would be able to find them in the morning. He undressed, folding his shirt in half, and placed it in the top drawer. Next came the shorts and boxers, placed on top of the shirt. He had only worn them a few hours, and by putting them in the drawer instead of the floor with his swim trunks, they would be good for a few more outings.

The TV was turned on, and a scan through the channels ended with what appeared to be a re-run of some soccer match. Not really interested in watching, it provided a little background noise as he adjusted to the solitude of the room. Sitting on the bed, but not yet turning it down, Ben laid his head back on the pillow and closed his eyes.

The room was very comfortable, the beach amazing, and his location just off the beach and near the dining area was perfect. It promised to be a great escape to the islands.

FIVE

....

IT WAS SATURDAY night in Dutch St. Maarten and a small crowd was beginning to accumulate at the largest casino on the island at Port de Plaisance. The resort and casino were located just on the Dutch side of the border separating French St. Martin from Dutch St. Maarten. Paul and his wife, Lisa, arrived at the casino around 9 p.m. and would again try to beat the odds. They were regulars at the casino. They had won a few big jackpots and continued to play each week on the casino's money.

The casino was managed by Dean Janson, who worked his way up into the powerful position of overseeing all functions and casino profitability. Janson's specialty, prior to becoming the overall head, was to observe the patrons for possible cheating scams. Dean still enjoyed his personal surveillance tours throughout the casino, relying on his years of observing and previously participating in his own cheating scams. He now protected the casino he had cheated out of hundreds of thousands of dollars in prior years.

"Good evening Paul. How are you and your lovely bride this evening? Planning to bring me to my knees tonight?" Dean had observed the duo for months before concluding their success as attributable to the remarkable card counting and constant recalculation-of-odds ability of the former certified public accountant.

"We are awesome! So glad to be here tonight," Lisa replied. Lisa was the more outgoing one of the attractive couple, eager to party and never meeting a stranger. "We'll be doing our best!" Lisa tipped the waitress who brought the first of several customary glasses of Pinot Grigio that Lisa enjoyed each week. Meanwhile, Paul kept sharp while having only an occasional beer.

Dean continued to circulate through the casino, the most lavish on the island. From the mammoth statue and fountain at the casino entrance, to the gold trim and ornate lighting inside, the casino exuded opulence throughout. Although some of the patrons wore casual clothing not typical for inside a casino, the Port de Plaisance casino still attracted a large majority of those looking to dress up for their evening of entertainment.

Dean stopped to observe one of the blackjack tables from a distance. Watching for a while, knowing a successful scam could take many hands where the scammer would play by the rules and lose a number of hands, it was important to watch the interaction of player with dealer. There were many variations of collusion between dealer and player, and Dean knew them all. He continued to observe the table for any signs of one of his dealers going bad before moving on. He continued to rotate through the dealer tables for an hour before making a cursory sweep of each of the stations of slot machines. The slot machines were much more secure than in past years after each had been retro-fitted for the latest software, foiling scams of misreading coins and bills, to the simple scam of attaching a coin to a string and pulling it back once touching to register. Again, Dean had seen them all.

Dean's possible only weak spot, which could potentially allow a scam to be successfully pulled, was his penchant for beautiful women. He recognized this weakness in himself, and typically did not allow himself to be distracted by the plunging necklines or hip-hugging miniskirts frequently worn by some of the vacationers. Dean had a very attractive wife who previously partnered with him in procuring large paydays from casinos and through other scams. Despite the beauty of his wife, Dean was never content. His roving eye was always there. If needed, Dean calculated how his suave appearance and use of his wealth would attract a new beautiful conquest.

Dean spotted the beautiful woman at one of the slot machines. He lingered, looking at her plunging neckline and the dangling gold pendant that now was securely wedged between her ample breasts. She had a glass of complimentary wine at the small table beside the machine. As he watched, he saw a spirit in her that was hard to resist. Several friends were gathered around to cheer her on each time she pulled the arm of the machine to activate the reels. Each time a spin came up a winner, her friends were rewarded by her opening her dress and flashing the goods. She would cradle each breast with a hand from below, move them up and down, and say in a falsetto voice "we won, we won" as if they were the puppets of her ventriloquism. She would then tuck the girls back in, smile at her adoring friends, and reach for the arm for another spin. While this was happening, elsewhere in the casino, the scam of the night was underway.

At the roulette table, the perpetrator had been profiting by his sleight-of-hand. The cheating scam was a practice called past posting. The talented player had the deft sleight-of-hand skills common to practiced magicians. He would place his bet on red or black by placing a stack of chips. When he chose the non-winning color, the magical cheat would do nothing. When he won, he would replace one or two of the chips at the bottom of his wager with a larger value chip. He would occasionally begin with a larger value chip at the bottom of the stack and allow it to be lost to reduce suspicion, intermittently having all of uniform value, and other times having larger values below the lower value chips stacked above. It was also important to position where the camera was blocked during the switch. After coming out ahead, the crooked magician ended his run at the table to cash in his chips. As he waited to receive several thousand dollars of winnings, the dealer also left the table and reported that there was a possible problem. He had not seen the trick to confirm what had been done, but knew the luck of such winnings would be extremely improbable.

Dean was notified. He saw Paul and Lisa and shared the dealer's suspicions with Paul. Paul was taking a break and sipping a Coors Light while Lisa squealed a victory cry with a nice jackpot at the machine. He smiled at Dean and shook his head in empathy.

The crooked magician was tall and slender, his 160 pounds spread over his 6'2" body. He gathered his winnings and walked out the grand casino entrance on his way to the dark parking lot.

As he neared his car, the tall man went down with a thud. Paul had waited in the shadows. In addition to being a CPA, Paul was also a former state wrestling champion. With the take-down, the thief was both lightheaded and nauseous, fading in and out of consciousness. Paul rolled him over onto his stomach, and planted a knee firmly into the small of his back.

He went through the crook's wallet and extracted only the thirty-two hundred dollars that was paid out at

the casino. As had been done several times before, half
would be given to Dean as recovery for the casino and half
retained by Paul as his collection fee. Before leaving, Paul
pulled the man off the ground, and folded him over the
trunk of his car. He remained there for several minutes
after Paul left, wondering what happened.

SIX

IT WAS A beautiful night in St. Martin. Ben reclined on
his bed and let his mind wander. After ten years as a bond
trader, he wondered about his future. Could he really face
going back, trying to survive the long pressure-filled days
and the worry-filled nights? His thoughts were interrupted
by a knock at the door.

"Just a minute." He looked in his small bag, grabbed
a faded pair of gym shorts, slipped them on and walked
to the door. He had not expected a visitor. Perhaps it was
Arnaud just making sure everything was well.

"Hi," she said as he opened the door. "Hope it's not
too late, but just wanted to stop by and maybe chat."

It was 10:30 p.m. He recognized her but did not know
her name. She appeared to be a little nervous, shifting her
weight from foot to foot.

"No. Come on in."

"Thanks. My name is Lauren…"

"Pleased to meet you Lauren. I'm Ben."

Ben had seen Lauren on the beach earlier in the day.
Tonight, Lauren wore a green t-back tank top and white,
mid-thigh shorts.

"Here, have a seat on the couch." Ben directed her
to the moderately comfortable pastel sleeper-sofa. His
unit consisted of a small bedroom, a smaller sitting area/

kitchen combination, and a generous sized bathroom with tub and shower.

Lauren gracefully crossed over to the couch and sat. Slipping out of her flip flops, she tucked her feet beneath her bottom.

Lauren looked about twenty-four years old. Her fair skin was slightly pink from the day of sunning, the hint of a tan beginning to show. Her blond hair, golden with a hint of red, was freshly shampooed and fell damply about her face. With a few freckles across her nose, she was the epitome of the All-American girl.

Ben sat in the chair that was positioned at a ninety-degree angle to the sofa. He was not sure what to say next.

Lauren began, "I saw you at the beach this afternoon, and again tonight having dinner with Mr. Temple. My friend was with me earlier, and will be going home tomorrow. I was just a little nervous about being alone here after she leaves, and a little bored tonight. I hope you don't mind my being forward and just stopping by unexpected."

Ben was thinking how nice-looking she was. "No, I'm glad you stopped by. How do you like the resort?"

"It's great! This is my first trip to St. Martin. It definitely won't be my last, though. What brings you to l'Hotel Lubrique?"

"I just needed a break. I've been working sixty-hour weeks much of the last three months and felt like I just had to get away for a while. Would you like something to eat or drink?"

"Oh, I'm fine. Are you having something?"

"Maybe a Red Stripe. Want one? Or maybe a soft drink?"

"Okay. Yeah. Maybe I'll have part of a Red Stripe."

Ben crossed over to the refrigerator to get the beers. "Would you like a glass? I can't vouch for how clean the glasses are."

"No, that's okay. A glass isn't necessary."

Ben returned with the two beers and again sat in the chair. He leaned toward her, giving her one of the cold Red Stripes.

"Thanks." Lauren took a sip. She remained very much a lady.

Ben took a couple of gulps, letting the beer bathe his throat. "No problem. Hope Red Stripe is okay. That's the only beer I've got right now. Maybe tomorrow I'll go to the local grocery and get a few things."

"This is fine. I didn't really come over to get something to drink, anyway." She took another sip. "Are you sure you don't mind me dropping in like this?"

"No, not at all. I was just kind of unwinding. Just sitting back, sort of meditating. Listening to the wind and the sea sounds. It's very relaxing."

He took another couple of swallows of beer. His was almost gone. "So, tell me Lauren. Where are you from?"

"I'm from a small town in Nebraska. What about you?"

"I'm from Florida. Been living there about twelve years now." With the statement, Ben began to think about the age difference. He must be a decade older than Lauren. "Have you ever been to Florida?"

"No. I'm sure it's great though. I've never even been to Disney in Orlando."

"What does one do for fun in Nebraska? Isn't that a big farming state?"

"Yeah. Nebraska is known as the Cornhusker state. For fun we have a big tractor pull each spring, right about now. In a tractor pull the drivers pull a weight-transfer shed, and whoever pulls the furthest, wins. Although the one we have isn't famous like the Boilermaker Tractor Pull, it's just as fun." She paused. "What do you do in Florida?"

"I'm a bond trader for a big insurance company. I also trade financial futures and options." As he said it, Ben felt his response sounded way too dry. He hoped he was not losing her to boredom. *But what could be more boring than a tractor pull? Was she kidding?* "How long are you going to be in St. Martin?"

"I got here a couple days ago. I'm scheduled to fly back after my two weeks are up."

Another twelve days sounded good. Ben made a mental note that her last day of vacation would be the same as his. He hoped she did not think he seemed boring.

Ben shifted in his chair, finished off his beer, and placed the bottle on the floor. He looked at Lauren as she took another sip. She was over half done with hers. "I might get one more. Are you sure you don't want a snack? What about a fresh beer?"

"No. I'm fine."

Ben opened the refrigerator and retrieved his second Red Stripe. He truly felt great. He looked at her as he sat, enjoying the beauty of her clear blue eyes. She seemed even better looking now. He was glad he was in pretty good shape. The age difference did not seem too bad.

"I see you have some books sticking out of your bag. Planning on doing a lot of reading?"

"I like to read. Adventures mostly. Don't know how much time I'll have to do it, though. But a few good books and an exotic getaway are a great combination."

"Yeah. My guess, though, is the books won't get much of a workout this week," Lauren said, smiling. "With the setting here and the opportunities this place has to offer, you should have your hands full." She looked into his deep brown eyes. "You enjoying that beer?"

"The first one was good. This one seems even better…"

Lauren stood, arched her back and stretched. "Well, I've been enjoying sharing a beer with you." She smiled and looked him over, returning to his eyes. "I probably ought to be heading back. The beer seems to have made me a little sleepy. I like to get an early start each day, so I should get back to my room for bed." She slid her feet back into her flip flops. "Don't want to wear out my welcome."

Ben wanted to persuade her to stay. As he stood, her hands reached his shoulders. On tiptoes, she kissed his cheek, brushing lightly against his bare chest. His involuntary response to her continued. "Won't you stay a while longer?"

"I better not." She smiled warmly, her hands sliding down his shoulders to his upper arms.

"I'd really like for you to stay if you will."

She gave Ben a knowing smile, then leaned against him and gave a quick hug. "Thanks, but I better be going."

"Let me walk you back."

"No, that's okay." She opened the door and stepped out. "But check me out tomorrow if you get a chance. The next move is yours."

"Consider it done."

"Goodnight." Lauren walked away to her unit, smiling. She believed Ben's interest in reading had taken a nosedive, and while she was in St. Martin, Lauren looked forward to keeping it that way.

SEVEN

ON SUNDAY MORNING Sylvie was driving her car away from Harrington's villa. She was frustrated at finding no useful information, but also relieved that she was not caught looking in the safe. Something did not seem right with Harrington, and she was concerned he may be suspicious. She would need to re-think her plan to get the hoped-for information. She felt certain Harrington was the key, and she wanted the money the information would bring her. How else could she get that which would undoubtedly make her very rich?

Sylvie drove the winding roads that would take her to La Playa Orient Bay Resort located centrally on Orient Beach and a comfortable walk from Lubrique. She would be checking in, moving from the Royal Palm. She had loved her stay at the Royal Palm in Simpson Bay, and especially loved the great variety of restaurants that were nearby. She would definitely stay there again, but the Royal Palm was not to her friend's liking. Her friend, Terri, would be flying in to meet her today, and her preference was La Playa. The Royal Palm seemingly catered to families, many with children, and some who owned a time-share interest there.

Terri wanted to stay at La Playa primarily because of its location on the premier beach. As a sun worshipper, Terri's objective to spend as much time as possible on the beach was enhanced by staying there. The deluxe hotel was small in scale with only 56 rooms in its eight towers. The two would be staying on the third floor of one of the buildings. As the top floor, there was still a sight line to beautiful Orient Beach above the vegetation that separated La Playa from the world-famous beach.

Sylvie parked in the small lot at La Playa. With parking everywhere on the island in short supply, it was nice to have adequate parking for her stay. She walked into the small open-air area for her check-in. "Bonjour, I am very early, but hoping my room might be ready. I booked the third-floor room of the third tower."

"I believe so, yes. And you are Terri?"

"No, I'm Sylvie and will be rooming with Terri. Here's the confirmation we received."

"Ah, yes. I'm Marie, no problem. I'm the manager of La Playa Orient Bay. Your room is ready. We have croissants, fresh fruit and a pot of coffee available just through here, where we also serve lunch. Please help yourself. Would you like any assistance with your bag? Claude would be happy to help you to your room."

"No, I'm fine, thank you. Just point me in the right direction."

Marie took a few steps and pointed out the room's location to Sylvie. She rolled her bag to the base of the stairs, then carried it up the flights to the third floor. Her key worked and her suite was beautiful. They would be sharing the king-size bed, and would be very comfortable at La Playa.

Sylvie used the next 30 minutes to unpack and neatly put away her belongings. There would be plenty of room for Terri to do the same. She next changed into her tiny red bikini, with a cover-up to allow her to have what was going to be a late breakfast downstairs, and catch some sun while she waited for Terri to arrive. Terri, like Sylvie, would be getting a rental from Hertz at the airport and would drive to La Playa after picking up a few items for the week.

* * *

While Sylvie settled into her room, Harrington's men began their search to locate her. She was away from the villa and out of sight before a tail could be put in place. However, with a small island, it was simply a matter of time before she would be found. Perhaps she would reach out to Harrington to discuss another get-together, this one more of a date as was expected when Sylvie followed him to his villa.

Harrington's men were accustomed to taking care of all tasks he requested. He paid well and they were pleased to get the money that not many jobs on the island could provide. They were also fearful of Harrington. If they failed or objected to a request, the consequences could be grave.

To begin the hunt for Sylvie, it was time to let a few people around the island know they wanted to find her, and that any sightings would be rewarded. Their first stop would be the Red Piano Bar, where she met Harrington. They would then make a few stops around the island, leaving messages at the popular tourist areas of Simpson Bay, Sunset Beach Bar in Maho Bay, a couple shops in Philipsburg, a high-end restaurant in Grand Case, the Princess Casino at Port de Plaisance, and the Esmeralda at Orient Beach. With additional eyes around the island, it could still take a few days, but the odds were much more favorable on her being found before Harrington's patience ended. They would be reporting their actions to Harrington before the day was done.

EIGHT

BEN WOKE AT 6:30 a.m. with the bright Caribbean
sun shining into the bedroom. He had failed to close the
blackout curtains, but was pleased as he was always an early
riser. He walked over to the kitchen counter and decided
to have a banana and a small box of cereal. They were
included as starter foods to welcome him to the resort. He
did not drink coffee, but popped open a can of Coke that
had also been provided in the refrigerator for his arrival.
He then brushed his teeth, shaved and had a quick shower.
Standing in front of the full-length mirror in the bedroom,
Ben began to apply the water-resistant SPF 30 sunscreen.
He began with his face, paying careful attention to ears and
forehead, and then methodically applied lotion down to
his toes. With his lotion fully applied, he stepped into his
swim trunks and was ready to step out. At just after seven,
he grabbed his beach towel, had his room key, and walked
barefoot out toward the beach.

The beach was very quiet, and the sun was already
warming the sand. Lubrique had set up a "front row" of
lounge chairs at the end of the resort closest to La Playa and
Alamanda, and left a wide area open on the southern end of
the beach near Papatwo. This allowed for impromptu gath-
erings of guests along the ocean-front without blocking the
view or otherwise distracting the lounging sunbathers as they

soaked up the sights and sounds of the beach. Ben walked down toward the southern end and spread his towel on the sand back away from the beach chairs, about twenty steps from the water. He was in a perfect spot to enjoy the beach views and early morning sun. Realizing he had forgotten to bring a book, he left his towel and walked back to the room with his key. Retrieving his adventure read, he also grabbed his sunglasses and the small water-proof box with string designed to hang around one's neck for securing the key.

Walking back, he was ready to enjoy the beach and sat on the sand as most others were taking leisurely beach walks. People were very friendly, speaking or nodding as they continued past. A sandy blonde female, also coming from the direction of Lubrique, was walking toward Ben. She smiled as she approached.

"Good morning," Ben said in response to her smile. "Beautiful morning for a walk."

As she was about to reach Ben, she cheerfully responded. "You're right. So why are you sitting and not walking?"

"I don't know, good question."

She continued walking, but slowed. "Then get up and walk. It's a perfect time of day, and there's not a more beautiful beach in the world to walk."

"You're right." Ben got to his feet, looking unsure of whether he was going for a walk, or might sit back in the sand.

"I've slowed, but I'm not waiting much longer. If you're going to walk, come on!" Ben moved quickly and fell in step. "That's much better," she said.

"I'm Ben, good to meet you."

"Good morning again, Ben. I'm Dee. I'll be walking the full length to the Mont Vernon on the other end of the beach. You're welcome to keep me company. You could even help me on the way back, if you weren't waiting on someone."

"That sounds good, thanks. I was just sitting back, enjoying the day. No one had arranged to meet me this morning. I'm not sure how I can help you on the way back, but will be happy to try."

"Great," she replied. "I'll hold you to it." They continued their walk, with Ben enjoying the company of his new friend. They reached the far end of the beach. "Okay, this is where I like to walk in the water for a while as I go back. It's extra exercise for my thighs and helps keep my glutes toned." She re-started her walk knee-deep in the water. She continued until they were about a quarter of a mile from where Ben had been sitting.

"Okay, this is where you can help me. I'm going to swim the rest of the way back. I'll stop about where you were sitting on your towel. Are you still willing to help?"

"Sure."

"Great, thanks." She walked up out of the water next to Ben. She then removed her swimsuit and handed the dry suit to him. Ben tried not to react. "We're in France. This is normal for the French and Dutch. It's mainly repressed Americans who are willing to sit around in wet swimsuits. I want to keep mine dry."

She splashed back into the ocean, and started her swim, with Ben walking along tracking her progress. When she was back in the vicinity of Ben's towel, she stopped. "Thanks for your help. Would you mind putting my suit on your towel?" Ben said nothing but did as she asked.

She continued treading the shoulder deep water. "Well, are you coming in?" Ben stood, indecisive as to whether he would go for a swim.

"What are you waiting for? Put your trunks on the towel and come on in. It's a nude beach, for goodness sake. What are you waiting on?"

Ben felt he had little choice after her challenging tone. He was waiting to see Lauren, but let her shame him into joining her. He stepped out of his trunks, tossed them on the towel, and hurried into the water. "That's great, isn't it! I just love swimming here. The water is so beautiful and clear. Why, I can even see your toes! Doesn't it feel like a dreamy reward after that long walk?" She continued talking with Ben mainly listening. Soon, she became flirtatious. Ben was even more unsure of how to react. He had just met Lauren, and really wanted to spend time with her. Instead, he was very uncomfortable with a woman being playful with him right in front of the resort.

A few minutes later, his discomfort increased dramatically. "Ben, is that you?" Ben turned and saw Lauren on the shore.

"Good morning, Lauren," he muttered.

"Ben, I was hoping to meet you here this morning. It looks like you got an early start without me." She made a pouty face. "I guess I'll go for a walk. Maybe I'll see you later."

"Hey, Lauren, wait up!"

"That's okay, I don't want to interfere. We can talk another time."

"No, seriously, hold up!" He waded as quickly as he could out of the water, never turning back to his swim mate. "I was hoping to see you this morning," he called as he was about to exit the water.

"It doesn't look like it! It looks like you were extremely happy cavorting with that woman." She turned her back to Ben.

"Seriously," he said, his voice lowered. "I don't even know her." He began babbling. "She was swimming and said something to me that made me think I needed to dip in, I know that sounds stupid. Won't you at least look at me?"

He grabbed each of her arms to turn her to face him. When she did, she was grinning broadly.

"Ben, I'd like you to meet Deana." Deana had stepped out of the water and was standing behind Ben. "She's my roommate who is going home today. I'm sorry, I was enjoying myself, seeing how flustered you were. When I saw her in the water with you, I knew she was being evil, but you were so sweet, I couldn't stop myself from being mean. Will you forgive me?"

Ben blew out his breath and had a hint of a smile on his face as Deana burst out laughing. "Lauren told me all about you last night. When I saw you sitting there this morning, I was certain you were looking forward to seeing her. I'm sorry for messing with you. And to help level the field, you should know Lauren thinks she's already falling in love."

"Deana, you are too much! Okay, Ben, I'm sorry, and I'm even more sorry for what is obviously a poor choice of my best friend," she kidded. She then gave Ben a big hug. "It's a beautiful morning. Please forgive me." She then turned to Deana. "I'll take you to the airport later if you go flirt with someone else now."

"Ben, why don't we go to your towel while the evil one goes for another walk?" They went back to his towel. "I really am sorry. That was unlike me. My crazy roommate rubbed off on me for a bit. Please tell me you forgive me."

Ben saw the humor in the orchestrated set-up and smiled. "You were evil, but I forgive you." She gave him a hug and a light kiss on the cheek.

"Okay, now that I'm forgiven, maybe you'll go for a swim with me. I need to take Deana back to the airport early afternoon, but want to enjoy the beach until then." She then mimicked Deana before walking into the water for a swim.

They enjoyed their time on the beach, then decided to get an early lunch. "I'll need to wear my trunks," said Ben, "but you're fine as is and we'll bring a towel for you to sit on. I think you owe me that discomfort after your antics this morning."

"All right, whatever! You've been a great sport this morning. If we go somewhere where it's fine, I'm good with it."

NINE

SYLVIE COMPLETED HER breakfast and walked to the beach where chairs were supplied by La Playa. Although nude use was allowed once again anywhere on the beach, there was typically little full nudity in front of La Playa. Instead, sunning there was predominantly by topless or fully covered bathers. Sylvie chose to walk south toward Lubrique, stopping just before that resort's property began. A large gathering of nude bathers typically enjoyed the beach there where the old Pedro's had been. Sylvie abhorred tan lines and this area was calling to her. She paid to rent a sun lounger, and secured her towel in the straps of the chair. She got out of her bikini, placed it in her beach bag, and lay back in the lounge. She was ready to begin some serious sunning. Instead of eating lunch, her late breakfast would hold her well until Terri arrived. Terri's plane was scheduled to land at 2:10 p.m. By the time it landed, and she got a cab, it would likely be close to 4:00 before she reached La Playa. Sylvie would go back before then to shower and be ready to greet Terri upon her arrival. They would go to the Greenhouse in Simpson Bay. Both Sylvie and Terri loved the Greenhouse, and would traditionally have their first dinner there when meeting in St. Maarten. The johnnycakes there were to die for. They weren't on the menu, but were complimentary to diners in the know. In addition to the johnnycakes, the special appetizers at half price and of course the 2-for-1 happy hour until 7:00 p.m., made the Greenhouse hard to beat. With music playing next door, sitting on the beach with great food and cold tropical drinks, what could be better!

As Sylvie sunned and waited for Terri's arrival, she watched part of an impromptu volleyball game that was taking place just to her north and a little inland. Watching naked volleyball was always entertaining. None of the players were any good, and none of them cared that they were not. Everyone was simply enjoying time with friends in the sun and frequently laughing. Moving around a little, chasing after a ball that would roll away from the court, and putting the ball in play occasionally was really the object of the game. If score was kept in a traditional manner, that did not determine the day's winners. The jiggling up top of the women, and of some of the men, in addition to the flopping and swinging of the men down below, was great sport for the participants and observers.

A great time was had by all. Occasionally, an intentionally over-dramatic play for the ball would occur. A dive would happen that would be more of a slow-motion laying down in the sand instead of a slide. Sometimes it would be headfirst with back on the ground, so that all the interesting parts could move even more freely. The few really talented players had perfected the pop-up following the headfirst back dive. This was where they would regain their feet, but the move would start with an arching of the back off the sand, pushing with elbows and then hands and feet, with the nether regions gloriously displayed at the height of the arch. A couple of those in a game made for a memorable match.

After a few drinks and dipping in the refreshing ocean several times, Sylvie decided to head back to her room. She gathered her towel from the chair and picked up her beach bag. She began her walk back, electing not to put her bikini back on, as to capture as many rays in as many places as possible for as long as possible.

As Sylvie walked back to her room, she saw several friends also enjoying the beach. She paused to talk to those she spotted while remaining mindful of her need to be back in time for Terri's arrival.

"Hey Sylvie, how is your Sunday going?" a friend asked.

"All great here." Sylvie really enjoyed talking to her friends. She was a pleasure to be around, and if there were new friends, Sylvie could easily keep a conversation going without periods of uncomfortable silence. "I'm staying at La Playa and Terri will be joining me soon later today. I had been at the Royal Palm, but Terri prefers staying on Orient. I really love Orient, too, and prefer it greatly over the man-made beach at the Royal Palm. Have you ever gotten in the water at the Royal Palm? It's okay, but the sand feels funny when you step in the water. It doesn't have the same consistency of most other beaches. I think it's because a lot of foreign dirt was brought in there, but that might not be true. Orient of course is way better for those of us who like total body tanning. It's rare that I've even seen anyone sunning topless at the Royal Palm beach. But I do love the location for the restaurants, being close to the Red Piano, and close to Topper's. Topper's is always fun. I like watching the karaoke there but rarely participate." Sylvie briefly paused. "How are you on this beautiful Sunday?"

"We are wonderful! With so many great beaches, this remains one of our favorites and worth the trip over from the Dutch side."

"Yes, this is my favorite beach, and am happy Terri wanted to stay on Orient at La Playa. I'm heading there now to be showered and ready when she gets here. We'll probably go to the Greenhouse for our ceremonial first dinner together to kick off the week. Feel free to head over there tonight if you don't have plans. Have fun today and look for me if you decide to go to the Greenhouse."

Sylvie continued back to La Playa, entered her third-floor room, locked the door behind her, and stepped into the shower. It had been a good day on the beach, and would be fun to see Terri. After showering, Sylvie brushed her teeth, dried her hair, and dressed. She walked out on the patio and looked out over the beach. The day remained clear, and the beach looked to be nearly full of happy people.

Sylvie thought back to the prior night at Harrington's villa. She had done her homework. She knew his routine and had expected he would be at his normal table at the Red Piano. She felt she had done a good job of setting up a seemingly chance meeting. Accentuating her good looks with one of her favorite dresses, she had waited for Harrington to take note of her before approaching him. She wanted the meeting to be based on his initiation, and she had successfully accomplished that.

The information she received was accurate; Harrington's safe was easily accessible in the study closet. Harrington's past activities with a series of casual encounters, many of which ended with a tryst at his villa, had resulted in a lot of information known by a number of young, attractive women. And the women shared information freely among the group, many trying to one up the others. Harrington's routines, habits, and even sleeping patterns had been chron-icled. Each woman thought sharing even more informa-tion not generally known would confirm her place to be acknowledged as Harrington's favorite.

The most important knowledge came from her friend Terri. Terri visited the island in the fall and Harrington had taken a great interest in her. She had a face and body unmatched by any that Harrington had ever seen. She had the same voluptuous look and naturally dark skin as Sophia Loren from a prior generation, but her face, while exotic, had more features typical of an American beauty. Harrington had invited her back to his villa. She had gone, but Harrington was disappointed that she was not succumbing to his charm. As Harrington tried to take additional steps to impress, he decided to show off some valuables in his safe. His suspicion of others had totally ceased. He was no longer thinking above his neck and let his guard down. Terri easily observed his safe combination. With that last piece of information, Sylvie had felt ready to enact her plan. The rumors of Harrington's wealth based on secret information that he used as leverage over the French and Dutch governments would most likely be in that safe, and Sylvie was ready to learn the secret. But now what? She had not been able to complete her mission and needed a new plan.

She decided to let her subconscious work on the problem. She got a book to read and sat on the patio passing the time until Terri arrived.

TEN

BEN WALKED BRISKLY to his room to grab some cash for lunch, put away everything other than the towel they were sitting on, and headed back to the beach. Lauren remained seated on the towel facing the water, her back to Ben as he approached. "Are you ready to get some lunch?"

Lauren looked at Ben, her eyes and mouth were smiling brightly. "I'm ready, let's do this!" She reached out her hands and Ben helped pull her to her feet. He gave her a quick hug, then walked a few feet away downwind and shook the sand out of the towel.

Ben held the towel in one hand and Lauren's hand in his other as they walked along the beach. They decided to eat at Chez Leandra. As they approached, they were greeted with the smells that were a testament to Chez Leandra being one of the best restaurants in St. Martin. They were glad that their early arrival would be ahead of the anticipated large lunch-time crowd. There were a few couples scattered at the covered dining area, but no one sitting at the tables set up as free-standing on the sand. As Lauren had no clothes to match the diners dressed in shirts, shorts and swimwear, Ben and Lauren elected to sit at a table on the sand. Lauren wrapped the towel around as a sarong before sitting down.

Ben and Lauren each ordered a lemon breeze to have with their meals. The drink was a refreshingly light combination of lime juice, lemon juice, vodka and Cointreau. The lunch was garlic shrimp, rice and beans, plantains and a salad. "Ben, thank you for a great morning. I had no idea of the fun and amazing food I would have."

Ben looked at Lauren and replied "It was certainly more than I imagined when I was the entertainment for you and your friend. I admit that was a good one. But my rollercoaster ride slowed to a nice smooth landing of our fun walk down the beach, followed by Leandra serving up a great early lunch." He looked at Lauren, afraid she might not have appreciated the analogy. "Don't misunderstand. I love a roller coaster ride. Especially when I know I survived and am safely back on the ground." Ben continued, "Looking back on it, I wouldn't change a thing." He made a face, as a light-hearted attempt to say "well, maybe not."

Lauren looked like she was good with all he said. "Unfortunately, I need to get on back. I promised Deana that I would drive her to the airport to see her off today." Ben remembered her commitment, his expected afternoon letdown without her about to become a reality. Ben nodded at Lauren that he accepted lunch was officially done. Leaving cash for the bill and tip, they stood up and waved their appreciation to the waiter for such good food and service.

They took the few steps to the water's edge to begin the walk back. Lauren re-fashioned her towel as a skirt and tied it at her waist. For the walk back, she again was next to the water. Ben held her right hand in his left while they walked. As they neared Ben's room, Deana could be seen a little further down the beach in front of the room she had shared with Lauren. "Hey Lauren, are you still good with taking me to the airport? I'm ready whenever you are." Without glancing in Ben's direction, Lauren called out to

Deana. "Yes, I'll be ready. My stuff is in Ben's room. I'll get it and be right over."

Deana watched as Ben and Lauren walked the remaining short distance to Ben's room and she slowly walked toward his room as well. The distance between Deana and Lauren narrowed to about twenty feet when Deana stopped her approach. Ben unlocked the door, reached inside, grabbed Lauren's bag and handed it to her.

"Ben, thanks for the great morning. I'll be back after taking Deana to the airport. Would you like to ride along?"

"No, I'll let you two have time together without me. I need to get a few items from the store. I also want to check on my rental car that should be delivered today. My friend Nico mentioned he would probably come by. I'll probably sit on the beach so I will be able to see him if he comes looking for me. I'll be enjoying how great it is here."

"Okay," she said and gave him a light kiss. "I'll be back soon!" She turned, walked toward Deana, and they headed back to their room. "Deana, give me just a couple of minutes. I'll rinse the sand off and be dressed in five minutes. I promise."

Lauren dressed and they walked out to the car. She got behind the wheel. As she pulled out onto the main road, she began sharing her thoughts. "As I told you last night, when you weren't feeling your best, I decided to step out. I had seen Ben at the beach, and again when we were eating at the 'let's mingle table'. I noticed him again eating with the resort owner. He seemed very reserved, not loud or falling down drunk, and just seemed like a respectable person. Knowing you would be leaving today, I decided to do something out of character. I screwed up my courage and decided to drop in on him. I saw him as he left dinner and went to his room. When I got there, he was very nice. I don't know many specific details of his life, but I feel like I know him. He wasn't pretending yesterday at the beach or at dinner last night. He didn't even know I was watching. He acted very stable and respectable, like someone I would like to know as a friend. After talking with him last night, I thought he might be somebody that I don't want to eliminate as a possibility for a more meaningful relationship. This morning he was so sweet and innocent when I pretended to catch him in the water with you. We spent time on the beach and had a great lunch at Chez Leandra. Not only was the food great, I really enjoyed being with Ben. I know I just met him, and I'm definitely not a boy-crazed thirteen-year-old, but as insane as it sounds, I'm really crazy about him. I'm eager to spend more time with him."

Nodding, Deana replied, "Yes, I saw how you were with him. You were more open with him on the beach than you were with me yesterday. And your 'I love you' puppy-dog eyes could have made a lesser person than me feel like barfing. But I'm happy for you, and I hope the rest of your time here will be everything you're hoping for."

Lauren smiled. "You know, we've been best friends for a long time. You were always the one entering wet t-shirt contests, and I was always the restrained one watching the fun instead of actively being part of the fun. Last night I saw how it was to be you and I liked it! I don't know if I'm going to be the next Deana, but I did enjoy stepping out of my comfort zone. Once I did, I just went with it and had a blast! I'm excited to see what happens next."

The drive was going as expected. As they came within a couple of miles of the Princess Juliana Airport, traffic slowed to a crawl as sometimes happens. They made it to the airport with a little time to spare. "I'll be expecting to get some updates from you this week on how everything is going, especially with Ben. Don't forget what I've taught you," she grinned. "Wish I could be here to give you some on-site coaching, but by the look of things, I don't think that's needed. Have fun and hope to talk to you soon!" Deanna grabbed her bag and walked into the airport.

Lauren pulled back out into traffic. It looked like whatever hold-up there was with traffic was impacting drivers in both directions. It promised to be a slow ride back.

ELEVEN

BEN QUICKLY TOOK delivery of his rental car and purchased basic supplies that he thought he might want for the coming week. It was now time to hit the beach again. He put on his blue swim trunks, gathered his towel, book, key and sunglasses, and returned to the beach. The beautiful weather was continuing and a peak afternoon crowd had gathered. It was a great time to sit back and marvel at his good fortune to be in the early part of his getaway. He thought about what he might do the coming days. He found himself thinking about Lauren. As he was lost in thought, he suddenly felt a hand on his shoulder. "Hello my friend, great to see you here." Nico had made it back to visit.

"Great to see you buddy. Glad you were able to make it back," Ben replied.

Nico was a self-sufficient survivor with many practical skills and experiences. He had spent much time in the Abacos in the Bahamas. There he was employed as a boat builder where he participated in building the much-respected Albury Brothers boats on Parrot Cay. The boats, along with Boston Whalers, made up the boats available for tourists. It was Ben's stay at the Abaco Inn that opened the door for Ben and Nico to meet. Ben had scheduled a five-day getaway at the Abaco Inn on Elbow Cay. No one used cars on the small island, so a boat rental was needed to get around. When he flew into Marsh Harbour, Nico had Ben's rental boat through Island Marine waiting for him. Nico welcomed Ben aboard at the airport and took them to Island Marine, where Ben exhibited the minimal knowledge needed to be turned loose with the boat. Nico got out at Island Marine and pointed the way to the Abaco Inn, which was the base for Ben's vacation. Ben enjoyed spending time with Nico while in the Abacos and their friendship continued after the vacation ended. Nico now spent much time in St. Maarten, where his general building skills helped him with building projects other than boats. Nico continued to have a love of boats, and with his time on boats in the Abacos, he was also an accomplished sailor.

"Ben, I have a proposal for you. I have a group that wants to take a boat tour tomorrow. I've arranged to captain a boat ride out of Simpson Bay Marina, off Billy Folly Road. I could really use your hands on board. My first choice would be a good lookin' first mate that would bring smiles to the group with her looks and service, but I don't have one of those. Maybe you would like a boat ride around the island tomorrow and help me out?" Nico did not often ask favors and Ben was reluctant to turn him down. "I think I could make it. I don't have much in the way of boat skills or any knowledge of the area, as you know, but can be available to take instructions."

"Great, you'll be fine. When I get a group like this, I don't expect anyone to be comfortable on running boats. You never know. But I'll enjoy spending time with you even if nothing is needed."

"Okay, sounds good. I'll need to get directions from you and a time to show up. Do you want me to do anything to help you prepare?"

"No, just show up about 8:30 a.m. and hop on the boat. We'll be back about 5:00 p.m., so a full day of fun.

You'll see the island from the water, so that can help you get to know it better. If you're like everybody else, you'll be coming back, and probably soon after you leave. Before you know it, you'll be touring others around and pointing out your special places." Nico continued, "I'll be heading over to Simpson Bay in a bit, thinking of having supper at Lee's. Would you be able to join me?"

"Yeah, I think so. I met a friend last night staying here and she was taking someone to the airport some time ago today. I should be here when she gets back. What time for dinner? Would you mind me inviting her to join us?"

"Your friend is my friend. A man can never have too many friends, bring her along. Just let me know what time is good. Maybe we can try for seven."

"Seven should work. I'll call you to confirm, but plan on seven."

"Good, good, everything's good." Nico got up to leave. "We'll have a good meal before boating tomorrow."

Nico left, leaving Ben to his thoughts. He had gotten most of what the sun had to offer for the day and decided to head back to his room to wait for Lauren. Ben walked into his room, and once again dropped his trunks on what was becoming the appointed spot on the floor. He showered, shaved, and dressed in a green pullover collared shirt with the blue shorts he had worn the night before. He decided to break out the same adventure book he had been carrying around but had not yet begun to read. He intended to read a few pages while he waited. He was not really in the mood to read, though, so sat back on his bed and began reliving the last twenty-four hours. He was not sure where it was headed, but was uncomfortable that his usual logical and methodical approach to facing life seemed to have run off the track. Ben always liked smart, strong women, and Lauren seemed to fit the bill. He did not know much about her, but she met the high level of intelligence that made her attractive to him. The break this afternoon acted as a mini cooling off period for Ben to regroup and take a more objective view of his new friendship.

TWELVE

TERRI PULLED INTO the parking area at La Playa. She was eager to see her good friend Sylvie and start having fun. She was sure Sylvie would be ready to party and that they would be enjoying happy hour soon. As Sylvie partied a little harder than Terri, Terri offered to drive them around for the night. It was 4:15 p.m. and she would freshen up before driving them to the Greenhouse. Sylvie's car would remain tucked away at La Playa, hampering Harrington's efforts to locate her.

Harrington received the call from his employees in charge of locating Sylvie. They shared what they had done, the search they had performed, and a listing of those they contacted to be on the look-out for Sylvie's car. Harrington recognized their great efforts to locate her, but also realized that finding her could take much longer than he hoped if she did not make contact with him first. He needed to be patient, comfortable that she had not discovered any information that could be harmful to him. His concern was more in finding out who had put her up to investigating him. He wanted to know who might be close to him who now represented a threat.

Nico returned to Simpson Bay and stopped by the Simpson Bay Marina. He confirmed that the 38-foot off-shore power boat with twin 225 horsepower engines was fueled and ready for the tour for the next morning. He looked at the list of guests for the charter. The charter was for the Northeast Florida Tiki Hut Association. There was a group of ten, that with captain and Ben as crew, would fill the boat to a comfortable capacity of twelve. Nico next went to get supplies to stock the boat.

Dean Janson was having a quiet Sunday afternoon. He had chosen to take his typical break from the casino on Sunday and Monday. This Sunday he received a call from Robert Vaughn. Vaughn was a land developer and identified himself as a sometimes business associate of Gregorio Harrington. The possibility that Vaughn was an associate of Harrington got Janson's attention. "I'd like to set up a time to visit with you tomorrow. I have a business proposal that I would like to discuss. Would it be possible for us to get together briefly tomorrow afternoon?"

Janson looked at his calendar and knew he could be available. Although his interest was piqued by the name dropping, Janson still wanted more information before blindly agreeing to meet. "What do you have in mind?"

"It's my understanding that you run a very successful casino. In fact, I'm told your casino is the largest and most lucrative in St. Maarten. I believe you have a large number of tourists who regularly enjoy your casino, and the house has a very good return based on percentage of wagers retained. I am in touch with some very large groups of tourists who enjoy the fun provided by casinos. In fact, these tourists are active elsewhere in the islands, but have not decided on a casino of preference in St. Maarten. I believe I have some influence with the tour groups, and could influence business your way. They love the excitement of the game, and your percentage retained could likely be increased even with the acquisition of this large tour group. Would you be interested in discussing how we might work together to bring happiness to the tour groups who would like to visit St. Maarten on a regular basis?"

Janson understood the message of a possible money laundering opportunity. "I have five restaurants at the casino. Would you be interested in meeting at the Grill tomorrow around 4:00? This would be a little before the evening meal service begins and could afford us some privacy for business discussions."

"That is a good suggestion. I look forward to meeting with you tomorrow."

Janson was excited at the prospect. He had run money through his casino previously, but had suspended the business when the risk of trouble to him had increased beyond an acceptable level. He would be eager to hear more, and to determine if the business opportunity might be attractive. If not, he would still be successful in expanding his sphere of business contacts.

THIRTEEN

LAUREN WORKED HER way through the outlandish traffic and finally arrived back at Lubrique. She was annoyed that the traffic had robbed her of several hours on the beach with Ben. She looked at the beach but did not see him and hoped that he was waiting for her in his room. She walked to his room and he stepped out to greet her. "Traffic was a nightmare. There was a major wreck that blocked traffic both ways, and it was then jammed where everyone was trying to go an alternate route."

"I'm sorry it was so bad. Thankfully, you made it back safely."

"What have you been doing while I was stuck in traffic?"

"I got my rental car that was delivered and got some stuff at the grocery store for the week. I then went back to the beach and sat where I was yesterday. My friend Nico had said he might come by, and he did. We visited for a while. Come on in and let me tell you about it."

Lauren walked in with some trepidation. It struck her as awkward that he said to come in and let him tell her about it. Her guard was up expecting some negative or disappointing information. "Have a seat. Would you like something to drink?"

"A water would be good if you have it."

"Sure." Ben handed her a bottle of water and sat across from her. "First, my friend Nico has done me favors in the past and he set up for me to be staying here. He asked if I could have dinner with him tonight, and also asked if I would help him with a boat trip tomorrow. I didn't feel like I could turn down his requests, so I agreed to both. I also told him I wanted to invite you to dinner tonight." Ben continued, "Would you want to go to dinner with me to meet Nico? He wants to go to a place in Simpson Bay called Lee's. I'm sure it's good or he wouldn't have suggested it."

"Thanks." Lauren paused before continuing. "It would probably be better if just you two did dinner tonight. I've already spent time with you, and he hasn't. I don't want to horn in. We can go to dinner a different night."

Lauren's reaction was not what Ben wanted, but was what he had feared. "Hey, I'd like you to go if you will. Nico said he'd like to meet you. Won't you go with me?"

"Thanks, but I'll pass."

Ben was disappointed. "Okay. Tomorrow I'm to go over to Simpson Bay to help Nico with a boat outing he put together. He's taking a group out and he wants me to help him. It's not something I asked to do, and I'm not sure I really want to, but I felt like I couldn't turn him down. I'm disappointed that I won't be seeing you instead."

"I understand. You just met me. Nico is a good friend and you should spend some time with him. I'll be around. There'll be plenty of time for us to get together again." She looked at him and tried to hide her disappointment. "You know where my room is." She then got up to leave.

"Lauren, this isn't going like I want it to. Please give me a chance to make it up to you." He took a couple of steps towards her as she turned and stepped out the door. "I'll call you when I get back. If you would, I'd like to see you then."

Lauren kept her back to Ben. "Give me a call. Have fun tonight. I'll see you soon." Ben let her walk away. He was not sure how he had gotten into such a bad spot, and did not know how to undo it.

After she left, Ben decided to go early to dinner. He would look around and see how long it took to reach the Simpson Bay Marina, make sure he could find it, and then go to Lee's. After the day had such a great start, his enthusiasm for St. Martin was temporarily gone. He hoped that a meal with his good friend would bring his spirits back up. Certainly the boat trip would be great. A good night's sleep followed by a boat trip in the Caribbean was on his itinerary. How could anyone not be excited to be part of a boat trip with a good friend exploring the beautiful Caribbean? He was certain his mood would improve.

Ben reached his car and headed out. He left Orient, going past Grand Case and all of its high-end restaurants. Grand Case had the reputation of being the culinary capital of the Caribbean. He hoped he could take Lauren there for a romantic dinner. Next, he rode past Marigot, seeing the remnants of the booths and a few late day tourists wanting to find some local treasures at the Marigot market. Finally, he reached the Simpson Bay area and followed the winding road down to the water to the marina. It was easy enough to find with Nico's directions, and he felt comfortable he could make the 8:30 morning meeting tomorrow without any anxiety. His mood was improving, so now to Lee's to wait for his friend.

Nico had arrived early, saw Ben, and waved him to his table. "How's it going? Where's your friend?"

"She decided not to come. Said something about letting us visit without her. I'm sorry she couldn't make it. I think you would like her."

"Yes man, I'm sure I would. Wish she had come. Hope to meet her another time." Changing the subject, he continued, "I hope you'll like it. They have great fresh fish with big amounts. It's happy hour, if you want a drink, it's two-for-one."

"Thanks, I'll probably get a beer." Ben decided to save the fruity tropical drinks for when he had some female company. "What do you recommend?"

The two friends each ordered grilled mahi mahi, potato salad and rice and beans. They lingered over their food, catching up after not having seen each other for the past year. The conversation turned to their time in the Bahamas, then boats, and then to the boat outing for the next day. Nico thanked him again for agreeing to help. Ben accepted the thanks and responded, "I'm looking forward to it. It will be great." His voice failed to convey much enthusiasm.

"You're going to like it. It's with a fun group from Florida. I've been talking with them for a while getting this set up. It seems like a good group."

The night had stretched to beyond nine and each decided it was time to go. It would be a fun but tiring day on the water tomorrow.

Ben got back to his car where he had parked in the small strip-shopping area just down the hill from Lee's. He took his time driving back, trying to let his mind empty of thoughts. He wondered if Lauren was in her room. Perhaps she had gone out and was having a great time. He would check in with her when he got back, hoping she had a great meal and would be back looking forward to seeing him.

FOURTEEN

SYLVIE AND TERRI were ready to enjoy their time at the Greenhouse. They had a table under a small tiki hut at the edge of the wide beach. "Good evening ladies. Welcome to the Greenhouse. Our happy hour tonight is two-for-one until 7:00. Could I get you started with something to drink?"

Sylvie looked at the young waiter. If he had been on the menu, she would have ordered him as appetizer, entrée and dessert. "I love the flavor of coconuts. Maybe a pina colada for me."

Terri added, "I'll do that as well. Just make it one to bring out two. We'll each drink those before ordering another to keep them from melting too fast." She continued, "And please bring us some johnnycakes to start."

"Yes, that sounds great. I love johnnycakes. And the johnnycakes here are the best." Sylvie was in a playful mood and her body language reflected it. She was ready to party. The handsome waiter was accustomed to a little extra attention from female patrons. He smiled a sexy smile. "Coming right up. I'll bring the johnnycakes with your drinks." He knew a little extra attention, as well as flattery, led to extra tips. It would be easy to be complimentary to these two. They were both stunning.

After their initial drinks, johnnycakes, and a second pina colada each, Sylvie and Terri were ready to order. Sylvie ordered the bang bang shrimp, Terri ordered a quesadilla with vegetables, and they opted to split some conch fritters. "Excellent choices. Could I get you another drink? We're past seven, so happy hour is officially over, but for you two, I'm sure I can slip it in."

The pina coladas were affecting Sylvie. She thought the waiter was very witty yet subtle, and believed his comment was intended as a compliment as well as a proposal. As he was looking at her when he spoke, she accepted his comment as he was hitting on her and not Terri. She was pleased. "I think I would like to switch to one of your specialty drinks. Do you have the list of drinks on you?"

"Sure, here you go."

Terri could see some celebratory drinking in the night for Sylvie and decided as the evening's driver she needed to slow her drinking pace. "I think I'll just have a water for now."

Sylvie scanned the list of drinks: Frozen Mudslide, Planters Punch, Bahama Mama, Pussers Painkiller, Baileys Banana Colada, and Tropicolada. At the top of the list was another one that caught her eye, however, not based on its ingredients of Island Oasis Pina Colada, Ice Cream, Kahlua, Rum, Baileys and Amaretto, but because of its name. "I think I'd like to have a Bushwhacker." She paused a beat, "Although it's just smooth sailing here. Is that something you'd recommend?"

"Oh yes, but it does have quite a kick. Seeing as your friend has switched to water, I say go for it!"

"Let's do it. I'd like to try it, and with my dinner, I think I can handle the second and still be able to walk out of here."

Terri and Sylvie enjoyed their meals. Terri stuck with water, and Sylvie was only able to finish half of her second

Bushwhacker. The evening had been great, but Sylvie was not ready to go back to La Playa. She felt like dancing. "Terri, let's go to the Red Piano. We can walk there from here."

Terri liked the idea. Although just arriving on island, she was not too tired to extend the evening. The alcohol impact from the two pina coladas had peaked and was now subsiding. She could keep an eye out for Sylvie, and the Red Piano was a safe place for meeting, drinking and dancing. It sounded like a plan. They paid their bill and left hefty tips for having monopolized the table much of the night. Sylvie also mentioned to the waiter that they were going over to the Red Piano and invited him to join them when his shift ended. The waiter agreed to do his best to make it there.

The girls walked down the hill the short distance to the Red Piano. It was located in the small strip of shops which included the Peli Deli Food Market and the Shipwreck Shop, which also had other locations on the island. There were several dozen people out walking in the area as was customary. It was a great gathering place for fun in St. Maarten.

Inside the Red Piano, partiers stood shoulder to shoulder. Tables were set up, and regulars who were Americans living on the island, were at tables unofficially reserved for them by the Red Piano management. As one walked in, there was a large "L" shaped bar on the right with stools that were occupied, and where other patrons would try to squeeze between those sitting to order drinks. Past the length of the bar was a small dance floor, and behind that a small area for live bands to set up to perform. This was a happening spot, where many old friends and friends still to meet, would congregate well into the early morning hours. With the time just past ten, the bar had gone from almost empty before 9:00 p.m. to maximum capacity. It was a regular but late crowd that enjoyed the best gathering spot in the area.

Sylvie and Terri mingled, striking up conversations as a twosome and individually, with the extremely friendly patrons. Both Sylvie and Terri felt at home, made easy with their good looks and outgoing personalities. They were both very smart and successful as well, and all loved them. They were respectful of all and genuinely interested in getting to know others.

The two partied, with each nursing one more drink over the next several hours. They walked through and around all of the bar. One of the bartenders took a break near midnight, stepped outside and made a phone call. "Mr. Harrington, this is Rollo from the Red Piano. I think I've spotted your girl tonight." He listened. "Yes, she's here now. She is here with a friend, a real looker."

"Please take a picture of the girl and her friend and send it to me," replied Harrington.

"I'll step in now and do it. They look like they're still going strong. I think they'll be here for a while longer." Rollo walked back in and seeing Sylvie and Terri in an animated conversation, snapped several pictures with his phone. He texted them to Harrington. Harrington received the pictures and sent them to his two primary employees in charge of tracking her. "Antonio, I just sent you and Baldo pictures. It's Sylvie. Interestingly, I also know the woman with her. Her name is Terri. They are at the Red Piano. I need you to head over now. There's a slight change of plans." He continued, "Follow them, but do not make contact. I want to know where they are staying. Let me know when you have that. I'll be waiting for your message. Then call it a night. I'll be back to you when it's time to do more."

Antonio called Baldo and went to pick him up in his sedan. They drove to the Red Piano, went inside and spotted the women. They took seats at the bar near the door and waited.

Around 1:00 a.m. Sylvie was wearing down. Terri had been ready to leave, but was always willing to party a little longer as any good friend would. They walked out of the bar and back to their car just outside of the Greenhouse. Antonio and Baldo also walked out, Antonio going to the car, and Baldo following on foot. Antonio drove and slowed to a stop when he spotted Baldo, with the girls thirty yards in front of Baldo. As the girls got in their car, Antonio eased forward, picked up Baldo, and waited to follow at a safe distance. Knowing the girls had been drinking, Antonio was comfortable that they would be unaware of being followed. He used normal caution, nonetheless.

FIFTEEN

BEN ARRIVED BACK at Lubrique. It had been a very good meal at Lee's and he enjoyed spending time with Nico. But now he was glad to be back in his room and wanted to see Lauren. He thought about dropping in on her, as she had done the prior night on him, but thought it could be scary for her to have an unannounced knock on the door. He decided to call. He went in his room and tried Lauren on his cell. It rang with no answer. He took off his shirt and stepped out of his flip flops. He brushed his teeth, passing a little time before trying her again by phone. There was still no answer. He turned on the TV and waited for another thirty minutes to pass before trying again. It was now after 11:00 p.m. He called and she still did not answer. This time he decided to leave a message. "Lauren, I'm back from dinner with Nico. I missed you. I hope you've been having a good time. I'm in for the night. Please call me or come over if you're up for it. I hope to talk to you soon."

Ben sat back. He was restless. He fidgeted for about thirty more minutes. He wanted to try Lauren again, but decided it would be inappropriate. Besides, he did not want to look over-anxious to someone he had just met, no matter how much fun it had been. After a few more minutes he decided to go to bed. He undressed and set his phone alarm for 6:30 a.m. If she called or came by, he would be happy to see her, but realized she might not try getting with him this late. He turned out the lights and got under the covers.

Ben slept little. He looked at his phone and saw it was after 1:00 a.m. He laid there a few minutes before getting up. He was curious why she had not called him back. He slipped into his swim trunks, put on a t-shirt, and decided to walk outside to see if he could tell anything about whether she was in or not. He walked over but did not see any lights. It was way too late to knock. He decided to walk back to his room but was not ready to go back just yet. It was a beautiful night with a clear sky and almost full moon. The walk along the beach was peaceful and he presumed it to be safe. He decided to walk further north along the beach, and just let his mind go blank. He became one with the beach with a heightened awareness of the night sounds in the quiet of the hour. He realized he was a solitary figure on the beach. All was quiet.

As Ben approached the mid-point of the white crescent beach, he heard talking and laughing. Two women were walking up a flight of stairs. Their voices carried in the night. They seemed to be having a good time and returning from a late night out. He continued walking slowly with his eyes directed toward the source of the only sounds other than those of the wind and water. He watched the women enter a room on the third floor. His view of them ended, and he moved his attention back toward the water's edge. It was then he spotted two more people who appeared to be large male figures. What held his gaze was that neither spoke nor made any other sounds. He slowed to almost a stop to observe. The men looked as if they were also watching the women. That did not seem unusual, because even at a distance, it was clear that they were both attractive, and could easily catch a man's eye. What was surprising was that once out of sight and probably out of earshot, there was no nudging between the men, or comments on how good-looking the women were. In fact, to have been following them with their look, it was very strange that nothing was said. They instead came to a complete stop, stood momentarily, and then turned to go back in the direction from which they had come. And still there was no discussion.

Ben decided to continue on his same course. His curiosity compelled him to watch, following the two men from a distance. He saw them turn and walk away for another fifty yards before getting into a sedan and driving away. Ben walked back to where he saw the girls go inside. He decided to check the name of the lodging, and made note of where the door was to check which room they were in during daylight hours. La Playa Orient Bay. Ben planned to return sometime before the next nightfall to confirm the room number.

At 2 a.m. he decided he had walked enough. It would be a tiring day of boating and he hoped he would be able to sleep. He walked by Lauren's room one more time and seeing no activity and no lights on, assumed she was sleeping. He knew he should be sleeping also. He went back to his room, undressed, and got back into bed. His phone on the nightstand set for 6:30, he had time for a few more hours of sleep. He closed his eyes and was quickly unconscious to the world.

At 6:30 his sleep alarm sounded. Ben always woke early, and with the early sunrise in St. Martin, he was fully awake and looking forward to a big day. Thinking Lauren may have been out late last night, he would not bother her with a call this morning. He hoped she got his message and would return his call. He wanted to renew his relationship with her.

Ben ate a muffin and had a Coke for his breakfast. It was not his usual breakfast which included juice and low-fat milk, but thought it was fine for on vacation. He showered, shaved and brushed his teeth. He then put on his 30 SPF sunscreen and was ready to go. He decided to take a quick walk along the beach because he had some time to spare. He hoped he might bump into Lauren, and would walk up to La Playa to check out the room number of the two women from the night before. There were a few clouds, and the forecast called for generally good weather, with a chance for brief showers. More importantly, the winds were calm and would make for a smooth boat ride. The tour group would have good weather for their around island tour. It had been a while since he had been on a boat and he looked forward to seeing Nico with full command of the vessel.

The walk up the beach was at a brisk pace, much faster than his last walk. As he got to La Playa, he decided he would walk up the stairs to see the room number. He did not think he would create fear or suspicion if he was seen. He would look and leave without knocking, as if realizing he was at the wrong room. He walked up the stairs at a normal pace, and reaching the top landing, he made mental note of the room number before retracing his steps back to the beach. He walked back at the same brisk pace. As he reached the beach in front of his room, he looked around, panning the area hoping to see Lauren. She was not out. He hung out for a couple more minutes, realizing it was time to leave to make it to the Simpson Bay Marina by 8:30 a.m.

He went into his room and grabbed his phone, wallet and a beach towel. He was set for the boat trip. Before leaving, he again considered giving in to the temptation to call Lauren. What would he say? He had already left a message asking her to give him a call or stop by. Instead of calling, he decided to send a quick text. "Sorry I missed you last night. Thought I might see you on the beach this morning. I'm heading over to the marina. Hope you are well. I'm asking you to go with me for a late dinner tonight. Send me a text or give me a call. Don't know if I'll have a cell signal on the boat. Thinking about you. Will call when back on shore. Sorry for long message." Ben walked out of his room and locked the door. He walked to his car and was ready for an adventure on the water.

SIXTEEN

··

THE GROUP WAS on the 38-foot boat at Simpson Bay Marina. After Ben boarded, Nico began the preliminary talk of basic boating, including where the life jackets were held on board available for all. Lunch would be served later on shore and there would be open bar on the boat with beer, rum punch, sodas and water. Snorkel masks and fins were available for the group along with noodles for floating in the beautiful sea. The boat would be doing a trip around the island with a couple stops for snorkeling, and an additional fun stop with more information to be shared about it at that time. There could also be another brief stop or two depending on how long the group wanted to stay at the snorkel spots.

The ten members of the Northeast Florida Tiki Hut Association took off their cover-ups and gave them to Ben for storage, and would get them back when the trip ended around 5:00 p.m. The group was comprised of island lovers who all had a zest for life. They were Jeanne and Chris, a married couple who were experienced boaters and avid fishermen, Paulie and Tammy, she a buxom blond and he her handsome and proud husband, Dale and Mary, he a lawyer and she a probate paralegal, Catherine and Mark, she a schoolteacher and he a technology expert, and two singles, Sara, a radiologist and the smartest of the very bright and successful group, and Kathy, a very attractive litigation paralegal. They were looking forward to a few ice-cold beers and refreshing rum punches as they explored the waters just off the coast of St. Maarten/St. Martin.

The boat trip began from the Simpson Bay area at Pelican Key, traveling east off the southern coast of Dutch St. Maarten. They made the northern turn, going past the Dutch capital of Philipsburg. Nico slowed the boat for picture taking, with Ben having custody of some of the cameras and taking pictures on command. He was also enjoying the tour of the island from the water. Ben took pictures of the full tiki group as they passed Philipsburg. Several large cruise ships docked in close proximity were in the background of the group photos. Next was the first scheduled stop of the day at a reef a bit off the shore of Dawn Beach. All decided to get in the water for snorkeling, including Ben, leaving just Nico on board. There were colorful fish and a sighting of a sea turtle. A few photos were taken by the snorkelers, and as each snorkeler climbed back aboard, the snorkeling gear was exchanged for either a cold Heineken or a clear plastic cup of rum punch. Starting at 11:00 a.m. was not too early to begin the refreshments. As the last snorkeler climbed on board, Ben again obliged the tiki hutters and captured a couple group photos.

With drinks in hand and amid discussions of the great snorkeling experience, they were underway again. They traveled northward along the eastern coast. The boat slowed along the Orient Beach coast, with individuals taking advantage of the slow movement of the boat for another prime photo opportunity. Ben could see Lubrique as they passed on their port side. He scanned the beach, hoping to spot Lauren, but did not see her. They continued further to the north, along the area of beach in front of La Playa. He was not sure he would recognize the two young ladies he had seen in the wee hours entering their room, but looked for them also. He did not see them, knowing that even if they were on Orient Beach, they could easily be somewhere other than in front of their lodging. The boat moved on, this time stopping at Green Cay for additional snorkeling. Green Cay was an uninhabited small island just off the coast of Orient. A strong swimmer could swim from Orient to Green Cay. As they anchored in the shallow water, there were a half dozen sunbathers scattered on the Green Cay beach facing Orient. There was also a banana boat group skirting the coast a little further to the north. Jeanne, Chris, Paulie, Tammy and Sara all decided to stay on the boat at this stop, with Jeanne, Chris and Sara all having their second beer, while Tammy and Paulie each enjoyed another rum punch. The other five opted for fifteen minutes of snorkeling. The snorkeling was again good, primarily with viewing tropical fish. The water depth was shallow, so there was no colorful coral to observe at either of the snorkel spots. Kathy was able to get a picture of a squid, and a good time was again had by each of the snorkelers, who quickly caught up with refreshing drinks upon re-entering the boat.

Next, they continued to the north, crossing the most northern point of the island, before continuing southwest along the coast. They prepared for their third stop which was at Happy Bay. Lunch would be served at Happy Bay. There were a few structures up the very steep hill overlooking the beach, but Happy Bay remained an unpeopled beach, with the few beach goers either arriving by boat, or by hiking across from Friar's Bay. Friar's Bay is a family-friendly beach with calm shallow water. Friar's and Happy are both on the French side, with topless sunning common at both, and a few naturists enjoying the isolated beach at Happy Bay. Also at Happy Bay was an enterprising islander who maintained a grill and prepared chicken and ribs for sale to the few people visiting that beach. A structure made of old wood with a sloping wooden roof served as the area for dining in the shade. Several old picnic tables were located there for common seating. The group of ten would all crowd hip to hip at one of the large tables.

Nico greeted the Happy Bay grillmaster. "Danny, thanks for preparing your ribs and chicken today. This is the group from Florida I told you about. They have been thirsty, and now they've all worked up an appetite." Nico and Ben assisted Danny with serving the meal of ribs, chicken, beans and rice, salad and some assorted fruit. The plates were taken the few steps to each of the seated diners, with Ben and Nico grabbing the last two plates and sitting at the adjoining picnic table. Everyone at the crowded picnic table had a beer or rum punch, with Ben opening his first beer of the day, while Nico had a Coke. There was lively talking among the group of close friends. "I'm so glad we got this trip organized where we're all doing St. Martin together. Nico, thanks so much for what has been a great start of the day," said Jeanne, who appeared to be one of the group leaders. "Danny, excellent job today, especially the ribs. They're one of my favorites." Danny was a man of few words, and nodded appreciation in response to the kind words.

The group finished their meals, and the plates and empty beer cans were dropped into the large trash can set up a little beyond the picnic area.

"It's now time for a St. Martin treat. Let's everybody go down to the beach." Nico led the group away from the shade of the picnic tables to a sunny area near the beach. "Okay," he continued, "lets gather in a circle and I'll explain what happens next. I used to do a stop in Tintamarre, which is an uninhabited island off of Orient. Visitors to

Tintamarre began participating in mud baths, where they would get mud similar to an expensive spa treatment, and rub on each other's bodies. The mud would dry, then dip in the water, and your skin would be soft like a baby. The mud baths got real popular, and St. Martin decided to stop them. Said they posed a health risk. Said the mud brought sickness. Never knew anybody got sick; think they just wanted it stopped before all the mud was gone. So now I stop at Happy Bay and bring my own special mud. We can do the Tintamarre mud bath here at Happy Bay. Now who wants a mud bath?"

"As the group doctor, my medical opinion is it would be bad for one's health to *not* have a mud bath. I don't think anyone wants to come back from this boat trip with skin not looking as soft and smooth as that of a baby. You can definitely count me in," said Sara. Everyone was eager to begin. Ben and Nico went back to the picnic area and brought back a cooler filled with the silky-smooth mud. "Okay," continued Nico, "you all been wearing swimsuits all day. That is good. It also good if you want full mud treatment, swimsuits are not needed on Happy Bay."

Tammy quickly got started, unleashing her award-winning assets and tossing her top to the sand. "These babies have been deprived of the sun on this trip, but they're not going to be deprived of the mud!" All of the girls joined in joyously, creating a stack of tops on the beach. The guys were appreciative of the initiative shown and each tossed his trunks onto the growing pile of discarded garments. As Dale and Paulie led the masculine unveiling, almost as one the girls continued their own disrobing and aimed their bottoms to the growing stack of clothes. Nico and Ben remained in trunks as the overseers of the beach mud spa operation.

"Ben, would you act as the group photographer and document the spa process for us with photos?" asked Mary. She had always seemed the most reserved of the group, but was now all-in, much to the delight of her husband Dale. "Yes, if you could get some pictures with each camera, but we can always share them with each other," added Catherine. "I'd also like to get a few pictures of Mark and me when we're fully mudded. We just finished a building project at home where we expanded our bedroom. We have some new wall space now where I'd like to put a couple of the pictures up. I think they'd be a great addition!" Mark smiled, thinking any false notions of him being geeky because of his technology knowledge had now been replaced with a new appreciation of him, as he was clearly an accomplished lover with a tigress for a wife.

"Sure, I'll be happy to take photos for you," replied Ben. "I'm here to help."

"Great," added Sara. "This will be awesome," said Kathy. "My golfing buddies at home are going to be so jealous!"

The group began to lather the mud on themselves and each other. There was much laughter and grins all around. But before the full mudding began, Jeanne got on her knees behind Chris, each of her hands caked in mud, and placed perfect palm prints with fingers pointed up on each of his butt cheeks. Chris then did the same to Jeanne, and an early picture of the hand printed duo was made by Ben at Chris's request.

All were mostly conservative, mudding those areas typically shielded from the sun without assistance from others. The exceptions were Mary and Catherine, who were seemingly enjoying their new competition as to who could be crowned as the mud queen leader. "It's early to be thinking about the Christmas holidays, but I'm having more fun than a five-year-old on Christmas morning," commented Catherine.

"Yes, indeed," continued Mary. "Speaking of holidays, this makes me think of gift wrapping, as I do most of the gift wrapping in our house. I think I'll start practicing my wrapping skills today. Dale, step on over here. I'll do some mud wrapping on that package you're no longer hiding. I believe it has my name on it."

Dale was speechless but did not object.

"Nice one," responded Catherine. "Mary, you are an inspiration. Mark, step over here and I'll help you with your mud."

The group finished mudding and more photos were taken. Paulie hoisted Tammy on his back, and she wrapped her legs around his waist, her chin on top of his head, and the weight of her upper body on his shoulders. Paulie's head was made into a Tammy sandwich, leaving him temporarily deaf but very happy.

Nico instructed them to all sit in a tight circle, with their feet in the center almost touching. Photos were made of the group capturing from knees to feet in an artistic shot.

After the mudding ended, Jeanne had become uncharacteristically quiet. "If there are no more pictures anybody wants, it's time to rinse off the mud and we'll get back on the boat," instructed Nico.

"Before we do that," began Jeanne, "I have one more photo idea. We've been staying at Villa Islandtude and having a great time this week. I'd like to make a special photo for leaving in the villa." Villa Islandtude was a villa overlooking Simpson Bay that preserved the traditional look and feel of a Caribbean villa, but was steeped in privacy and luxury. The open concept with a large 20' by 40' pool and a huge sunning deck had facilitated great fun during the week. "There are ten of us," continued

Jeanne, "and there are ten letters in the word 'Islandtude'. I propose we spell out 'Islandtude' by each of us forming a letter with our bodies. Here, I'll show you." Jeanne then turned her back to the group, bent over at the waist, and resting her elbows on her knees, clasped her hands together, forming the letter 'A' with her body. The group loved the idea and Jeanne's 'A'.

Jeanne took charge of the group again, having them form a straight line in front of the calm sea, and each took her instruction on forming the letters spelling 'Islandtude'. Dale began, standing tall and straight as the 'I'. Sara formed the 'S' by having her feet to knees on the ground with body raised and curved forward while holding her head. Mark was the 'L' by standing straight on his knees, his knees to feet forming the bottom of the letter. A space was reserved for Jeanne to be the 'A'. Mary was the 'N' by doing a girl's pushup on her knees, then having her feet pointed skyward. To form the two 'Ds' were the double D girls of Tammy and Kathy, where each rested their knees to feet on the ground and arched their backs, letting their hands fall behind them to touch their heels. Chris formed the 'T' by standing tall and holding his elbows out from his sides parallel to the ground. Catherine formed the 'U' by lying on the ground on her back, raising her feet in the air with rear to the camera. Paulie was the final letter, forming an 'E' by standing with feet to knees on the ground, his right arm down from the shoulder and then out, and his left arm out parallel with the ground at head level. Once they were all in place, Ben again was the photographer and captured the tribute to Villa Islandtude.

The group dipped and swam, rubbing the final places where mud continued to cling. Once they were close to mud-free, they went ashore and gathered their suits. They dressed and waded back to the boat.

Nico addressed the happy group. "Everybody, have a drink. We have time for one more stop." Ben passed beers to all the beer drinkers, then poured fresh rum punch for all the rum drinkers. The boat continued almost due west, passing Nettle Bay, Bay Rouge and then Plum Bay before turning south and then southeast following the coast. They passed picturesque Long Bay, Cupecoy and Mullet Bay. They then came to the Maho area where they could see the Sunset Beach Bar where tourists loved to congregate to watch the planes land. The planes approach the landing strip from over the beach, at times so low it would look like the beachgoers might need to duck. It was now after 4:00 in the afternoon and there was one more major airplane scheduled to land soon.

Nico made them aware of the large jumbo jet that could be seen approaching in the distance. Ben jumped in the water with a water-proof camera to capture the event, angling past the bow toward the incoming plane. He stopped far enough away to capture everyone in the group, but still close to the boat. Jeanne had continued her leadership role, instructing all in the group to set down their drinks to form a tight line to welcome the new guests that would be landing. As the plane was almost to the boat, upon Jeanne's command, the group bowed, pulled down their bottoms to moon the captain and passengers, then continued with enthusiastic waves. Ben clicked the frames, capturing the ten-person nautical salute, and again as each waved with their hands extended high over their heads. It had been a great day at sea and the boat headed back to the marina.

Back at the marina, the happy cruisers thanked Nico for the great day and headed back to their cars. They planned to continue the day at the Villa Islandtude pool, and to call Vesna of Vesna's Taverna, to see if it would be possible to have dinner delivered to them.

Ben stayed to help Nico wash down the boat. "Thanks for your help today Ben."

'It was a great day. I needed this. It was a total escape. You had a super group and it was a lot of fun. Thank you so much for inviting me."

"Glad you had fun. Now you go on and take off. I can finish here. You need to get back and see that new friend of yours."

"Thanks Nico. You're the best." The old friends hugged and Ben was glad there was still a little daylight left. He got in his car and drove toward Orient Beach.

SEVENTEEN

SYLVIE AND TERRI slept in until 10:00 a.m. It had been a fun evening, and Terri had mostly recovered from the long day of travel followed by the late night of partying with Sylvie. Today was expected to be a sun on the beach day.

The girls got up and leisurely took turns showering. After showering, they applied their sunscreen, helping with each other's back. They put on their bikinis, grabbed a cover-up and sandals, and walked down to the resort's informal dining area. Only a couple of others were seated in the open-air dining room. They each opted for a croissant, fruit and orange juice. They chatted as they enjoyed their food. They were on island time. "Good morning," greeted the manager and owner, Marie. "Is your room okay? Is there anything you need?"

"No, everything is great," responded Sylvie. "We slept in after a late night of fun and are planning to relax on the beach today. Does it look like a busy day for you?"

"No, I have a couple rooms checking out today, and three rooms coming in, so quiet today."

The girls lingered at their table a few more minutes, then went back to their room. They brushed their teeth, each grabbed a towel, and they shared a beach bag for their key, combs, cash and books. They put their sunglasses on and decided to walk down barefoot. There was no need for beach shoes for the short walk to the beach. They decided to stop for a while at the chairs set up for guest use by La Playa. Later in the afternoon they would walk further down the beach where tourists had a tendency to gather. For the late morning, however, they closed their eyes and chatted, never reaching into the beach bag for their books. They rarely read books on the beach. Instead, the options of lying back luxuriating in the sun, dipping in the ocean, chatting and meeting new friends, all ranked much higher than book reading. Today was no different. Terri shared with Sylvie all her news from home, and Sylvie enjoyed Terri's company. After several hours, they decided it was time to walk the beach before setting up further to the south. They left their beach bag on the chairs tucked under one of the towels. They had a little cash in the bag as the only item of value and were comfortable that their belongings would be left undisturbed. Terri grabbed the key, and they began their walk. They started toward the less populated end where the far point of the beach was anchored by the Mont Vernon. It had gone through several stages of own-ership, and was currently operating somewhat like a time-share arrangement, but with some units being individually owned and not part of the time-share pool. Once reaching the Mont Vernon, they reversed course, and walked toward the end of the beach once occupied by Club Orient that was now home of the new mini-resort Lubrique.

As they ventured south, they made note of the new restaurants that had opened as well as the old favorites. "I really miss Baywatch, or Andy's Place, or whatever it was last called," said Terri. She continued, "There was nothing else on the beach to compare. With all the license plates decorating the wooden open-air structure, to the cheerful greeting with kisses that one could always count on from

Cheryl, one of the owners, to the incredible cooking provided by Andy, it was an institution."

"Yes, it was," replied Sylvie. "I remember stopping for breakfast there several times. And the lunches were to die for. There are other great places around, but I really miss that place. I remember going there from the beach. You could go up the few wooden steps to eat and have a seat at the wooden tables. It was fine if you were wearing a bikini, monokini, just had a wrap around your waist, or no kini at all, for men and women, it was all fine. Everyone was welcomed. I hope Cheryl is doing well. I'd really love to see her smiling face again."

"Yes, not to get too nostalgic, but I remember eating there on the fourth of July one year. The nude fourth of July beach parade had ended, that's another story on its own, and many of the parade participants were loving life enjoying their late lunch in their parade uniforms. It was all great! Wow, how I'd love to have that one more time!"

"This is certainly a magical place. I don't think it's just this French girl," continued Sylvie, referring to herself. "The friendliest people in the world must come to St. Martin, or the magic of the island makes them that way. Most of my closest friends are friendships that began right here in St. Martin. And of course, we met here, and immediately became great friends. All of my friends have similar stories of quickly making lasting friendships with people they met here."

The girls completed their trip down memory lane and at the far southern point of the beach, turned to return to their chairs. There they laid back for a few minutes resting from the roundtrip walk of two and a half miles. With the time now after 2:00 p.m., they decided to begin several hours of power sunning. They each re-applied their lotion, gathered their belongings, and walked a short distance down to the open area of the beach where, without chairs, people were congregating.

Terri and Sylvie placed their towels on the sand. They placed their beach bag down between the towels, and leaned back, propping their upper bodies up on their elbows. They watched the crowd for a few minutes. It was time to get in the water. They each came out of their bikinis, tucking the tiny bits of fabric into the side of the beach bag. They both knew the benefits of avoiding a wet swimsuit. Neither would ever consider returning to wearing wet swimwear unless it was absolutely required.

"This water is perfect," called Sylvie. "I don't know why I waited so long to get in."

"Yes, still got some sun to warm the air and only a light breeze. This is as good as it gets." They splashed, swam around, and talked to others as they would get in the water near them. The people at Orient must be some of the friendliest people in the world. They never seemed to meet a stranger. Unless someone gave off unmistakable signals of not wanting to have their thoughts interrupted, everyone welcomed a greeting from someone who could easily become a new friend. Orient Beach was a special place. After standing and swimming in the water for about forty-five minutes, they decided to get out and take a short walk. They glanced back at the beach bag and towels, and began to walk north for about five minutes, then turned around for the walk back. Instead of stopping at their towels, they walked to the southern-most point and then returned. It was hard to describe the delicious feeling of getting out of the ocean, walking unencumbered, and letting your hair and body dry in the light ocean breeze. "Life is great," smiled Sylvie. "It's been another phenomenal day in paradise. Island time, island breezes, great friends and salty kisses." She gave Terri an innocent kiss on her cheek as they got back to their towels. "I feel like a child again. Every time I come here, I think it can't get better, and I wonder how I can ever leave this place."

Terri took that opportunity to turn the discussion to a more serious subject. "Sylvie, do you want to talk about your adventure Saturday night at Gregorio Harrington's place? I know I shared earlier how he had invited me there. He seemed totally uncaring when he opened his safe and took no precautions on my seeing the combination. When you acted like you didn't believe me, I told you the combination to show you I wasn't making it up. But I didn't think you would actually try to use the combination for any reason."

"Well, I had a long time to think about it. The more I thought, the more determined I was to check out that safe. You've heard the same rumors as me, and if they are true, I wanted to know. A little evidence from that safe could make me a wealthy girl. I'd never leave this island again."

"Yes, but you knew it was a long shot. And what would you have done if you were caught?"

"Well, I wasn't caught, and he was none the wiser. Now, I just need to come up with a plan B. When I have the plan, and his secret, I'll share my new wealth with you. Neither of us will ever have to leave this island again."

"Okay, Sylvie." Terri was not sure if she was kidding, completely serious, or somewhere in-between. "When you have your plan, let me know. You know you can always count on me if you need anything. What are friends for!" Terri stopped talking and let the thought hang in the air. Sylvie did not respond, and Terri still did not know if Sylvie was at all serious. She would let it drop unless Sylvie brought it up again.

It was now after 5:00 in the afternoon. The sun was low in the sky, and the beach chairs had been gathered. Sylvie and Terri gathered their belongings from the beach and walked back to La Playa. They did not have any plans for the evening, but that was not a problem. They were on the island and living on island time. They were confident a plan would happen without them trying to create one. That was how it always worked when the two of them were together in St. Martin. They were comfortable with each other as best friends and knew anything they did would be great.

Once back in the room, Sylvie suggested Terri shower first. Terri was quick in and out of the shower. She wrapped a towel around herself in lieu of drying, combed out her hair and continued to get ready for whatever would be next. Sylvie stepped into the shower and enjoyed the hot spray as it washed away the salt and sand of the day. She re-lived much of the day as she lathered and let the hot water run down her body. It had been a great day, and she had little doubt the evening would be equally as fun. She was lucky to have Terri as her best friend, and thought about different restaurants. She would let Terri pick tonight. Terri was a trooper going dancing with her at the Red Piano after just arriving earlier in the day. She was certainly tired and probably would have preferred an earlier evening. Sylvie would finish her shower and would soon be ready for another night of fun.

EIGHTEEN

DEAN JANSON LOOKED forward to the scheduled afternoon meeting with Robert Vaughn. He spent the morning looking over the casino books. The casino was a cash cow, and the revenues had increased dramatically each of the last three years. The prospect of easy money from Vaughn piqued his curiosity. He was told the contact was through Harrington, but why? He and Harrington were well aware of each other, and knew the other generally travelled within a different circle of business associates. Was this really Harrington reaching out to him? If so, what did he want in return? He did not want to be indebted to Harrington.

Dean's wife was still off island and would not be back for another few weeks. His roving eye was creating a problem, one which he wanted to deal with directly. He had approached the beautiful blond who had distracted him while the theft occurred at the roulette table. She was at the casino with friends and not with a significant other. Of course she had a boyfriend. What beautiful woman would not have several men vying for her. But she was unattached and still enjoyed fishing for more. She was flattered when he asked for her number, and she gladly provided it to him.

At noon Dean decided to call the beautiful blond. "Hello Debi, this is Dean from the casino. I enjoyed meeting you Saturday night. How are you today?"

Debi was pleased to receive the call. She loved that Dean had fallen under her spell, and believed as an added bonus, he had money. Lots of money. "Well good afternoon. I'm well. I'm enjoying the St. Martin sun on the beach right now."

"I hope I'm not disturbing you."

"No, not at all. I can sun and talk at the same time even though I am a blond." She giggled. "And my hair is already covering my ears, so the phone won't cause any tan lines." She laughed, knowing she was not a blond with no brain, but was actually very smart and very funny.

"Great, I'm glad I got the chance to call you today. I thought about you yesterday and apologize for not calling sooner. I had some business I was working on, where I have a couple deals in the works, and got tied up. But I promise I did not forget you. I'm preparing for a business meeting now scheduled for 4:00 this afternoon. I'm expecting it to go well, and after it's done, I'm going to need someone to help me celebrate. I know it is very short notice, and I apologize for that, but I would be honored if you would allow me to take you to dinner tonight. You name the place and we'll be there."

"Well Dean, what would you think of me if I accept your invitation on such short notice? Would you be comfortable if I abandoned my friends tonight to accept a better offer?"

Dean chuckled. "I would be honored if you abandon your friends tonight. But I have a plan to make it where you are not abandoning them, but helping them. You simply tell them that the handsome gentleman from the casino called. He had several propositions, one of which I hope you tell them you are very interested in accepting. But you are also doing it for them, because he is going to set each of them up with chips at the casino, a dinner at one of the five restaurants there, and excellent tickets for the Vegas-style show for tomorrow night. But to get those things for them, you must accompany me tonight."

Debi was pleased. Not only would she be getting what she wanted, Dean had given her an easy way to accept. She was impressed with his quick mind. "I believe my friends would be upset if I declined your generous offer. I love my friends dearly," she said, her voice becoming playful, "and will do what is needed of me for their benefit."

Dean loved her response and tone. The evening was looking up. "I will give you a call as soon as this afternoon's business is concluded. I should be able to pick you up around seven. Is that good for you?"

"Yes, but where are we going? I'll need to know to be dressed appropriately."

"You can surprise me. But if you don't have a selection, my recommendation is we go to Spiga in Grand Case. It is always excellent, and I can make a reservation for 7:30."

"That sounds good. I'll look for your call and will be ready for you at seven tonight." They ended the call, with each expecting a rewarding end to the evening.

Dean continued his preparation for his meeting with Vaughn. His final preparation was to make certain the listening devices at the table in the Grill were fully functioning, and that the conversation would be recorded in his office for later review. Although potentially risky, maintaining the recorded conversations could be beneficial as leverage as proven in the past. Dean was an accomplished businessman, and he was preparing to maintain an upper hand in any deal he might enter into with Vaughn.

At 3:45 p.m. Dean walked into the Grill Restaurant of his casino. There were a few customers, and his table was marked *Reserved* for the meeting. He had also given instructions that all nearby tables be marked as well. No diners would be allowed within earshot of their conversation.

Robert Vaughn arrived for the meeting promptly at 4:00 p.m. and the obligatory pleasantries were exchanged. "Mr. Vaughn, pleased to meet you. Before we get started, would you like me to give you a brief tour of the property?"

"That won't be necessary," replied Vaughn. "I believe I am well enough acquainted for our preliminary discussions. I do have a few questions for you, however. I've received some general information on the size of your operation. It is common knowledge that yours is the biggest casino on the island. If we do business together, I would agree to a trial basis at first, in order to see how it goes. After that, we can see where it goes from there."

The discussion continued for more than an hour. Dean provided information which was mostly accurate, and to the extent he was comfortable sharing. A general plan was reached for the coming month, starting out very small. A steady stream of associates of Mr. Vaughn would be coming into the casino and purchasing chips with money from their operations. After playing for a while, the chips would then be cashed reflecting the house cut of winnings, and a receipt would be provided for the amount of the remaining money. These receipts would be the basis for reporting as winnings to make the cash 'clean'. There would also be a few larger winnings that would be included as well, with the casino laundering the cash by issuing checks for winnings. If all were to go well, there would be an acceleration of the program, with the possibility of other business projects that could be run through the casino.

The gentlemen concluded their meeting with an understanding for beginning their business arrangement. "Mr. Janson, if your offer to show me around your property is still open, I would greatly enjoy taking that tour now. I am familiar with your casino, but would like to learn more about your five restaurants that are part of the property. I do believe they could become part of an expanded business relationship if all goes well."

"Certainly, let's begin." The two men continued with light discussion as the tour was underway. At 6:15 p.m., Dean was ready to end the business discussions to make his dinner appointment without being late. "Mr. Vaughn, I hope you have enjoyed the tour and I hope I've provided the information you were seeking. I look forward to future discussions, but I have another meeting at dinner that I need to make. I hope you understand."

"Certainly, this has been a good start. I look forward to what could be a long and profitable relationship." The men shook hands, and Vaughn departed. It was time for Dean to quickly get ready for his evening with Debi.

NINETEEN

....

BEN HURRIED BACK to Orient Beach. He had two pressing goals. One was to meet up with Lauren. The second was to check in on the two ladies he had seen entering La Playa around 1:30 a.m. He had tried calling Lauren when he reached his car, and he still did not get an answer.

He was inside his room and tried Lauren again. "Hello," Lauren answered.

"Hey, Lauren, I've been trying to reach you. Is everything okay?"

"Yes, sure, how are you?"

"I'm fine, and glad you're okay. I've been trying to reach you last night and today. I'm just getting back from helping Nico. Did you get my messages?"

"Yes, but I don't keep my phone on me. I checked this afternoon and saw that you called. How was your dinner and boat trip with your friend?"

"They were fine. I'd like to have dinner with you tonight if you don't have other plans." He was reluctant to mention his other priority, but sunlight was limited and he felt he needed to check in on the ladies soon. He did not want to stop by after dark and possibly be viewed as some kind of threat to them. "I have a quick errand that I need to take care of, but it shouldn't take more than thirty minutes, forty-five minutes tops, but can get ready real quick. Are you up for dinner with me tonight?"

"Call me when you're done. I should be here." They ended the call and Ben hurried out the door. He strode up the beach, a combination of fast walk and slow jog. He slowed as he reached La Playa, made sure he was not sweating and his breathing was at a normal pace, then took the stairs to the third floor. He knocked, hoping for an answer, but not sure how he would introduce himself or the very strange purpose of his visit. Thankfully, everyone he had met on Orient Beach had been very friendly, so he hoped these women would give him a chance to talk to them.

"Just a minute." Terri opened the door about a foot, and looked at Ben, her towel still wrapped around her.

"Hey, I'm Ben Carlisle. I'm a neighbor of yours just down the beach. I'm so sorry for coming by unannounced, I've been on a boat trip all day, just got back, and wanted to talk to you briefly about something from late last night, actually early this morning, if you have just a couple minutes."

"Um, okay, I guess. I met a lot of people last night at the Red Piano, but I'm sorry I don't remember you. Maybe you were talking with Sylvie. You look harmless enough. Come on in and I'll get Sylvie." Terri turned toward the bathroom and heard the shower spray end. "Sylvie, we have a visitor. Ben from last night."

Sylvie walked out of the shower, grabbed a towel and started drying her hair as she stepped into the living area. "Hello Ben from last night." Sylvie stood in Ben's view as she unhurriedly dried her face, and then her body, before wrapping the towel around herself as Terri had done. "As you can see, we both just finished showers, but please, have a seat." Ben sat in the chair as Terri and Sylvie moved to sit on the couch across from him. Sylvie continued, "To what do we owe this pleasure?"

"Well, thank you. I'm Ben Carlisle. Thank you for inviting me in. I just finished with a boat trip, and apologize I haven't yet showered, so I apologize I'm still in need of a shower. I have a date in a bit for dinner, so not trying to take too much of your time, but just wanted a couple minutes. I saw both of you last night, but not at the Red Piano. I've never been to the Red Piano, but maybe I should check it out sometime." Ben paused, then continued. "I saw you last night, technically this morning. I'm staying just down the beach at Lubrique. Well anyway, without getting into all kinds of details that you wouldn't care about, I was having a hard time sleeping. So, in the wee hours this morning, I took a walk on the beach. That's when I saw both of you. It looked like you were coming in from being out for the night. And it may not be anything, I was still a ways down the beach when I saw you. There wasn't much activity around at that time, so I just saw you. Well, that's part of why I stopped by just now. In addition to seeing the two of you, I saw you coming in, going up the steps, going in your room, but in addition to that, I saw a couple other people. And, this is the weird part, to get to why I'm imposing on you now, there were two guys that I also saw. They were a little behind you. When you were going in your room, they stopped, and it looked like they were watching. That's not all that unusual, I guess, because you're both very attractive, and I'm sure guys look at you all the time. But the strange part about this is they just stood and watched. They didn't say anything. And then, after you went in, they didn't continue walking in the same direction. Instead, they just stopped, then turned and went back from the direction they were coming from. It was like they weren't staying here, either, because I saw them walk to a car, get in, and then leave. I imagine this sounds really crazy. And I assure you it seems crazy to me, too, so I wanted to let you know what I saw. I'm not trying to alarm you and it may be nothing. I promise this isn't some hair-brained idea I came up with to meet you, and I promise I'm not some kind of stalker, but thought I needed to take the chance that even though you might think I'm crazy or some perverted guy, I just wanted you to know." Ben was relieved he had gotten it all out.

Terri looked confused by what Ben had shared. Sylvie tried to maintain an aloof appearance. She was not sure if she should be concerned, but after her Saturday night adventure at Harrington's villa, she was not ready to dismiss the whole of Ben's story as a crazy fabrication. "Wow, that was a mouthful," said Sylvie. "I'm not sure what to say or how to respond. I appreciate you coming by. I always like making new friends. And if you're staying just down the beach, there's a good chance we'll run into each other on the beach this week. We haven't made plans for the night, but as you have a date to start soon, I won't invite you to meet us wherever we end up going tonight. But it is good to meet you Ben Carlisle." With that Sylvie stood, and Ben took the cue to move toward the door to leave. "I'm Sylvie, and this is Terri. I'll look for you on the beach. If you see me, please be sure to say hi."

Ben walked to the door, opened it and stepped out. Before closing the door behind him, he said "I hope ya'll have a great night. Thanks for inviting me in. I'll see you on the beach." He closed the door, walked down the stairs, and hurried back to his room. He quickly undressed, showered, shaved and brushed his teeth. He called Lauren and was relieved when she answered.

"Hey, I just got out of the shower and am about ready. Does it suit for me to come by there in five minutes and we go to dinner?"

"Yes, that sounds good. Where do you want to go?"

"I heard that Vesna Taverna in Simpson Bay is one of the better restaurants on the island. They have a variety with fish, beef and pasta, and great desserts. Does that sound okay with you?"

"Sounds good, I'll see you in a few."

Ben put on a pullover knit shirt, shorts and flip flops. He walked over to Lauren's room. She was stepping out as he walked up, they greeted briefly, and walked to his car. The drive to Simpson Bay was pleasant but quiet. The electricity of a few days ago was missing. Ben understood she might be disappointed with the choices he made, going two straight days to be with Nico, but thought that it could not have been avoided. Besides, Nico was his friend, and he enjoyed his time with him. The time on the boat was a real escape and helped him get his mind back in a festive vacation mode. Although things seemed to have cooled down with Lauren, he hoped and thought that they would both be feeling better about each other soon. A good meal should help. They pulled up to the restaurant and were able to park right in front. They were greeted by Sally, who showed them to a great table for two. They ordered a couple glasses of cabernet, and settled in for what looked like a promising evening with a great meal in a perfect setting.

"So, while I was working helping out Nico, what did you do today? I hope you had fun."

"Yes, it was a good day. I met some people at the 'meeting table' last night for supper, and we decided to get together at the beach today. It was fun. We had a few showers, but none lasted long. When the rain would come up, we would huddle together under an umbrella to stay dry and warm. Then dry off our chairs when it quit, sit for a while, and then huddle again during the next shower. It was fun, we laughed a lot, and just enjoyed the day."

"That sounds good." Ben was curious. "Who did you meet? Are they staying at Lubrique?"

"It was a group at dinner last night. I think there were seven of us. Only four of us met at the beach today. The other three decided to go into Philipsburg to do some shopping today with the spotty rain. We talked today, and although it was fun at the beach, we were thinking of going into Philipsburg tomorrow. I'd like to do a little looking around and shop for a few souvenirs. But tell me about your day."

Ben did not like how Lauren did not say who she had spent the day with, and did not like that she might have made plans without him for shopping tomorrow. The evening was not going as well as he had hoped. "Well, I just helped Nico. He had a group of ten traveling together, and they stopped a couple places for snorkeling, then for lunch and a little beach time, then stopped briefly where the planes come in. The boat went around the island, I helped a little with the boat, got drinks for the customers, helped serve lunch, and took pictures with their cameras and phones for them. I tried to help them have a good time, and Nico needed a couple more hands."

Their wine came and they sat silently sipping on it as they waited for their meal. They each ordered the grilled salmon for their entrée and found it delicious. They ended up getting a bottle of wine, and had crème brulee for dessert. The great food and wine had helped improve the mood at the table. Vesna, the owner of the restaurant, came to the table and greeted them warmly as if now including them as among her friends. She provided a perfect atmosphere and spectacular meal. They paid, went to the car, and drove back to Orient. Once back, Ben put his arm around Lauren and walked her to her room. They stood outside briefly. The silence was uncomfortable. "Do you want to come in?"

"Yes, that would be great. I'm tired from working with Nico, but have been wanting to see you."

They went in, Ben sitting on the couch, and Lauren sitting across from him in the chair. "The meal was great tonight. Thank you very much. Whoever recommended Vesna's made a great recommendation."

"Yes, it was good. I'm so glad you were available to have dinner with me. I would have been very disappointed to miss you again tonight." Ben paused before continuing. "I'd like to have a beach day tomorrow. Have you decided if you're going to the beach or going shopping?"

"I'd like to do both. If I ditch my new friends tomorrow, would you be willing to take me to Philipsburg? Maybe shop in the morning? I wouldn't mind having a quick lunch in town, and then coming back to the beach for the afternoon."

"It's a date," Ben said quickly. He realized on the drive back to Orient from the restaurant how badly he wanted to spend most of his vacation time with Lauren. He was thrilled. He thought the awkward moments from earlier in the evening were over. He felt like celebrating. "Hey, I'd really like you to take a walk on the beach with me. Are you up for it?"

"That sounds great. Let's do it." They hugged, slipped out of their shoes, and walked out on the sand.

TWENTY

AFTER BEN LEFT their room, Sylvie and Terri sat and talked. "Well, what do you think?" asked Terri.

"I hope it's nothing," Sylvie responded. "But I don't know what to think. I don't know what it would be about, unless it has something to do with Harrington. But as I said, he saw nothing, did nothing. I left Sunday morning and nothing was unusual. I find it hard to believe it has to do with my plan there."

"I hope you're right. But what if you're wrong? Or what if it is totally unrelated. Is there anything else going on with you that could be creating a little drama? A secret admirer?"

Sylvie thought. "I don't know. I meet a lot of people. Maybe somebody is interested and doesn't know normal social graces. Maybe it's somebody who is a little creepy. If so, probably just a nuisance, no big deal." Sylvie paused. "What about you? I haven't had anything out of the ordinary here. This came on the first night after you got on island. So, what about you? Any past dalliances that might have somebody interested in re-connecting with you? Anybody that might be interested in you that might also be visiting St. Martin now? If there is anything to the story we just heard from our new friend, it may have nothing to do with me, but might be all about you."

Terri sat and thought. The more they thought about it, the more silly it started to seem. Ben had seemed very sincere, but maybe he was a total nutjob. They started laughing. "You know," began Sylvie, "it's tough being a young sexy girl in the Caribbean. Men are crawling out of their hiding places wanting to get near us, before long we'll probably wake up and there will be a long line of would-be suitors waiting to get a glimpse of us as we leave our room each morning."

"And who could blame them?" added Terri. They both laughed. "Now that we know this is just the beginning, that we'll have men all over us every time we step out, what should we do for food tonight? I'm starving!"

"Let's finish getting ready and then decide. I'm good with wherever you want to go. You went with me to the Red Piano last night, so you decide. What should we wear? Is it a t-shirt and shorts kind of night? Or do we decorate the Christmas tree in something slinky, let all those men wonder if there might be a present under the tree for them?" Sylvie was back to feeling playful. She was ready for a no-holds barred night of fun.

Terri smiled. "Why don't we go with something in-between. I don't want to go with just a t-shirt, but maybe not put on the full man-catcher either. Let's look like two gorgeous but respectable ladies who are fishing only for the best catches, but not to be confused with an easy mark." She smiled before continuing, "Even though you may be!" She continued her good friend smile. Sylvie laughed out loud, a slight snort of surprised laughter sneaking out.

"Oh, you so know me. That's why you love me, enough to fly halfway around the world to be part of my crazy life!" They got ready for what was planned to be another great night. Tonight, they would leave the car parked and walk to the Orient Beach village square, the area comprised of

restaurants hosting fun activities convenient for those staying near or on Orient Beach. Of the nearly dozen restaurants there, Terri and Sylvie decided on Le Piment, which
Terri considered as one of the better restaurants of the outstanding choices. They were handed tablets containing the
menu while ordering a Pino Grigio and a Sauvignon Blanc.
A basket of bread with butter came first, followed by their
entrees of mahi mahi for Sylvie and lasagna for Terri. The
meal was exquisite.

As they dined, Antonio placed his call to give an
update on his surveillance of the girls. "Mr. Harrington, it's
been a quiet day today. Little movement. Didn't leave the
room until late morning, then on the beach the rest of the
day. No interaction with others on the beach, other than
what is believed to be casual greetings. The only contact
was of a man going to the room between 5:30 and 6:00,
about six feet tall, 180 to 200. He went in. Was inside for
twenty minutes."

"Follow him, may be nothing, keep contact with him
for a few days."

"Baldo is keeping an eye there. Looks like his base is
in a resort just south on the beach. From there he went to
Simpson Bay. Looks like normal meal. I am keeping watch
on your primary friends. Nothing interesting. Right now,
they are having a meal locally. Long meal, no contacts,
nothing happening."

"Good work, continue, I will want another update
tomorrow. As always, anything meaningful, do not delay."
The connection was broken. Antonio continued his watch,
while Baldo maintained his watch of Ben.

After the great meal and wine, Terri and Sylvie were
ready to continue the evening of fun. It was time to walk to
the Bikini Beach Bar. There was a small gathering of tourists
that was expected to grow into a good crowd for late night.

A DJ was there to keep everyone involved. He took song requests from the growing gathering and played them when he was able. The group consisted of a base of regulars, with a rotation of tourists discovering and enjoying the bar; as a group left at vacation's end, it was replaced with new vacationers. There was karaoke, dancing, some people watching and much drinking, with everyone having a great time. The evening became more fun for all when Sylvie and Terri arrived. They walked up to the bar, and each decided to go with Pinot Grigio for the rest of the night. They found a table to sit and drink. Ten minutes later, they left their drinks on the table. It was time to dance.

Terri and Sylvie were very comfortable moving to the dance floor, with each other as a partner, to the extent a partner was needed. They were having a blast and danced to several songs before going back to their drinks. They finished their first glasses and ordered refills. They sat for a while, talking as they waited for more wine. As their night progressed, and unnoticed by them, Antonio continued to discreetly watch from a distance.

Now armed with their second glass of wine, the girls looked around and surveyed the crowd. It was a good group, but there was no one who caught the attention of either of them as someone they needed to get to know better. It looked like an ordinary gathering. They decided it was time to get back to the dance floor. They each loved moving to the beat of the music, as they became an extension of the songs the DJ played. They lost themselves in the music, and the incredible setting of being beach-front on one of the ten best beaches in the world. They were feeling lucky, two of the earth's favored creatures, and they were drinking it all in. After several more dances, they were ready for more wine to further fuel their night. They kept the wine coming, Sylvie more so than Terri, but both felt unconstrained with no driving needed and their room a short walk away.

"I've figured it out," said Sylvie.

"What are you talking about?"

"I've got a plan. I'm planning to be rich beyond my wildest dreams this week. I now have a plan to make that happen."

Terri looked at her, still not certain what she was talking about. "Does this have something to do with Gregorio?" whispered Terri. "I thought you were over that."

"Well, I'm not. And I have a great plan. Let's go back to the room and I'll lay it out for you. You'll see, it's pure genius."

The girls finished their glasses of wine and paid their tab. It had been a fun night at the Bikini Beach Bar. The night had crossed into Tuesday morning and they walked back to their room. Once inside, Sylvie laid out her plan to Terri.

"And you think this plan will work?"

"Of course, I've thought it all through. There's basically no downside. I can't be caught. The worst that would happen is I come up empty again and don't find out the information I believe I'll find."

"For this to work, you want help from our new friend, Ben. You really think he'll help you with this?"

"Of course, don't you?"

"I don't know. Why do you think he'll be willing to help?" asked Terri.

"Did you see his reaction when I came out of the shower? It was obvious he liked the view." She smiled a knowing smile. "And besides, if he didn't make up the story he told us, he's a boy scout. He came here trying to protect us. If he thinks he can help, he'll have a hard time turning me down."

"Let's say you put your plan in motion and Ben agrees to play his part. What happens if your plan actually works?

Are you prepared if he reacts poorly? He feels deceived and you have a new set of trouble?"

"Look, after he helps me be successful, I'll let him know I owe him. I'll offer to do something for him that will make him happy. You could help me. I'll be sharing my new wealth with you. You can in return help smooth out any speed bumps after the victory. Our new friend Ben might be pleased just to have helped, and that's that." She paused, then continued "If not, I'm sure we could make him happy. A four hands massage might be a good start." Her smile turned into a wide, toothy grin. "I'm sure he won't be a problem."

"For your plan to work, first you need to find him. If you're lucky, he'll be on the beach tomorrow." Terri looked at Sylvie, her look communicating that she did not want to discuss the crazy plan any longer. "For now, I'm exhausted and need to go to bed. I was up most of the night before I flew in, up too late last night, and it's way late again, we're well into morning! If I don't get more sleep soon, I won't be able to function tomorrow."

The girls got undressed, turned out the light and got in bed. Terri went immediately to sleep. Sylvie was too excited to sleep. She lay in bed, her mind reviewing her plan multiple times, and then finally drifted off.

TWENTY-ONE

DEAN JANSON WAS excited. He had what promised to be an incredible business opportunity. He felt like Scrooge McDuck rolling around on a bed filled with cash. There would be so much cash that it would spill out of the bed and fill the room, and then fill the entire dwelling. He could envision a geyser spewing an unlimited supply of cash, and it was all for him. As if that was not enough, he could not believe he had a romantic evening ahead with a beautiful woman. This would not be his first tryst away from his wife. His prior encounters were also with beautiful women, but this one could be the most gorgeous of them all.

He was greeted with a warm hug from Debi, her body melting into his. When the embrace ended, she gave him a light kiss on the cheek before getting in his car for the drive to Spiga. The drive went quickly with Debi entertaining him with her stories and humor. It was a challenge to keep his eyes on the road and his hands on the steering wheel. His treasure was beside him. It had been a remarkable day.

A parking space was available on the street near the Spiga restaurant. Dean got out of the car and walked around to open Debi's door. She got out and he could no longer contain himself. "You are stunning! Oh my, yes!" He moved inside her personal space and gave her a long kiss. He then gave a strong hug, letting his hands wander down her back and below. Debi did not break the embrace, but remained firmly in his hungry grip. He finally loosened his hold on her, made a show as if straightening his clothes, and then walked hand-in-hand with her into Spiga.

It was a beautiful evening with a cool breeze following the day's sporadic showers. They were seated at a romantic table for two on the front porch area of the restaurant. Other diners on the porch were seated a comfortable distance from them. The ambience of outside dining enhanced the couple's focus on each other.

"As I said, you are absolutely stunning! Thank you so much for accepting my invitation."

Debi looked into his eyes and smiled. "So, when do I get all the goodies for my friends? You know I'm here because you bribed me with offers for them of cash, food and entertainment. And so far, not one mention of your promises. Instead, it's this," she said kiddingly, opening her arms to the amazing atmosphere. She continued, "Thank you very much for rescuing me tonight. You're treating me like a princess. May I encourage you to continue?" She leaned forward slightly, arching her back.

"You certainly may continue to encourage me. The encouragement is greatly appreciated!" Dean looked at her as if eyeing a prized possession.

They ordered pre-meal drinks, a Wiser's Canadian Whiskey for him, and a Pinot Grigio for her. While continuing to enjoy each other's company, they looked over the expansive menu. Spiga prided itself on selecting the highest quality ingredients from Italy, as well as local fruits and spices, making for an incredible dining experience. There are many amazing restaurants in St. Martin, and Spiga consistently ranks as one of the best. They each ordered the Insalata Della Casa Salad of mixed greens, tomato and homemade vinaigrette. For his entree, Dean chose the Pork Chop Bolognese, a pounded breaded pork chop topped with meat sauce and melted mozzarella. Debi selected a traditional pasta of Tagliatelle Bolognese. The meal was exquisite and was followed with an additional glass of wine and Canadian whiskey. Before leaving, an after-dinner bottle of local flavorful rum was placed on the table with bottomless shot glasses. Spiga had been a favorite restaurant enjoyed by Dean on special occasions, and quickly became a favorite for Debi as well. The entire dining experience could not have been better.

The bill was paid, they thanked the waiter, and left. They walked over to the car. Dean walked to the passenger side and prepared to open the door for Debi. "After such exceptional company, I don't want the evening to end. Do you need to get back to your hotel?"

"Unfortunately, I don't think I have a choice." Debi watched Dean, his shoulders sagging, and his face looking as if he had received a gut punch. "What choice do I have?" she asked coyly. She paused before continuing. "I haven't gotten my hands on the goodies yet. What kind of reception do you think I'd get if I came back empty-handed? All talk of your promises to my friends has been non-existent, even after I brought it up. After such a marvelous dinner, I think we shouldn't delay any longer. It's time for me to get my hands on the merchandise," she said, insinuating more than the gifts for her friends. "How long am I expected to remain empty-handed?"

Dean was jolted by the electricity of the moment. Normally quiet, he was now speechless. He looked at her in response, his involuntary smile reflecting his excitement. Without saying anything, he opened the passenger door for her, and she gracefully slid in and buckled her seat belt. Dean got in and recovered his voice. "I have a rental property I'd like to show you. It's above the theatres, up

the small mountain in Simpson Bay. I hope you'll like it."
He drove quickly from Spiga in Grand Case to Cole Bay in
the Simpson Bay area where the rental was located. The
four-bedroom villa was accessed via the steep straight road
that ran up the mountainside, sitting well above the theatres, and offering a spectacular view of the bay below. He
parked the car, opened her door for her, and fumbled for
the key to the villa. Finding the key, he unlocked the door
and cut on several lights. He gave her a cursory tour of the
layout of the villa as he led her to the balcony area in back.
There was a large pool, tile decking for expansive day-time
sunning, and a multi-million-dollar view.

Debi followed him out onto the pool deck and looked
down at the lights and boats below. It was certainly a phenomenal view. After silently drinking in the view for several minutes, Debi turned her look toward Dean. He was
intently watching her, as a cat about to pounce on a squirrel.
Before he could pounce, Debi moved to him, grabbed his
face with both hands, and delivered a passionate kiss. He
was excited by her bold aggression and overwhelmed that
he was the recipient. He reacted, but instead of becoming
the aggressor as had always been his role, he remained the
more submissive partner. It was an incredible compliment
that he was receiving, and he did not want his new role to
end. Her hands mimicked his from earlier in the night,
as she first gave him a powerful bear hug, never breaking
the kiss, with her hands massaging his back before moving lower. Dean felt that the sixteen-year-old version of
himself was inhabiting his body, and he was drunk with
the feeling. When Debi allowed him to come up for air, he
raised his hand asking for the shortest of possible breaks.
He huskily gave her a hug as if completing a slow dance,
but instead of ending the embrace, he continued the hug as
he slow-danced her inside to the master bedroom.

TWENTY-TWO

MONDAY NIGHT HAD turned into Tuesday morning for Lauren and Ben. They walked on the beach, first holding hands, then he with his arm around her shoulder, her arm around his waist. "This might be one of the most beautiful nights I've ever seen," Lauren said softly. "The sky and stars are amazing." The sand was cool beneath her feet, gently massaging them with each step.

"I'm really glad you let me take you to dinner tonight. I'm sorry I wasn't around today and that we had separate obligations after lunch yesterday, but I'm thinking tomorrow will be a lot of fun. I won't lie, shopping is not one of my favorite activities, but I do want to see Philipsburg, so some shopping and a light lunch in town will be good. Is there anything special you want to look for?"

"Oh, I want to look in some jewelry stores, and some clothes shopping is always fun. Then I'd like to look for some souvenirs, like a t-shirt of St. Maarten, and maybe some knick knacks to decorate with at home. I'm not looking for any glassware or crystal, but I read where those are a good value here, so I wouldn't mind looking. I think there is a local market, too, where there might be some trinkets. I wouldn't mind getting a St. Maarten license plate, maybe some island spices, some artwork made on the island, and if they have one I like, maybe a pareo or two for on the

beach. I could also use an island dress if I find a good one.
I would like to have a few actually, I think I could get used
to being here and would be better prepared for coming
back if I found a few of those dresses." She paused, realizing
she had given a very lengthy list of items to fulfill her shopping desires. "Are you sure you want to go shopping with
me? I may have so much on my wish-to-shop-for list, that
there won't be time for what you might be interested in."

Ben smiled. "I'm more interested in you than shopping. Your shopping list is my shopping list. If we don't
find everything tomorrow morning, maybe we could go
again later in the week." Ben could not believe he had just
opened himself up for a possible second shopping day.

Lauren looked at Ben and smiled. She still believed he
was insensitive to her earlier, but she could not help but grin,
thinking that despite that, he really was a good and caring
guy. She was feeling closer to him. "Well, we'll just have to
see. You might have so much fun shopping tomorrow that
you'll be begging me to come again the next day." She gave
him a mischievous grin, letting him know she was kidding.

He smiled in return. "You just never know. I didn't
have any plans for this trip. I was just going to sit on the
beach, rest, read a few pleasure books, swim, eat some
great seafood, and do it again the next day. Life often
doesn't follow a plan, and I guess that's okay." He then
added, trying to compliment her without making it too
heavy, "Maybe even better."

They looked at each other, leaned in, and kissed their
first real kiss. They had an affectionate hug and looked out
over the ocean. "This is a special place. Thanks for dinner tonight, and thanks for taking me shopping tomorrow.
I think tomorrow will be a great day." They walked the
rest of the beach, to the far end at the Mont Vernon, and
turned around. It was a slow walk to cover the mile back

to Lubrique. They went back to her room. "It's late, but do you want to come in for a few minutes?"

"Yes, that would be great. I need to get my shoes from inside."

They walked in and both sat on the couch. Ben put his arm around her shoulder, and she leaned into him comfortably, resting her head on his chest as if settling in to sleep. "I like this," Ben said, his words continuing to understate his true thoughts. Lauren responded by simply moving her head up and down slightly while continuing to rest it on his chest.

"I guess I better be getting back to my room. What if I come by around eight in the morning? We could get a little breakfast and then be in Philipsburg about the time the stores open."

"I like that." She lifted her head and stood, reaching her hands down to him to help lift him up from the couch. Ben slipped his shoes on, and they walked to the door. There Lauren initiated their second kiss and wanted Ben to be interested in the two of them as a couple. She hoped her kiss communicated that. Ben broke the kiss and got ready to step out. "Not quite yet," said Lauren, leaning into him, kissing him again, this time with more passion with her hands on his back pulling him into her. Ben responded by wrapping his arms around her and lifting her in the air as they kissed. He set her back on her feet and looked down into her eyes. He reached behind him for the doorknob and opened the door. "I'll be here at eight. Be ready for a great day." He gave her a final light kiss before walking back to his room. Both Ben and Lauren expected to have happy dreams.

TWENTY-THREE

DEBI AWOKE EARLY Tuesday morning. Dean, with a history of being a womanizer, had been overmatched by the amazingly sensual being. He was left with a reaction similar to that of Julius, the character played by Arnold Schwarzenegger in the movie 'Twins', when he lost his virginity to Kelly Preston. It was a life-changing experience for Dean. Debi turned toward her exhausted but happy new friend, a look of more fun to come on her face. "Good morning, Dean. I trust you had sweet dreams." She lifted her upper body, hovering over him, the fingers of her right hand playfully grazing his chest. "Do you keep coffee and tea in your villa for all your guests? This girl is no coffee drinker, but I do enjoy a cup of tea in the morning. But, I'm no sweet southern belle looking for a glass of iced tea." She purred, "I like it hot."

She sat up in bed and kicked back the sheet that had been covering her. She stood unabashedly relaxed, then placed her palms flat on the bed beside Dean. She exuded confidence, knowing Dean was exhilarated by the view she was presenting. "So do you have some tea to keep your guest happy?"

"Yes, tea and coffee are available in the kitchen. Do you want me to show you where everything is?"

"No, you lay back and rest up a little longer. I'm comfortable exploring to get what I want. Would you like me to bring you a cup?"

"No, but maybe we can go out and get a light breakfast this morning before I have to get back to work."

"That sounds great, love. I'll have a cup of hot tea first and then breakfast with you would be wonderful." She stood and turned her back to him to go into the kitchen. Before moving forward, she stood in place wiggling her hips playfully. She looked back as she took her first step. "Now don't you be ogling me as I walk to the kitchen."

Dean stared in open lust. He had hit the jackpot. He lay there paralyzed, reliving his night. Dean heard her going through the kitchen and preparing her cup of tea. Soon she returned to his bedside, holding the cup of tea with her right hand on the cup ring and her left holding the saucer in which it sat. She held the tea high, careful not to block any of his view. "The tea is excellent, thank you. I think I'll take it out poolside and sit at the table there to enjoy the view for a few minutes. Last night it looked like any views of neighbors are obstructed, so I trust I'm fine as is." She did a 360-degree twirl before walking out to the pool deck. There she placed the tea on the small table, sat in a chair facing out over the water, and enjoyed her tea.

Debi finished her tea and was luxuriating in the early morning sunshine. It looked to be the start of another great Caribbean day. She went back inside, rinsed out her cup, and placed the cup and saucer in the dishwasher. She returned to the doorway of the master bedroom, where Dean was now sitting in bed. "I'm going to take a very quick shower," she said. "I brought a change of clothes with me in my bag last night. It's another island dress. It weighs next to nothing and takes up very little space in my bag. I didn't know if I'd need it, but I was hopeful."

She turned to go to the shower, then turned back. She smiled and added, "In case I didn't mention it, I enjoyed last night. I'll be back in a jiffy. Maybe then we can go by the casino on the way to breakfast. I'd like to get the show tickets to give to my friends this morning. They'll kid me about not making it back last night. After they see I got them tickets to the show, they may suggest I not come home to them again tonight." Debi smiled seductively, then wiggled her way to the shower.

As she showered, she thought that Dean's once sated appetite would now be at a fever pitch. It was her intention to keep it that way, and she would leave for breakfast without offering up anything more than a playful kiss. Debi always exuded supreme confidence and she looked forward to increasing her hold on Dean. She completed her shower, dried her body, and slipped the fresh dress over her head. As was typical, she did not include underwear as part of her attire. She walked back to the bedroom doorway. Dean was getting out of bed. "I'll be out on the pool deck waiting for you. I hope you're not one of those guys who takes longer to get ready than a woman. I don't think so. You're too manly for that."

Dean quickly showered, shaved and brushed his teeth. In less than fifteen minutes, he was dressed for the day and greeted her on the deck. Grabbing her hand, he said, "Let's go. We have a breakfast date. And before that, I have an important stop to make." He paused for effect. "I need to go by the casino, pick up some promised show tickets, restaurant vouchers, and a hefty stack of chips. I believe there are a couple extra show tickets that if you will, I would be pleased to have you as my guest for dinner tonight and the show. And I suggest you bring an extra dress." He smiled hopefully at her.

"Why Dean, I would be honored to accept your invitation. You can be thinking if there is anything else you'd like tonight. I'll bring an extra dress."

They went to his car and he drove them to the casino. They both went inside, and the promised goodies were collected before they continued to breakfast. They were within a few minutes of La Croissanterie Restaurant in the Marina Royale in Marigot. The Croissanterie was a fixture in Marigot and highly regarded for its exceptional breakfasts and lunches. It had been owned and operated by a pair of brothers from France for over twenty years until Hurricane Irma hit the island in September of 2017. After the hurricane, a long-time employee purchased the restaurant from the brothers, kept all the recipes that had made it so successful, and re-established it as the place for breakfast in Marigot.

"This is exceptional," commented Debi. "I worked up an appetite last night, and this is delicious. These French pastries are the best I've ever had."

"I'm glad you're enjoying your breakfast. With the Croissanterie so close to the casino, I like to come here when my schedule permits. It's very peaceful sitting here looking out over the water and boats. After we finish, I'll deliver you to your friends."

"I want to thank you again for a wonderful time. This has become a vacation to remember."

The two walked back to his car, and he drove Debi back to her friends. He pulled into a parking space, stepped out and opened Debi's door for her. "I will be back at 6:30 this evening to retrieve you. We'll have time for dinner before attending the show."

Debi kissed him goodbye without hugging, but let her hands trail down his arms to his hips, giving him a playful squeeze before going to see her friends.

Dean drove to the nearby casino, with work to be completed before evening. He had a full day planned, first his normal routine, then making all arrangements necessary for the implementation of the new project with Robert Vaughn. All appeared to be going well for Dean. He now focused on the business and took care of the details needed for ensuring his new venture with Vaughn would be extremely successful. Without the immediate distraction presented by Debi, Dean again became the ruthless businessman that had made him wealthy.

TWENTY-FOUR

BEN WENT TO Lauren's room on Tuesday morning. As he was about to knock on her door a little before eight, she opened the door and stepped out. She was ready to go. Her face reflected her excitement. Ben looked down to her feet, and saw she was wearing tennis shoes. She was ready to do a lot of walking and was also prepared to keep up with his longer strides. Ben looked at Lauren and gave her a goofy smile. He loved seeing how happy she looked.

They held hands like children protecting one another while waiting to cross a busy street. They drove the fifteen minutes into Philipsburg and parked at a relatively convenient place on the Salt Pond. From there they walked to the boardwalk. Standing out was Barefoot Terrace. The large building was painted a canary yellow, with the words 'Barefoot Restaurant' painted in bright blue large script. Between the words, in bright pink, were two bare feet painted toes up. The restaurant had a white decorative railing adorned with multi-color signs. It screamed out 'fun Caribbean restaurant' to Lauren and Ben. They sat at the railing of the open-air restaurant with a great view of the boardwalk and the beautiful ocean harbor.

They enjoyed a leisurely breakfast, and were ready to begin the power shopping Lauren had planned. They first walked along the boardwalk, enjoying the sights of the freshly painted shop fronts and the small but increasing foot traffic of other early morning shoppers. Then they went to Front Street to begin their shopping. "Let's go in the Shipwreck Shop. I want to get a t-shirt and maybe a nice trinket or two." They walked in after seeing the Heineken Regatta shirts in the front window. Ben and Lauren each bought a pullover regatta collared shirt in matching green. Lauren also bought a regatta tank top. "That was a great store," exclaimed Lauren as they left. "I will definitely recommend it to my friends. It's a little early to start jewelry shopping for the day, but because it is right here next to the Shipwreck Shop, let's stop in at Royal Jewelers." Entering the store, they were warmly greeted by Vince, the handsome jewelry store owner. He made her comfortable, provided a few suggestions, and showed her the pieces of jewelry she pointed out. "Thanks so much. I really like that necklace. I'll keep it in mind and may come back later this morning to get it." They walked out and Lauren was very animated. "I love that necklace and it's a great price, but I want to look at a few more jewelry stores before I make a final decision." Ben got into the shopping spirit and decided he wanted to stop in Gulmohar's. The store offered low prices on an extremely wide selection of liquors and had very friendly employees to assist without being pushy. Ben made a couple of alcohol purchases and they continued with their shopping. They checked out several other jewelry stores and Lauren looked around in each for about ten minutes. As they exited their third jewelry store of the morning, Lauren turned to Ben and said, "I'm not going to wait any longer. Let's go back to Royal Jewelers. I want to get that necklace." They walked back to Royal Jewelers and Vince grinned at them as they entered. "I'm ready to buy that necklace."

Vince got the necklace she wanted with the cut-out of the island. "This will be the perfect reminder of my great time here." Ben had remained quiet during the entire jewelry shopping experience in each of the jewelry stores. As Vince placed the necklace around her neck to wear out of the store, Ben pulled out his Visa to pay for the inexpensive necklace. "I'd like to buy you a souvenir. Let me." He handed Vince his Visa credit card.

"I wasn't planning on you buying that for me." She broke out her credit card to hand to Vince.

"No, I want to." Ben pushed the card down she was holding and handed his card to Vince. Vince ran the purchase through on Ben's card, and Lauren promised she would be a regular customer as they left the shop.

"Ben, I didn't want to make a scene, but I'll pay you back."

"No," Ben said immediately. "It's a small gift. Please let me do it. I am having more fun than I thought I could shopping. I'd like to know I bought you something that you really like." Lauren tiptoed and gave Ben a light kiss, signifying the discussion of payment was finished, and thanking him for the gift. They were ready to continue their shopping.

"I know we're about to the end of our allotted shopping time, but I haven't even looked for any clothes yet. I'd like to look at a clothes store before we get a snack lunch."

There were many clothing stores on Front Street. The one that caught their eye was Color Freak, a store with primarily women's clothes. They walked into the Color Freak store. The outfits in the window that commanded their attention were in bright colors and sexy cuts. They walked inside, with most of the outfits seemingly designed for when not wearing underwear. Cut down to here and up to there, any underwear worn would be more visible than covered.

Lauren grinned at Ben between browsing at the daring dresses. She tried on several, and Ben nodded his approval with each dress she tried. She narrowed her selection down to two, and unable to comfortably eliminate either, she purchased both. The minimum shopping to satisfy Lauren for the day had been completed. They looked to get a quick lunch before going back to spend time on the beach.

Still walking on Front Street, Lauren and Ben came to the Lazy Lizard Beach Bar and Grill. They could not resist eating at a restaurant called the Lazy Lizard. The service was very quick. They feasted on voodoo shrimp, which was butterflied shrimp served with a voodoo dipping sauce, and fried calamari rings with a curry mayo. Some rice and beans completed their meal. The meal was the crowning touch on what had been a great but very quick shopping trip. Lauren looked at the bags containing shirts, alcohol and dresses. She fingered the necklace she was wearing. "That was a great shopping trip. I loved it. Thanks for bringing me." She beamed. "Breakfast and lunch were both excellent and fun. It was a great morning. But now I'm ready for us to go back, put this stuff away, and hit the beach. It'll be a great afternoon."

They walked back to their car, again holding hands as they walked. They were both very happy. The trip back took a little longer as traffic had increased. They arrived back just after one and put the bags in Lauren's room. Ben left to put on his blue swim trunks while Lauren put on her sunscreen. She had been prepared with her bikini on under her t-shirt and shorts that were worn for shopping. Ben slipped into his suit and walked back to Lauren's room. She was ready and they walked down to the beach. They were both a little tired from the shopping and decided to take advantage of the Lubrique chairs. They put towels on two chairs paired together with an umbrella and reclined.

"This is very relaxing," said Ben. "I'm ready to chill for a while." They laid back quietly, glancing at each other on occasion, letting the sun beam down on a perfect Caribbean day. Fifteen minutes later, Lauren noticed her friends talking and laughing in the water, a short distance up the beach.

"Hey, I see some of my friends up the beach. I think I should go over and talk with them a few minutes. After ditching them this morning, I want to make sure there are no hard feelings."

"Okay, I'll be here. Take your time. I'll see you when you get back."

Lauren walked up the beach to where her friends were splashing in the shallow water. They saw her as she approached and waved her in. Lauren waded into the waist deep water and joined them. "How is everyone? I appreciate you understanding about me backing out on shopping with you this morning. Did you make it to Philipsburg?" asked Lauren.

"Yes, but we just stayed a couple hours. We decided the weather was too good to shop any longer," replied one of the friends. "I see why you dumped us." The group looked down the beach toward Ben.

"I'm sorry, I'm glad you're not mad. We went out last night and I was having a good time. Since we didn't have totally set plans, I was bad and went with him this morning. I'm sorry, I shouldn't have."

"You don't need to make excuses. I think we all would have made the same decision if given a choice."

As Lauren was talking with her friends, Sylvie was walking the beach between La Playa and Lubrique. She had come down to the beach early, hoping she would see Ben and was disappointed not to find him. Her concocted plan had included seeing him, waiting for a time when he was alone, then approaching him. She was pleased that after spotting him, it was only a few minutes before he now sat by himself. Without delay, she walked, at a pace she believed to be normal for a solitary walker, with her path to take her past his beach chair. She continued with her plan.

As Sylvie approached Ben's chair, he had his head back with his eyes closed and did not see her. She pretended her bag slipped from her hand next to Ben's chair, with its few contents spilling out onto the sand. Ben looked up and saw it was Sylvie. "Oh, hi," he said, reaching down to help her gather her bag contents.

"Hey Ben, I really need to talk to you. It is very important, critical actually," she said in a hushed tone as she knelt on the sand picking up the last of the items and placing it in her bag. "I'm going to continue walking another minute, then turn and go to my room to re-apply lotion. Please, please, please come to my room. I need help and need to talk to you. Will you come?"

Sylvie began to get up to resume her walk. "Uh, yeah, I can meet you. I'll be there in a few minutes."

Sylvie walked a little further south before reversing course. She passed Ben, purposely not speaking or making eye contact, and continued to her room. Ben was intrigued at Sylvie's request, but also a little uncomfortable. Lauren was still in the water talking to her friends, and he did not know what he should tell her. He decided he would start walking toward La Playa, tell Lauren he was taking a walk up the beach, and that he would meet her back at the chairs in a bit. Ben started his walk and slowed as he approached the area where Lauren was visiting with her friends. She saw him and smiled. "Hey, I'm going for a walk, I'll be back in a bit. I'll stop by on my way back. If you're not here, I'll meet you at the chairs." Ben waved. Lauren smiled her acknowledgement and returned his wave. Ben continued on to La Playa, took the stairs up to the third floor, and knocked on Sylvie's door.

Sylvie came to the door, opened it about a foot, saw it was Ben and waved him in. Her bikini was on the floor and she held a tube of suntan lotion in her hand. "Come in. Thanks so much for coming. You're a lifesaver!" she said in a quiet voice. Ben stepped inside, and Sylvie closed the door behind him. "Come on over and have a seat." She gestured toward the couch. As Ben sat, Sylvie set the suntan lotion down, placed a beach towel on the straight chair, and sat directly across from him. She placed her feet flat on the floor, had her hands resting on her knees, and leaned forward slightly at the waist to talk. Ben tried to look only into her eyes, but was unsuccessful. His gaze continued to take in the rest of what Sylvie made available for him to see.

Sylvie and Terri had discussed the event of Saturday night that prompted the warning from Ben. They were certain that they were not followed from the Red Piano, and thought it funny that Ben was so concerned. Although convinced there were no concerns, Sylvie had prepared a different story for Ben.

"Ben, you were right. I was being followed. I was later contacted, maybe by who you saw, I don't know. But I'm being blackmailed!"

Ben sat and listened. It made sense to him based on what he saw Saturday night. He wondered how something so outlandish could be happening, and it felt unreal that he was somehow now involved. "What do they want? Money? How are they blackmailing you?"

"Ben, I'm so ashamed. You've just met me, but you can see I'm a bit of a partier. I have done some things that, if made known, would be embarrassing even to me. I have an idea that I know will work. I will be able to retrieve the blackmail material, but to be certain I'll be successful, I could really use your help." She placed one of her hands on Ben's knee and did her best to exude sincerity. If her naked body and touch had his brain processing information less effectively, all the better.

Ben's mind was on overload. He still could not believe that what he saw was really happening. He had the sick feeling of dread that he had once before when he was in a car wreck. He saw the wreck about to happen, knew it would total his car, but was powerless to move his vehicle out of harm's way. He was beginning to brace for impact. "How can I help?"

"Oh, Ben, thank you so much!" A tear slipped out of Sylvie's eye. "I could really use a hug." She stood and opened her arms to Ben. Ben was moved by her despair. He moved in and embraced her. She allowed her body to melt into his and made sure her tears were on his neck and upper chest. She snuggled her face against his chest and gave a big hug of seeming desperation. She continued her hug, reluctant to break, knowing he was hooked. He would never be able to turn down a naked crying woman.

Sylvie finally disengaged from the hug. She patted the couch, and Ben sat on command. She sat next to him, her hip pushed up against his hip and leg, her face at his chest, with one of her arms reaching as far as she could around his shoulders, her other hand resting on the inside of his thigh.

"What can I do to help?"

"There is a bad man who has something that belongs to me. They are pictures from a previous life and I need to get them. My dear friend Terri also agreed to help me. She knows this man is attracted to her, so she is going to contact him, and ask to meet him at the Red Piano. While she is keeping him occupied, I will go into his house and get my belongings. Your part will be a very simple but critical task. I would like for you to drive me there and stay at the car as a look-out. If you see anyone coming along to go in the house, you call me on my phone. I will then get out of the house right away, leaving through the back if necessary, to avoid being seen. If no one comes, as I believe it will be, I will come back out and you drive me home."

"I can do that. When do you want to go get your pictures?"

"Now that you have agreed, I will confirm with Terri that she is ready. I would like to go get the pictures tonight. The Red Piano doesn't get busy until about nine, so thinking about ten we could go to the house, I'll retrieve my pictures, and we'll be back here before eleven." She stood and got her phone. "Here, put your number in my phone. I'll call you and you'll have my number." Ben did as he was instructed. "Meet me here tonight at ten."

"Okay." Ben stood to leave. Sylvie put her phone down and gave him another hug as her version of a handshake sealing the deal. "I'll be here at ten," he said. "I can come up and get you, I'll have my car here, and we can go and get this taken care of."

"Great! I will be so relieved. I am indebted to you, and I promise if I can ever do anything for you, just ask. In fact, you don't even need to ask. Once this is over, if I think I can help you with anything, I'll do it before you can even ask! You are a rare find!"

Sylvie reached down to where she had placed her sunscreen. "Now, one last thing. I came here also to re-apply my sunscreen. Would you be a dear and do my back?" She handed him the bottle of sunscreen and walked into the bathroom to the sink. Looking into the mirror, she placed her hands on the basin and leaned forward slightly. "Okay, I'm ready for you. You are such a dear."

Ben ignored any messages she may have been sending to him other than the request for application of the suntan lotion. He squirted the lotion into his hand for it to be warm, and methodically applied the lotion to her back, making sure no spot was missed. When the job was finished, he said, "Okay, all done. I've got to get back to Lauren. She may be wondering where I've been for so long. But I'll be back here at ten sharp."

"Thank you, thank you, thank you! When this is done, be ready to celebrate with Terri and me! I will be so relieved."

Ben made his way to the door and stepped out. He hurried back toward the chairs, looking first in the water where Lauren had been talking to her friends. He continued to the chairs and was excited to see her. "Did you have a good visit with your friends?"

"Yes, it was good to talk to them for a few minutes. How was your walk?"

Ben wondered what all he should share. As he was walking back to their chairs, he realized he had never mentioned to her seeing two men following a couple women he had never met, or that he had later alerted them. How could he now tell her he had arranged a meeting for tonight and was in their room making the plan while she thought he was on a walk along the beach? "Oh, it was fine. I'm glad to be back now. I'd like to just enjoy the rest of the afternoon with you. Any additional beach walks, I want you coming with me." The subject was closed for now. Ben would figure out something and tell her before he left to meet Sylvie at ten.

TWENTY-FIVE

DEBI WALKED INTO the two-bedroom rental unit at the Royal Palm and greeted her three travel mates. "Where the hell have you been?" asked Jodi. "We were worried, but not worried sick. We figured you were having a good time and may not make it back last night." Jodi grinned at Debi.

"First off, yes, I had a great time! And you'll be glad I went." She opened up her purse and pulled out several items. "I have for each of you a ticket to the show at the casino tonight." She placed the tickets in their hands. She reached back into her purse and pulled out another piece of paper. "Next, I have a voucher for all of you for meals at any of the five restaurants, all food and drinks complimentary, thanks to my new very good friend Dean." Debi made a show of putting her purse on the floor, and reaching in for a third time. "And now, for the finale, you have chips. It looks like about $300 worth of chips for each of you. Did I do good or what?"

Jodi answered for the others, "Wow, that is awesome! You did a great job of taking care of us."

"Yes, I did. I did an even better job of taking care of Dean!" Debi laughed a hearty laugh. "I've decided to make him a project. Not just any old project, but *the* project! I really like him, and it is easy. You wouldn't believe his place. The view is amazing. I could really like it there."

"What do you know about this guy?"

"Let's see. He's successful, he has a lot of money and he just got a new business deal where he is going to make a lot of money even to him. He has a great place, but more importantly, he's good-looking and he's really into me. He was kind and generous. And I'm going out with him again tonight."

"Is he married?"

"I hope not. There's a good chance I'll find out more about that tonight. If he is married, I'll find out his intentions for how long. He could be married, separated or divorced. I'm not sure, but he took me out to a very nice restaurant, also a very public restaurant, and did nothing to act like we were hiding that we were together. That was a good sign."

"We were getting ready to go to the beach. Do you want to come with us, or do you have other plans?"

"Count me in. That would be fun! I'll go put some suntan lotion on and I'll be ready to go. What beach are we going to?"

Jodi replied, "Karen wants to go to Cupecoy and Jan wants to go to Baie Rouge. We'd like to try them all, but I think today we're going to Baie Rouge."

"That's fine, anything is good with me. It will be fun to try a new beach." Debi went into the bathroom and applied her sunscreen. She got help with her back, then put on her bikini and cover-up, and was ready. "Let's go, this will be fun." They all got in Jodi's car, and in about fifteen minutes they were at Baie Rouge. Baie Rouge is one of the lesser known beaches, but has two great extremely informal restaurants there, Gus's and Raymond's. They had both been there for years, were destroyed by hurricane Irma, and were involved in some controversy afterwards. All the issues had now been resolved, and both restaurants were back up and running better than ever before.

The beach attendants sat up in a wooden structure overlooking the beach. To access the beach, one would descend several flights of steps to the thick sand of Rouge. The sand had a reddish tint, giving the beach its name. One of the attendants, Ishmael, set up chairs for them. They requested chairs be placed on the open beach about fifty yards to the left of the stairs facing the beach. It was away from the restaurants, very quiet, and looked like the typical vision of a wonderful remote tropical beach. The girls loved the location and would be able to get lunch and drinks from either of the two restaurants.

They waded into the clear water, being careful not to slip on the large shelf of rock next to the primary entry point near their chairs. The water was relatively calm, and with a rock ledge on part of the beach, attracted many colorful fish. If they came back another day, they would need to bring snorkel masks to take advantage of what looked to be good snorkeling right off the beach. The girls splashed and played, enjoying their time together. They went back to their chairs and let the hot sun bake them dry. Once dry, it was time to walk down for lunch. They stopped at Raymond's and each ordered a cheeseburger with fries, as well as the best strawberry banana daiquiris they had ever tasted. Their server was Raymond's daughter. She told them about the happy hour for that afternoon. Each afternoon, Raymond would blow into a large conch shell, with its resounding sound alerting all on the beach that happy hour had begun. The girls were always interested in a happy hour and wanted to stay long enough to hear the conch call.

They took their strawberry banana daiquiris back to their chairs, enjoyed their drinks, and got down to some serious sunning. "It's great to be able to remain tan-line free," said Debi. "I think Dean will appreciate the work I am putting in today." Each of the girls had brought a beach read book, and enjoyed reading, flipping every few chapters. The afternoon went by quickly, when at 4:00 p.m. they heard a new and very loud sound. It was the melodic call of happy hour being played out on the large conch.

"I love it! That made the trip here today uniquely special," said Karen. "Of course, to make it complete, we'll need to get our happy hour drinks. The experiences here and the stories we'll have when we go back from vacation will be memories of a lifetime. I absolutely love St. Martin!"

The girls dressed in their swimsuits, went to Raymond's and each ordered another strawberry banana daiquiri, which was really two with the two-for-one happy hour. They broke out their phones, and took pictures of the beautiful beach, Raymond's and Gus's. They handed their phones to other patrons to take several pictures of them with their drinks, using Raymond's and the beach as scenic backdrops. They finished their drinks, then walked back to their chairs.

"We should probably get ready to head back to the Royal Palm before too long," said Debi. "You all have a show and dinner to get ready for, and I have an evening planned with Dean. He mentioned dinner and that we could also go to the show, but I'm thinking a leisurely dinner followed by some time at his villa might be even better. I really enjoyed the view there and I plan to make sure he enjoys his view! Ladies, no need to wait up for me!"

The girls gathered their books and towels and walked in the deep sand back to the stairs, each step with the soft, thick sand giving their legs a workout, where each foot would sink well below the sand's surface. Baie Rouge had certainly been a unique beach experience.

They arrived back at the Royal Palm and took turns getting in the two showers. With having maxed out their time at the beach, they needed to quickly get ready for their planned entertainment for the night. They were happy with their beach day and equally excited about the anticipated night-time fun.

TWENTY-SIX

....

SYLVIE WALKED BACK down the beach to where
Terri had been waiting. "How did it go?"

"It went great! Ben is on board and will be picking me
up from our room at ten. I'll need you to get with Harrington
at the Red Piano so we can get this done. Have you thought
about what you're going to say and how you're going to be
able to convince him to meet you at the Red Piano?"

"Yes, I've got that worked out. I'm going to be somewhat truthful. Why tell a lie when the truth will work fine?
I'll start off the call by letting him know I'm here visiting
with you, and that you said you had met him at the Red
Piano. I'll go into more detail with him, but by the time I'm
finished, he'll definitely be at the Red Piano at ten." Terri
continued, "Tell me more about Ben's willingness to help.
If your plan works and he learns you were not being blackmailed, I still think he's going to be mad that you used him."

"I've been thinking about that some more. I have a
new approach on how I'll share the truth with him, and
I'll do so in a way that he'll be pleased by the time I finish explaining. After that, if he wants to celebrate with
me more into the future, we'll just see how it all goes. I
wouldn't be opposed to spending some time with him on a
regular basis after all this is done."

"So Ben agreed right away? No problems?"

"That's right. He's a great guy. I explained that I needed his help. He asked how he could help me. I told him and he agreed. Just to make sure, and because it was fun whether needed or not, I just happened to be at my most vulnerable. No clothes and needing help with my lotion. We sat close. He was attentive, very attentive, and immediately accepted my request for help. He liked what he saw before, and I gave him a little reminder. I actually think that was more for me than him. I'm pretty sure he would have agreed to help without my extra effort of convincing needed. But what was I to do? I enjoyed it, maybe even more than him."

"Then it's all set. I'll go back to the room in a few minutes and call Gregorio. After it's set, which shouldn't take long, I'll come back here and let you know how it went."

As Terri started to their room, Antonio began his update call to Harrington. "Mr. Harrington, there have been a couple of developments. We've continued a loose watch on them. Earlier today, the girl had a brief encounter with that same man, either by chance or intended, very briefly on the beach. Right after that, she went to her room, and he went there also a few minutes later. After about thirty minutes, the man left and joined a different female on the beach. The girl also left and separately rejoined with her roommate."

"Very good. Thank you for the update. Please keep a watch on the girl. I don't know what is going on with the man, but please have Baldo continue with his surveillance, also. Please update me again tomorrow unless something comes up before then." They disconnected and Antonio resumed his surveillance.

Within a few minutes of ending his call, Harrington's phone again rang. "Gregorio, this is Terri. It's been a while since we've talked. Am I calling at a bad time?"

"No, it's always a pleasure to hear your voice."

"Great, it's been a while, but I am now back on island. I'm hoping you'll be able to make some time to see me while I'm here. I'm visiting with a friend, and while we were talking last night, she mentioned that she had met you. As we talked more, I'm a little embarrassed to tell you this, but I reminded her of the good girls' code, where two friends don't actively pursue the same guy. Well, I was maybe too presumptuous, but I felt like you and I had made a connection, or at least the beginning of a connection. I strongly suggested to her that if she had oats to sow, she needed to look elsewhere to sow them. I hope you're not displeased or mad at me for asking her to back away."

"Why, I must say I am flattered. I assume you are talking about my dear Sylvie. I certainly enjoyed the minimal time I spent with her, but if you are offering yourself as a replacement, I am pleased with the boldness of your call."

"Excellent, I was with Sylvie at the beach earlier today when I decided to address our discussion in a forthright manner and give you a call. When we hang up, I am be going back to the beach to inform her of our conversation. I am going to tell her that it is now official and that she should seek companionship elsewhere."

"I endorse that discussion."

"Great! With that settled, when can we resume our connection?"

"Is tonight too quick?"

"No, I would love to meet you tonight. I promised Sylvie I would eat with her this evening. She has been trying to attract another man that she saw on the beach today, but I don't think she has successfully won him over," she paused, for added emphasis, "yet! She's not giving up on him, especially after the discussion we had pertaining to you. In fact, she lured him into our room earlier today, but I don't think she got all she was after. But she is persistent, so I'm sure she'll keep trying. But I am available after I help Sylvie strategize over dinner. I could meet you at the Red Piano if you'll be there."

"That sounds grand. I will be at my table and eagerly awaiting your arrival."

"I'll see you tonight. I should be there around nine, and certainly no later than ten."

"I'll be waiting."

Terri was very pleased with how the call had gone, and truthfully, she did find Gregorio attractive. Spending time with him would not be a hardship for her. She walked back out of their room to update Sylvie.

Harrington called Antonio. "Please keep the watch on the girl. Tell Baldo he can drop his watch of the man on the beach. I just received information that eases my suspicion of him. But if I am wrong, surveillance of the girl could include future meetings with him. And if there is a problem, both will pay dearly." Antonio relayed the message to Baldo and continued his watch of the girl.

"It went great, it couldn't have gone better," Terri told Sylvie as she joined her on the beach. Terri then relayed the details of her conversation with Harrington. "We are on for tonight. If anything goes wrong, and he leaves the Red Piano before eleven, I will call you. But you need to get in, take care of your business, and be out of there before eleven. I still don't like this, and the sooner you're done, the better. I want this to be over."

"Fantastic! Now, let's free our minds of worry and enjoy this beautiful afternoon." They sat back for a few minutes, but Sylvie was too excited about her plan to stay in her beach chair. "Let's go for a walk." Terri agreed, and the two walked most of the beach, turning around before they reached the Mont Vernon. By the time they got back to their chairs, Sylvie had rid herself of some of her nervous energy. They leaned back and caught a few more tanning rays. They spoke no further of the plan, but as they were lounging, Sylvie could not stop herself from playing out the plan again in her mind. She was not nervous, but very eager. Wanting to work on their tans, they stayed on the beach until five.

After cleaning up from their long afternoon at the beach, Terri and Sylvie decided on an early dinner. With neither girl being very hungry, and with the anticipation of their evening activities, it was a fairly uneventful meal before the momentous evening.

TWENTY-SEVEN

WHEN THE GROUP traveling as the Northeast Florida Tiki Hut Association awoke on Tuesday, they began reliving their adventures from the previous day. They planned their activities for their last scheduled day of vacation.

Most of the group decided to do the Topper's Rhum tour located near the villa where they were staying. Sara and Kathy were committed beer drinkers, and although they were sure they would enjoy the tour, they wanted to have their group picture printed and framed to leave in the villa. They volunteered to take care of the picture project while the others enjoyed the tour.

The group discussed one more time if everyone was comfortable sharing with future guests the fun picture of the word 'ISLANDTUDE' spelled with their mud-covered bodies. "You bet your A," exclaimed Jeanne, who had proudly contributed the 'A' in 'ISLANDTUDE.' There was an immediate enthusiastic unanimous agreement for the picture to be left on display.

Sara and Kathy drove to Pete's Photo, the long-standing photography store on the island for decades. Pete's was very helpful, making an 11" x 14" print while they waited. They picked out a blue frame to match the interior colors of the villa and were pleased with the final product. They would send an email to the villa owner to make sure he approved, but expected the group picture to be welcomed. It had been a successful trip to Pete's.

When Kathy and Sara left for Pete's, the rest of the group drove to enjoy Topper's Rhum Tour. Upon arrival, everyone was greeted with an ice-cold rum punch. They enjoyed their drinks as they waited for the rum presentation to begin. The prepared remarks on the history of rum and rum making, with the fun facts provided, was entertaining to the group. They then watched the bottling process which included an inspector confirming the proper quantity in each bottle. The bottles were then sealed for delivery. After seeing the process in action, everyone was invited to a rum tasting. Each selected six flavors of rum from those in development, as well as tasting three of the flavors currently being marketed. The Topper's Rhum had won awards for its quality and taste, and the group agreed that each was a very smooth rum. At the conclusion of the rum tasting, the group purchased bottles of rum to take back to Florida. They all agreed that the Topper's Rhum Tour was a great addition to their vacation.

The group reassembled for lunch and a day at the swimming pool. Their last day passed quickly, with fun splashing and floating on the Frontgate floats, while listening to the reggae music being played. It had been an outstanding vacation, and for their final meal, they decided to go to Topper's. It had been recommended as one of the more fun places on the island. Topper's was also known for its karaoke, and the group wanted to participate.

Once there and with the karaoke beginning, Paulie addressed the patrons at Topper's. "I know everyone is familiar with the Alan Jackson song Five O'clock Somewhere. Well, our song selection is much like that, in that we know it's Tuesday night, but every night here is like a Saturday night. So, with that, we'll begin our song by the Bay City Rollers!

S-A-T-U-R-D-A-Y night!
S-A-T-U-R-D-A-Y night!
S-A-T-U-R-D-A-Y night!
S-A-T-U-R-D-A-Y night!
Gonna keep on dancing
To the rock and roll
On Saturday night, Saturday night
Dancin' to the rhythm
In our heart and soul
On Saturday night, Saturday night."

The crowd went crazy over the campy rendition. The group led the karaoke, but part way through the song, almost everyone at Topper's was singing along. The song selection was a smashing success.

The group returned to Villa Islandtude, some with tears in their eyes, partly from happiness over a great trip, and some of sadness that it was about to end.

"Let's extend our stay!" exclaimed Mark. "I'm not ready to go home."

"I'd love to stay longer," replied Kathy, the litigation paralegal. "But I have a big trial on Monday and I have to get back to finish the trial preparation."

"I could stay longer," added Sara the radiologist, "but there's a local politician I met at a diner in Jacksonville Beach who is very interested in me. He's been sending me messages the whole time I've been here. I probably need to get back soon or he'll die of a broken heart!"

The rest of the group decided to try to extend their stay. They contacted the villa owner and asked if there was a vacancy where they could extend for another week. They received approval to prominently display their picture in the villa, and were able to work out the requested extension. The Northeast Florida Tiki Hut Association would be continuing its vacation.

TWENTY-EIGHT

BEN WAS ENJOYING the afternoon at the beach with Lauren. He was not sure how to broach the subject of his intention to help Sylvie. Should he mention it now, wait until he and Lauren went inside, or bring it up over dinner? None of the choices were attractive, but to go ahead and get it behind him, he decided sooner rather than later would be better.

"I have some strange information to share with you. Do you remember the other day when I said I had an errand to run? Let me give you some background. The night I had dinner with Nico, I came back, couldn't reach you, and had trouble sleeping. I took a very late walk on the beach that night because I couldn't sleep. While out, I saw some suspicious behavior. Two men were following a couple girls and stood back watching them as they entered their room at La Playa. They were following very quietly and unknown to the girls. My errand that I mentioned was that I needed to make them aware that something bad could be happening to warn them to be careful. I did that, there was nothing further, and I thought it was over. I forgot about it. But today when you were in the water visiting with your friends, one of the girls walked by and spoke to me. She is very concerned, and told me that she is being blackmailed, and wants to get back whatever blackmail material someone has on her. She was contacted, and guesses it was one of the two men I saw that contacted her. She seemed desperate and was crying, and asked if I could help. She thinks she can get the blackmail material while the man is away from his house, but wants me to watch outside the house to call her if I see anyone approaching. I said I would, and am supposed to do that at ten o'clock tonight. I know this all sounds crazy, it sounds crazy to me, but I saw the guys and believe the story. I want us to go out to dinner tonight, but I need to help as I promised and then it should be all over. I should be back before eleven. Maybe I'll have a great story to share with you and then we can get on with our late evening."

"Wow, as you said, that is a lot of strange information. Give me a few minutes to process what you just said."

"Fair enough." Ben tried to relax while Lauren sat silently for a short time. The two then discussed further, each taking turns not believing what was said was real, but finally reaching a decision that it would be treated as real, and that Ben's involvement would be to drive Sylvie to the house, remain as a lookout while she was inside, then drive the two of them back. Lauren would be waiting in her room, and Ben would go by her room as soon as he was back.

With the discussion of Sylvie's problem completed, the two remained in their beach chairs to try to enjoy the sun, but neither one was enjoying the day as before. There was too much to think about and they were now both on edge. After sitting there for another thirty minutes, they decided to go in and get ready for their evening meal together. They each went to their rooms, completed getting ready, and Ben walked over to Lauren's room to pick her up. They decided they would stay at Lubrique and eat at Papatwo. The meal was fine, the food was probably very good, but neither of them was in a good mood.

They each wondered why this was happening. Ben had not looked to get involved in any problems, but was in St. Martin for what had been planned as a complete escape to the islands. There would be no worries, he would walk the beach and eat seafood, rest and read. It was the prescription he needed after too much work without a vacation for way too long. Ben hoped that at eleven o'clock, he would be back on vacation full-time. He tried to be optimistic, thinking all he would be doing was driving, sitting for a few minutes, and then driving back. All should go smoothly, and he kept trying to convince himself that it was a logical conclusion and that he needed to stop worrying illogically.

After completing their meal, they went to Ben's room. It was 8:30 p.m. and he still had an hour and a half until he was scheduled to pick up Sylvie. Ben and Lauren sat on the couch quietly. "I'll turn on the TV and see if there is anything worth watching." He turned on the TV, adjusted the volume, and began scrolling through the channels. Nothing held any interest for them so Ben selected a music channel instead.

"I don't want to interfere or distract you once you're underway, but please call me as soon as you're on your way back if you can. I'm going to be worried until I hear from you."

"I will, but if for some reason I don't call, please don't assume something bad has happened. It may be that I can't get cell service, or maybe I'm just wanting to get out of there as quickly as possible. It may be Sylvie has stuff to say, or maybe it won't be good for her to hear what I'm saying. There could be a lot of okay reasons why I don't call before I get back. If that happens, I'll just come to your room as soon as I'm back."

"Okay, I'll try to be patient."

TWENTY-NINE

DEBI WAITED FOR Dean to pick her up for their date. She was dressed in sandals and a thin island dress that accentuated her curves. Dean would be pleased. At 6:30 p.m. Dean was knocking at her door. "Hey Dean, come on in. The girls left about thirty minutes ago."

Dean walked in and greeted her with a kiss. "You look great! It's so good to see you again."

"It's great to see you. I'm glad you didn't have to work late tonight. I've been looking forward to this all day." Debi stayed inside of Dean's personal space as she talked. "If you're not wedded to going to tonight's show, I was thinking instead, we could have a leisurely dinner, and then relax for a while, have a little music on, and enjoy a few after-dinner drinks. I'd rather spend the time getting to know you better." She leaned in and gave him a kiss, but not one of invitation calculated to delay their dinner.

"That is an excellent idea. I am all in favor. With this improvement to our plans, I recommend we go back to Grand Case, but this time to La Villa. La Villa is rated each year as one of St. Martin's best restaurants. I know the owners and am certain we will get a prime table."

To heat things up a bit, Debi re-thought her previous kiss, and kissed Dean again, this time with added gusto. "That sounds like a great selection. Let me get my bag."

She walked out of the room and back in with her bag and set it on the counter. She then walked back out of the room, coming back while holding up at eye-level a bright yellow dress, cut down to the waist in back and almost as low in the front. She folded the dress and placed it in her bag. "Now I'm ready."

Dean beamed. Debi was thinking how easy it was to have the upper hand in a relationship with a man. She glowingly smiled back at Dean, and they left the Royal Palm to dine in Grand Case. Parking in Grand Case near La Villa was limited, but there was still paid parking room in the nearby grass lot. After parking, Dean grabbed Debi's hand and they walked hand in hand to the restaurant. Florence and Christophe, the owners, greeted Dean and his date. They prided themselves not only on exceptional food, but also focused on providing a memorable dining experience with their personal service and intimate setting. They played a major part in keeping Grand Case the gourmet capital of the Caribbean.

Dean and Debi were escorted to a very private and intimate table where their server immediately appeared, offering them a drink before their meal. Debi seemed very impressed. Their meal began with a chilled creamy cucumber soup, followed by a salad of mixed greens. Dean's entrée was the Branzino sea bass with mashed sweet potatoes, while Debi chose the pan-seared duck. They ordered desserts, sharing hot chocolate profiteroles and caramelized pineapple crumble and mango sorbet. Everything tasted extraordinary. They lingered with after dinner drinks, then the customary bottle of flavored rum was brought out for them to enjoy. It was a meal to remember.

Feeling the effects of the alcohol consumed, they walked a little unsteadily back to the car. Upon sitting, they felt like teenagers, and gave in to the temptation to comport themselves as if they were. It was a little after ten when they pulled out of the grass lot to go to Dean's rental house.

"Dean, I'm sure you know I am having a great time with you. You are truly wonderful, and so kind and handsome. I've been telling you all about me, but I don't know much about you, your childhood, some of your interests, general information that might be learned over an extended period of time. But I'm really liking you, and I'd like to compress the timeline on learning all the fun facts. Why don't you use the drive back to tell me all about yourself." Debi began with the easy questions: what's your favorite color, what's your favorite food, do you like sports, what's your favorite sport, and how do you like no winter in St. Martin. She then eased into more personal questions with asking where were you born, how long have you lived in St. Martin, and how did you get involved with the casino? She was working her way up to finding out about a possible marriage. She decided she had done enough in laying the groundwork. Later she would ask the tougher questions of his personal life and marriage. Before they reached his rental house, she stopped asking questions. She decided the answers to the more important questions might be more forthcoming if she first gave him a reward for the progress already achieved. So, she turned the conversation to herself. "You know, when I first saw you at the casino, I thought you were very handsome. I was extremely pleased when you approached me, and I think my friends are very jealous of the attention you've given me. I'm so glad this vacation is not about to end. I want you to know I'm having a very good time."

They arrived at Dean's house. "I'd like a glass of Pinot Grigio. Would you be a dear and get me one?" Dean went to get the wine, returning with a bottle and two glasses. They sat on an inside couch looking out over the patio. Dean poured the wine and they sat in silence enjoying each other's company. After she finished her glass of wine, Debi decided it was time to begin rewarding Dean for answering her questions during the drive. Dean was ready to be rewarded.

THIRTY

TERRI AND SYLVIE were back in their room from dinner at nine o'clock. Sylvie changed into a dark blue pair of shorts, a comfortable gray t-shirt and tennis shoes. She would be able to move quickly and was ready to go. At nine fifteen, after hugging and wishing each other luck, Terri left to drive to the Red Piano. She anticipated being there about nine forty-five. She was dressed for drawing attention. Her bright orange dress accentuated her dark skin, and fit as if custom made for her. Her stunning appearance would command Harrington's complete focus.

Upon arriving, she saw Harrington already seated at his usual table. She walked over to him and tapped him on the shoulder. "Hey handsome, I'm here and thirsty."

He laughed, signaled the waitress and ordered a glass of wine for Terri and a Red Stripe for himself. "The wait was worth it," he said. "You look beautiful tonight. I'm very glad that you called."

The waitress brought the drinks and added them to his tab. "Cheers." He tipped his beer in Terri's direction, and she tapped her glass to his bottle.

"It's a great crowd tonight. It's great to be back on island. What's been going on with you while I've been away."

"I continue to have a lot of work coming in and my shipping business has been very active. For a break from the work world, I still enjoy a few nights out here. It continues to be a major meeting place for those of us living here. It also remains very popular for vacationers who are enjoying a week or two in St. Maarten."

It was almost ten o'clock when Terri finished her glass of wine. She accepted Harrington's offer to order her another, and the waitress quickly brought her drink. "Thanks, I will drink this one a little more slowly." Terri continued, "I haven't had a night of dancing in a long time. I hope you're wearing your dancing shoes tonight."

He reached across the table and touched her hand. "I'm sure you'll be able to convince me."

Harrington knew many people at the Red Piano. Many of his friends and acquaintances circulated throughout the crowded bar, stopping by the table to say hi. Everyone wanted to be introduced to the beautiful woman who sat across from him. Terri enjoyed the attention she was receiving in the Red Piano. She took her commitment to Sylvie's plan seriously, but was enjoying the night out. She would have wanted to be at the Red Piano even if she was not helping Sylvie. She found Harrington extremely attractive and was thoroughly enjoying his company. She prepared herself to be at the Red Piano for a very long time.

THIRTY-ONE

AS LAUREN AND Ben continued to sit and wait, Ben had an idea. "Would you like to help me with this? I've come up with a wrinkle that may help improve on Sylvie's plan. If you're willing, I could use your help."

"Of course, tell me what to do."

"Here is my car key. I want you to drive my car over to the Mont Vernon and park. If Sylvie is being followed, I want to make it harder on them. Leave the car key under the driver's side mat. It's early enough that people are still enjoying evening walks on the beach. I want you to walk back, staying in sight of others as you walk. To be on the safe side, don't come back to my room. Go straight to your room and wait for me to come by when this is all done."

"Alright, I'll do it."

"Let me call Sylvie and alert her to the change." He called and she picked up on the first ring. "Hey, it's Ben. I have an idea. My car will be parked at the Mont Vernon. If you are being followed, I want to try to get away from here without being seen. In about fifteen minutes, I want you to walk the beach to the Mont Vernon. I will be walking the beach behind you but not too close. Dress as you would for a beach walk, and have tennis shoes and anything else you might want in your bag. I'll close the gap between us and pass you for the end of the walk. You can watch me from a distance, seeing me get in my car. I'll duck out of sight behind the wheel, wait for you to hop in, and drive you to Harrington's. If someone follows you on the beach, they'll likely have a long way back to their car. They won't be anticipating you catching a ride from the other end of the beach."

Sylvie loved the idea. She still did not think anyone was following her, but as time drew closer, she was becoming more nervous. "That sounds great. Terri left for the Red Piano around 9:15. I'll leave here at 9:45. I will see you shortly," she said and ended the call.

Lauren took the car key, gave Ben a big hug, and went to her room to dress for her beach walk back. Within five minutes, she was driving Ben's car to the Mont Vernon.

After Lauren left, Ben exchanged his flip flops for socks and tennis shoes. He was ready for action, feeling much better about the plan. He stepped out of his room to begin the 1.2 mile walk from his room to the Mont Vernon. He left at 9:45, the same time Sylvie started her walk. He was moving along the beach faster than normal, confident he was quickly closing in on Sylvie. After five minutes, he could see her ahead. Ben passed Lauren as she was heading back. He stayed much closer to the water in passing, with neither acknowledging the other. He continued to reduce the distance he trailed Sylvie, finally passing her with about a quarter of a mile to go. Sylvie followed Ben, and when she reached the end of the beach, saw him enter his car. She stepped onto the parking area, made a bee line to Ben's vehicle and hopped in. Ben had retrieved the key from under the mat, and they were on their way. Sylvie gave directions to Harrington's villa, and they arrived at the beginning of his street at around 10:20. Sylvie got out, having changed into her tennis shoes, and began walking toward the house. Ben continued driving and passed the house before circling back to the beginning of the street. He pulled to the side of the road and waited.

Sylvie walked along the street, hoping to look like she was enjoying a late-night walk. She reached Harrington's villa, and walked around the perimeter, choosing a section of fence in the back to pull herself over. The fence was merely decorative and not a deterrent to entry. Her plan was to access through the back sliding glass door that he had left unlocked when she was there. If that was not unlocked, the backup plan was to try to enter through the small laundry room window. It was the only window of a thickness that she felt comfortable she could break. She had an oversize beach towel in her bag that would muffle the sound and protect her while going through the window. She reached the sliding glass door. The theft gods were on her side, and she slid the door open just enough to scurry in.

She walked in and listening, heard no sounds. The house seemed to be vacant. She quickly walked into the office, and to the closet housing the safe. Sylvie carefully entered the combination to the safe and it opened as before.

As Sylvie was opening the safe in his study, Harrington's phone rang. Harrington excused himself from Terri to accept the call. "Mr. Harrington, it's Alberto. I followed the girl on a beach walk tonight, but instead of going back to her place, she left the far end of the beach by car. I'm now in my car, but I'm not able to follow her."

"Go to the house. I don't know what she's planning, but get over there now. Call me back."

Harrington stepped back inside after his call. "Terri, my dear, something important has come up. Unfortunately, I am going to have to cut our evening short. Please excuse me but I must be leaving now." He placed a one-hundred-dollar bill on the table. "Please take care of my tab for me. I am so sorry but I will be in touch."

"Gregorio, do you have time for at least one dance? You know my heart was set on dancing the night away with you. You don't want to leave me with a disappointing ending to an evening that started with such promise, do you?"

"Unfortunately, it cannot be avoided." He started toward the door. He said again as he was leaving, "I will be in touch."

As Harrington walked out the door, Terri called Sylvie. She walked to the bathroom to get away from the bar noise, and not chancing that Harrington would see her on the phone if she walked outside.

Sylvie answered. "Get out. To be on the safe side, leave in fifteen minutes or less. Harrington just left and I think he's on his way there. No time to explain, just do it!"

Sylvie hung up. "Shit! I've got to find it now!" she exclaimed to herself. She dialed Ben. "I think Harrington is on his way here. I'll meet you in fifteen if not sooner. Be ready!"

Ben looked behind the car to the house, then back ahead. What if someone comes before she gets back? He grabbed the steering wheel lock bar that was on the passenger floorboard, and got out of the car. Turning the volume to vibrate on his phone, he put the car key and phone in his pocket and began walking in the direction of the house. He went just past the house and kneeled behind some shrubbery.

Meanwhile, Sylvie grabbed a stack of files that she had not looked through on her last visit. Not needing to be quiet, she glanced through them with great speed. Ten minutes later, she thought she had something. With no time to make pictures of each page, she grabbed the file and shoved it into her bag. She stacked the other files, stuffed them back into the safe, closed the safe door, and started toward the sliding glass door to leave.

Suddenly, car lights turned onto the street to the villa. The car parked in front of Harrington's villa, and a burly man got out. Ben stayed motionless behind the hedge. He saw the man walking toward the front door. Not having seen Sylvie leave, and not knowing what to do, Ben sprang into action. He came up behind the man, and Alberto heard him. As Alberto began to turn to face Ben, Ben lifted the makeshift club overhead and cracked Alberto on the side of his skull. Alberto went straight down, exhaling a loud groan.

Sylvie was coming from the back of the house and saw Ben use the club. They both took off running to the car. Ben quickly threw the club back into the floorboard and started the car. They eased off with the intention of maintaining a lawful speed on the way back. He would need to clean the club.

When they were a just a few blocks away on the main road, Sylvie thought she saw Harrington driving toward the villa. "Ben, let's not do anything crazy, but get me back to La Playa as quickly as possible." Ben accelerated, now driving as if late for an appointment.

"I think we need another change in the plan," said Ben. "We'll stop by La Playa, you grab a few things for overnight, and you'll need to stay with me. We've got to talk about what just happened and figure more of this out."

They pulled into La Playa, and Sylvie jumped out and ran up the stairs to her room. Meanwhile, Ben dialed Lauren. "Hey, everything is fine. Both Sylvie and I are safe, but it got more complicated. Sylvie was almost caught. I don't want to tell you anything more out of an abundance of caution for your own safety. I told Sylvie she must stay in my room tonight. We need to figure out what to do next. I'll call you later. I don't think I'll be over tonight, but let's plan on breakfast tomorrow."

"Please call me."

"I will and don't worry. Everything will be all right, but I think Sylvie needs to do something, I don't know what, before she can resume her normal activities." They hung up as Sylvie got back in the car with her small travel bag. They drove to Lubrique, parked, and hurried into Ben's room, Sylvie with her bag and Ben with the club.

THIRTY-TWO

....

IT WAS APPROACHING midnight on Tuesday night and Debi and Dean were in the master bedroom relaxing. They sat in bed, with the sheet up to their waists. Dean looked at Debi as a servant would to his benevolent queen. Debi looked back at Dean. "Aw shucks, is that look for me?" she kidded in her impression of a deep southern drawl. "Why, I just hope you aren't planning to end this party any-time soon. I'm feeling some of that same loving feeling as you, and I think we have a lot more partying to do."

Dean was pleased beyond any high expectations that he had when he first saw Debi. He was addicted and did not want her to ever get away. Debi continued, "We don't have to talk about this now, but my stay on the island ends fairly soon. You live here year-round and I am not sure what is going to happen with us."

Dean did not like thinking of her being separated from him for long. "We need to talk about that. You are correct, but I think we can reach a solution that will be mutually satisfying. I'm not prepared for you to be leaving anytime soon. You think on it, and let me know what you want. We can make that our priority project tomorrow."

Debi liked how the evening had been going and loved Dean's acknowledgement that he did not want her to leave. She was not sure of her bargaining power in the daylight hours, but liked the shift of power that as of now was in her favor.

"Dean, while we are in this intermission period, would you like me to get you one of your favorite Wiser's Canadian whiskeys? I, for one, have worked up a thirst, and could use a fresh glass of wine." Debi slid out of bed without waiting for his response. "I will be back in a minute with refreshments. You sit back and conserve your energy for when this intermission is over."

Debi continued the show for Dean, pretending not to know what direction to go for the drinks. She put one hand to her chin as if in deep thought, and twisted her body in several directions as if trying to peer around corners to find the alcohol. "Why, I do believe it is in this direction. Please forgive my momentary confusion." She did a little curtsy, then turned her back to walk out of the bedroom. She was confident that she had successfully kept his motor revved.

She returned with the drinks, placing Dean's on a coaster on his nightstand, then carefully sat back in bed with her glass of wine. They sat sipping their drinks and enjoying being in the proximity of one another. Dean finished his drink and extended his arm to place the empty glass back on the coaster. "Let me help you with that." Debi reached across Dean for his empty drink. As she did so, she pretended that her movement caused her to tilt her glass, spilling wine on Dean's chest. Hovering over Dean, she looked at him playfully. "Oh my, it looks like I was messy. I am so sorry for spilling my drink." She began lowering her face, while purposefully pouring the remaining wine on his chest. "It looks like I have a lot of cleaning up to do."

THIRTY-THREE

BEN AND SYLVIE were relieved to be in the safety of his room. Ben walked into the bathroom and with hot water and soap from the shower, cleaned the club. He dried it, it looked fine, but decided to do it again. He walked back to the car and placed the club on the floorboard where it had been before.

Sylvie's demeaner was hard for Ben to read. "You should call Terri and let her know you're okay. Also let her know you will be staying here tonight. She should be safe as she was with Harrington, so she should not be viewed as a problem to be dealt with."

Sylvie called Terri and she answered right away. Sylvie assured her that both she and Ben were fine. They needed to do some more planning and were unsure as to what they needed to do. She told Terri she would see her in the morning, but for the night, she felt comfortable staying in Ben's room. "If you're nervous being there by yourself, I'm sure Ben would invite you to stay with us for the night." Ben was not so sure of that, as he thought that Terri not staying in her own room would look suspicious if Harrington found out. How could that be explained, especially if it came to light that she was hiding out with Ben and Sylvie? Ben was relieved when Terri turned down the invitation.

Sylvie ended the call, then hugged Ben. "You may have saved my life tonight. I can't thank you enough."

Ben's mind was racing, trying to think of any next steps. "Now that we're back, my first question is, did you get what you were after?"

"I think so." Sylvie wanted to tell Ben the whole truth about the escapade, but was not sure how to do it, and fearful of Ben's reaction. She quickly decided she would tell him everything, but not yet. "I just grabbed what I thought I was after, slammed it into my bag, and didn't take time to really review what I had. But I'm pretty certain it's good."

"Then let's think through what we'll need to do. We can't be sure that one or both of us wasn't seen. And when Harrington discovers what is missing, he'll feel certain it was you who broke in. We may need to come up with several plans, one of which will be a worst-case scenario. If things go really bad, we need to figure out where we go and what we do. We can't stay holed up here indefinitely. I have a friend, Nico, who lives here. I'm going to call him and ask for any suggestions he might have." Sylvie agreed with his idea.

Ben called and shared a summary with Nico. "Harrington is a big man on the island," cautioned Nico. "He is not somebody to cross. I have someone in mind for you, might be good on your side, if you need muscle. I'll get with him tomorrow. If you need somewhere else to stay, I will call the group on our boat trip. They are staying at a very private villa, with security at the entrance of the neighborhood. Maybe they have room." Ben thanked Nico and anticipated an update call from him in the morning.

"Alright, I'm glad Nico is working on it. I honestly don't know what I'm doing. I don't know what other plans should be made. I don't know how we'll find out if a serious plan is needed, if we're all clear, or if it's something in between. Any thoughts?"

"No, I like to have a good time. I don't go around chased by bad guys. I've got no experience in something like this, I'm a lover, not a fighter. I really just want to go along with whatever you think will be best. I think you've done a great job so far. Let's keep going with what you think. You're the brains of this operation. I'm just lucky you're my friend."

Ben and Sylvie leaned back on the sofa. They both felt more secure with the lights off and the curtains closed to any outside eyes that might want to take revenge on them. "I have some Bimbo cookies, the vanilla creme cookies from Puerto Rico. Would you like any? I also have some chips and salsa. I need a snack, maybe help fuel some more thoughts."

"I'd like some chips and salsa. I'll get them." Sylvie poured some chips on a plate and placed them on the coffee table. She poured the salsa and emptied a third of the bottle into a small bowl. Without asking, she got two cold Heinekens, opened them and placed them on the coffee table next to the chips. They ate and drank in silence for a few minutes.

"Any ideas?" asked Ben after a while.

"Not really. We could go back to our normal routines. What could someone do, shoot us? Maybe the best way to see if everything is normal is to just do it, and see what happens."

"That's certainly an option. I think we can consider that as the base case. Whatever Nico might come up with might be taking the most precautions, hiring muscle and going into hiding, but if we did that, how would we know if it is ever safe to come out of hiding? I'd like for us to

ESCAPE TO THE ISLANDS

come up with a strategy that is somewhere in between the two approaches."

"Let's see what happens tonight," suggested Sylvie. If nothing unusual happens here, and nothing is reported by Terri, maybe we keep a low profile just for a few days. We could hang out in high population settings, on the beach, at crowded restaurants, and avoid any out-of-the-way places where someone could be emboldened to try to take revenge."

"I have no better idea. Let's try that. We'll lay low tonight. If nothing happens to give us a scare, and we hear nothing troubling from Terri, we'll tiptoe back toward normal. If nothing else occurs, we'll keep stretching out our activities until, hopefully, we are in the normal zone."

"Sounds good, we've got a plan." It was after midnight, and they were both tired. The adrenalin rush from earlier was gone. "If you don't mind, I'd like to take a shower and go to bed," said Sylvie.

"That's fine, I'll be right after you." Sylvie showered, and came out wearing an oversize t-shirt as a night shirt. She brushed her teeth in the sink outside of the bathroom as Ben stepped into the shower. He dried off, wrapped a towel around his waist, and brushed his teeth. He saw Sylvie curled on her side on the starboard side of the bed. She looked to be asleep or close to it. He went back in the bathroom and hung up his towel, then went to his suitcase of clothes still on the floor. "Are you coming to bed?" asked Sylvie. "I will feel much safer once you're in here with the covers up to my neck."

Ben was startled. He grabbed a pair of gray gym shorts and stepped into them. "I'll sack out on the couch, but I'll be right here if I'm needed. Try to sleep and we'll start getting back to normal in the morning." He walked over to the couch, opting to sleep on it without pulling it open to make an additional bed.

They both were exhausted and fell asleep quickly. As had occurred several times on the trip, heavy rain moved over the area between 2:00 and 4:00 in the morning, pounding the roof. On previous nights it had sounded calming and melodious for sleeping. Tonight, it was not comforting. Awakened by the rain, both of them worried that nature's sounds could be masking sounds generated from unwanted activity. "Do you hear anything?" whispered Sylvie. "I don't like it. I'm scared."

Ben got off the couch and sat on the floor next to Sylvie. "I don't hear anything. I think everything is okay." They both continued to speak no louder than a whisper.

"But you can't tell, can you?" asked Sylvie.

"No, but I don't think anyone is out there in this downpour."

"You're probably right," responded Sylvie. "I think a hired killer coming to get me would tell Harrington 'no way, not tonight, I'm scared of the rain!'"

Sylvie's sarcastic logic registered with Ben. He also felt nervous and very vulnerable. He got up from the floor, crept to the other side of the bed, and slipped under the cover. He got up close to her and whispered. "Okay, I'm in. Now if someone shoots through the window, we can both be killed with one shot."

Sylvie found Ben's comment funny and somehow reassuring. It was comforting to have someone close at a time of high stress. She nudged back in the bed, stopping when she was firmly resting against Ben's body. "That's much better. I might even be able to sleep now. I'll be quiet and very sensitive to any sounds or movement. Thanks for being a good friend. First you agree to help me when I was upset. Then you saved my life. And now, you're comforting me trying to keep me from panicking." She reached back, found his hand, and pulled his arm over her body, tucking his hand up under her left armpit. "That's much better. I don't deserve you as a friend, but I thank you for continuing to help me and being my guardian angel. When I got in the bed tonight, I prayed to God, that no matter what happens to me, He keeps you safe." Sylvie stopped talking, snuggled into his arm, and fell asleep. Ben also found the touch of another person comforting. He was trying to think of a better plan as he also quickly fell asleep.

THIRTY-FOUR

....

DEAN AND DEBI woke early on Wednesday morning. Dean was in lust, and he wondered if he was in love. He was certain he wanted to continue to see Debi after her vacation ended. "Good morning, I am getting accustomed to having you around. I have a full schedule again today, but would love to take you to dinner again tonight."

"I could probably do dinner tonight. I love being with you, but my friends may decide to disown me if I stop seeing them this trip. Do you think we should take a break? I don't want to monopolize all of your free time. I should probably check in with my friends to see if they will still include me in their plans."

"Perhaps I should agree to separation for the night, but to be clear, I do not like sharing. We planned to discuss a mutually satisfying solution to our problem of separation with your vacation ending soon. We have not had that much needed discussion. Maybe we can discuss that tonight."

Debi was calculating in her response, wanting to press her advantage that she had created, but also needing to be careful to not lose that advantage by overplaying her hand. She did not want to appear demanding. For a successful negotiation, she wanted the first proposal to come from Dean. Although she believed she had the upper hand, she did not anticipate his first offer would be the best offer she could receive. He was still a powerful and at times ruthless businessman. If his offer was not the ultimate, she could then entice a better offer with the prospect of more fun times as they had been experiencing. "Oh Dean, you flatter me and make me feel so special. You not wanting to share me with others is very touching. And your willingness to say it is so sweet. You deserve somebody who feels that same way about you. I think you've seen that I'm eager to meet your needs, and that your needs match with mine very nicely." She smiled coquettishly. "Going forward, you deserve nothing less. You don't want me to stray, and deserve my commitment to you, where I don't want to share you, either."

"Let's celebrate how wonderful we are together and our new understanding. Now, I'm going to take a short break and see what I can cook up in the kitchen. You stay put, I'll be back soon." She held the sheet, which was at her waist, and leaned forward as if to uncover her feet. However, instead of kicking off the covers which could remove the sheet from Dean, she brought her feet up toward the pillow, her face moving down to the foot of the bed. She secured the sheet on Dean, with a new moon rising. Grinning, she got out of bed and headed toward the kitchen to begin making breakfast for them.

She carried a tray back into the bedroom with two plates of scrambled eggs, bacon and buttered toast. Returning to the kitchen, she retrieved her hot tea and coffee for Dean. They sat in bed, sheet to their waists, and enjoyed the hot breakfast. Dean relished all the attention he was receiving. He was not focused on work as would have been typical. As he ate his breakfast, however, he started thinking about all the new revenue he would be receiving from his arrangement with Vaughn. After the operation was running smoothly, perhaps he would hire an assistant for all the detail work

needed at the casino. It could free up time for more breakfasts in bed, where he advanced to a higher level of oversight
only. He would be involved in handling minor details less
frequently, reserving his time for when unique projects or
problems arose. His ascent on the island as a power figure
had blossomed the last few years. Dean could approach sta-
tus similar to that of Harrington if his work with Vaughn
developed as expected.

Finishing their breakfast, Debi took the tray with the
empty plates back to the kitchen and placed them in the
dishwasher. "Would you like some more coffee?"

"Yes, maybe a half cup. Then we can discuss our new
arrangement. I have had much success in quickly address-
ing opportunities as they arise. Now is a good time for us
to discuss."

Debi took her empty teacup to place in the dishwasher, and got his coffee cup for a refill. She returned and
placed his coffee on his nightstand. She crawled got back
in bed from where she stood by his nightstand, crawling
across Dean to her side of the bed. She tucked herself in
and waited for him to begin.

"First, thanks for an amazing breakfast in bed. I
have to say, you are one delightful woman to wake up to.
Certainly a woman of many talents. But, let's get down to
business. How do you see our relationship going forward?"

Debi responded, maintaining her formal negotiation
tone. "I am also enjoying myself. This has been fun for
both of us. When finding something good, it only makes
sense to hold it dear. I have treasured our time together,
with my vacation to end soon. I know you are a very
smart businessman, and have structured many successful
business deals. I'd like to take advantage of your experience in business, and hear your thoughts. I have con-

fidence that you will propose something where we will both be very happy."

"Well, I definitely do not want to discontinue our relationship when your vacation ends. Are we in agreement with that?"

"Yes, I would also like for this to last longer."

"Okay, we agree on where we are now, and we have a common goal. Both of those are important, because without one, we wouldn't be able to reach a mutually agreeable solution. So now we need to assess each of our situations. Are you able to return here on a frequent basis?"

"Not really. I have a small company that I love to manage. It provides me a great opportunity to be with people that I enjoy spending time with, and I like the feeling of accomplishment of running my own business."

"Would you entertain moving your business here? I could assist in getting a location for your office and business, assist with contacts needed, or anything else to help you have the same success as you currently enjoy."

"It is possible to transition my business to here. However, at home I am much more than my business. I spend a lot of time with my family and friends. I don't want to move my business here and give up my family and friends. Not unless there was a good replacement."

"I am sure in no time you will develop great friendships here, some more dear and lasting than those you already have. And your family could always come for an occasional visit."

"I'm sure you're right. But I would be undertaking a big risk. My only lasting connection to this island is you. What if you tire of me? I will have uprooted my life, alienated my friends, and separated myself from my family. That would be both an emotional and financial hardship for me. That is a big risk for me to take. Although it has been less than a week, I know my level of commitment to you. I believe your commitment level to me matches mine, but what if I'm mistaken? What if someone comes along that you think can serve the bacon better than me?"

"I have to admit, you are a very wise woman. It is not only your looks and enthusiasm that I find attractive. I believe you could be an asset for me in all areas. Let me think through this some more. Are you willing to risk insulting your friends again tonight by standing them up for dinner with me instead? I want us to have a long and meaningful discussion, and dinner would be a great opportunity to discuss our future."

"I can risk it for another dinner. When you take me back, I'll explain to my friends that I will unfortunately miss them for one more night. Now, before you have to leave for work, is there anything else I can do to help?"

THIRTY-FIVE

BEN HEARD SYLVIE'S phone ring in her bag, while Sylvie continued to sleep. It was seven o'clock and he picked up his phone to call Lauren. "Hey," he said, "I'm up, but Sylvie is still sleeping. Are you doing okay?"

"Yes, I'm fine."

"If it's okay with you, I'll clean up real quick and come over. I'd like to talk about what's happened so far, and get your thoughts on what you'd like to do."

"Sure, come on over when you're ready."

Ben ended the call and walked into the bathroom to get ready. While Ben was in the shower, Sylvie woke up and checked her phone in her purse. She saw that Terri had called. She called Terri back and kept the conversation short, assuring her they were fine, and would talk again soon.

Sylvie walked into the bathroom to let Ben know she was up. "Okay, I'll be right out, then it's all yours." He toweled dry and wrapped the towel around his waist now that he knew Sylvie was awake. "How did you sleep?" Ben asked as he went to retrieve shorts and a t-shirt.

"I slept fine, what are the plans for this morning?"

"I just talked to Lauren briefly and I'm going to her room to bring her up to date on all that has happened. You can get ready while I'm there. I'll come back in a bit and we can see what we should do next. There is some food here if you want, or when I get back, we can see if we think it's okay to step out for breakfast. I don't know what we should do, but having the morning sunshine makes everything seem better. I'll be back in probably thirty minutes."

Ben left to go see Lauren. Once he left, Sylvie reached into her bag and retrieved the papers she had stolen. She took a picture of each page with her phone. The pictures would be saved on the small removable memory chip in her android phone. She began to read the papers in detail. She was elated to see she had hit the jackpot, but now needed to think through how she could best use the information. She placed the papers back in her bag and began to get ready.

Lauren opened the door to Ben immediately as he arrived. He hurried in happy to see her and gave her a long hug. "I think everything is okay, but I want to tell you everything that happened. We'll need to discuss what you'll be comfortable doing, looking at any risks that I might have and assessing if they might transfer to you, and trying to minimize those." Ben went through everything that had occurred, ending with his return with Sylvie from the night before. He also told her how he had clubbed some guy with his wheel lock who had driven up before Sylvie was out of the house. "We discussed my call to Nico for advice, and right now we're thinking of trying to resume being normal but being watchful for trouble. I think Nico will call me later this morning with any ideas he might have."

Lauren listened attentively, shocked and upset that it had not gone as expected, and very disturbed that they had been caught in the act. She was especially worried over Ben's needed surprise attack for Sylvie to get away, worried that his actions had greatly increased the seriousness of the evening. Believing Ben's participation in Sylvie's plan was unknown to Harrington, Lauren wanted to continue as if she and Ben were not in danger. They would remain alert, however, for signs of possible trouble. "Okay, I need to go back to my room and update Sylvie and see what she plans to do. As soon as I'm done talking with her, I'll be back, and we can go get some breakfast." He hugged Lauren, and they shared a caring kiss.

When Ben went back into his room, Sylvie was dressed and ready for the day. "I called Terri to let her know I'm okay. I think it would be best if I go back to our room. We plan to be careful, but think we can resume our normal activities. If anything changes, we'll let you know. To be on the safe side, it would probably be good if we don't run into each other for a few days. You have my number, so call me if there is anything you think I should be aware of." Sylvie paused before asking a favor. "Would you mind me using your safe for a few items? I have my passport and some jewelry that I gathered up last night. I'd feel better if I stored that stuff in your safe instead of mine." Sylvie had removed the memory chip from her phone and placed it in her locket among the jewelry she would place in the safe.

"Sure, that's fine." Ben opened his safe and she tucked her items inside. However, she kept the original papers in her bag. If caught, she knew Harrington would do whatever it took to retrieve the papers, and if needed, she would make it easy for him to get them.

"Thanks," Sylvie said as Ben secured the safe. She stood, genuine tears beginning to form. "You don't know how much you have helped me. I have a special place in my heart for you. I hope one day you will forgive me for everything I've done. I plan to reward you when this is all over, and I hope you'll accept that, as well as my apology." She gave Ben a big hug. He was moved by her words, and pleased that she and Terri would try to resume their lives normally, but continue to be alert for any problems.

She broke the hug and left Ben's room, beginning her walk along the street to La Playa.

Ben walked back to Lauren's room. Once inside, they hugged for a long time. "It went well with Sylvie. She decided to go back to her room. It went better than I thought it would, and Sylvie reached her decision while I was here with you. We agreed to avoid any contact with each other, and I feel as if my responsibility in this is over. I just want to resume my vacation, and especially want to resume it with you. Let's go get some breakfast."

Lauren loved hearing what Ben had just said. She was also ready to pretend none of the craziness had ever happened. They stepped out to get some breakfast at Papatwo. They were greeted by the manager and owner. "Good morning Ben, I trust you are enjoying your stay. And who is this beautiful lady in your company?"

"Arnaud, this beautiful girl is Lauren. And yes, we are both loving our stay here. Your place is magnificent! I am sorry I have not seen you since I first arrived, but everything is great!"

"It is a pleasure to meet you, Lauren. I hope you continue to enjoy your stay here but please call on me if I can add to your enjoyment."

Ben and Lauren were seated at a table and ordered scrambled eggs, fruit and fresh orange juice. "What would you like to do today? I feel like I have messed up your vacation with the things I've been doing, and I want to make it up to you. I'd love to spend a worry-free day with you. You name it, and I'll do my best to do it."

"That sounds like an offer I might have received from you on Saturday night. It's hard to believe it's Wednesday already. I'm good with anything, but seeing as how it's my choice, I'd like to start the day on the beach, have a late lunch and then go to the market in Marigot. I think the busiest days at the Marigot market are Saturdays and Wednesdays. I don't have anything specific in mind, but I would really just like to look around."

"That all sounds great! I think it will all be fun. I haven't been to Marigot, so I'd like to see what it's like. And I'm not opposed to shopping. I totally enjoyed shopping with you in Philipsburg, and I think the market sounds like a lot of fun with all the items made on the island."

They finished their breakfast and walked back to their rooms. Ben looked at Lauren before they went their separate ways. "Hey, why don't you get your suit and bring it over to my room. I'll help you with putting suntan lotion on your back, and you can help me. I always find it easier to put the lotion on inside where you don't have to worry about sand blowing all over you and making the lotion gritty when I put it on your back." Ben gave a huge grin, feeling young again, temporarily forgetting about all the stress from the night before.

"Okay," Lauren laughed, "I won't make you beg. I'll be right over."

Ben got undressed and started putting lotion on his face and ears while he waited for Lauren. They had already seen each other undressed, and with the prevailing St. Martin attitude of nudity not equated with sexuality, applying lotion on each other was less licentious than if in the U.S. She gave one knock before opening the door. "I'm here. I hope my lotion assistant is ready. And when you do my back, put it in your hands first to warm it. I don't like cold lotion squirted directly on me and then rubbed in."

"Definitely, come on over and I'll get you started." Ben applied the lotion and hoped that Lauren would be impressed with the restraint he was challenged to maintain. Slipping into their suits, they grabbed two beach towels and walked out to the beach. They did not bother to take books, thinking there would be little time to read.

They found two chairs, and arranging their towels, they sat back and smiled at the world. Around 9:30 a.m. Ben suggested they walk the length of the beach. Standing up, Ben reached to pull her into a hug before twirling her in a youthful dance. They started up the beach holding hands, leisurely walking in the shallow water as they worked their way toward the Mont Vernon.

As they reached La Playa, Ben saw Sylvie and Terri sunning on the beach, but there was no greeting, as they ignored each other as agreed. After another hundred steps, Ben mentioned he had seen Terri and Sylvie on the beach in front of La Playa, and described them so Lauren would recognize them on the walk back. He cautioned her not to stare as they walked back by them.

They continued their care-free walk and turned around when the beach ended. "That's a long walk. I may need a ride back." Lauren jumped on Ben's back for a piggyback ride, and he carried her for about a block before panting and putting her down. "That was a great ride, thanks. You are very chivalrous!"

"I try to please, Ma'am. In about five minutes we'll be back in front of La Playa. When we're about fifty feet from Sylvie and Terri, I'll not say anything, but I'll give your hand a squeeze so you'll know it's them." They walked on, and Ben squeezed her hand, confirming their identity.

They were back at their chairs before they spoke again. "I didn't see anyone on the beach that looked like they might be following us. I think we've been left alone today. I'm certain the guy I surprised did not see me, so there may be no one interested in following us. It's probably good to still be cautious, but I think we can relax for the most part and have a good time."

They waded out in the water, splashed and talked. The water felt great, and they were in no hurry to get out. Around eleven they went back to their chairs and enjoyed the sun's warming rays. Nearing one in the afternoon, they walked over to Papatwo, had a light lunch and went back to shower off before going into Marigot.

Lauren and Ben found a parking place on the main road along the waterfront. The market was full of activity, with individual booths set up for several hundred of the island residents to present their goods. Lauren and Ben first stopped at the booth with spices, purchasing Magic Spice, a combination of a number of spices, for sprinkling on hamburgers and chicken. They also purchased a special combination of spices in a bottle labeled 'Fish Spice' made specifically for enhancing the flavor of any type of fish. Next, they came to a table of rums of many flavors, all in decorative hand-painted bottles. A couple of those for decorating at home were a must. There were t-shirts, towels, dresses, shorts, shirts, jewelry made with shells, paintings, carvings, linens, beach bags and so much more. They each bought a couple of colorful pareos, and Lauren got a new bag for carrying to the beach. She came across a booth selling license plates that she was hoping to find. Instead of small fake signs of 'I Love St. Martin' printed on them, these license plates were actually used on island vehicles and removed by enterprising islanders to sell to tourists. Ben and Lauren each bought one, with Lauren scoring a rare find of a license plate used many years ago and stamped with Mullet Bay as the background of the plate.

"That was fun! I love the Marigot market. Before we leave, I want you to take a picture of me with the statue of the market lady." They walked over to the statue presiding over the market booths, and Ben snapped her picture. He flagged down a tourist who was happy to assist him by taking a picture of both of them with the statue, and another one of them with the waterfront in the background.

The happy couple walked back to their car and drove back to Lubrique, the trip taking less than twenty minutes. "Come on over to my room and let's plan what we want to do for dinner tonight. We need a great meal to top off a great day!" They walked over to Ben's room and once inside, they put the bags of purchased treasures on the floor next to Ben's suitcase.

"Okay, now to pick a restaurant. Let's sit on the bed and scroll through the guidebook for recommendations. Lauren, let me know if you see anything you want us to try." As they began their search, Ben's cell phone rang. It was Nico.

THIRTY-SIX

SYLVIE AND TERRI enjoyed the beach at Orient. They walked into the water after seeing Ben and Lauren walk past for the second time. "Well?" asked Terri.

"Well what?"

"Did you get what you were after? Are we going to be rich?"

Sylvie gave her a solemn look. "I found some papers, and at first, they looked like they might be what I was after," she said, her voice trailing off as with disappointment. "But then," she paused, "I looked again, and I was sure I had the motherload!" She took the two steps that separated them in the water, wrapped her arms around Terri, and lifted her out of the water with her biggest hug. "We're going to be rich," she said, keeping her voice low. "I know it's what I was after, and I know it will make us rich. Now I need to think through the details on how I cash in this winning hand."

"That is awesome," Terri replied, also keeping her voice down so no one nearby could hear their conversation. "We will have to celebrate." They hugged again.

"Yes, it is looking like a fairy tale with a happy ending. I can't believe it!" She changed the subject before continuing. "When we saw Ben walk by, he appeared to be enjoying himself. I'm glad. He has been amazing for me. After

a few days, I hope we are all able to get together. I want
to share everything and tell him when I cash in, he will
be greatly rewarded. He earned a healthy split. I hope he
forgives me for deceiving him to get his help. I want us all
to be wildly happy!"

"I think he will be upset at first, but he'll forgive you.
Nobody can stay mad at you, Sylvie."

"I hope you're right. I want us to be close friends."
They walked out of the water and laid out for the sun to dry
them. "I would like to go to Philipsburg for a few items.
Would you mind going with me?" asked Sylvie.

"No, that will be fun. I think going shopping is just
what we need. We can get a quick bite and then look around.
Maybe I will get a little something to celebrate. I think we
should eat here tonight and discuss what we should do to
cash in safely. I'm getting excited. It doesn't seem real!"

The girls went inside to shower and get ready for their
trip to town. They were in Philipsburg a short time later
and found a parking place in one of the large flat parking
lots off the main road. They walked toward Front Street
and saw a food vendor and drinks. They stopped, had a
snack, and continued on to Front Street. Sylvie wanted
to get a replacement memory chip for her phone. They
went into Boolchand's at 50 Front Street, where there was
a large selection of cameras, electronics and computers.
Sylvie purchased the chip and the Boolchand's employee
inserted it into her phone. Close by, at 43 Front Street,
was the Shipwreck Shop. There Sylvie purchased a packet
of large envelopes. She walked outside the store, inserted
the stolen papers in an envelope, sealed it and then
inserted it into another envelope. She threw away the
rest of the purchased envelopes and secured the envelope
containing the papers in her bag. Her most important

purchase of the day had been completed. "What would you like to shop for Terri?"

"I don't have anything specific in mind, but will enjoy looking around. I'd like to get something as a special memory for this trip. I guess that means either clothes or jewelry," she laughed. "Let's go into this jewelry store." Royal Jewelers was next to the Shipwreck shop at 44 Front Street. Upon entering, they were greeted by Rakhee, the beautiful wife of the store owner. She chose a necklace with a citrine pendant as her birthstone, encircled in diamonds, and wore it out of the store. She was ecstatic with her purchase and enjoyed talking with Rakhee, who she already was beginning to think of as a friend. She would definitely shop again at Royal Jewelers.

The girls decided to move along the shops on Front Street, and next looked at t-shirts and swimsuits. Although there was a large selection in each shop, nothing jumped out at them to buy. Terri was content with what she had already purchased, and did not need to continue shopping for herself. However, she insisted Sylvie look for something that would be a traditional gift before their shopping ended. They walked into Gift World at 21 Front Street. "Sylvie, maybe you'll find that special memory of St. Martin here. It looks like this store has a wide variety of items."

They looked around the store. Terri watched the people around her and wondered if she had seen some of them before, perhaps shopping in other stores. "Question for you, Sylvie. We're having a good time, and I've been pretty relaxed. You look like you have been, too. Have you noticed anybody that maybe we've seen before, not just shopping in the same stores as us?"

Sylvie tensed. "I don't know. I haven't seen anybody that I'd say was suspicious. I've felt like maybe, but it's just been a feeling after what I've been through. I haven't identified anybody that I could point to."

"Okay, let's just be careful." They shopped around in Gift World, where Sylvie decided to purchase a St. Martin beach towel. It was thicker than those advertised as two for ten dollars and was a very nice towel. Saying she was cheap to shop for, Sylvie completed the purchase and they walked out of the store.

"Is there anywhere else you'd like to shop?'" asked Terri.

"No, I think I'm happy with just my towel. We can look at the store fronts as we go back to our car, but I think I'm done. What about you?"

"No, I'm good. Let's head back. If we leave now, we can be back in time to catch a little more sun today."

The girls started walking back along Front Street. To return to their car, they needed to cross over Back Street and C.A. Cannegieter Street, bringing them back to the main Walter A. Nisbeth Road. They would also need to cross the main road before reaching the parking lot adjacent to the Great Salt Pond. They cut perpendicular to Front Street, walking through a narrow alley for walkers but not paved for vehicular traffic. It was at that point their fears were realized. Two fit-looking men, late thirties, turned into the alley behind them. They were fifty feet behind them and without others around, did not hide their focus on the girls.

"Sylvie, let's pick up the pace." They accelerated to a brisk walk, but the men walked faster, closing the gap to thirty feet as they came to Back Street. Instead of continuing on toward the car through the alley, Sylvie reached for Terri and they turned to mingle among other shoppers on Back Street. The men kept within view, but lagged behind. Terri and Sylvie hoped they would blend in and be lost to them, or that the men would lose interest. After slipping in and out of several stores, they looked up and down Back Street but could not see the two men.

"Let's head back to the car," suggested Terri. "We've still got a couple hours of daylight left. I don't want to be walking back to the car at dusk. We're fairly close to the car, and if we need to, we can run as we get closer."

They walked on Back Street to their crossover point, going north toward their car and continuing to look over their shoulders. They came to C.A. Cannegieter Street without incident, and continued toward the Great Salt Pond and their car. All was still fine, there was no threat to their safety. They crossed the street, seeing the parking lot and their car up ahead. They made a beeline for their car, breaking into a jog the last several yards and got in. "Whew! It's good to be back. That unnerved me," said Sylvie, sitting in the driver's seat and looking at Terri.

Terri responded, "Let's get out of here and back to La Playa." Sylvie had the car key in hand and went to turn the ignition. Just as she did, she saw the same two men at her window, one with a gun visible. He motioned for her to roll down her window. She did what she was told, rolling it down about six inches.

"I believe you have something that doesn't belong to you," said the man with the gun. "We need to return it to its owner."

"What are you talking about?"

"We're not going to stand here discussing this. As you can see, I have with me something that ends all talking, permanently. So tell us where it is."

"I don't know what you're talking about."

"You ladies need to step out of the car. You're going to take a little trip with us. But don't worry, I assure you I will return you to the Salt Pond. It will be my pleasure. Now step out. There's no need to dirty up a perfectly good rental car. Blood stains are hard to remove."

Still holding the car key, Sylvie reached for the car handle to open the door. As she did, she saw a blur of movement. The man with the gun went down, his face smashing into the metal door frame, with blood spurting from his broken nose. His companion, standing at the back door, had also gone down in a heap, his body bouncing off the body of the car. An unknown man had propelled himself sidelong into the two men, knocking the wind out of the second would-be assailant. The unknown man jumped into the back seat. "Drive!" he ordered. Sylvie obeyed and quickly pulled away into the flow of traffic. "You're driving to the Kooyman Store not too far from here. My car is there. We'll talk on the way."

Sylvie drove, too scared to talk. "You are in luck. Your guardian angel asked me to look out for you ladies today. When we get to Kooyman, I will get out and follow you back to La Playa. There, you will both gather any valuables you have that you would like to be assured you will be able to keep, and give them to me. I will deliver them to your friend Ben for safekeeping."

Sylvie and Terri were trying to process all that just happened. "You know Ben?" asked Terri.

"No, but we have a mutual friend. You are both okay, for now."

At the Kooyman store, the stranger got out of the car and followed Sylvie to La Playa.

"Terri, I've already given Ben my passport and jewelry. They're in his safe. I recommend you do the same," said Sylvie before getting out of the car. The girls went to their room, Terri retrieved her passport and some jewelry, and put them in Sylvie's large outer envelope holding the sealed envelope with stolen papers. Sylvie sealed the outside envelope and the two girls hurried back down the stairs to the waiting stranger. Sylvie handed the envelope to the stranger.

"You can trust me. I just saved your lives. I'm not demanding you give me anything. If you want to keep these items with you, they are yours to keep." He handed the envelope back. Sylvie pushed the envelope back to the stranger. "Okay, I do not want these items. They will be with Ben soon. Enjoy the rest of your evening. You will be hearing from Ben later tonight. Do not try to contact him. If you need to get in touch with someone, here's a number you can call. He knows what is going on and can give you guidance. You should consider finding a different place to stay." The stranger got in his car and drove away.

Terri and Sylvie were very shaken. Instead of going back to the beach, they went into their third-floor room and locked the door. They played some island music, and had a glass of wine to try to relax.

THIRTY-SEVEN

BEN ANSWERED HIS phone. "Nico, I was expecting your call. Lauren and I are just sitting here trying to decide where to go for dinner."

"You should eat at Mario Bistro. It is at Cupecoy. After your call last night, I made a few phone calls and found a friend to help. He has been busy today and will be at Mario Bistro at seven tonight. You should meet him there for dinner. He helped Sylvie today and has something to give you."

"Okay, who am I meeting?"

His name is Paul. His beautiful wife Lisa will be with him, so you should have Lauren there, too. You two will like them. He looks mild-mannered, but do not misjudge him. He is trained in specialized defense, which was valuable to Sylvie. He could be valuable again."

"Okay, we'll meet them there at seven. Nico, you're a great friend, I look forward to talking with them tonight. I'll keep in touch." With that, he ended the call.

"I guess you heard? Are you okay with us trying the place in Cupecoy?"

"Yes, that sounds fine. Let's see if it's in the dining guide." They flipped through and Lauren spotted it. "This looks great! It shows an amazing atmosphere, French, seafood and European dishes, and has outstanding reviews.

I'm liking Paul and Lisa already. This should be fun! Now that that's settled, let's take a long leisurely walk down the beach. I feel like celebrating. While you're getting into your swim trunks, I'll change into one of my new pareos."

Dressed for the beach, they stepped out, carrying only the room key in the water-proof box dangling from Ben's neck. The late afternoon sun, mixed with the light breeze from the ocean, was refreshing, and they walked with their feet in the water at ankle depth. Lauren looked at Ben, thinking that something magical could be starting. "Ben, what are you thinking about?"

"I don't know. Nothing really. Just trying to live here in the moment after all that has happened since I got here on Saturday. A lot more than I ever imagined."

"Are you glad I came over and introduced myself that Saturday night?"

"Of course I am. You're the highlight of my trip. Thank you for coming over on Saturday night." Ben thought for a minute before continuing. "Now, for a tougher question, with all that has happened, with the craziness that has touched you because I didn't simply mind my own business, do you wish you had introduced yourself to someone else?"

"Let me think about it." She made an exaggerated show as if pondering a deep question. "Well, I guess when I weigh it all, and recognizing the jury is still out, I would have to say going over to see you Saturday night was one of my better decisions. We'll see how dinner goes tonight to confirm. You might be on probation if the meal is disappointing." She grinned up at Ben, and then wrapped her arms around him. Ben picked her up and spun her in a circle, placing her back down on the sand where she began. "Okay, I promise to be on my best behavior at dinner tonight so that you won't think you made a bad mistake." They continued happily on their beach walk. When they got to the end of the beach, they turned and marveled at how beautiful it all was. "This has got to be one of the most beautiful beaches in the world," said Lauren. "Thank you for walking it with me. I'm working up an appetite, so I'm glad we're going to a great place tonight."

The two continued to make small talk all the way back to Ben's room. Lauren went in long enough to grab her shopping bags before leaving to get ready for dinner. "I'll be ready a little after six so come over and pick me up then." Lauren and Ben each showered and were ready to eat a fancy meal at Mario Bistro. They arrived a little before seven, stopping at the hostess station. "We're here to meet another couple, Paul and Lisa. Do you know if they're here yet?"

"Right this way." They were led to a quiet table where they saw the attractive couple already seated. "Hi," said Paul, "you must be Ben and Lauren. Pleased to meet you. This is my wife Lisa. Thank you for meeting us tonight." The couples exchanged the usual pleasantries before settling into a comfortable conversation. They placed their orders and Paul ordered a bottle of wine to be brought to the table.

"I have something for you." Paul brought out the sealed envelope with the items from Sylvie and Terri. "Your friends would like you to hang on to this for them. I met them today in Philipsburg." He continued by sharing that Nico had requested his help and that he watched over Sylvie and Terri for the day. He explained how they were followed by two men and almost forced to accompany them, and how he was able to help. He concluded by telling Ben and Lauren he had followed the girls back to La Playa, where they had given the envelope to him for Ben's safekeeping. "Ben, I told them that you would call them tonight. I don't think either of you should have any concerns. I'm comfortable you were followed and they know you both were in Marigot when the plan in Philipsburg didn't go as expected for Harrington. You two should be off the radar, but I believe Sylvie and Terri will be targeted again. It's not my intention to be involved with this any further, but you can reach out to me if you need me."

"I'm not sure what I'm to do. I have a couple of things from Sylvie already in my room safe, and will put this envelope there also. I'll call Sylvie tonight and ask what her plans are. It seems to me that they should get some protection, or move somewhere unknown in case they continue to be followed. It doesn't seem like there is a good solution."

"After you talk with Sylvie, you can call me. It looks like our food is on its way, so let's enjoy a great meal." The food was served, and Paul made a toast. "To new friends. May the rest of your time in St. Martin be everything you hoped it would be." The foursome enjoyed the food and getting to know one another, but the enthusiasm of the group was curbed by the threat to Sylvie and Terri.

After the meal, Ben and Lauren rode solemnly back to Lubrique. "Now what?" asked Lauren. "As long as you have their stuff, this isn't over. What are you planning to do?"

"I don't know. When we get back, we'll call Sylvie. I want you to hear everything. I'll ask Sylvie if she has any suggestions, but then a decision will be needed. I don't want to be involved anymore with any of this. Let's see if there is a way for us to no longer be involved and they have a happy ending."

They made it back to Lubrique and went in Ben's room. "Ben, do we need to call Sylvie now?"

"We probably should, but first, I've got an idea. How would you like a day trip to St. Barts?"

THIRTY-EIGHT

DEAN DROVE DEBI back to the Royal Palm. They both had some thinking to do before dinner on Wednesday night. "Hello everybody, I'm home," called Debi as she entered their unit. "Did you miss me?"

"Who are you and what are you doing barging into our room? Do I need to call security? Oh wait... I think I remember you. Are you dumbass? No, ditch girl? No, Debi, yes Debi, that's right. Welcome back Debi, how have you been? Enjoying your vacation?" asked Karen.

"Good one. I had that coming. Are you guys going to forgive me and let me hang with you today?"

"Did you bring us more show tickets, free dinners or cold, hard cash? I'm sure we could be bribed into forgiving you for ditching us again."

"I'm sorry, I came back empty-handed. And I'll go ahead and tell you that I have separate dinner plans again tonight. Does that eliminate me from being with you until then?"

"I guess not. We went to Rouge yesterday, so today is going to be a Cupecoy day. Are you okay with going to Cupecoy Beach with us?"

"That's fine, if I'm invited, I accept."

"Okay, Cupecoy is supposedly more of an afternoon beach than a morning beach. People like to go there to see the sunset, and a chance to see the green flash. Dany

186

has his bar there, and cooks food on the grill. Maybe we should get there a little after noon, get some chairs, put in an order for some ribs, and catch some rays. Is everybody good with that?" asked Karen.

Jodi, Jan and Debi were all excited to try the new beach. They got ready, dressed in bikinis under their shorts and t-shirts, and were out the door. "Before we leave, I don't want to mess up anybody's plans. Dean is picking me up tonight at seven, so I want to be back by six. Is everybody okay with being back then, or should I drive separately?"

"Let's take two cars. That way everybody can decide later if they want to stay or be back by six," replied Karen.

"It's a deal. Jan, would you mind riding over with me? I'd like to give you an update on what's going on with me and Dean. You can feel free to give advice if you'd like."

The four girls drove over to Cupecoy near the unsightly big, blue mall. St. Maarten is a beautiful place, but one of the few negatives was the mall across the street from the entrance to Cupecoy. Unfortunately, buildings like that are a part of progress that probably cannot be avoided. The girls parked and walked down to the beach. It was quiet with only a dozen people on the beach. The beach at Cupecoy for some years has changed from day-to-day, with a full, white sand beach one day, to only rocks along the shore the next. They were rewarded with a beach large enough for several rows of chairs.

"This is beautiful," declared Karen. "I think I've found my new home." The girls walked to Dany's bar and requested four chairs. Dany pointed them to some chairs open down the beach. They took that as an invitation to claim those as theirs for the day, with payment to come later. The few people on the beach were friendly, much like the beach goers at Orient. The water was rougher than the calm sea at Orient, but there was a natural rock pool where the girls enjoyed dipping. After a while, Dany came by asking if they wanted anything. They ordered two rib lunches to split, and four Red Stripes. It looked like a Red Stripe type of beach. They enjoyed the food and solitude of Cupecoy, and primarily laid out on their chairs talking within the group. As the day wore on, Debi reminded the others that she would be leaving a little after five. The rest of the group decided they would stay and enjoy the sunset around six before going back to the resort. At five Debi gathered her belongings and gave some cash to Karen to cover her part of the expenses. It had been a restful day, giving Debi time to think more about her strategy when discussing future plans with Dean.

Debi showered and dressed well before Dean arrived. She decided the night of negotiation called for a change in approach that would take Dean off guard. She had not packed many conservative outfits for her tropical getaway, but selected a dress that showed off her body without putting as much on display. She was ready to conduct a successful negotiation.

Just before seven o'clock, Dean arrived. Debi answered the door wearing a big grin. "You look great tonight, as always," Dean said in greeting. I hope you've had a good day."

"Yes, it was fun. I had to do some begging and groveling to be part of my friends' group, but then we had a lot of fun. We went to Cupecoy for the day."

"I am so glad you had a good day with friends. Where would you like to eat tonight?"

"I thought maybe we could stay here and eat. The waterfront restaurant behind the Royal Palm looks good, and I want to try it before going back. Is that okay with you?"

"I am happy to try it. Any meal with you will be a good meal."

They walked to the Palms restaurant that was part of the Royal Palm Resort. It was a nice open-air restaurant, and they were seated at a quiet table overlooking the beach.

As they waited for a server, Debi began the discussion. "I hope you weren't too busy with work and that you had time to give thought to what happens when my vacation ends."

"Yes, and I am prepared for us to reach a happy decision. Have you given it any more thought?" The waitress came over, and Dean ordered a bottle of wine for the table.

"Yes, I had a great chance to think at the beach today. I have smart friends who are an asset in keeping me grounded. The discussion today led to talk of marriage. Not my marriage, but yours. They are under the impression that you are married, and that I should not be making a commitment to you. Is it true?"

"I will not lie to you. I am married, but it is a marriage based on business. It is not something that I want to be a concern."

Debi decided to go full bore. "That is not a concern for me if it isn't for you. I am looking forward to another delightful meal, but I won't be making any commitments. When I return on future vacations, I would certainly like to enjoy your company if we are both available."

"I understand your position, but I believe I can satisfactorily explain that I am committing to you, even while maintaining my marriage. I hope you will hear me out before making a final decision."

The meal was served, and discussion continued as they ate. At the conclusion of the meal, they each had an after-dinner drink. It was almost time to leave the restaurant. Debi began her closing argument, maintaining her formal business approach. "Thank you for yet another great meal. To briefly summarize, I am not asking for a marriage commitment to me, as I am not close to ready for marriage. To highlight what I bring to you, is the ability to do more than be a great dinner date and best lay of your life. I run my own business and have a set of skills that I have honed to great success. A future arrangement would be to combine our business talents as well. You said you are beginning new business arrangements, and I believe I can get results in ways that you cannot. And with the dramatic pick-up in revenues to come, you can easily end your marriage business relationship, and already have new deals to more than offset any losses you might suffer doing that. For a commitment that I will be available when it suits, you must establish your sincerity by ending your current business relationship in the form of a marriage. My friends should be back now, and I will be hanging out with them for the rest of this evening. I hope you'll give my proposal ample thought, and will let me know your decision after you've had time to think it through. I am not open to any additional negotiation, but am prepared to accept whatever your decision is as final. I will be leaving in a few days, and as a good businessman, I am certain you appreciate the value of being decisive. When a great opportunity presents itself, you must be prepared to act. As I've always heard, if you snooze, you lose."

They left the table and Dean walked Debi back to her room in silence. "You are a strong woman and it certainly has been a pleasure. I will be in touch, and for now, wish you well."

Debi leaned in and the two had a chaste kiss goodnight. The night ended with Debi having played all of her cards.

THIRTY-NINE

....

BEN PLACED A call to Sylvie. He had the call on speaker to add Lauren to the conversation. "Hey Sylvie. I have the sealed envelope that you handed over to give to me. Everything is in my safe."

"Oh, thank you. Did you hear what happened?"

Yes, I got a call from Nico, who told me high level, and we just finished dinner with your rescuer. He gave us a detailed version. You were very lucky that Nico asked for help and his friend was there when needed."

"So what do we do next?"

"I've given it some thought, and I have a couple ideas. The attack earlier today was pretty bold. As much as I'd like to think it won't happen again, I'm afraid they won't give up. You both need to stay very diligent, watchful in everything you do. I'm so sorry, and know that's an awful way to spend a vacation. But here are my ideas. One, I think you could stay close here, and maybe alert La Playa to see if they can increase their security until you go home. Or two, I may have an idea where you could still have some fun away from the beach. Lauren and I are thinking of going to St. Barts for a day, and maybe you two can go also. I've heard it's beautiful, and it would be fun to explore there a bit."

"If we wanted to try St. Barts, how would we get there?"

"I could work on that. My idea is that I arrange for you to go over by boat, maybe with a scheduled group. Instead of driving to the boat and being followed, you could take a taxi. By getting on the boat unexpectedly, it would make it harder for someone to find you over in St. Barts. They would know where you're going, but would have to find you again after you're over there. Here's the next part that I'd have to work through, and I don't know if you'd like it. I could ask Nico to meet you in St. Barts, and he could take you by boat back to St. Martin. If someone chooses not to go after you separately to St. Barts, you could have the day without being watched, and they would be thrown off when you didn't return with the group. They would have to start over trying to find you. To delay them finding you, you probably should find somewhere else to stay. What do you think about the ideas?

"It's a lot to think about. I don't know what to do. I'll talk it over with Terri and call you back. I'd like to go into more detail on some stuff with you later, and when this is all over, I want to repay you for blindly helping like you've done. I will be in a position to give you a large financial reward. Let me talk to Terri and I'll call you back."

They ended the call. "Lauren, thanks for going along with all of this. As Paul said, it's a pretty good bet we are free and clear now. I feel an obligation to finish what I started, but I hate dragging you along, putting a damper on your vacation. If you want to drop out of this and spend time with your friends, I understand. And as soon as this is over, I'll be tracking you down."

"I do wish it was all over, but I can't imagine any vacation ever being like this one. I think years down the road I'd still be regretting it if I didn't stay for the ride. If they decide to hang out on the beach, what are you thinking we'd do?"

"Anything you want. There would be nothing more for me to do here. We could stay here at the beach and enjoy it, but that would be independent of them. Or we could make a day of going anywhere else you'd like to go. Whatever you decide, we'll do it."

"Of course, if they go to St. Barts, I'm on board with going there. It would be fun even if the crazy situation wasn't going on." Lauren continued, "Do you need to make any calls to try to arrange a St. Barts trip in case that's what they want to do? Is it too late to get that arranged for tomorrow?"

"I'm not sure. Let's make some calls and find out."

Ben called Nico. He updated him on the dinner meeting with Paul and Lisa, and then shared his ideas. He wanted to know if Nico could help get Sylvie and Terri on a boat scheduled to go to St. Barts tomorrow. If they did want to go, Ben also asked if Nico would be available for a boat trip taking just Lauren and Ben over, but bringing Sylvie and Terri back with them. He also asked if he had any suggested places where Sylvie and Terri could stay once back in St. Martin if they left La Playa.

Nico said he could make a few calls, and that probably a trip scheduled to St. Barts would have room for two more. "It's the islands, man. People say they go, but they no show. Room for two more to replace them. If everyone is a go, it's still the islands. We sit a little closer and make room, as long as we don't sink the boat." Ben was encouraged and eager for Sylvie to call him back.

"Well Lauren, now it's time to try to be patient and wait for Sylvie to call us back. Why don't we walk down to the beach, enjoy the sound and smell of the ocean, and try to relax? It's beautiful weather, and that might help pass the time."

They walked barefoot outside, slowly up the beach and purposefully turning around before they reached La

Playa. They did not have to wait long before getting the call on Ben's cell phone from Sylvie. "Hey," Ben began, cutting her off before she could get started. "We're on the beach walking back now. We should be back in five minutes. I'll call you as soon as we're back." Ben hung up before she had a chance to say anything. He knew it was an impossibly small chance that someone would hear her voice talking to him on the beach, but it was a chance he would not take.

They walked into Ben's room, sat on the bed, and Ben called Sylvie on speaker so Lauren could hear. "Have you guys decided what you'd like to do?"

"We're concerned if we stay here we'll be looking for trouble and we won't be able to relax. We also think staying here any longer than necessary is not very smart. We'd like to try going to St. Barts. Do you think that can be worked out for tomorrow?"

"I'm pretty sure it can. I talked to Nico, and he said it wouldn't be a problem. I'll call him back and get him to work out the details. If I do, are you willing to go along with whatever he works out? He's a good guy, and I don't think he would arrange something that you would object to."

"Yes, definitely," responded Terri before Sylvie had a chance to answer. "That makes it unanimous then," added Sylvie. "We'll look forward to a day adventure to St. Barts. Please call me back with the details. I'll walk down now and mention to the manager that we will want a taxi in the morning and see what we need to do to get one. We'll be ready to go when you tell us."

"Okay, I'll call him now, then call you back tonight with details. I don't think it will be long."

Ben called Nico. Nico had already added Terri and Sylvie to a boat outing. "That was no problem. If they were a no show, the boat would still go. Glad that is set. I'll have somewhere arranged for them to stay, bring them back on my boat and take them there. I may invite Paul and Lisa to go too. He could be a help if needed."

"What time and where on the boat trip?"

"Sylvie and Terri are to get on a boat at the Oyster Bay Marina. Captain Paul has a boat trip out of that marina tomorrow. They should be there by eight in the morning to leave at eight-thirty."

"You need to come to Simpson Bay Marina at that same time where I have my boat and we will also leave around eight-thirty. Normally you bring passports to go to St. Barts, but this will be unofficial for all of us. I've worked out this special arrangement with Paul. Everybody just needs to bring themselves."

Ben called Sylvie and updated her. She promised to be ready in the morning for a boat trip.

FORTY

HARRINGTON WAS LIVID. Antonio was recovering from the blow to the head from Ben. Doctor Rick was called to attend to Antonio. He was resting and would begin light activities soon based on his treadmill test.

Harrington called Antonio. "How did two capable men get taken from behind? I can't believe they were so careless. You need to deal with them. Have Baldo start his assignment with Sylvie. I want her brought in." Antonio placed a call to Baldo and gave the instructions from Harrington.

Harrington had discovered what papers were missing and he was prepared to take whatever steps necessary to recover them, any copies made and ultimately, eliminate anyone involved in taking them. He had much work to do, and temporarily lost all interest in Terri. He would resume his relationship with her once the missing papers were returned and those who participated in taking them were eliminated.

Next, he placed a call to Robert Vaughn. "Robert, it's Gregorio. I trust you are well."

"Yes, Gregorio, it's a pleasure to hear from you. What can I do for you today?"

"I have a small problem. Someone is trying to insert himself in my business. What are you hearing?" Harrington knew Vaughn had many connections with his import/

export business. Harrington was determined to learn who might be involved. There could be an outside source working with Sylvie who had the business connections needed to profit from the missing information. Perhaps Robert Vaughn was working directly with Sylvie to try to get a cut of Harrington's business. Lastly, and least logical, was that Sylvie was acting on her own.

"I've not seen anything, nor have I been approached by any of the big players. As a favor to you, I will of course tell you if someone tries to go through my network to go after you. If I hear anything, perhaps there could be a business venture that we could work on together."

"Thank you, Robert. Your cooperation would be appreciated."

"Absolutely, Gregorio. If I hear it, you will know it."

Harrington ended the call. Harrington believed that Vaughn truly knew nothing. Harrington and Vaughn had done business deals together before, and he could not detect anything in his voice indicating he was involved. It was also unlikely that if someone was involved with Sylvie, that Vaughn would not be aware of it. It was looking like an attempt by Sylvie without any sophisticated help. He would concentrate on Sylvie to get what information he needed.

Harrington placed a call directly to Baldo, an unusual move in bypassing Antonio. "Baldo, did you get your instructions from Antonio?" Harrington listened. "Okay, here are your additional instructions. Maintain the surveillance. Pay a visit to Sylvie after dark. That will increase the speed of her cooperation. Get in her room, or take her to a special place, but I need a quick and silent interrogation with results. After that, do as you wish, just get rid of it." After failure from Antonio to prevent the theft, and the failure in Philipsburg, Harrington was turning up the heat.

FORTY-ONE

AFTER ENDING HER dinner date with Dean, Debi entered the two-bedroom unit at the Royal Palm to the surprise of her roommates. "What are you doing here?" asked Jan. "We weren't expecting to see you before tomorrow afternoon."

"I may have ended my time with Dean. I made a demand of him that he might not meet. I'm prepared for this to be the end, but I'll just have to wait and see." Shrugging with disappointment, she continued. "What are you guys planning for tomorrow?"

"We're trying to figure that out now. You remember that cute guy Karen was flirting with at Cupecoy?" Jan was interrupted by Karen's protest. "I was not flirting. I was merely talking with him as well as talking to everybody else on the beach. It just so happened that we had a lot of interesting things to talk about."

Jan continued, "Yeah, he seems to be quite the ladies' man. There were a number of women on the beach competing for his attention. Well, Karen is desperate to go back to Cupecoy before Rick has been picked up by somebody else."

"That is not true. I do want to go back to Cupecoy, it's a beautiful beach. And you're right, Rick is definitely handsome. But I would want to go back to Cupecoy whether he

198

is there or not, although I might be a tinge disappointed if it turns out he's not there."

Jodi interjected, "The problem is we signed up for a boat trip for tomorrow. Karen doesn't want to go, and I would probably enjoy a day on the beach more than a boat ride. We're still trying to figure it out."

"I'm good doing either," insisted Jan, "but Jodi doesn't want to spend the day alone on the beach if Karen is going to be hooking up there with Rick. If she goes to the beach, I probably should tag along to keep her company. We all know Karen will act like she doesn't even know who we are with Rick in the picture," kidded Jan. They all laughed.

"Well, tell me about the boat trip."

Jodi began, "It leaves tomorrow from Oyster Bay Marina. It's on a boat nearly forty feet long. It's a fast boat with two big engines. You go for a boat ride for about thirty minutes, then you stop on an isolated beach. Everybody gets out of the boat and swims and suns on the beach for a short while. Then the boat trip continues, with the next stop at Gustavia, the capital of Saint Barthelemy. There everybody goes into town, looks through the trendy and pricy shops of St. Barts, and has lunch on their own. When everybody goes into town, the captain and first mate take care of customs. Then everybody gets back on the boat, there's a stop at a beautiful beach, Anse de Grande Saline, and then the boat ride back. It makes for a full day."

"That sounds like a great trip. I would be interested in doing that. If you three have reserved spots, I'm guessing I could go and take one of your places if you don't go."

Jodi replied, "I'm sure you could. Why would they care if it was one of us or you? I'm sure you'd be welcomed. When we checked on it, most people just sign up, don't know anybody else on the boat, and at the end of the day, may have made new lifelong friendships."

"I think I'll try it instead of being leisurely on a beach, thinking too much about what Dean might do. It would be great for me to be active with other people and just have a blast! Karen, I guess you've decided you're going to Cupecoy. Jodi, it sounds like you want to go to Cupecoy, so I'm guessing Jan will too. If you guys don't care, I'll go on the boat trip and get with you afterward."

Jan replied, "That sounds like a plan. I'll keep Jodi company, Karen can follow her heart, and Debi, you can check out the boat trip. One last detail I didn't mention, the boat trip is clothing optional."

"That makes it even better," exclaimed Debi. "If I was on the fence before, I'm definitely one hundred percent ready to go on the boat trip now. I think it will be amazing! What time am I supposed to be there?"

"The brochure said eight-thirty. I don't remember if that is the time to arrive, or the time it starts." Jan paused. "I recommend you try to be there by eight. We put down small deposits that we'll forfeit, but maybe he'll let you apply one of the deposits to your trip. I think it will end about five, but being in the islands, I'm guessing it might be closer to five-thirty. Do you want to meet back here and get with the three of us for supper? That is, if there are three of us. Karen may be the next Debi and ditch us for dinner plans with Rick."

Debi laughed. "Okay, I'll plan to meet the two of you, and if Karen happens to join, that will be a bonus. But, of course, plans can change here in the islands. Who knows, I might meet the next Dean on the boat and miss dinner. We'll just have to see."

Debi's friends were pleased that Debi was not letting any disappointment over Dean break her spirit. The girls were very supportive of each other and looked out for each other's well-being.

"Okay, our plans are set. Debi, I'll see you after your boat trip, depending on if you meet the next Dean, and depending on if Rick insists I eat with him. You two will already be together," Karen said, referring to Jodi and Jan.

"All right, Jodi and I will be here until six-thirty tomorrow night. Anybody not here then will be assumed to be eating on their own." The girls had made their plans, and they were all excited for the next day.

FORTY-TWO

....

SYLVIE AND TERRI were eager to go on the boat trip to St. Barts. They had a restless night and were up early and ready to go. Sylvie had thought more about their arrival time, and decided she wanted to minimize the time between their arrival at the Oyster Bay Marina and their departure from there by boat, to make it more difficult for anyone who might be following her. She decided to call the marina and reached Paul, the boat captain. "Yes, I am familiar with your reservation for two. Nico asked that you be added last night. The boat will be leaving at eight-thirty. Guests are asked to arrive at eight to sign their waiver, get fitted for fins and get a snorkel included with the trip, and listen to the briefing about the boat and where the life jackets are located. If you'd like, I can get your fin sizes and have the fins and snorkels set for you. I won't worry about the waiver as I know Nico well. If you are here at eight twenty-five, you can simply step on the boat and we'll go."

Sylvie thanked Captain Paul and became genuinely excited. She called Marie at the front desk and asked that a taxi be available at eight. It would take about fifteen minutes to get to the marina, and she was allowing a little time for the cab to be late. Marie called for the cab, and it arrived at just after eight. Sylvie and Terri waited until eight-ten to go to the cab, apologized for the wait, and they were off. The taxi driver did not mind the short wait, and the healthy tip made a friend of the driver.

Debi had a longer drive from the Royal Palm to the Oyster Bay Marina. She left at seven-fifteen and arrived before eight. She spoke to Captain Paul and the first mate Elisa, and introduced herself to the other boat guests as they arrived. Debi and the other six passengers went on board. Paul began, "Welcome everybody to our clothing optional boat trip. We have calm seas today and should have a relatively smooth trip. We will be stopping at a beach just before we get to St. Barts, where we can swim and go ashore for a short while. The trip over is rougher than the trip back, when we will be going with the current. If you need anything just ask Elisa or me to help. We will have open bar on the boat all day. If there are no questions, we'll get started shortly, but I'm expecting two more passengers. As soon as they arrive, we will get underway."

It was almost eight-thirty when Sylvie and Terri got out of the taxi and hustled to the boat. Paul and Elisa greeted them and instructed they take their shoes off and place them in the shoe bin to be stored below on the boat. They were welcomed, took a seat next to Debi, and the boat was untied and underway.

Within thirty seconds the boat stopped. They were at a buoy. Captain Paul addressed the nine passengers. "As you can see, we are stopped. We call this the naked buoy. Elisa will be collecting your swimsuits and will store them for you. They will be returned just before we reach Gustavia, then collected again when leaving, to be returned once again at the end of the trip." He continued kiddingly, "When we get back, all of your clothes will be washed before they are returned." Sylvie and Terri were unaware that the trip was clothing optional. When they heard this, they were excited. "Terri, this trip just got even better!"

Captain Paul, Elisa and all nine passengers stripped off and gave their clothes to Elisa. Everyone was naked and happy as they motored away toward St. Barts.

Captain Paul did a great job of minimizing the waves as they went against the current. There was not much talking during the thirty minutes ride because of the engine noise and having to hang on as the waves crested and splashed the passengers. Soon they arrived at the promised beach. Everyone disembarked in the shallow water off the boat and waded ashore.

Once ashore, Debi introduced herself to Sylvie and Terri. They sat together on the beach. "We can be modern day Charlie's Angels," giggled Sylvie to Debi, welcoming her to join as a member of a three-person team. Debi was appreciative of their willingness to adopt her, and the three quickly became friends. Debi found herself telling Sylvie and Terri about Dean, his role with the casino, and how she had quickly gotten close to him. Sylvie and Terri listened attentively, especially Sylvie. She wondered if Debi would be not only a great friend, but a possible ally to help her collect her newfound wealth.

Ben and Lauren were up early and ready for the day, dressed in their bathing suits under t-shirts and shorts. They were at Simpson Bay Marina before eight, and were pleased that already on the dock were Lisa and Paul, Nico, and another woman they had not met. "Ben, Lauren, I want to introduce you to Jenny. I decided that I shouldn't be the only single on the boat. Jenny and I are both from the Bahamas and have been spending time together here in Saint Martin. This is going to be a fun day, and as Jenny and I are spending more time together, I wanted to intro-duce her to my good friends."

"That is great," said Ben. "Jenny, we are excited to meet you. Lauren and I are spending more time together also. You being here will make the trip even more fun."

"The boat is stocked and ready to go," said Nico. "All aboard." The trip to St. Barts was bumpy as expected, but not so much as to make anyone sick. They came to the beach where Nico knew Captain Paul would be making his first stop. They saw Captain Paul's boat anchored in the distance, with its passengers wading toward the shore. The beach was about seventy yards long, so they would all be able to interact naturally on the beach. Nico anchored at the far end of the beach from Captain Paul's boat. As they anchored, several of Captain Paul's passengers stepped onto the beach and waved a friendly greeting, as is customary among boaters in St. Martin.

"Hey look," said Lauren. "Everybody on the beach is naked." Lauren looked at Lisa, and saw that she had already removed her suit and was grinning broadly. "Welcome to the islands," said Lisa, "where nobody likes to sit around in a wet bathing suit. This is going to be a great day!" Everyone followed Lisa's lead.

They swam and waded to shore, with Nico carrying a basket on his shoulder out of the water, keeping their towels dry. They set their towels on the sand about thirty feet from the group with Captain Paul. As they sat on their towels, Nico addressed the group. "We are here to have a good time. We all know that we have some other plans to help out our new friends Sylvie and Terri, but that is just going to make this day better! Paul is the captain of that boat, not to be confused with Lisa's Paul, so I will try to remember to refer to him as Captain Paul so as not to confuse anyone. Captain Paul works with Captain Alan, and their group provides premier boat outings on island, both textile and clothing optional. I highly recommend you book a boat trip with them. I do an occasional boat trip, but it is primarily when asked for a special occasion, so booking a boat trip with Captain Paul or Captain Alan will not hurt my feelings. I highly recommend it. While talking about the name Paul, if all goes as expected, you will be meeting a third Paul, who goes by the name Paulie. He is part of the boating group from Florida that I took out earlier. He is a great guy, and to keep it from being confusing, I will always refer to him as Paulie. As you all know, it is not only normal, but it is expected, that everyone in this part of the world be friendly. So do not let any reservations you may have because of a second purpose of our trip get in the way of being very friendly with all. It is no problem! So, with that, I recommend we all go over and greet our neighbors!"

Paul, Lisa, Ben, Lauren, Nico and Jenny walked over first to where Debi, Sylvie and Terri were chatting. Introductions were made, and after a few minutes, they continued over to wave and speak to the others in Captain Paul's group. Nico and Jenny lingered with Captain Paul and his mate Elisa, while the others moved back down the beach. "Pull up some sand!" shouted Terri. "How about joining our circle?" They did, and the group of three beautiful women expanded to seven friends. After a few minutes, Lisa, Paul and Debi went to play in the shallow water, leaving Ben and Lauren sitting with Sylvie and Terri.

"Ben, Lauren, thank you so much for helping Terri and me, primarily me," began Sylvie. "We are relaxed and having a good time today. It is great to feel like I am on vacation again. I want to come clean with you. You've both been amazing and have sacrificed your vacation for me. So first, I want you to know I will be rewarding you two in some small way to try to make up for my deception and for intruding on your vacations."

"Okay," said Ben quizzically. "What are you about to come clean on?"

"This is very difficult, but I can't keep deceiving you. You have been very caring and welcomed me as a friend. I value your friendship more than I can express, so I hope you will forgive me."

"It can't be that bad," replied Lauren. "Out with it. We'll then all hug and continue with a great day."

"Well, here goes. Ben, when you warned me about being followed, you were right. I was unaware of being followed, and you have literally saved my life. There is some blackmail going on, but I am not being blackmailed. I had heard some rumors about Gregorio Harrington, and that some of his great wealth is from some secrets he knows. Instead of going to retrieve blackmail pictures, I was searching for the bad secrets contributing to his wealth. I found the secrets and now have evidence of his participation in a corrupt scheme."

"Several high-ranking government officials, both French and Dutch, have conspired to make great amounts of money in their holdings in Dutch Sint Maarten and French Saint Martin. There is an oil exploration deal that was reached in the Dutch Antilles. Dutch Sint Maarten is part of the Netherlands. They are more open to oil exploration than France and French Saint Martin. The mega oil exploration project underway is partially in French Saint Martin, which would not be approved by France. There is a coverup on this, and what is being presented as official boundary lines have been doctored, differing from the original charters. There is not much difference, but it makes all the difference needed in allowing the oil project to go forward. French and Dutch officials here on island were involved to set this up. Harrington became aware, and is a partner in the deal, adding to his many other business interests. I found all this out from papers confirming this when I was in Harrington's villa. He is now likely after me and will probably do away with me if I don't cooperate with him."

Ben was stunned to hear all that Sylvie shared. He and Lauren remained silent.

"I cannot undo what I have done. And because I am being completely honest, I really would not want to undo it if I could. This type of corruption is widespread in every country of the world, so much so that it is the basis of great amounts of what would otherwise be legitimate business. I know I am rationalizing my position, but I stand to participate in the venture, and now that I am deeply involved, I plan to receive a small share of the profits that the politicians are pocketing to create their great wealth."

"I'm in no position to judge you," replied Ben. "I don't think it is something I would have done, but what's done is done. Maybe I'm rationalizing as well, but you are nonetheless in serious danger. I will continue to try to help you stay safe, and whatever you decide on these business dealings will be your business, not mine. I'll need to tell Nico. I don't want to keep this from him and deceive him. I'll go talk with him now."

Ben walked over to Nico and Jenny. "Nico, can I have a minute with you? I have something I'd like to discuss." Nico separated from Jenny, and Ben and Nico talked. Ben relayed much of the story he had just heard from Sylvie.

"Ben, you are my good friend. Sylvie is a friend to you. Any friend you have is my friend. I want to help keep her safe. I don't want her to be harmed. Let's see this through."

Ben went back to where Sylvie, Terri and Lauren were still sitting. "Let's take a dip. Nothing has changed. We are going to have a great day and keep you and Terri safe. No more talk of stuff that is solely your business."

Ben looked at Lauren and could tell she looked more reluctant than Ben to move forward after the startling confession. "Lauren, hop on my back, the Ben shuttle is ready to take you to the water." His hope to create a spirit of fun was only a partial success. Ben leaned down, Lauren hopped aboard, and he took several steps into the water before Lauren would allow herself to smile. Ben squatted in the water until Lauren's feet were almost touching bottom, and she slid off. They held hands, chatted, and gradually Lauren recovered most of her enthusiasm for the day. She agreed to continue on with the help planned for Sylvie and Terri, but wanted nothing to do with any decision made by Sylvie and did not want a reward for any involvement. She promised Ben she would not let the news negatively impact their day together.

Next to hear the update were Paul and Lisa. Ben saw the two of them alone walking out of the water to their towels. He coaxed Lauren to hop again on his back and went to meet them. Ben gave a brief summary as the two couples sat together on the towels. Paul and Lisa were surprised but agreed to withhold judgment. "I have seen many things, and this development is mild compared to other requests I've received. I promised my help to Nico, and I am 100% committed to the safety of Sylvie and Terri." Paul looked at Lisa and she nodded in agreement. Everyone had renewed their endorsement of the actions to be taken on Sylvie's behalf.

After another thirty minutes of sunning and splashing, the group got back on Nico's boat. Debi, Terri and Sylvie returned to Captain Paul's boat, where everyone dressed before the two boats arrived at the dock in Gustavia ten minutes later. Captain Paul and Elisa presented passports to Customs for their group, without a disclosure of Sylvie and Terri who did not have passports to present. Customs did not raise an eyebrow to any of this.

Debi continued to pal with Sylvie and Terri, looking through the trendy shops. Paul and Lisa remained with Ben and Lauren, while Nico wanted some alone time with Jenny. After eating lunch, they returned to the dock at one o'clock. As per the plan, Sylvie and Terri did not re-board Captain Paul's boat in Gustavia, but stepped onto Nico's boat. Captain Paul could truthfully tell, if asked, that they elected not to stay with his group when leaving Gustavia. Everyone was ready for the short ride to Anse de Grand Saline, the famous clothing optional beach in St. Barts. After pulling away from the dock, they all disrobed for the remainder of the outing. When anchoring off the beach, everyone jumped in, leaving the towels aboard for drying at the end of their swim. Everyone was getting along, and any remaining ill will toward Sylvie had mostly disappeared. It was great fun at the beach, and new significant friendships had been cemented. At three o'clock, it was time for the next part of the plan for Sylvie and Terri. While others on Paul's boat would remain at the beach until four-thirty before returning to the Oyster Bay Marina, Sylvie and Terri swam back toward Nico's boat to leave at three. However, there was a new wrinkle to the plan. Sylvie, Terri and Debi had quickly bonded on the trip, and Sylvie confided much more to Debi than Ben would have approved. It could not be undone, so when Debi swam toward Nico's boat at three, the decision was made to continue as planned, but with Debi also part of Sylvie's rescue team. Her belongings were retrieved from Captain Paul's boat.

FORTY-THREE

WHEN DEBI LEFT Thursday morning for her boating adventure, Karen, Jodi and Jan were up and preparing breakfast. They loved the spacious kitchen they had at the Royal Palm as they enjoyed the convenience of having breakfast in their unit while looking at the magnificent ocean view.

Karen was eager to get to the beach. Jodi and Jan made good-natured jokes, exaggerating her desire to make a connection with Rick. All three looked forward to Cupecoy, being the entertainment and the entertained. They collaborated on what they should wear. They each wore a bikini bottom and shorts. Karen decided to fashion a top out of a pareo around her neck, crisscrossing over her chest and tying in the back. Jan went with a white blouse, unbuttoned and left open, but tied at her navel. Jodi opted for a loose-fitting top that had an extremely deep V neckline. Their outfits would be comparable to what other well-dressed women would be wearing at Cupecoy.

At eleven, they could not wait any longer and were ready to go. Cupecoy Beach was a short drive from the Royal Palm. When they arrived, a few people were there, but Rick was not. They stopped at Dany's Bar, had a drink and talked with the Cupecoy regulars. After about an hour they placed orders with Dany for food and went down to the beach. Karen removed her shorts and placed them in her beach bag beside her chair. She planned to stay dressed in her pareo top and bikini bottom until Rick arrived. She would wait until he was talking to her before she would remove the rest of her garments for effect. Jodi and Jan did not have anyone in mind that brought out their flirtatious best. Instead, they went to their chairs and immediately began enhancing their full tans. They made sure their chairs were not shaded by an umbrella, while Karen sat close under an umbrella until she had her full unveiling.

There were not many early lunch orders and their lunches were delivered shortly after they returned to their chairs. After eating, Karen volunteered to dispose of their plates and napkins and walked back up the stairs from the beach to Dany's Bar. Just as she turned to leave, she was rewarded with Rick arriving and watched him park his car. Before he opened his car door to get out, Karen turned away and walked back to her chair. She would lay in wait until Rick ambled down the stairs to the beach.

Karen kept an eye on Rick from the periphery of her sunglasses as he stepped off the last concrete step to the beach sand. He surveyed the crowd, spotted Karen, and began walking toward her. Rick was something of a lady's man, but he had taken particular notice of Karen on their previous meeting at Cupecoy, and it was obvious he liked what he saw.

He walked over to where they were lined up in chairs, with Jan first, Jodi in the middle, and Karen on the other end. "Ladies," he began, "It's great to see you enjoying another beautiful day at Cupecoy." He then leaned down, and greeted each, in order of their seats, with a kiss. Jan and Jodi both cooed appropriately. Karen used the kiss as her cue to stand and return the greeting by giving Rick a light hug.

They stood away from the others and talked for a few minutes. Karen grinned at Rick. "Rick, I haven't been in the water yet. I'm thinking of dipping in. Do you want come?"

"Sure, sounds good."

Karen took that opportunity to undo the tie of her pareo, letting the garment slide seductively off her body. She leaned to her chair and delicately placed the pareo on her towel. She stood upright, saying, "The water looks so refreshing," and slid her bikini bottom down, stepping out of it and placing it on the pareo. Reaching for Rick's hand, she led him to the water. Once they were at the water's edge, Jodi and Jan could no longer contain their laughter. "I'd have to say, that was certainly well played," snickered Jodi.

"Oh yes, it couldn't have gone better. It looks like Karen won't be joining us for dinner tonight!" They laughed again, happy for their dear friend Karen, and loving being entertained at Cupecoy.

FORTY-FOUR

NICO WAS THE first one back to the boat and helped the others board. The boat now had the original six: Nico, Jenny, Lisa, Paul, Lauren and Ben. Joining them were Sylvie, Terri, and unexpectedly, Debi. Each climbed the boat ladder, grabbed a towel, dried and took a seat. There had been little drinking on the trip, but an executive decision was made by Nico that everyone aboard had earned one rum punch, including the captain. They sat sipping their drinks, while Nico raised the anchor and began the trip back. The trip back would take about fifty minutes and would be a smoother ride with the current helping them. The group was soon laughing and reliving the best parts of their day. The coming together during the ride back solidified their loyalty to help Sylvie.

When they were within fifteen minutes of the marina, Nico slowed the boat so everyone could get dressed. It was time to start preparing mentally for the next step. Nico discussed with Debi his plan to have someone retrieve her car and return it to the Royal Palm. She agreed and gave Nico her key, the car description and where it was parked.

They arrived at Simpson Bay Marina, tying up the boat but not taking out time to wash it down. They walked to Nico's van and all piled in, with Terri and Sylvie out of sight in the back. Their next stop was Almond Grove.

Nico had called Chris with the Florida Tiki Hut Group that had the boat trip with him, and asked a favor. Before they could respond, he asked that the members of the group discuss his request to place two friends with them to be tucked away for several days. Fifteen minutes later, Nico received the return phone call and the unanimous invitation for Sylvie and Terri to stay with them. They had the essential toiletries for the girls, and if they wanted to borrow any clothes, each of the tiki ladies wanted to be the one to share. They were all set.

Nico came to the entrance of Almond Grove Estates and exchanged greetings with the security guard. Jeanne had alerted the guard that guests were expected. Nico was waved through and drove halfway up the small mountain to Villa Islandtude, lot 167. The boaters walked up the steps to the villa gate where they were warmly greeted by the tiki hut group staying in the villa.

Recognizing that their guests would not have eaten dinner, Jeanne and Chris called and placed an order with Vesna's Taverna. Vesna delivered a variety of foods, enough to feed thirty people, even though there were only seventeen. There were eight from the friendly Florida group and nine from the boat trip. There would be a feast, alcohol, and skinny dipping after dessert. An assortment of beer, red and white wine, and several gallons of rum punch were ready to be served. The seventeen sat at tables bordering the expansive pool deck, and Mark and Catherine played hosts by bringing their drink orders. Dale and Mary followed, taking each person's food order, with the choice of beef or fish, served with rice, vegetables and salad. Crème Brulee and lemon cheesecake were brought to the tables for dessert. The boaters were treated as heroes returning from war. When the meal was finished, the cleanup was handled by Paulie and Tammy.

Chris tuned in the non-stop reggae station on the Bose Music Box and Jeanne turned on the pool lights for ambience. She then invited everyone into the large heated pool. As the primary guest of honor, Sylvie began the procession of skinny dippers into the pool.

Around ten o'clock, Debi proposed a toast. "This is to the best friends I could ever imagine. I know we've just met, but all of you have welcomed me into your hearts. So, this toast is to the best friends, who are St. Martin friends." Everyone cheered and toasted. Ben could not remember a party with so much fun. Lauren, who was also having her best day of the trip, swam over to Sylvie, and without saying anything, gave her a long heart-felt hug. Sylvie thanked her and hugged her in return.

Ben and Lauren floated over to Paul and Lisa in the pool. Ben was becoming great friends with Paul, and Lauren was thinking similarly of Lisa. Ben thanked Paul for all of his help and was extremely appreciative of the added protection he felt with Paul's presence. Ben and Lauren swam over to see Nico and Jenny. Ben gave Nico a big bear hug. He had never had a more loyal friend. Ben thought to himself that if Jenny and Nico were becoming serious, Jenny could not have found a better man.

As it neared eleven o'clock, the group of boaters was wearing down from the full day of boating and sun, plus the anxiety they had been experiencing. It was time for one final round of drinks and one last toast before ending the fun with their newly committed friends.

Sylvie and Terri would be staying in the Happy Bay bedroom, with each bedroom in the villa named after one of the island's great beaches. At the entrance of the villa was the first bedroom named Baie Rouge, and up the steps to the pool deck was the second bedroom, Cupecoy. The master bedroom, Orient, was followed by Happy Bay, also on the pool deck, with the fifth bedroom named Mullet Bay down a flight of stairs.

Everyone got out of the pool, with the seven boaters getting dressed before getting back in the van. After the goodbye hugs, they drove out of Almond Grove as it neared midnight, leaving Sylvie and Terri behind. Nico drove to the Royal Palm and made sure Debi was back safely in her room. Next, he drove back to Simpson Bay Marina to everyone's cars. Paul and Lisa drove back to their home at Cupecoy Beach, while Ben drove Lauren back to Lubrique. When they were back, Lauren wanted to stop in her room to brush her teeth before they went to Ben's room. She laid down on the bed as Ben went in the bath and showered. He came out and found Lauren soundly sleeping on top of the covers. He got a spare spread from the closet, covered her with it, and laid down behind her. As he was falling asleep, he wrapped his arms around her, hugging the person who was becoming more important to him than he could have imagined.

FORTY-FIVE

JODI AND JAN enjoyed Thursday afternoon meeting a lot of new friends at Cupecoy Beach. A major attraction of Cupecoy was watching the sun set over the ocean. They stayed for the classic event, with Jan proclaiming she witnessed the elusive green flash, that meteorological phenomena where a distinct green spot is briefly visible above the upper rim of the sun. Whether there was truly a green flash or not, the sunset was indeed a beautiful sight.

Rick and Karen remained at Cupecoy all afternoon as well, spending much of the afternoon together, but enjoying some time individually talking with others on the beach. As time for sunset neared, Rick made sure he had circled back to Karen.

"This must be the most beautiful place on earth," said Karen in a hushed and reverent tone, mesmerized by the amazing sunset.

Rick, with his arm around her waist, tightened his grip as they peered out over the horizon. "It is certainly a magnificent sunset, a fitting ending to what has been a beautiful day." They continued to watch the sun slowly slide into the ocean, highlighted by a few clouds but otherwise, an orange sky. As the sun disappeared, Rick turned to Karen and asked, "Would you like to grab a bite to eat with me? I'm going to want to eat some dinner soon."

"That sounds great. Let me talk with Jan and Jodi for a couple minutes, then I'll be ready to go." She walked over to Jodi and Jan and let them know she would not be joining them for dinner. The two dropped their jaws, their mouths remaining wide open in pretend shock at Karen's pronouncement. "Okay, we were counting on you eating with us," said Jodi, continuing with kidding sarcasm, "but somehow we will make do at dinner without you."

"Have fun," added Jan. "Although we'll miss you, I think you've made a good decision. We'll probably go back to our rooms and eat at the Palms Restaurant behind the resort. If you're not back too late, we'll look to see you after your dinner."

"Thanks. I don't think I'll be out that late. It's been a long day. We'll probably eat somewhere fairly casual since we've been on the beach all day. I'm also eager to get back to clean up. Maybe I can convince Rick to come in and visit with us for a while when he drops me off."

Karen walked back over to Rick, squeezed his hand, and said she was ready to go. They climbed the steps from the beach back up to Dany's Beach Bar and its dirt parking lot. Rick steered Karen to his car, not knowing Karen had watched him park earlier in the day, and opened the door for her. "Where would you like to eat?" asked Rick.

"Let's eat somewhere casual. Would you be okay with eating at Lee's? It is very close by."

"Lee's it is." In less than fifteen minutes they had parked and were shown to a table.

"Rick, this is great. Thank you very much. Oh look, a band is setting up."

The band, Island Dreamers, was getting ready to go on stage. Their lead singer was Dave, whose voice sounded much like Lou Rawls. Kerry was on the keyboard. They played a wide variety of island music as well as easy listening tunes from all decades going back to the 1960s.

"I love them, they are amazing. I don't think I've told you, but I sing in a band from time to time," said Karen.

"Oh really," replied Rick. "I have been in a band for a long time. I don't do much singing, but I'm pretty good at playing the keyboard. Maybe we should ask them if we can play a song when the band takes a break."

"That would be a lot of fun!" Their food arrived, and they enjoyed eating and listening while the Island Dreamers performed non-stop. As they finished their meal, Dave surprised them by coming over to Rick and Karen's table and started singing "The Way You Look Tonight" by Frank Sinatra. It was beautifully performed and brought the house down as Dave concluded. Turning to Karen, Dave asked her if she had a song request. Now it was his turn to be surprised. Not only did she have a song request, but she wanted to sing it and wanted Rick to play the keyboard. Dave and Kerry were happy to oblige and ushered the two on stage. They selected a song popularly performed by Third World that seemed fitting. When Karen began singing, with the first line, *"Now that we found love what are we going to do with it?"*, Rick's whole body beamed. Rick and Karen had found their soul mates.

While Rick and Karen were entertaining the crowd at Lee's, Gregorio Harrington sat at a table nearby with Baldo. It was unusual for the two men to meet in public together. Baldo shared how Sylvie had taken a taxi to Oyster Pond and boarded a boat bound for St. Barts. He had placed a call to a contact on St. Barts to try to pick up the tail when the boat arrived, but his contact never spotted her. When Baldo was waiting at the Oyster Pond Marina for the boat to return, he saw that she was not on the boat. Baldo approached Captain Paul and asked about the girl.

Captain Paul said that she and her friend got off the boat in Gustavia, but did not get back on. He did not know where they had gone. Somewhere after leaving the marina, Sylvie and her friend Terri had made an unscheduled exit.

Harrington commanded Baldo to have a thorough search of St. Barts and to keep an eye on Sylvie's room at La Playa. Since Baldo did not see them carrying any bags, they may return for their possessions. He was also to find out if they had already checked out, and if not, their scheduled check-out date. Harrington would coordinate with a larger group to be on the look-out for her on St. Martin as well. He needed Sylvie found very quickly.

After wowing the crowd at Lee's, Rick and Karen ordered after dinner drinks. Karen wanted to share her happiness with Jan and Jodi, and invited Rick to the Royal Palm. Rick was more than happy to spend more time with Karen.

Back at the Royal Palm, Rick, Karen, Jodi and Jan all sat around telling stories of their time on the island and found a second wind from all the stories and laughter. They were still going strong when Debi returned.

Debi was beaming when she walked into the sitting room. "You're not going to believe the amazing day I just had! I had an incredible boat trip to St. Barts, went to two different nude beaches, and ended the day at an amazing villa where I had a gourmet meal, drinks, and finished with skinny dipping in a huge pool overlooking Simpson Bay. All of this with some amazing people I met on the boat! It couldn't have been a better time!"

Everyone enjoyed hearing about Debi's adventures. One by one each gave the highlights of their day's events. Recognizing Rick from Cupecoy earlier in the week, Debi said, "Rick, I may need your help soon. I don't know how I'll do it, but I might want to arrange a meeting with Dean, who if he had any sense would devote the rest of his life to me. I might want to introduce you to him as my new love interest to make him jealous. You could pose like you're my new island husband."

Rick clearly was completely captivated by Karen, but if Karen had no objections, he would be happy to help another beautiful woman in distress. He thought it could be fun. "You come up with the plan and I'm in. I'd be happy to help you pull a trick on Dean."

As the others continued sharing their encounters on island, Debi began to drift away with thoughts of what her next step should be with Dean. She had been careful not to disclose any information that she had learned from her new friend Sylvie, and purposefully never mentioned her name or the name of the villa with this group. Sylvie had not asked Debi for help, but Debi could see a clear path where the two new friends could be invaluable to each other. If she could add Rick to her plan, she would know that she had maximized her chances of getting everything she wanted from Dean. She made a mental note to call Sylvie soon. She believed she could easily convince Sylvie to accept her help.

The Thursday night gathering at the Royal Palm, spilling over into Friday morning, was winding down. There were no more bursts of adrenalin to fuel any further partying. Karen walked Rick to his car and Rick left after kissing her goodnight. They all slept soundly under the spell cast by St. Martin and their earlier day's events.

FORTY-SIX

ALL DAY THURSDAY Dean debated calling Debi. He would reach for the phone, then change his mind as he had nothing prepared to say. Instead of calling Debi, he went about his business, and reviewed the early results from the developing relationship with Robert Vaughn. Everything was going smoothly, and he was certain that this new arrangement would prove to be very lucrative in the coming months. Instead of waiting for Vaughn to present additional ideas where Dean could profit from his start-up laundering business, he decided to pursue additional business outside of what was brought to him by Vaughn. He spent much of the day working on his new business plan. Thursday turned into Friday morning and Dean had heard nothing from Debi after their Wednesday night dinner. He had known he would miss her companionship, but he missed her even more than he had anticipated. He knew he needed to present a plan to Debi that she would accept. He found it difficult to concentrate on his business interests, and knew he needed to rectify the problem soon.

Once Dean had come up with a plan, he would request another meeting with Debi. Perhaps he could invite her to a meal at one of the casino restaurants, give her a tour of the operation, and entice her with some sort of a business interest. Her demand to dissolve his marriage was extreme, and was a demand he did not envision accepting. Perhaps he could provide something that would resonate with her as a suitable substitute, but he was at a loss as to a plan. He felt certain he would eventually devise such a plan out of necessity, but it was yet to materialize. He wished he had someone to confide in for advice, but that person was missing from his life. He knew it was too soon in their relationship to be logically thinking in such a way, but he wondered, and at least half believed, that Debi could be that person he was hunting for. She was correct in her assessment of herself. Not only was she capable of providing companionship beyond what he had previously thought possible, she had demonstrated that she was very shrewd. He could use someone with a skillful mind like hers to enhance his business dealings. It was clear what he needed, but he had not come around to accepting the high price that was presented to him for having it. He would try to reach her soon and would work out a deal that they hopefully both would find attractive. He had to make it happen.

As Dean was working on his plan, Debi was working on a plan of her own. It was only seven in the morning, and she knew after such a full day and late night, both she and Sylvie should still be asleep. But not wanting to wait any longer to call, she dialed Sylvie and hoped she would not wake her. If she did, she would apologize, but thought once Sylvie heard her out, she would be glad to have been awakened.

Sylvie answered the call immediately. "Sylvie, this is Debi. I hope I'm not waking you."

"No, I was awake. I've been thinking through what I need to try to do next. It was a great day yesterday, as was last night. But I can't just hide out forever. I need to finish my project I started and begin every day like I did yesterday."

"That's why I'm calling. First, I want to thank you and Terri for taking me in yesterday. You two are amazing! You including me had me totally forgetting any other concerns I had. And, I really appreciate being included to go to the villa last night. That was one great party! I think we all have gained some more real friends." Debi paused before continuing, "Besides thanking you, I wanted to run something by you. I don't have all the answers for you on your next steps, but I do have an idea that might help both of us. Don't be afraid to tell me to mind my own business, because I will. I hope you're willing to listen to a few ideas I have, where you and I can help each other in a very big way. If you like my basic idea, I want your suggestions on how we can improve on it."

"Wow Debi, I can't thank you enough for the call. I am all ears!"

Debi presented her basic idea to Sylvie and she readily agreed that they could mutually benefit from working with each other. Her idea was a definite go. They talked on, debating if Rick should be a part of the plan, and if so, how he could best be utilized. Before hanging up, they had finalized their plan. Debi would be calling Sylvie later in the day to update her on if she was successful in getting the plan started. Debi and Sylvie ended the call, with both optimistic that their fortunes would take a dramatic upturn very soon.

Sylvie updated Terri and Terri agreed that the plan seemed perfect. "So, after this is done, when will I get my riches?"

"I still need to work through a few more details. The plan with Debi overcomes one of my biggest obstacles. Now, I just need to stay alive long enough to collect. While we are here, I feel perfectly safe. If I need to hide out, I can't imagine a place where I would rather do it. Why don't we

grab a little breakfast and spend a few morning hours poolside while I think on my next step for contacting Gregorio."

They got out of bed and grabbed their beach towels before padding to the main building that housed the
kitchen. After having a light breakfast, they walked out to
the pool deck and enjoyed the early morning sun in the
poolside lounge chairs. Sylvie laid back trying to finalize
the last piece of her plan, while Terri was dreaming of what
she might do with a lot more money.

FORTY-SEVEN

BEN AWOKE BEFORE Lauren and was careful when getting up not to disturb her. She was still sleeping soundly. He dressed, and when he saw it was only seven o'clock, decided he should let Lauren sleep a while longer. He sat in the chair, staring at her, and decided he could not wait any longer. He walked over to her and gently nudged her. She stirred slightly, but continued to lay peacefully on the bed. He next kissed her on the forehead, and when she still did not wake up, he continued to kiss her face until she did. "Good morning," she said sleepily. "What a nice way to wake up this morning. What time is it?"

"It's already after seven. If we're not careful, we'll sleep the whole day away," he teased.

She gradually pulled herself into a sitting position, took note of the spread that was covering her, and grinned at Ben. "I think I was pretty tired last night. I remember you going in to shower, and it's a blank after that. What a day and what a party! That was easily the best day of my vacation. What an amazing island this is, and what an amazing adventure. I'm over all the worrying. It seems like there are a lot of capable people who are now helping Sylvie and Terri. I'm fine if we stay involved, but it's nice to have others share in the responsibility. So, what should we do today?"

"I was thinking we could go to Mullet Bay Beach today for a change of beach. After talking with Paul and Lisa last night, I know they planned to sleep in and most likely won't be up before about ten. Maybe we could get a leisurely breakfast, have a walk on our beach, and then call them to see if they want to meet us at Mullet."

"That all sounds good to me. Lisa told me she doesn't have any calls today, so I think that might work. If you hadn't suggested going to the beach with them, I was thinking about asking Lisa if she wanted to go to Philipsburg. I could look around a few hours and give you a break from shopping."

"You've got to be kidding. You know I love shopping. What could be better than coming to a tropical island with beautiful beaches, calm breezes, swaying palm trees, the aroma of rum in the air, than some power shopping in Philipsburg?" His tone made clear he was not serious. "But despite all those reasons, the most compelling is that although I'm happy for you to spend time with Lisa, I'm not ready for you to take a break from me, even if it means me having to go shopping. So why don't we go get some breakfast and I'll take you into Philipsburg. We can still call Lisa and Paul and see if they'll meet us at Mullet Bay Beach this afternoon."

Lauren got up from bed and started walking toward the door. "You drive a hard bargain, but you've got a deal. I'm going back to my room and get presentable. I never even showered after all that beach time yesterday. Give me about thirty minutes and I'll be back. I promise to be here no later than eight." She planted a happy kiss square on his mouth and walked out to her room.

Ben used the time to shave and also get ready. After such an active day yesterday, he was thinking a leisurely day would be great today. It was not the vacation he expected, but turned out to be so much more.

At eight o'clock Ben was ready and waiting when Lauren returned. They decided to make it a longer trip than necessary by first going to the Croissanterie in Marigot for breakfast. Once there, they feasted on some of the best tasting croissants ever of ham, egg and cheese. After finishing breakfast, they went in the Boutique Ananas that was next to the breakfast spot. Lauren purchased two purses that started out as a zipper wound into a cone, but when zipped, made into a full-size purse. She picked up some wonderfully scented soaps, and a couple more pareos.

"I have an idea that I think you'll like. If you go with me over to the Marigot market for a short visit, I suggest we skip Philipsburg and go back to the beach with those swaying palm trees."

"Lady, you have a deal. Let's do it." They got in the car and drove the few blocks to the market. While there, they met Micka, an artist displaying some of her unique artwork. They both chose a mouse pad with a scene of Orient Beach on it, with a man and woman lounging under yellow umbrellas. After making the purchases from Micka, they were both ready to head back.

"We should be back about ten-thirty. When we get back, I'll call Lisa and see if she and Paul want to meet us at Mullet. We can take a walk on Orient until they're ready to meet."

When they parked at Lubrique, they sat in their car and Lauren placed the call to Lisa. Lisa answered the phone and agreed to meet. She also suggested they eat lunch at Daleo's Snack Bar Restaurant on Mullet Bay Beach. The restaurant had been in business for over twenty years, and in addition to being a great restaurant, provided chairs and umbrellas available for rent. Lauren agreed they would meet and ended the call.

"We have about an hour before we need to leave for Mullet. Ben, do you still want to take that walk?"

"That sounds great. Let's put our stuff away and I'll be ready." Meeting back at Ben's room, they started their walk. It was a relatively quiet day on Orient, and it seemed strange to Ben not to see Sylvie and Terri. He started to mention that thought, but decided against it. He did not want to bring up any reminders of stressful times.

When they had walked about half the beach, they decided to turn back to sit in some chairs for a few minutes. Before they could do it, however, Lauren decided she wanted to do a little more shopping. She had still not looked at the small area of shops along Orient Beach. She suggested they look briefly, still giving them time to get ready to leave for Mullet. Ben was willing to continue keeping Lauren company while she shopped. They looked at t-shirts, paintings and swimsuits, but did not find anything of interest to buy. As it was nearing noon, they went back, put on their swimsuits, shorts and t-shirts, and left for Mullet Bay.

Mullet Bay Beach was a beautiful white sand beach with clear, calm water. The slight gradual drop-off and minimal waves looked inviting to Lauren and Ben when they arrived. Not seeing Lisa and Paul, they decided to get four chairs ready and wait for them. They were wading in the calm water when Lisa and Paul arrived. They stepped out of the water and waved them over to the chairs. Lisa and Lauren sat next to each other, while Ben and Paul sat in the next two chairs.

As Lauren told Lisa all about the shopping she had done during her vacation, Paul and Ben began discussing the events that had brought them together.

"What do you think happens next?" asked Paul.

"I don't know, but it is clearly not over. And I am definitely not out of it. I have Sylvie's and Terri's passports in my room. At some point I need to get those to them, as well as some jewelry and whatever else they gave to me for safekeeping. I really want this whole thing to end, but I don't see it ending until Sylvie has left the island."

"I agree. I think we will be more involved than Lisa and Lauren will want. Nico called this morning and asked if I would be willing to help if needed. He is still concerned about them. Of course I said I would help. I don't have a plan on how this ends, but will be available to whatever extent I'm needed."

"Why don't we take a break from the crazy stuff and grab some lunch? Lauren, Lisa, are ya'll hungry?" asked Ben. "I think I'm ready for a burger from Daleo."

They walked to the open-air restaurant, lined in front with picnic tables on the sand for dining. Next to Daleo's was a similar restaurant, Rosie's. Rosie's had ribs as one of the restaurant specials, while Daleo's main lunch items were hamburgers, hotdogs and French fries. They each got a burger, fries and soft drinks for lunch and sat down to eat at one of the picnic tables.

"I love sitting at the picnic table eating a hamburger. It makes me feel like a kid again," said Lauren.

"Yeah, I'm enjoying it here at Mullet too," added Lisa. "It has a very wholesome family atmosphere and is one of my favorite beaches. It's also a great walking beach. After lunch, let's walk down the beach so you see it all. Back in the 80's and 90's there was what was possibly the best beach resort on the island a little further down the beach. Everyone staying there would typically come here for swimming. The resort was spread out and there was a shuttle available to take you to the different parts. It was an amazing place, with a number of two-bedroom units spread out over the grounds. The only golf course on the island was also part of the resort. The resort was badly damaged by Hurricane Luis in 1995. It is a shame that it has never been rebuilt. For years, the exterior of the buildings continued to crumble from exposure to the elements and no upkeep. There would be April Fool's newspaper articles that a new buyer had emerged and that the resort was going to be built back. But unfortunately, after all these years, there has never been on St. Maarten a resort comparable to the old Mullet Bay Resort. If I had an unlimited amount of money, one of the first things I would do is build the Mullet Bay Resort back just the way it was!"

"I would love to walk down the beach with you and hear more about the history of this area. I'm thinking Ben and Paul can stay at the chairs, talk about sports and watch our stuff."

Everyone enjoyed their lunch, gathered their trash, and walked it to the large trashcan at the corner of the restaurant. The firm sand beyond the shade of the trees where the picnic tables sat was extremely hot to the touch, almost burning their feet as they walked from the picnic table area to the cool damp sand closer to the water. After taking a few steps, Lauren broke into a trot for the comfort of the damp sand at the water's edge with Lisa following close behind. Ben tried to find shade patches as he gingerly walked faster, while Paul continued with a tough exterior, walking normally, as if impervious to the burning sand. Lauren continued her pace into the refreshing water, running in as if a child. Lisa, laughing, followed her in.

"I'm loving this beach," said Ben. After a fantastic day, and a lot of drama and adult themes yesterday, it really makes me happy seeing Lauren shift gears and seeming more carefree today. I hope it continues."

Ben and Paul walked into the shallow area, where the water was calm and small seashells could be seen on the sand in the water where they stepped. A few shells were gathered as souvenirs. "I hadn't thought about it, but seeing these shells made me think how I haven't seen any shells at any of the other beaches we've been to. Here's something else that distinguishes Mullet as a great beach." Ben scooped another shell and handed it to Lauren. "This shell is the best one so far. Maybe you can put it in your beach bag before you and Lisa go for your walk."

Lauren took the hint. She walked the beautiful shell up to the chairs and tucked it securely in the bag before returning to the water. "Now that I did your work for you, how about giving me a piggyback ride. You've given them to me on Orient, and that might be the new requirement any time we break in a new beach." Paul and Ben hoisted the girls onto their backs and carried them around in the water. Lisa and Lauren jumped off after a few minutes to start on their walk the length of the beach and back. Paul and Ben went back to their chairs.

FORTY-EIGHT

KAREN AWOKE EARLY Friday morning after a sound sleep and happy dreams of Rick. She saw that her roommate, Debi, was already up and out of the room. She knew Debi was an early riser and thought it very considerate that she had not disturbed her when she got out of bed after the late night. It was only seven-thirty and she wondered what time Debi had started her day.

Karen was hoping to hear from Rick soon and possibly meet up with him again before the day ended. Thoughts of returning to Cupecoy were pushing out other plans for her day. Not sure if Jan and Jodi would want to go again, she would see what their plans were before deciding. Debi was more of a wild card for the day. She had been spending days with them, but her nights had been separate for the second half of the trip. Debi clearly loved her time yesterday and last night with her new friends. Karen wondered if Debi would be planning something on her own, if she would do something with Jan and Jodi, or if she might invite all of them to meet her new friends. Karen got out of bed and walked into the living area and saw Debi was sitting on the couch, looking deep in thought.

"Penny for your thoughts," offered Karen as she walked in greeting Debi.

"Good morning, Karen. You're up early, too. I'm just sitting here thinking about how much fun I had yesterday. I'm also trying to decide what I want with Dean. I would love to see him today, but I want to do whatever is best, whatever that might be. I could see my time with him as a great time while on vacation, magical actually. Or I could even see spending a lot more time with him for a long time to come. I guess a lot is going to depend on what happens over the next few days." Debi paused, then changed the subject. "Rick was clearly smitten with you. That was so cute. Have the two of you made plans for today?"

"No, when he left, I think we both assumed that we would spend time together today, but we didn't make any actual plans. I'm guessing he will call me this morning after he thinks it's not too early to call, and we'll decide something then. Would you want to do something with us if I do get with Rick today?"

"Thanks for the invitation. I'm not sure what I'll do yet. I'll see what Jodi and Jan are doing after they get up. I called Sylvie this morning to chat about some stuff, but I didn't ask her if she would want to get together. I might call her back and see what she's doing today."

Debi and Karen sat quietly for a few minutes, each in her own world of thoughts. Karen's phone rang. "It's Rick calling," said Karen, holding her phone up, as she walked back into the bedroom to talk to Rick. Debi grinned, thinking Karen reminded her of when she was a young teen and would get a call from a boy. She definitely did not want anyone to overhear their conversation. Karen walked into the bedroom and closed the door. Debi shook her head and laughed. It looked like Karen would be spending much more of her time with Rick. She would consider spending some time with the two of them, but did not want to be a third wheel if there would not be any others. She guessed they would be going back to Cupecoy Beach some-time during the day. Debi was not sure if she wanted to go again. She liked it, and it was a beautiful beach, but she thought she might prefer something different for the day.

She heard Jan and Jodi stirring in their bedroom. It was not yet eight o'clock and everyone was up despite not getting in bed until around two. Debi found it amazing about the difference between how little sleep one needed while on vacation, as opposed to a normal work week.

Jodi greeted Debi as she walked into the living room. "Good morning, Debi, have you eaten yet?"

"No, I was waiting for everybody to get up before eating. I'm thinking of making some bacon and eggs. Would you want some?"

"Yes, sounds good. Let me ask Jan." Jodi stepped back in her bedroom and was quickly back. "Jan would like some, too. What's up with Karen this morning?"

"Oh, she's up." Debi joked, "Rick called a couple minutes ago, she asked me to leave the bedroom, and I think Rick and Karen are having phone sex." Jodi shook her head and grinned. "You should have seen her yesterday laying the trap for him. You might have been kidding about the phone sex, but I wouldn't be surprised!" Both girls were laughing as Jan walked in.

"What's so funny?"

"We're just laughing, thinking Karen is going through adolescence again," said Debi. "I'll fix some bacon and eggs for her, too. She may have worked up an appetite when we see her next." Debi snorted, and Jan and Jodi joined in laughing, gleeful that Karen was so excited about her time with Rick.

Since the girls were so close, they knew Karen would not mind them having a little fun on her behalf. They would enjoy their breakfast before planning the day's activities. Just as the eggs and bacon were ready, Karen walked into the kitchen.

"Wow, something smells great! I'm starving!"

Debi, Jan, and Jodi erupted with laughter. "What's wrong with you guys? Have you lost your minds?"

Debi could barely talk, choking on her laughter, but managed to respond, "We're just all feeling silly this morning. It's another beautiful day in the islands. Let Doctor Debi serve you up some breakfast to build your strength back up." They continued to snicker, with Karen shaking her head.

"Karen, now that I'm feeding you, I have a favor to ask." Debi had regained her composure. "First, are you planning to get with Rick today?"

"Yes, he's coming over and we are planning to go to Cupecoy. If any of you want to go, we'd love for you to come with us."

"Thanks, but now for my favor. Would you and Rick mind if I borrow him for about an hour, two hours tops? I want to call Dean to see if I can stop by his casino office to see him for about fifteen minutes. I think it would be very effective if I had Rick with me. Would you call him and make sure you'd both be okay with it? Then I'll call Dean and try to arrange it, maybe for around eleven or eleven-thirty today."

"Okay, I'll call him now. Debi, come on in the bedroom with me and I'll put him on speaker phone so you can answer any questions he might have."

"Great, thanks! Finish your breakfast and let's make that call."

The conversation with Rick went well for Debi. She explained her plan, and said she would call back as soon as she confirmed Dean could meet her.

It was now Debi's turn to be alone in the bedroom for a phone call with her man. Dialing Dean's number, he picked up right away.

"Debi, it's great to hear from you. Ironically, I was planning to call you later today."

"Great, Dean, I have really missed you! I'm hoping you have a few minutes where I could have some private time with you in your office. I'd like to offer you something special that I'm not making available to anybody but you," she purred. "I'm thinking you're not going to want me to leave your office without jumping on it. I don't know about you, but I don't want to wait long. Would it be okay if I came over about eleven this morning? I don't think you'll be disappointed."

Dean was floored. Waiting her out for her to call him had gotten better results than he had imagined. He could not agree soon enough. "Absolutely, I have no meetings, and if I did after hearing this, I would clear my calendar. You know where my office is. The door will be unlocked. Come on in, and I promise I'll be ready for you!"

"Sounds great, love, see you soon!"

Debi could hardly contain her excitement. She called Rick, and he agreed to be at the Royal Palm at ten-thirty. They would be at Dean's office before eleven.

FORTY-NINE

EVERYONE WAS UP early at Villa Islandtude and on their way to the kitchen to get breakfast, they passed by Sylvie and Terri, who were already working on their all-over tans. Grabbing their food, they went outside to eat poolside with the two newest members of their group.

"You guys are getting a jump on the tanning time today," said Chris, not even trying to hide his delight. "I'm sure others of us will be joining you soon!"

"Ditto," said Mark.

"Double ditto," said Dale.

Paulie chose to be a man of no words, and as the others were talking, he had pulled up his lounge chair and had joined them. Tammy and Catherine were the first wives out, pretending first to slap their husbands Paulie and Mark, then grinning.

"Paulie," began Tammy, "it looks like you are getting your engine revved again today. Be careful not to get too much sun on those tender parts. And remember, the closer you get to the sun, the more intense those burning rays become, so try to keep it under control."

They all had a good laugh. Jeanne and Mary were the last to arrive poolside. They had completed their breakfast before walking out with beach towels, each swirling them show-girl style in unison overhead. They were wearing big grins and nothing else. Everyone was in an extremely good mood Friday morning.

They all had chairs gathered closely together, with everyone sunning and dipping in the pool amidst the lively bantering. "You folks are the very best," declared Terri. "It's hard to believe we just met this time yesterday, and today I feel like we're all best friends. I can't imagine a better vacation!"

"That's for sure," added Sylvie. "You people were crazy enough to take a chance on me, and I'm overwhelmed. Just like Terri, I cannot imagine being with a better group of friends. I know I need to keep out of sight, so may not be getting out for a while, but I don't want any of you to change your plans to babysit me. I'm very happy just to sit here at the pool with the incredible view of Simpson Bay."

"This is awesome," echoed Jeanne. "I'm having a blast too. Last night will be hard to top, but I think we'll do what we can to match it!"

Tammy had an idea. "Now hear me out before anybody says no. Terri and Sylvie told us all about their boat trip yesterday and how much fun they had! Us tiki hut people had our own boat trip, and it was pretty special. I just wonder, would it be too much risk to charter a boat with just the people in our group and take another boat trip tomorrow? The only time we'd need to be careful is when we board the boat, and when we leave the boat to get in cars to come back to Islandtude."

"Should we see if we can put together a charter that quick?" Mary continued, "I'll be disappointed if we decide to go only to find we can't get a boat to take us."

"I think we could call Captain Paul and see if he could work it out for us. He may already be booked for tomorrow, but I know from yesterday they have more than one boat that they take out. If we charter a full boat, even if

Captain Paul is captaining a boat already, maybe he would get a substitute captain to take his place with that boat and take us instead."

"I think that's a great idea," said Jeanne. "If Captain Paul agrees, I'm good with going. We could minimize our risk by going before any other boats go out. It gets light about six o'clock. As someone who loves fishing, I'm used to getting up early for trips on my boat. We could plan to leave from Oyster Bay Marina at seven o'clock before any other people would be arriving for a boat trip. That cuts our risk to only when we come back. I think we could simply be very careful, and as we approached the dock on our return, Sylvie and Terri could stay down below until the all clear is given. What does everybody think about that?"

There were nods all around with no objections. "It looks like we're all good with the plan," said Chris. "I'll call Captain Paul now since everyone is in agreement."

As there were still no objections, Chris picked up his phone to call Captain Paul. Answering his phone, Captain Paul talked with Chris for a while, making sure everyone was comfortable with the risk that would be taken. Chris assured him that the group had thoroughly discussed it and were all on board. Captain Paul agreed to have the boat ready to pull away from the dock at seven. He would have everything on board and would skip all the customary preliminaries to expedite their departure. Chris agreed they would have the cash in hand upon boarding, and the deal was done.

The group had resumed their early morning sunning when Sylvie received a call from Debi. Sylvie felt no need to keep any secrets from the group, so stayed on the chair and talked. Debi told in great detail of her plan for later that morning. They agreed it could be a huge positive for both of them if it went well, which they both believed would happen. Paulie was trying to get Sylvie's attention midway through their phone conversation. He whispered to other tiki hutters, and everyone nodded. He tried again to get Sylvie's attention.

"Debi, hold on just a sec." She put her phone on mute.

"Why don't you tell Debi our plans and see if she wants to join us?"

"Paulie, are you sure?"

Paulie nodded.

"Is everybody else good with me asking her to join in on our boat trip?"

Everyone chimed in with their approval. Sylvie was thrilled and took Debi off mute and put her on speaker. "Sorry about that, but I just got a suggestion from the group this morning. We're all sitting around the pool loving another day in the islands. They want me to ask if you'd consider joining us on a boat trip tomorrow."

"Yes! I'm all in."

"Great, but before you fully commit, let me tell you the details. We'll be meeting at the Oyster Bay Marina at seven tomorrow morning. We will be pushing off immediately once we are all on board. Are you still good with it?"

"Absolutely! It will be a blast! I can't wait!"

"You could come over here first if you'd like, but you're already close to the marina, and it would be a long way out of your way to go back over to the marina."

"That's okay, I'll do it. And if you don't mind, I have a suggestion. What about me coming over today after my meeting with Dean? If you could let me squeeze in the king size bed with you and Terri for one night, I'll just spend the night and be ready to go with everyone else when the rest of the group is ready to go. I can bring some food with me when I come over."

Everyone heard Debi's idea and everyone was enthusiastically in favor of it. "Come on over when you're ready. We can hardly wait!"

The tiki hut group continued to sit poolside sunning and planning. For the trip to the marina, Dale suggested renting a van. He volunteered to turn in his Corolla at the car rental and replace it with a van for the remainder of the trip. The group had extended their stay until the coming Wednesday. Dale left for the nearby Hertz, turned in the Corolla, and drove back in a six-passenger van. They were all set for the big boat outing on Saturday.

With Dale's return, they were eagerly awaiting Debi's arrival. It promised to be another memorable party.

FIFTY

DEBI WAS READY for Rick when he arrived at the Royal Palm at ten-thirty. They rehearsed her plan for several minutes and were ready to go. Rick drove Debi the ten minutes to the casino. Rick looked handsome in his burnt orange linen shirt, khaki shorts and docksider shoes. Debi was at her alluring best, with the minimal amount of cloth of her dress barely covering the absolute essentials. Even in laissez-faire St. Martin, she was a candidate for being arrested for having too much on display.

Walking hand in hand into the casino, Debi led the way to Dean's office. As they approached his office, Debi called out. "Dean, are you here?"

"Come on in," he responded cheerfully.

They pushed the door open and walked in together, Debi's body in constant contact with Rick's as they moved toward Dean.

"Dean, I'd like you to meet Rick. Rick is an old friend that I recently discovered was also visiting St. Maarten. He heard I was here and looked me up. Rick, this is Dean, the manager of this casino."

Rick stuck his hand out to shake. "Pleased to meet you, Dean."

Dean was caught flat-footed. It took him a couple seconds to recover his composure. He slowly reached out and shook Rick's waiting hand.

Debi asked, "Dean, do you mind if we have a seat?" Without waiting for Dean's response, Debi and Rick sat in the two chairs across the desk from Dean. As Debi sat, both breasts popped out of the too deeply cut dress and converged in the middle. Debi murmured, "Oops, sorry about that." She quickly tried to push them back behind the thin fabric.

"As I mentioned on the phone this morning, I have something for you that I think you'll want to jump all over. It's a great opportunity, and I know you can be very decisive when a situation presents itself. So, please take a minute to listen and let me know your thoughts. My good friend Rick," she paused, giving his arm a loving squeeze, "was talking with me and I told him all about you and how successful you are with the casino. Now I know not to say too much, but as we were talking, it occurred to me that I might be able to broker a deal between you two esteemed businessmen. It may be likely that there is an opportunity to do some business with your casino. Rick, how much are you thinking about?"

"I believe there's about $10 million that I could steer your way. I recognize that might be a big number, so I'm prepared for you to earn a reasonable commission on this business."

Dean was reeling anew. He looked pale and was struggling for words. "Well, I am certainly interested in talking with you. When do you think this deal would be ready?"

"I think it will move quickly, less than thirty days. But I don't want to waste any time nitpicking over the details. And above all, Debi said you are a great businessman, and very decisive. I understand this is a lot for you to swallow. But I'm going to ask you for a decision based on your friendship with Debi, and your knowledge that she's as sharp as she is good to look at. Debi and I have discussed, and I've shared everything I know. I think it's a good deal. Debi, what's your assessment? Do you think this is a good deal for Dean?

Debi looked at Dean but addressed Rick. "Rick, I have never been surer in my life. I believe before we walk out of this room, we will have us a deal. But if Dean is not ready to shake on this now, based on his blind faith in me, I suggest we excuse ourselves immediately. I have another person who I know well that I am certain will be interested, an up and comer, and if he hears that Dean turned this down, he will be all over it and wanting to rub Dean's face in the one that got away."

"Well Dean," asked Rick, "What do you say? Do we have us a deal?"

"Well, I'd like to ask a few questions. That's a lot of money and little information. I'm sure you'll want some assurances and details as well before anything is agreed upon.

"Thank you, Dean. Debi, I believe we need to leave Dean to think this one over. There may a misunderstanding on the type of deal we're discussing." Rick looked quizzically at Dean as if Dean might not understand the opportunity presented was a money laundering deal. Debi added her look of exasperation, her hands held out and her face perplexed. Rick continued. "These deals don't require a bunch of lawyers and fancy paperwork. Dean, I'm willing to risk you're a reasonable man based on Debi's recommendation, and willing to let it ride with you that there won't be any details to get in the way." Rick looked at Debi before continuing. "Debi, while Dean is trying to get to that same level of comfort with your recommendation, I suggest we leave for that up and comer that I thought was going to be our business partner. I'm happy I gave Dean a shot at it per your insistence. Dean, it was good to meet you. We will be on our way."

Debi and Rick slid back their chairs, stood, and turned to leave. Debi looked back at Dean as she was leaving. "Sorry Dean, I can't wait any longer for you to make a decision."

"Rick, would you mind if I have one minute alone to talk with Debi?"

"Why of course not, take two minutes if you need them. I'll be waiting just outside." Rick stepped out of Dean's office and closed the door behind him.

"Debi, I had been thinking about our situation ever since you called and I wanted to tell you the decision I made yesterday. After a lot of thought, I'm prepared to meet your terms. It's going to take a while for a divorce to go through, but I'll show you the papers when I file. I'll also make a cash contribution to an account in your name that will belong to you as you wait for it to be final. I want you as a partner, in every sense of the word. What do you say?"

"Before I answer, here's your first test. I have Rick's deal that could make a couple million dollars. Do you trust me enough to agree to the deal, or do you still need more time for thought?"

"Before I answer, here's the test for you. If I say yes, are you dropping Rick and partnering with me?"

"That would be the deal."

"Then please ask Rick to step back in."

Rick returned to Dean's office. "Rick, we have a deal. As part of that deal, we need to be clear where Debi stands on this. Debi?"

"Rick, I have to be honest with you. Even though you are a dear friend, and I will always have a special place in my heart for you, I will be working with Dean as we move forward. I appreciate your understanding, but Dean and I have begun a special relationship. Going forward, I plan to represent Dean in any discussions to bring the $10 million deal to fruition. Any involvement that you have going forward will need to be with the person who will be getting clean money in return, and not with me. So, do we all have a deal?"

"I understand perfectly," said Rick, extending his hand to Dean. "Let's seal this deal."

"We have an agreement," responded Dean, shaking Rick's hand. "Debi, this is your deal to handle."

Debi turned to Dean. "I will be meeting with the money person for the next couple days. By Monday morning, I plan to have all the details worked out. I will be reaching out to you then. Please be prepared to celebrate accordingly!" Debi beamed as she and Rick left Dean's office.

FIFTY-ONE

RICK AND DEBI reached Rick's car and remained stoic until they pulled away from the casino. During the short drive back to the Royal Palm, they marveled on how smoothly the plan went and was pulled off without a hitch. Once parked, they looked at each other and the celebration began. Debi hugged Rick and thanked him profusely for his help. Rick congratulated Debi, told her how phenomenal her acting was, and that she truly was as brilliant as she was beautiful. Karen was waiting on them and they quickly gave her the run down on how well it went. After congratulatory hugs all around, Rick and Karen prepared to go to Cupecoy, while Debi prepared to get ready to leave for Villa Islandtude and stop on her way for food.

Debi placed a quick call. "Sylvie, it went great! I'm stopping by to get pizzas for everybody for lunch. Let everyone know that I'll be there soon and will tell you all about it. Start thinking of what you want to do with all that money!" Debi hung up, grabbed her overnight bag and headed to Pizza Del Sol in Simpson Bay. Once on her way to Villa Islandtude, it was a quick seven-minute drive. As she drove, she got a call from Jodi and Jan wanting to know how it had gone with Dean. Debi enjoyed telling how well she and Rick had performed. "Hey, I just got to the villa and am taking lunch in for everybody, so I'll need to talk later. Love you guys!" She ended the call, gathered the stack of pizza boxes, and climbed the stairs to the villa. The gate was unlocked, and she walked in, again amazed by the beautiful view of the ocean, harbor, and of Princess Juliana Airport. She encountered the group in the pool, laughing and already drinking.

"Debi, great you're here! Thanks for bringing the pizzas. Put them on a table and I'll grab some plates while you take a seat. What can I get you to drink?" asked Chris.

"I'd love a glass of Pinot Grigio, please."

"Sure, I'll bring the bottle and a glass for you. Make yourself comfortable and relax," said Chris.

One by one, the others stepped out of the pool, dried off and started to pull chairs to the table to eat. All eleven crowded around the table intended for eight diners, never giving any thought to the seating being tight. The pizza and a new reveler brought on a new burst of energy throughout the group.

After pizza, Debi went back down the stairs to retrieve her overnight bag. After storing it in the room she would share with Terri and Sylvie, she rejoined the gathering at the table and sat next to Sylvie.

"Sylvie, it went great," Debi said quietly. "When you're ready, let's go inside and I'll tell you all about it." While others continued to eat and talk, the girls slipped away to the bedroom, and Debi gave Sylvie a recap of the meeting with Dean.

"That's great," said Sylvie. "I now have a way to convert money that I believe my information is worth. But my problem of trying to stay safe and at the same time get Gregorio's agreement to pay, is the final piece. To keep safe, I need someone to act on my behalf, but I don't know who would be willing to help with it."

"Here are my thoughts, based on what I've seen in movies. Gregorio has presented himself as threatening your physical safety. The best way to end that is to surprise him, and I suggest you do that by having him think there is a threat to his physical safety. You can't do that by yourself, but maybe you have someone you trust who is willing to help. That person can get a message to Gregorio that if anything happens to you, the information will go public, and whatever happens to you will happen to him. If you like this idea, let's think of someone you can trust and ask that person for help."

"I like your idea. I might try calling in yet another favor from Ben. I can't think of anybody I can trust more than him." They stayed in the bedroom and Sylvie placed the call to Ben. "Hey Ben, how is your day going?" asked Sylvie.

"It's going great. Lauren and I are at Mullet Bay Beach with Lisa and Paul. Lauren and Lisa are on a walk, and Paul and I are sitting back resting from giving the girls piggyback rides. What's up with you?"

"I'm having a good time at the villa. You guys are the best. I can't thank you enough, and all the people here from Florida have treated me better than family."

"That's great to hear."

"I'm glad you're having a good time. I've been giving more thought to ending all the craziness I got you involved in. I think I have a way to finish this all up."

"That's also good to hear," said Ben.

"Thanks, I thought you would be glad. But there is one catch. I hate to do this, but there isn't anyone I trust as much as you, and I need hopefully one last favor," she said, cringing as she finished the sentence.

"Oh," Ben said hesitantly. "What is it?"

"Well, you know my former friend, Gregorio Harrington, is a regular at the Red Piano. I need someone to go to the Red Piano. All of the bartenders are close with Gregorio. I want to get a message to him through one of them that I am willing to work a deal and that I hope he'll be reasonable. I believe it was his guys who were threatening me, and that he believes he has all the power because I'm scared of what they might do. But I want him to think the person delivering the note will have my back. If he does not agree to a deal, I want him to think that his safety could also be in danger."

"And how do you propose I do that?"

"I thought that if you could take the note in a sealed envelope addressed to him, maybe you could leave it at the bar when it is really busy so no one would see you leave it. The bartender would then see it and contact Gregorio. He would get the note, and hopefully there will be a possibility that we could work out a deal."

"As I mentioned, I'm here with Paul. I'll talk to Paul, get his thoughts, and we can call you back."

"Ben, you and Paul have each literally saved my life. If you could see yourself clear to do this, I can't ever repay you enough for saving my life, but I will be here to help you anytime, anywhere, for as long as I live. You ask and I'll do it!"

"All right, I'm going to talk with Paul. We'll call you back." Hanging up, Ben looked at Paul.

"I heard," said Paul. "Let me think about it." After pausing, he continued. "It would be good if we can figure this out and call her back before the girls return from their walk. I think between the two of us, we can do it. We'll need to prepare what is appropriate to include in the note. I can handle that. My suggestion is you and Lauren meet Lisa and me at the Red Piano tonight. Ben, it will be important to keep suspicion off of you. This is more my area. While you are at one end of the bar, you can be talking with the bartender, distracting him, while I deliver the note on the other end of the bar. The bartender won't know who delivered it, but he'll know it wasn't you."

"If we do this, should we tell Lauren and Lisa?" asked Ben.

"No. I work alone every time possible. If they know nothing, they cannot act nervous or unusual to bring any suspicion our way. I'll prepare the note and make the delivery. Even you won't know when it happened."

Ben called Sylvie. "Consider it done. The note will be delivered before the night ends. I don't know what will be in the note, but am leaving that to someone who knows how to handle this kind of thing. Someone other than me will get in touch with you later when you need to be contacted. Whatever you do, do not mention this to anyone."

"Thank you, Ben. I will use my best discretion." They hung up. "Debi, you heard nothing, right?" Debi nodded yes. "Our lives may depend on it. You did great with Dean so I'm trusting you on this one hundred percent."

"I won't let you down. Remember, when this works, not only will I have locked in Dean, I will have made more money than I've had in my entire lifetime. This secret will go with me to my grave."

With the best assurance possible, Sylvie headed back to be part of the partying group, with Debi following closely behind her. "Did we miss anything?" called out Sylvie.

"No, we are just organizing our group for the next activity," replied Catherine. "Based on the collages of pictures inside, it looks like prior guests have left pictures of their vacations while at the villa. The owner asks visitors to submit pictures made of their vacations while here. We want to oblige and submit some pictures for inclusion in a new collage of pictures for display in the villa for future visitors' enjoyment. Come on over and let's get creative!"

Jeanne organized the first picture, with Catherine's husband Mark taking a turn as photographer. Sylvie, Terri, Debi, Jeanne, Catherine, Mary and Tammy all lined up at the railing facing north. Looking out at the undisturbed beauty of the green mountainside, they posed with their backs to the camera, dressed only in floppy Islandtude hats. Mark clicked a dozen shots. He exclaimed, "That is going to be tough to top and still be permissible to display!" Chris, Dale and Paulie all agreed.

Tammy arranged the next shot on the large sunning area northwest of the spa and pool. They gathered seven of the thick Frontgate floats and placed them on the pool tile deck. The girls changed into red Islandtude visors, then laid down facing the camera with their feet toward where the sun would set. Each propped up on her elbows, smiling big for the camera. The picture captured Simpson Bay and the ocean in the background. Mark again took multiple pictures of the pose. They all believed the essence of their time at the villa had been captured.

More pictures were taken in a spirit of fun as everyone loved celebrating their time at the villa. After including everyone in the pictures, it was time to put the cameras and phones away and cool down in the pool. Several decks of waterproof playing cards were brought out to the pool. Floats were used as card tables. Beer, wine and rum continued to be consumed as the afternoon party continued. Reggae music complemented the sound of water spilling over from the spa to the pool. The afternoon fun continued, with only bathroom breaks or the need to bring a new round of drinks as the only reasons for leaving the pool. When intermission was reached in the pool card championship series, Terri decided it was time for some snacks. Retrieving two large bags of chips and two bowls of salsa, she brought them out to the large outside table located under the porch covering. Everyone observed the intermission by leaving the pool temporarily to enjoy the snack break. Sylvie trooped back to the kitchen and mixed up another gallon of rum punch made with Topper's award-winning rum and poured the rum-drinkers refills. After the intermission, the leftover chips and salsa were put away and everyone hopped back in the pool. The card players at times made up new rules during their games where no one cared who won or lost, but exemplified that all of the fun was in the playing of the game. After thirty minutes of play, Debi and Terri were crowned as Villa Islandtude Card Co-Champions. They posed for their championship photos, with each having four ace cards inserted to stick up above the brim of their visors. They held each other's hand high above their heads signifying the championship. They exited the pool, and one by one each of the supposedly defeated players lay face down on the deck, where the two girls placed a foot on the back of the prone body in a pose that would have made the producers of World Wrestling Entertainment proud. The fun of the day matched that of their night-time party.

After all the championship revelry ended, the cameras and phones were again put away and a few revelers returned to the pool while others took a break to lay in the Caribbean sun on the poolside lounge chairs. They were mesmerized by the beauty of Dutch Sint Maarten from the privacy of the expansive deck. Reggae music floated through the air providing an appropriate tropical backdrop.

"Debi, I'm glad you came on over today," said Terri, "even if it did cost me the sole card championship. This has been a great day!"

The afternoon flights were arriving at the Princess Juliana Airport in the distance. The partiers took delight in watching the departing flights take off toward them, then turning before they reached the villa.

Discussion turned to plans of the around island boat trip planned for the next day. "I know most of you have already done an around island boat trip during your vacation. Thanks for agreeing to do another," said Debi.

"Of course," replied Paulie. "I imagine the trip tomorrow with Captain Paul could highlight a few places that the trip captained by Nico did not include. Even if it didn't, who wouldn't want to go on another boat trip around Dutch Sint Maarten and French Saint Martin? It will be another phenomenal day!"

"I propose a toast to Caribbean boat trips, pool parties, and the best friends a person could ever imagine," said Dale. "The best friends are St. Martin friends!"

Everyone agreed with the toast. "I can't believe how much fun I've had," said Dale's wife Mary. "We're going to have to create an expanded Tiki Hut Association to include our new friends. Friendships in St. Martin are truly the best."

The day became a relaxing afternoon with the anticipation of another beautiful sunset to be viewed over Simpson Bay. All got their phones and cameras to record the beautiful ending to the day.

FIFTY-TWO

....

BEN GREETED LAUREN and Lisa as they returned from their walk. "Did you girls enjoy yourselves?"

"Yes, it was great," replied Lauren. "You two should have come with us. Did you miss me?"

"Of course I did. I'm thinking of dipping in. Do you want to come in with me?"

"Sure." Lauren and Ben walked hand in hand into the shallow water. The water was very calm, and the clear water looked like a lake of silver tequila. Even their steps in the shallows did not make the intoxicating water murky.

"This beach is hotter than Orient. It would probably be a good alternative to Orient on windy days. What did you and Paul talk about while we were gone?"

"Not much. He did mention about going to the Red Piano tonight. Would you want to meet them there?"

"That would be fun, especially since we haven't gone out anywhere at night other than to dinner."

Okay, let's go see what time would suit them." Ben and Lauren walked back to their chairs. "Hey, I talked to Lauren and we're thinking of checking out the Red Piano tonight. We'd love for you guys to meet us there if you can."

Paul looked at Lisa. "That sounds good to me. There's a dance floor there, and at times it's so crowded that people are more or less standing instead of dancing. But even that's not enough to get Paul out on the floor. Lauren, is Ben going to dance with you?"

"I don't know. We've never been anywhere with dancing. I was just telling him, we've been out to dinner, but other than a restaurant, we haven't been out anywhere on the island at night."

"It'll be fun tonight. I don't know about the dancing, though. We'll see what the music is like. I might follow Paul's lead on that," said Ben smiling.

"You guys are awful," responded Lisa. "I don't know if there's much I can do about Paul, but Lauren, you still have time to break Ben in right. I want to see you two out on the dance floor. And if Paul excuses himself for whatever reasons he always seems to come up with, maybe I'll join the two of you. Ben, you might be the envy of everyone in the Red Piano with two women wanting to dance with you."

"Okay, okay, we'll see. What time do ya'll want to meet there?"

"It doesn't start to get active until after nine o'clock. Why don't you come sometime after nine and look for us? We'll be easy to spot. I'll be the guy content to sit and watch the crowd and Lisa will be dancing in her chair, trying to convince me to get out on the floor."

"That sounds good. Lauren had mentioned she wanted to go to Philipsburg the other day for a second day of shopping there. Since the afternoon is winding down, if Lauren still wants to do it, I might take her into Philipsburg, look around for a very short while, then head back to our side of the island to get ready for dinner. Lauren, does that sound okay with you? We could then meet Paul and Lisa a little after nine at the Red Piano."

"That sounds great, but don't think volunteering to take me to Philipsburg lets you off the hook for dancing tonight. You must really not want to dance to try to get me to go easy on you by offering me the chance to go shopping."

Ben grinned at Lauren. "It was worth a shot. Now it looks like I'll be going shopping *and* dancing. Lauren, I don't know how you've done it, but two activities that I don't normally do, you're somehow getting me to do. This is a little scary!"

They all sat and talked a few more minutes before Ben and Lauren stood up to drive to Philipsburg. "We'll see you guys tonight," called Lauren as they walked to their car.

"We're looking forward to it," responded Lisa. "Ben, don't wear yourself out shopping. You may be dancing for two." Ben grinned and waved.

As Ben and Lauren left for Philipsburg, Lisa and Paul continued to enjoy their time at Mullet Bay Beach. "Paul, I just got a message from someone wanting to have a coaching call later today. Would you mind us going back home so I can work in this call?"

"No, that's fine. It's been a fun day and will likely be a late night. I was thinking it was getting close to time to go back anyway."

Gathering their towels, they left the beach, Lisa to make a coaching call to a client, and Paul to prepare a note for delivery at the Red Piano.

FIFTY-THREE

WHILE BALDO WAS keeping a lookout on Sylvie's room at La Playa for her possible return, Robert Vaughn was keeping a watch on Baldo. It was unusual for Harrington to call Vaughn, so he was comfortable it was significant. He had someone watching Antonio, but Antonio was very inactive, prompting Vaughn to focus his energy on Baldo instead. If there was someone trying to get business from Harrington, Vaughn would make that person a priority to find. He watched the building in Baldo's scope. There were seven units, three on the ground floor, three on the second floor, and one on the third floor. It was easy to determine which Baldo was watching, as people were in and out of the first and second floor units, but Baldo never left his post. Vaughn decided to pay a visit to his old friend Marie, the owner and manager of La Playa.

"Hello Marie, how is your Friday treating you?"

"All is well with me, Robert. How are you and what brings you to La Playa Orient Bay?"

"As you know, I have business contacts who love visiting St. Martin. I have a group interested in coming soon, and I'm scoping out some possible places for them to stay. Your lodging here has always been popular with some of my clients. I'm looking in particular at your top floor. I know the top floor is a little more expensive, but my clients do not like the possibility of hearing footsteps of other renters on their ceiling. Would your top floor units be available for my clients to consider?"

"Yes, sure. In fact, seven of the eight are currently open. I have reservation requests for next week with a preference for the top floor, which is why I was holding them open. They are merely requests, and they will accept the second floor if the top floor is unavailable."

"The other top floor unit, when is it scheduled to be vacated?"

"Let me look." She pulled the file. "It looks like they are scheduled to check out on Wednesday."

"Hmm, I wonder if those guests would consider swapping rooms if there were a financial incentive to do so?"

"Robert, I can ask them. I haven't seen much of them lately, so they might agree." As she looked to make a note in the file, Vaughn was able to see the names of the tenants.

"That would be great. Before you go to the trouble, let me place a call to the group interested in coming. If they won't commit to accepting the rooms beginning on Monday, I don't want to trouble you or your guests. I'll go check with them now, and if I get a commitment, I'll give you a call tonight."

"Okay, just let me know."

Vaughn left with an important piece of the puzzle. He could quickly do some research to have a high level of confidence as to which of the two women Harrington was concerned about. If he was not able to determine if it was one more so than the other, he would merely seek out both, expecting them to be together. He placed a few calls and hit paydirt quickly when he called Rollo, the bartender at the Red Piano.

"Rollo, this is Robert. I'm trying to reach a couple of ladies, and knowing how your bar has received honors each of the last few years from the Daily Herald as being the best piano bar, the best live music venue, and having one of the best pool rooms and best bartenders, I thought you might be able to help me." He continued to talk with the bartender Rollo and provided the names of those he was wanting to find.

"It's a small world. You're not the only person hunting for Sylvie. In fact, I took a picture of them the other night and sent it to someone."

"Do you still have that picture? Would you mind sending it to me also?"

"I've still got it. Hold on a minute, here it is, I'll send it to you now."

"That's great, Rollo. How is everything going for you? Is the Red Piano still treating you the way you deserve? You know, if you decide you want a change of scenery some time, just let me know. I have a lot of people who ask me about young enterprising talent."

"Thanks, Robert, but I have a good set-up here. I don't think I'll be looking to leave anytime soon."

"Okay, well let me know if you have a change of heart. And if you do see Sylvie, would you let me know? I think it could be worth your while." The two ended the call. Vaughn had made great progress in a short period of time.

Vaughn went to his office and continued to work. He alerted his troops about who he was trying to find, and sent the picture of both Sylvie and Terri. "Start making inquiries, find out where and when they were last seen, and let's see how fast we can find them."

Although Vaughn had a good network, he decided to try to fast track his search. He placed a call to another old friend, the head of the Gendarmerie in French St. Martin. "Jacques, this is Robert, how are you?" After making small talk, Vaughn got to the point. "Jacques, are you still doing traffic stops these days? Yes? Well, when you're patrolling at the stops, would you mind doing me a small favor? I'm looking for a couple people, nothing real important, but some family is wanting to make sure they are behaving, but don't want them to know about it. If I send you a picture, could you let me know if these two young ladies are spotted? They will probably be easy to spot as they are both real lookers. I don't want them detained, I would just appreciate a description of the vehicle and the tag if possible. Thanks in advance for your help."

Vaughn felt good about the progress he had made. He called several more people as he continued his search, now having lined up help from his employed network as well as the head of the French Police.

Vaughn got a steady stream of updates from his men. They were actively looking, and someone had been placed at La Playa to watch the room. The only information he received on their whereabouts was old. He did not receive any reports of them being seen for several days. Vaughn decided to place one more call.

"Gregorio, it's Robert. How are you? I thought I might owe you a call. You had asked if I had heard anything about someone trying to get into your business. I want to let you know that, unfortunately, I have still heard nothing to that effect. Is there anything I can do to help you? No, well, I'll make my team aware that you could have a situation, and if anything is heard, to let me know. As you know, Gregorio, I am always happy to lend you a hand. We need to schedule a time to get together again. It's been too long."

The call ended, and Vaughn was pleased that he had made Harrington aware of his willingness to help. It served as an insurance policy for Vaughn. He wanted a cover story in place in the event that Harrington became aware that Vaughn was potentially getting into his business.

FIFTY-FOUR

BEN WAS RELIEVED when the shopping in Philipsburg had ended. He was not sure how or when Paul would create the note to leave for Harrington, but wanted to make sure he and Lauren were out of the way, and decided he might as well do something that would please Lauren.

As Ben drove back to Orient from Philipsburg, Paul completed his notes to Harrington. Paul and Lisa had an understanding that Paul would have necessary errands on occasion, and when he did, she would not have any questions. He would only tell the expected time of his return, and Lisa had learned over the last few years not to worry. As she prepared for her coaching call, Paul let her know that he had a few errands to run, but would be back in time for dinner. With that, he left their home in the Cliff. She would not communicate with him until he returned.

Paul was on his way to Orient Beach. He located Baldo's parked car, walked the distance necessary to confirm that Baldo was deep into his surveillance watch, and returned to the car. Within seconds a door was unlocked, and the sealed note was placed under the driver's side foot mat. The door was relocked and Paul was on his way back to the Cliff.

When Ben and Lauren were back at Lubrique, each went to shower and get ready for dinner, followed by a night of dancing at the Red Piano. They chose the Italian-

Sicilian restaurant Al Dente located a short distance from Orient in Cul de Sac on the French side. They arrived a little after six o'clock, which was before the restaurant became very busy. They were directed to a table set for two, in a corner of the main dining room. They faced the large tree that grew in the restaurant, where there was a hole in the ceiling with the ceiling built around the top portion of the tree's trunk. It was a one-of-a-kind on the island. They each ordered a meat lasagna with a Caesar salad. Ben had decided it would be a long night, and in deference to his role in helping distract while the note to Harrington was delivered, he decided to limit his alcohol consumption to one glass of red wine. He ordered flat water for the table. The salads were served and Ben and Lauren ate with little discussion.

"Ben, is everything okay tonight?"

"Yes, I'm great, thanks. How are you feeling tonight?"

"I'm fine, you just seem quieter than normal. I'm glad you're okay. I'll chalk up you being quiet to your resting up for all that dancing you'll be doing," she kidded.

"Yes, I wasn't able to hide it." He paused, then continued. "Hey, I'm sorry for worrying you. I'm feeling great, this is a beautiful setting with the best company I could hope to have, and I'm confident the meal will be great. We haven't had a meal on island that has been less than excellent. I promise I'll start speaking up. We have our night planned for a lot of fun. It's probably presumptuous of me, but I'm thinking that for the rest of this trip, I'm thinking that we'll be spending it together. Maybe that's inappropriate of me, but I hope you feel the same way."

"Yes, somewhere along the way, my vacation turned into our vacation. But don't get overconfident. You know you're only as good as your last meal. One misstep, mister, and I'll have to check my calendar before you can consider me part of your plans."

"Yes, I'm aware and I'll be trying to stay on relatively good behavior." Ben looked at Lauren, a rare serious look on his face. "You've asked me why I came to St. Martin. I told you how I was tired from working and was just looking to take a break. My plan was to do little, eat a lot, and hang out at the beach. Of course, it's not turned out the way I anticipated. Thank goodness God stepped in and did a better job of planning my life than I did. So, with all that, you've never told me what brought you to the island."

"Like you, I'm taking a break. Unlike you, instead of taking a break from working too many hours, I'm taking a break from school. I'm in my last year of law school, and before graduating and preparing to take the bar exam, I'm taking what might be my last vacation for a while. I'm thankful that our paths crossed, and I hope you're thankful that I made the first move to seek you out."

Ben loved that memory. "Yes, I am thrilled that you came to me first. I am honored, and glad you didn't give up on me. I thought I came across as pretty boring, and I'm glad you tolerated it."

"Well, it was out of character for me, both that Saturday night, and again on Sunday morning. I tried to be more like my lifelong best friend who was always more willing to take those types of risks. I think since we've been spending time together, you're seeing more of the real me."

"The real you is the one I want to spend time with."

The lasagna was brought to the table. As anticipated, it was delicious, and Ben sipped his wine while intermittently drinking a lot of water. "Let's see what they have for dessert. We've still got a lot of time until we go to the Red Piano." They looked at the dessert menu and both ordered the crème brulee. They became much more talkative as the dinner continued. The dessert was finished and the bill was paid. It was only eight-fifteen, and they would be early to the Red Piano.

"Are you tired of shopping? If not, we can stop in the Maho area and look at the shops that are open there."

"Ben, I believe you may secretly like shopping more than me. But before you take it back, I'm not tired of shopping, and I think it would be great!"

They left the restaurant and drove toward the Red Piano. They stopped in the Maho area and parked in the small parking garage there. They walked over to the Lord and Hunter store, a store in the Shipwreck Shop family. "I love the walk shops here. Thanks for offering to take me shopping yet again."

"I think this is fun, too. It's not like power shopping for me, this is part of the adventure and discovering all that the island has to offer." They left the Lord and Hunter, then walked into a jewelry store just to pass the time. After browsing there briefly, they crossed the street and looked in a t-shirt shop a couple doors down from the pharmacy. Ben bought each of them a souvenir t-shirt. It was almost nine-thirty and time to go to the Red Piano.

They parked and entered the piano bar at nine-forty. They saw Paul and Lisa, and walked over to them, where everyone greeted with hugs. It was loud, and everyone had to project their voices to be heard over the noise of the crowd. As Lisa talked with Lauren, Paul spoke quietly to Ben. "It changes nothing, but I see Harrington is here tonight. It looks like he has a new female friend with him on display. I'll still deliver the note, but now we'll have a chance to see his reaction when he receives it. I'm going to greet him in a few minutes. Later, I'll introduce you to him. After that, please try to not be watching him or monitoring his behavior. It would probably be best if you do as

Lauren wishes and spend time on the dance floor with her, avoiding eye contact with him. You'll want to not change your normal behavior."

A few minutes later, Paul projected to the small group. "I'm going to get a beer. Would anyone else like anything?"

Lisa replied, "The waitress will be over in a bit, I'll wait for her to come by." Ben and Lauren said they would wait a bit as well.

Paul walked toward the bar to place his order. As he worked his way there, he moved closer to Harrington, the men made eye contact with one another, and Paul edged over to greet him. "Gregorio, it's good to see you. Who is your beautiful friend?"

"Good evening Paul. I'd like you to meet Michele. Michele, this is Paul, he also lives on the island. Michele has just moved here, and I'm showing her around. I'm glad you're here. I'd like to introduce her to people and make her feel at home."

"Michele, it's good to meet you. My wife, Lisa, is just over there. She's cornered a couple of tourists here for the week just now. After she comes up for air, I'll introduce you to her."

"That would be great, thanks. It's good to meet you Paul."

Paul continued to the bar, got a Coors Light, and slowly made his way back to Lisa, who was still enjoying telling Lauren about her afternoon. "Lisa, in a bit, I'd like to introduce you to someone who just moved to the island. Perhaps you could be yet again St. Martin neighborly and offer to include her in some of your social activities the coming weeks."

Paul looked at Ben, then glanced at the dance floor. Ben looked at Paul and saw him again look at the dance floor.

"Lauren, let's get this party started. Would you like to dance?"

"Shopping and dancing, who are you Ben Carlisle? Yes, absolutely!" As Ben and Lauren moved to the dance floor, Paul took Lisa over to introduce her to Michele. The two quickly got to know one another and were enjoying their time at the Red Piano. As they chatted, Paul edged away and greeted others he knew. Ben and Lauren were on the dance floor for an extended time before Paul saw Ben lead Lauren over to the bar for drinks. The two of them were enjoying focusing on each other, and despite all the activity around them, were close to oblivious to the world outside of the two of them. After they had drinks, Paul watched as they returned to the dance floor. They had been on the floor for several songs when Paul modified the plan. He saw an empty beer bottle with tip placed underneath it at the bar. He palmed the note for Harrington, and with the sleight of hand of a practiced magician, was able to place the note under the tip money as he passed. He returned to Lisa and was being introduced to a new friend she had met when the tip and note were picked up by the bartender, Rollo. Rollo saw the note was addressed to Harrington, called a waitress over, and sent the note and a drink to Harrington, keeping watch until he saw the delivery was completed. Rollo then stepped outside. He sent a message to Harrington that he had just discovered the note on the bar and had not seen anyone place it there. He waited, Harrington acknowledged his message, and Rollo returned to his post.

At eleven-thirty, Paul decided it was the right time to leave. Instead of telling Ben and Lauren goodbye, he and Lisa stepped out, entered their car, and then he sent a terse message to Ben. "We're good, heading home, have a good night." Ben felt his phone vibrate, saw the message, and pocketed his phone. He and Lauren went back to the dance floor for several more dances. At twelve-thirty the crowd had thinned some but was still going strong. Ben and Lauren decided they had danced their last dance of the night and left the Red Piano.

"Ben, I had a great time. Thanks for everything tonight. The Red Piano was a lot of fun."

"Yes, I'm glad we tried it. I'm ready for some quiet time now back at Orient. It's been a fun and full day." The happy couple drove back to their vacation home on Orient Beach.

FIFTY-FIVE

FRIDAY NIGHT AFTER the sun had set, the group at Islandtude made a dinner of the food from Vesna's left from the prior night. The pace of drinking had tapered off significantly as all were aware of an early start and full day planned for Saturday. After dinner, the group did something it had not done on the entire trip. Leaving the glass wall to the entertainment room open to the night as normal, they went inside and turned on the big screen TV for the first time during the trip. They decided it would be a great night to have a movie night. Instead of choosing a movie available on one of the movie channels, however, they loaded all of their pictures and videos taken during the trip and had a showing on the big screen. Several hours passed as they watched, paused, and rehashed all the fun of the trip. It had been another great day and night at Islandtude, and approaching eleven, all were ready to get in bed for the night.

Debi, Terri and Sylvie went to their bedroom, but instead of getting in bed, they were wound up and continued to talk. At midnight, Sylvie got a call. She saw it was from Paul. "Sylvie, I have an update for you. I suggest you have a place of privacy for us to talk."

"Sure, hold on a second." Sylvie put the call on mute. "Hey, it's Paul. He wants to talk to me where I won't be overheard. I don't care if you hear everything, but I think I should do as he asks."

"Absolutely, you can step out poolside and talk. That's good with us," responded Terri. Sylvie stepped out, sat in a chair next to the spa, and took the call off mute. "Hey Paul, it's good here for me to talk. Thanks for calling."

"Here's what you need to know. I strongly caution you not to share, even with a best friend. Everyone performs more naturally when they have no knowledge of information that they should not know. Understood?"

"Yes, I'll not share with Terri, Debi or anyone else unless you say I should."

"Here's where we are. A note was delivered to Harrington about thirty minutes ago. It directed him to a note that he will find in an employee's vehicle. I am certain he has already contacted the employee and has read the second note, or will read it shortly. I did some analysis before creating the demand in the note. Harrington will not agree to the demand, but the plan is for him to agree to a lesser demand that will make you very happy. Based on the enterprise value he receives from the oil production that would be shut down, and the companies that he would lose if the French government exercised its rights, Harrington can afford a hefty amount to you to continue with his business. He has several Dutch oil production and distribution companies. The smallest of these is to be transferred to your ownership. I will set up your holding company for you to take ownership. The company is currently worth about ten million dollars and will generate a steady stream of revenues and profits in future years for you. I have proposed transfer of this company, as well as a substantial cash payment. The demand is for thirty million, but that is an amount he will never consider. Your goal will be to get something in the neighborhood of ten, but I recommend a floor of five. That will be on your negotiating skills. He will take the demand seriously, and I expect there will be tension, but the playing field has been made more level. As long as you do nothing stupid, which I know you won't if you remember being greeted at your car by men with a gun, you should be able to soon return to a more normal life."

"The second note for Harrington states that you will be calling him. You are aware he is an early riser and often begins his workday before six in the morning. I think he will start even earlier tomorrow. I suggest you call him no later than six in the morning and try to negotiate a deal. You do not need to get into details. Let him know that the details for transfers will be provided shortly after the deal in concept is reached. For a small fee, I will have a team handle all details. The name of the company to be transferred to your newly formed holding company is Dutch Energy Production Company, referred to as DEP. I have shared a lot of information, and Lisa continues to be totally unaware of any of this. She is in another room and will remain oblivious to any of these dealings. The only people who will know are you, Harrington, Ben and me, and Ben will not know details unless you choose to provide them. Now, it is your turn to ask me questions and make sure you are completely ready for your call tomorrow morning. Ask away."

Paul and Sylvie continued to discuss, she was coached on what to expect during her discussion with Harrington, how she should react, and how it would be critical to complete the negotiation quickly. "This could be concluded before your call tomorrow morning ends. Remember, after the general agreement, my team will handle all the details and will reach out to Harrington."

Sylvie ended the call and was excited but nervous. She went back into the bedroom where Debi and Terri were still talking. "Okay, I'm going to make an early call tomorrow morning before we go on the boat trip. I've been cautioned to the point of feeling threatened not to share any information with anyone. So I'll tell you this, I'm hoping this is over soon, and when it is, I'll be sharing with you a reward for your help. Debi, I hope to need some assistance from you as well for Dean's help that I would like you to coordinate."

All of the girls accepted that discussion of the topic had concluded. Debi said, "Well, if it's okay with you, I'm going to bed now. It will be time for our boat trip soon, and I'm excited to have a super day to look forward to tomorrow." They all were soon asleep.

FIFTY-SIX

SYLVIE AWOKE EARLY. They would be leaving at six-thirty to start their boat trip. At five o'clock, Sylvie showered and put on a skimpy bikini, and put a colorful tropical print rayon dress over it as a cover-up. She was ready for the trip. She went back outside to the chair she sat in next to the spa when she talked to Paul. It was five-twenty, the sun had not risen, but she prepared to call Harrington. "Gregorio, good morning, it's Sylvie. I trust you were already up as usual."

"Yes, Sylvie."

"And I trust you have received my notes?"

"Yes, I have."

"Shall we talk? I'd like to get your agreement to my proposal."

"Sylvie, Sylvie, Sylvie. You break into my house. You steal from me, and now you want me to reward you? Have you had trouble sleeping lately?"

"Gregorio, you are right. You have stolen from others. You are making much money from your deceptions, but you are finding fault with me? Would you like to start over?"

"You are a brash one. You know we could have been very good friends. What you are hoping to receive, you could have had plus so much more. All you needed to do was continue as you seemingly wanted when we met. Was it all a ruse?"

"No, Gregorio. You are a very attractive man, and I hope when our business is concluded we can be friends, maybe even very good friends. At a minimum, however, I believe we are both in a position that if we make missteps toward the other, there will be serious consequences. I'm suggesting we have an alliance where we happily co-exist, where we each can enjoy long and fulfilling lives."

"Sylvie, your demands are absurd. Where did you come up with such nonsense?"

"I have very sophisticated people as advisors. You are correct, I am not knowledgeable on such matters, but thankfully I have very strong support who are knowledgeable. The demands presented are extremely reasonable, a very small share in our new partnership, where you remain the vast majority stakeholder of our dealings. I would like quick action, as I am beholden to others. If I cannot reach an agreement with you quickly, I will remain tucked away until I have been assured that I have nothing to fear. Unfortunately for you, that assurance would come at a very high cost to you, an event from which you will not recover. I've possibly made mistakes, but with the guidance I am receiving from my advisors, they will not allow a do over where we all pretend nothing happened." Sylvie paused. "Are you ready to discuss with me, or would you prefer to negotiate with others? You know I have no experience with such matters, but I am prepared to move forward anyway. It is your choice, but if you choose not to discuss with me until we agree, I will end the call and place my next call to my advisors. You're a powerful man, and to have become so powerful, clearly a smart man. Please let me know your choice, as I am on a deadline to make a call that I have either reached agreement, or that I am turning it over to the professionals to handle."

Harrington knew the notes were prepared by knowledgeable people who most likely were not playing games. He decided to negotiate with Sylvie. Once he agreed to the transfer of DEP and a one-time payment of six million, Sylvie said someone else would be contacting him for completion of the deal. Sylvie called Paul, and Paul gave assurances that all details would be handled for the transfers. Sylvie insisted that Debi be credited for steering the cash through Dean's operations when creating good funds. Paul agreed and the deal was left for him to finish.

At six o'clock, Sylvie returned to her bedroom where both Debi and Terri were awake and getting ready. She said she believed they were all safe to enjoy the day, and that she hoped in the next few days to have more information as to when and how much they would be receiving.

With Sylvie's belief that the matter with Harrington was concluded, she was ready to focus on the boat trip. She told Debi and Terri that she did not want to have any more discussion, and especially with the rest of the group, as to the deal she hoped was reached with Harrington. Terri and Debi were both happy to agree and glad to focus on the fun in front of them.

At six-twenty, all eleven at the villa had congregated at the pool deck and were ready to go. They boarded the van driven by Dale, with Sylvie and Terri tucked out of sight in the back, and with five in the vehicle driven by Mark. They were off and pulled out of the driveway headed to the Oyster Bay Marina. Turning right out of the Almond Grove neighborhood, they quickly came to the French-Dutch border and the roundabout to enter Marigot on the way to the dock. Traffic was slowed, as a stop and inspection was ahead. They slowed as they approached the gendarme. Several cars were on the side of the road for inspection before being allowed to continue. Mark drove first

as he proceeded through the stop. The gendarme looked
in the car and signaled them through. Behind Mark, the
van was signaled to pull off the road to the shoulder. Two
of the French police came over to inspect, asked everyone
to step out, and Dale displayed his driver's license when
asked. After the gendarme made a radio call, they were
clear to move on. The delay took only a few moments,
and Dale caught up with Mark, who had slowed waiting
for Dale to get back on the road. They arrived just before
seven, walked onto the boat, and were ready to leave. The
boat was untied, and as they edged away from the dock,
Captain Paul and Elisa welcomed them all aboard. Within
two minutes they reached the naked buoy, where all provided their garments to Elisa for storage, to be returned at
day's end. It was a sunny day with calm seas. Their escape
in the islands was getting off to a great start.

Mark began kidding Dale. "Dale, were you sporting
your most criminal scowl this morning? What was up with
the traffic stop?"

"They were stopping some cars, and we were one
of the lucky ones chosen. They asked to see my license,
everyone got out of the van so they could look inside, and
I guess they didn't find what they were looking for, so we
were told to move on."

"Well, I'm glad you didn't get hauled in to one of the
French jails. That would have made for a great story later,
though. The charges might have been you were impeding
traffic for driving too slow in a roundabout. That would
have been a hoot."

The boat headed north, with Captain Paul slowing
as everyone enjoyed viewing Orient Bay from the water.
As the Florida group had been to Green Cay off of Orient
when on the boat trip captained by Nico, he took them
instead to nearby Tintamarre Island. He anchored in shal-

low water and everyone went ashore. It was early in the morning and no other boating visitors were on the island. Jeanne and Tammy wrote on the sand "Welcome from the NE FL Tikiers" where the group gathered behind the writing for a picture. Captain Paul was the photographer. The first picture was of the original eight members, then Debi, Terri and Sylvie joined for the next picture commemorating their honorary induction into the group. A third picture was taken by Captain Paul to include Elisa at the group's urging. The group walked the short beach, and because not wearing shoes, chose to not explore the remainder of the island. After thirty minutes, they all waded back to the boat. On board, breakfast croissants were broken out, with the early morning drinks of choice of water and sodas. After the croissants, they continued the tour. They next anchored out in the vicinity of Anse Marcel. Elisa showed them an area where there would be good snorkeling and handed out snorkels and fins. Everyone snorkeled a bit, then came back aboard for a photo to document their visit. They lined up sitting on the edge of the boat, as if they were about to dive backwards headfirst, with Elisa capturing the view from the water. After the short snorkel, they were ready to resume the around island tour. They motored past Grand Case and took a few pictures of the brightly painted buildings. They next passed Happy Bay, where they had eaten lunch when sailing with Nico, before nearing the beautiful beaches of Rouge and Plum. They stopped briefly to enjoy the sights, and decided they were about ready for lunch. The boat's next stop, as they had made it halfway around the island, was Cupecoy. They all looked forward to the stop. As they approached, a small contingent of about thirty sunbathers at Cupecoy hurriedly lined up, backs to the boat, and on command, mooned the boat in unison. It was a hilarious sight and worthy of a picture. They had received a ceremonial welcome from the people of Cupecoy. They anchored and swam ashore, where two of those to welcome them were Karen and Rick. Debi made the introductions, and soon everyone on the beach was mingling with the visitors from the boat. Captain Paul brought towels and drinks ashore in several baskets, keeping the towels dry. Lunch was being prepared for them by Dany, and everyone sat on towels in the sand eating a great Caribbean meal washed down by rum punch and beer. The group decided that the name "Dany" was synonymous with beach grilling excellence, as the grilled lunch they had at Happy Bay was prepared by another person named "Danny." "Dany" of "Dany's Beach Bar" had met the expectations set by his counterpart on Happy Bay.

After lunch, the group swam back to the boat to finish their trip. A quick sweep around the rest of the Dutch side of the island brought them to Dawn Beach for a few pictures of the area from the water, before it was time to return to the Oyster Bay Marina. They arrived at the Naked Buoy, and everyone dressed to go ashore. Captain Paul was aware they did not want to tarry and needed to be gone before the other boats were due to return.

"Captain Paul and Elisa, as president of the Northeast Florida Tiki Hut Association, we want to thank you for an incredible day." Jeanne looked at the group who all nodded their agreement. "We are making both of you honorary members of our Association, and hope one day your travels will bring you to Florida, where you will be warmly welcomed."

All eleven on board with Captain Paul and Elisa hugged their captain and first mate before stepping down to the dock. They hurried to their vehicles, with Sylvie and Terri once again safely out of sight in the back of the van. It was time for the drive back to Villa Islandtude.

FIFTY-SEVEN

BEN RECEIVED AN early morning call from Paul. Paul shared with Ben what he would need to know on the development with Sylvie and her general agreement with Harrington. He let Ben know that all the details were good as done, without sharing with Ben that his group would be handling and doing all the cleanup work needed. Ben was relieved. He was eager to be able to return to Sylvie and Terri the possessions they had left in his care.

Ben asked, "Would you and Lisa want to come to Orient today to celebrate? I'm relieved, and know Lauren will be too, that this has been basically wrapped up."

"Thanks for the invitation. I think Lisa has a few calls today, and I'm unfortunately going to be tied up also. Hopefully we will be able to see you again before you both leave to go home."

Ben thought it was too early to wake Lauren after their late night. He tried to go back to sleep but could not. At seven-thirty, Ben got up for an early start to the day. He and Lauren had planned to relax on the beach most of the day, and wanted to eat a leisurely lunch at one of the great restaurants available right on Orient Beach. At eight-thirty, Ben decided he had waited long enough. He called Lauren and she immediately answered. "Did I wake you up?"

"No, I've been awake for a while and couldn't go back to sleep. I'm ready to start the day. You?"

"I'm on my way over. I'll put on a shirt and we can get some breakfast. See you in two minutes."

Lauren was waiting for Ben. They decided to get breakfast at Papatwo. The sun had been up for several hours, and it was already a very warm morning. They walked into the restaurant. "I feel like a big breakfast today. I think I'll have scrambled eggs, bacon, toast and fruit. Lauren, what do you want?"

"I think I'll get the pancakes." A waitress came over and collected their breakfast orders.

Lauren began, "It's Saturday morning, a traditional travel day. I'm so glad it's not a travel day for us. I'm going to be content to spend the whole day laying on the beach if that's good with you. We have been very active, and I want to relish every minute of this day."

"That sounds perfect to me. A low-key day of lazing around will be awesome!"

They finished breakfast and were ready to start the hard-core sunning before ten o'clock. They went back to get the beach bag, suntan lotion and pleasure books. Ben had still not read on the trip, and today was setting up for a little reading. They stopped at the Lubrique chairs and secured their towels to the chairs. They both reclined at a sitting position of thirty degrees with books in hand. They read and looked at each other on occasion. After thirty minutes of paradise, Ben became restless. "Why don't we walk down the beach? We can scope out what's happening elsewhere and pick a spot for later to eat lunch."

Lauren was happy to take a walk. Ben placed the waterproof box containing the key and cash around his neck and they started out. They held hands, dipped in the water a few times as they walked, and thirty minutes later made it to the far end of the beach.

"Ben, what do you think the tiki hut group from Florida is doing today? I miss them and their crazy antics."

"Oh, I don't know. Maybe they'll come around here sometime. They are a lot of fun, but this is perfect for me today with just us." They walked a few steps in silence, before Ben continued, "That was fun at the Red Piano last night. After getting there, we sure didn't see much of Lisa and Paul."

"Yes, that was fun." Lauren agreed with Ben. "It was strange that they left and didn't say good-bye. I guess they saw us having a good time and were ready to go. At the time, I kind of forgot that we had gone there to meet them and didn't think anything of it. That was fun, though, just you and me."

"Where do you want to eat lunch today? We could eat at Leandra's again, or try something new. What do you want to do?"

"Leandra's was great, but I'd like to try something new. I'd like either Le String that is next to Leandra's or Orange Fever. The one we don't eat at today, I'd like to eat at maybe tomorrow."

"Sounds good. Let's try Le String today, and Orange Fever tomorrow." They went back to their chairs and dipped in the water. The water was refreshing as the heat of the day set in. They talked while cooling down in the shallow water. Wading out of the water, they headed to their chairs for the sun to dry them before going to lunch. The lunch at Le String was a feast. John the waiter brought each a welcoming rum punch. They had shrimp tempura, mahi mahi, calamari and mozzarella sticks. "This is amazing. Everything was absolutely great! And to be able to eat all that super food while wearing a swimsuit with your feet in the sand is special. I love Orient Beach. I can't imagine a better beach anywhere in the world."

"Ben, I agree. I would say it was on par with Leandra's. It's hard to believe that there are two restaurants that good together on Orient Beach!"

After eating lunch, they walked the short distance back to their chairs and laid back. They closed their eyes and were close to drifting off to sleep. "Hey you guys, wake up!" It was a familiar voice. They looked up to see Lisa and a friend.

"Hey Lisa," said Lauren. "I'm surprised to see you here."

"Yes, I had calls scheduled for today, but my afternoon call got cancelled. I thought you might be here. Lauren, Ben, I'd like you to meet Michele. I met her last night at the Red Piano. She's recently moved here and was with Gregorio last night. We exchanged numbers, and when my afternoon work call was cancelled, I took a chance on calling her to see if she would want to come over to Orient with me today. I tried calling you, but got no answer. I guess you don't have your phone with you."

"Hey Michele," answered Lauren. "Great to meet you. Sorry, I left my phone in my room this morning and haven't been back to get it. Congratulations," she continued, looking at Michele. "That's exciting to move here. This is my first visit, but I love everything about this island. I think you're very lucky to live here."

"Mind if we pull some chairs up and sit with you guys?" asked Michele.

Lauren looked at Ben for his reaction, knowing he had planned on just the two of them.

"That would be fine," said Ben.

"I have a request," added Lauren. "Ben and I have been having a great day, but we don't have any pictures to remind us how great it's been. Would you mind, if you have your phone, taking a few pictures of Ben with me and sending them to me? Let me give you my phone number and email address."

"Sure, happy to do it! Why don't you two stand over there with the water in the background and I'll snap one of you."

They got out of their chairs and hugged with the beach in the background. "Now maybe if you go in the water, I'll get some pretend candid ones while you're there."

"That sounds fun. Ben, give me a piggyback ride into the water!" Ben obliged and his enthusiasm for having his day interrupted began to improve. "When we get in the water, I'll slide down, and then you can kiss me like you mean it!"

Ben was pleased that the impromptu photo session had taken a marked turn for the better. "Come on, Ben," called Michele. "You can do better than that." Ben kissed Lauren, and knew it meant more than a typical kiss.

After a few minutes Michele walked to the edge of the water. "I have an idea for one more. I'll move the chairs out of the way, and I think you'll like this. I'd like the two of you to sit in the sand with your feet in the water and your backs to me. I'll go back up on the sand and take a few photos."

Ben and Lauren posed as Michele instructed. Lisa and Michele slid the chairs away from the yellow umbrella, and Michele stood back, capturing the umbrella in the picture along with Lauren and Ben. That picture included the umbrella, beach, the different shades of blue of the water, and Green Cay in the background. One picture even captured a sailboat as it passed by Green Cay. "Okay, that's a wrap! You guys come take a look."

Ben and Lauren came up to the umbrella and held Michele's phone in the shade to be able to see the pictures.

Lauren loved all the pictures, and especially the last one of Ben and Lauren sitting in the sand. "Michele, you are an amazing photographer. I love all the pictures, and especially the last one of us sitting in the sand. That could be the cover of a book!"

At that moment both Lauren and Ben were grateful their day had been interrupted by Michele and Lisa. As an added bonus, Michele had made a new friend in Lauren.

FIFTY-EIGHT

DALE AND MARK drove the group back to Almond Grove. They waved to the security guard at the neighborhood entrance and continued to the villa. As they approached the villa, a white van was parked, partially blocking the driveway and preventing Dale and Mark from entering. They both pulled past the white van to the other side of the driveway, where they parked along the road in front of the villa.

"Who blocked our driveway? I guess if it's not moved soon, we can call security and ask for that van to be moved," said Mark. "We'll need to walk up the hill from here. Dale and I can move the cars into the driveway later."

They exited their vehicles and began walking up the driveway to the entrance of the villa. As they were walking up the drive, someone called out to Sylvie, who was last in the procession. "Hey, Sylvie, how are you? It's good to see you."

Sylvie stopped and turned. "Hello to you. I'm well, thanks." She paused, not sure who the handsome young man was who greeted her.

"Hey, do you remember me? I'm Samuel from the Red Piano, Sam. I certainly remember you." He paused, seeing Sylvie was trying to recall their meeting. "Hey, no problem. It probably happens with you a lot. You're very memorable, where I'm much easier to forget. I was visiting a friend in the neighborhood."

The rest of the group continued up the steps to the villa entrance as Sylvie talked to the young man. "I'll be up in a sec," Sylvie called out. "I'm sorry, I feel like I should remember you, but I'm struggling after a full day of boating and my share of alcohol. It's good to meet you again." Sylvie stuck out her hand in greeting. He accepted her handshake, but also leaned in to greet her with alternating kisses to the cheek. As he began to pull away, he suddenly placed a hand over her mouth, and with his other hand applied pressure to her carotid artery, stopping the blood flow to her brain. Seconds later she had gone limp. He continued to hold her up, then dragged her the few steps to his van blocking the driveway. He drove away, with the unconscious Sylvie leaned back in the passenger seat in a sleeping position.

Twenty minutes later Terri stepped down the stairs to see if Sylvie was ready to eat. She did not see Sylvie, and noticed that the van was gone. She hurried back up the stairs and told the group that the van was gone and so was Sylvie. Not certain if the two were connected, Chris decided to call Nico for advice on this new development. Nico assured him everything was probably fine, that he would call him back soon, and to try not to worry.

Debi called her roommates at the Royal Palm. She let them know that Sylvie had gone missing and that she would be spending another night at Villa Islandtude.

Nico called Paul immediately. "I was afraid of that," said Paul. "Call them back and let them know it is being handled. I will call you later. There is nothing further for them to do. They are not to call the police, but let them know everything possible is being done."

Paul called Harrington. "Gregorio, good evening. I hope I'm not catching you at a bad time."

"It's fine Paul. What can I help you with?"

"I have been hired to assist in a transaction with DEP. I have received papers for a transfer of ownership, and would like to schedule a time for your execution. In addition, I have just received word that a shareholder of the acquiring company is temporarily unreachable. Would you have any knowledge about that?"

"Thank you, Paul, for your call. I will be available on Monday to review the papers. As to anyone with the acquiring company, I have no knowledge of how you might best be able to reach them."

"Thank you, Gregorio. I will have the papers delivered on Monday for your signature. If you become aware of any information on the other matter, please reach out to me. The instructions I received were that you were pivotal, and that wherever the acquiring party might be found, you would also be found there shortly thereafter. Have a good evening."

Paul ended the call and called the lead member of his team. "I need information. You had surveillance on the villa. Find out everything and call me back. We need this transaction to be completed."

Sylvie's abductor drove to the small shopping strip where the Red Piano was on one end and the Peli Deli on the opposite end. One of the businesses between the two anchor tenants was closed and undergoing renovation. Sylvie's abductor took her there, and secured her to a chair in the small, closed off office in the back of the store. She was blindfolded and gagged. "Sylvie, I'm sorry for having to bring you here this evening. It is my understanding that this ordeal will be over shortly. Someone should be along soon who will have some questions that he believes you will be able to answer. After you answer his questions, you will be free to go about your business and return to your friends." Sylvie was left in the dark office, and could hear the sound of fading footsteps and a door closing and locking.

While Paul waited to receive a call providing needed information, he decided to call Ben. It was about six o'clock, and Ben and Lauren had returned to his room after a long afternoon on the beach. "Ben, it's Paul. I need to make you aware of a new development. Your friend Sylvie has disappeared. I am organizing a group of potential rescuers. If all goes well, here's what I'll need you to do." Paul gave his instructions to Ben, as Lauren looking on wondered why Ben had suddenly turned pale. Hanging up, Ben relayed Paul's bad news. Ben, upon seeing Lauren was visibly shaken, pulled her to him and gave her a strong, comforting hug.

Samuel left Sylvie locked securely away and returned to his vehicle. Once inside, he placed a call to Robert Vaughn. "You were correct. The white van stopped for the license check was a rental to someone staying at Villa Islandtude in Almond Grove. I was stationed there, and when the van returned, I was successful in securing the missing person. She is sitting in the designated place waiting to answer your questions."

"Well done. There will be nothing further." Vaughn decided to let Sylvie wait for a while secured in the small, dark office. A little waiting time was expected to heighten her anxiety and help her decide to answer his questions. At ten o'clock on Saturday night, Vaughn decided Sylvie had waited long enough. He drove over to the shopping center, unlocked the back office, and found her bound, gagged and sitting blindfolded in the chair as described.

"Good evening, Sylvie. I am so sorry for your inconvenience. I would like to think very shortly we can both put this behind us, and not waste any more time on such a beautiful evening on the island. I apologize for the gag, as I am sure it is uncomfortable, but I don't think either of us would like what happens immediately if you were to scream. Please think of the gag as a life insurance policy for you. Without it, you could possibly forget the rules, and may emit a scream before you remember you were told not to do that. Fortunately for you, you have that gag that is saving your life if you were to be forgetful. If you understand, please nod your head up and down." Sylvie nodded.

"Very good. I believe we have both agreed to the rules for this little game. You will remain blindfolded and gagged for now. For my first question, I would like to know if you are right-handed or left-handed. I am going to ask you the question, and you will either nod up and down or side to side. Sylvie, are you right-handed?" Sylvie nodded in answer.

"That was easy, was it not? Now, I am going to start out nice. You've probably read about interrogation techniques where someone could be injured for failure to answer or for providing incorrect answers. I'm now asking that question. Please nod your head accordingly, are you familiar with interrogation techniques where a bad answer leads to a body part being cut off, such as perhaps a right hand?"

Sylvie froze but nodded yes. "Good, that is very good. I'm now going to leave you for a bit and let you be thinking about that. I want us to get back to our lives, but I also don't want to rush. I've rushed before, and too many hands have been lost unnecessarily. That led me to wonder, if I had let people think about the question longer, would they have saved their hands? So I'm going to step out while you give that some thought. When I come back, we'll see how much you like your hand." Vaughn walked out of the office and locked the door behind him. He hoped it would not be a long night. He returned to his car for a short drive before he would return.

Around eleven that night, Vaughn was back to check on Sylvie. "My dear Sylvie, I hope you have been enjoying the opportunity to consider what will be best for your future. We're going to see if we can keep your right hand attached at the wrist. Does that sound good?" Sylvie nodded. "Excellent, you even responded before I instructed you that you must. I believe you could be a very smart girl, Sylvie."

"Next, I am going to do something very unusual. I am going to get a pen and a pad and bring them to you. I am then going to untie your right hand, but your right arm will be secured from your elbow up to your shoulder. That should allow you to write. Do you understand?" Sylvie again nodded.

"Excellent. We are making very good progress. Hold on as I get the pen and pad for you." Returning with the pen and paper, he placed them in front of her.

"Okay, now I am going to untie your hand. Feel free to wriggle it around. It feels good attached to the wrist, I am sure. Now, here is the pen and the pad is below. Don't worry, you will not be getting a grade on your penmanship. So, here's your first question. Have you been trying to get involved in anybody's business lately?" Sylvie nodded.

"Very good, but we need to follow the rules. We are now going to write our answers. This is a test, would you please write your response?" Sylvie very slowly and shakily wrote the word "yes."

"Excellent, now my next question is this: whose business have you recently attempted to be involved in?"

Sylvie hesitated. She then began to scribble "Gregorio."

"Oh Sylvie, this is going so well. I'm now going to tie your hand down again. There, that's done. I'm going to take back this pad and pen as well. Next, because you've done so well, I believe my allowing you to think a while before continuing has been excellent for both of us. I will be leaving you again for a bit. When I return, we will continue, with you still attached to your hand." Vaughn left and locked the office, returned to his car and again took a ride. He was looking forward to more answers when he returned.

He was not gone long when he returned for additional questioning. He went in the office and locked the door behind him. "Sylvie, I'm back. It's time we make significant progress. I am going to untie your hand and you are going to write the answers to my questions." Vaughn untied her hand and began.

"What type of business do you want from Harrington?"

Sylvie wrote the word "oil."

"Do you know much about the oil business?"

She wrote "no, but know he makes a lot of money in oil."

"Are you doing this on your own, or was this someone else's idea?"

She wrote "it was my idea."

"Why did you have that idea?"

It took her a long time to write her response which was "he stole some oil business. I heard he stole some oil business. I wanted to threaten him that I had heard he was an oil thief."

"Did he get worried that you were threatening him?"

She wrote, "I made initial contact and he tried to kill me. Two men, a gun. I got away and was in hiding. Trying to think how I could try again without being killed."

"Why do you think he stole oil?"

"I was not sure at first. He then tried to have me killed. That convinced me I was right. Now I was going to try to find out more."

"Sylvie, I'm not sure how this information can help me. I think we need a refresher course. I am sure you

would like to keep your hand. What I am going to do next,
I'm going to leave you one final time for you to think what
information you believe you can get, and where it is, and
I'm going to ask you to beg for your life by writing in great
detail how you will help me get this oil." He tied her hand
back down and left for the final time.

FIFTY-NINE

PAUL HEARD FROM his informant. The surveillance of the villa included a description of the vehicle parked in the vicinity and its license tag which was traced. A name and address for the vehicle were provided to Paul.

He was on his way. He passed slowly by the address and saw the white van. Finding a dirt lot several blocks away, he pulled his car well off the road. Hurrying out of his car, he headed back to where the white van was parked. Ten minutes later, Paul had entered the back of the dwelling and soundlessly walked through the house. A nude man was lying on his side in bed, breathing heavily and obviously asleep. Going behind the prone form, Paul applied a choke hold, and very quickly Samuel was rendered unconscious. Paul rolled the man on his stomach, and injected the dose of ketamine into his buttocks to keep him unresponsive for the time needed.

Paul calmly exited the back of the house and returned to his car. He drove to the side of the house and angled behind the van that was parked just off the road. Popping open the trunk, Paul re-entered the house and hoisted the two-hundred-pound dead weight of the man onto his shoulders. Lugging him to his car, he dumped him into the trunk. He drove to the abandoned warehouse and prepared it for his guest. After everything was in place,

Paul returned to the car, opened the trunk and placed a blanket on the ground. Realizing he would have difficulty lifting the man from the awkward position of the trunk, he grabbed and pulled him, easing him down onto the blanket. The man was easily dragged into the warehouse atop the blanket.

Samuel began to regain consciousness. As he did, Paul addressed him. "Good evening. Allow me to update you on your present circumstances. Your hands are tied behind you around a steel support column. You are blindfolded and your head has been taped to the steel column so that you are incapable of moving your head. You are also incapable of speaking as you have been very securely gagged, a rubber ball in your mouth and your mouth taped shut. I recommend you not struggle to try to speak, because you could then suffocate before I could correct your problem. You are facing the corner of a building where you are sitting naked on a concrete floor. The two adjoining walls forming the corner you are facing each contain a very heavy metal hook. Each of your legs is tied and secured to those metal hooks, which has your legs flat to the concrete and spread at a ninety-degree angle. As this registers with you, I'm sure you realize you are in a very vulnerable position."

"I will be asking questions and you will be answering them. You will have five seconds to answer each question. If you delay more than five seconds, you will not be killed, but you will wish you were. I will limit the damage to one body part per your failure to respond quickly and truthfully. As you are very much fully secured and immobile, you are left with three primary body parts which will be severed for bad answers. First, you will lose one testicle, and as you may know, you can recover from that and continue to have a fairly normal life. A second bad answer will result in amputation of your second testicle, which you will so desperately want to hang on to after losing the first. After that, I don't think you'll care what happens next, so additional questions will require an immediate answer before the last slice completes the dismembering."

"I am going to make sure you understand. If you understand what I have said, please clinch your gluteus maximus if you want to keep your cock and balls." Samuel clinched as if his unborn children were riding on it.

"In my haste to tell you what you can expect, I left out one important part. You are located in the corner of an abandoned warehouse. When I remove the gag from your mouth so that you can avoid emasculation, feel free to scream as loud and as long as you like. As I don't have much time, at any point during the scream, I will treat that scream first as one bad answer, then a second bad answer and quickly a third. So, to make sure you understand, even though you won't be heard, I will be thoroughly irritated, and you will immediately lose all your manly parts. If we have an agreement that you will do everything in your power to prevent that from happening, you can now tell me that by clinching your butt muscles and keeping them clinched for a full twenty seconds. You may begin at any time." Samuel clinched and did not stop until he was told he could stop.

Paul ripped the tape from Samuel's mouth and removed the ball gag. "Samuel, who asked you to take Sylvie from her friends? One thousand one. One thousand two."

"Robert Vaughn."

"Good answer. Before my next question, I want you to know that we are not the only living creatures in this warehouse. There are also rats, some of which are the size of a small cat. They may be hungry. So your full cooperation may save your life from those rats. Tell me now where I can find Sylvie."

"If I tell you, you're going to kill me anyway."

"That's a bad answer Samuel." Paul reached into his packet of tools, and pulled out a pair of pliers and a syringe of lidocaine. He fastened the pliers on a testicle and tightened. He then injected lidocaine to simulate the burning of an amputation followed by numbing of the area. Samuel screamed.

"Okay, okay, she's near the Red Piano. It's a building between Red Piano and Peli Deli, in a locked office in the back of the business being renovated."

Paul knew exactly where he was being told. "Samuel, you have one chance. If I get there and she is there and alive, you have my word that I will be back to cut you loose. It will be up to you to explain to others why you are here and how you will get home."

Paul put the ball gag back in Samuel's mouth and taped his mouth shut. He was about ten minutes from the Red Piano.

SIXTY

THE GROUP AT Villa Islandtude was distraught. They had pizza delivered in to eat and limited their drinking to sodas and water. What had started as a great day with an amazing boat trip had ended in disaster. They were trying to think what else could be done. Nico had called back and gave the message that everything that could be done was being done. They were in the helpless position of sitting back and doing nothing, and that was agonizing.

Mark and Dale went down to the vehicles and parked them in the driveway. They were left to pace and keep their phones on for a reassuring call that they hoped would be received very soon.

Ben and Lauren were also sickened over Sylvie's disappearance. They decided they would stay in the area for dinner, and opted to go to the Papatwo for their meal. They watched the other diners and how happy and carefree they all appeared. Ben and Lauren placed their orders, then could barely remember what they requested. The food came and they ate with little discussion during the meal. After eating, they decided to go for a walk on the beach. They walked to the vicinity of La Playa, and Lauren began to cry. Ben wrapped his arms around her as she sobbed into his chest.

"Lauren, I know Sylvie is missing, but we need to be hopeful. Paul sounded very encouraging when he called. He didn't give me instructions if something were to happen to Sylvie. His instructions were to be followed when Sylvie is found. I have confidence that if anyone can find Sylvie, it's Paul."

Lauren's crying slowed to sniffles, and grabbing her hand, they began their walk back to Lubrique. "Lauren, what are you going to do if Sylvie decided she was going partying tonight and didn't tell the others, or she thought she told them, and they didn't hear or misunderstood?"

"I'm going to kill her. I'm going to first give her a huge hug, and then I'm going to kill her. I can't believe she would leave and not tell anybody what she was doing. You don't believe that either, do you?"

"No, under the circumstances, that's hard to believe. But we just don't know what happened yet. Let's stay positive. What should we do when she is safely found and we get together? Do you think we could have a party that's twice as good as the party we had at the villa?"

"Absolutely, Ben! We will have a party that's the party of the decade. I'm ready to get the call to break out the party favors."

Ben and Lauren walked all the way back, went in Ben's room and sat and waited. There would not be much talking and no more walks until they knew what had happened to Sylvie.

SIXTY-ONE

PAUL PREPARED HIMSELF for anything he might find. He had been on rescue missions before, and knew it was critical to minimize any emotional thoughts to maximize the chances for success. Lisa had learned from her time with Paul not to anticipate the worst.

Paul arrived at the shopping strip containing the Red Piano. He tried to assess the situation with Sylvie. The only business open in the strip was the Red Piano. There was no line to get in the bar and no people were standing outside as if taking a fresh air break from the bar. He looked to the back of the building and thought he saw what appeared to be security guards there, but was unaware of the Red Piano ever hiring outside security. He had to proceed as if the muscle was part of Vaughn's team keeping guard on Sylvie. He did not know what torture might be underway inside, but he knew he needed to be careful but act quickly. He decided to go to the front of the Red Piano and move from there as if he were just exiting. He had seen two men who could be guards. He made a show of rounding the corner of the building and stepping into the shadows where both men would see him. He walked near the first man, and bumped him as if by accident. "Sorry buddy," he slurred. "It sure is a big crowd in there tonight. There's even a line a mile long for the men's bathroom." Paul began to unzip his pants, but instead of facing away from the man he had moved close to, he angled his body toward the first guard.

"Hey, buddy, if you gotta go, you need to face away from me. Don't be spraying me."

Paul continued to act as if he was drunk and could not wait for an inside bathroom. "Hey, buddy, yourself." Paul stopped unzipping his pants and acted as if he was becoming irate. "Can't you see that if a man's gotta go, he's gotta go. I don't need no help from you dictating where I go."

The second guard who was watching all of this, started over toward Paul and the first guard. He raised his voice as he walked. "You, moron! What's your problem? You need to learn some manners."

"Oh, I'm terribly sorry sir," Paul responded in a mocking voice. Continuing to direct his words toward the second guard, "I didn't see Captain Crunch over there waiting for his mama. Come on over. You can help me too. You and your buddy can arm wrestle to see who gets the honor of unzipping my pants!"

"Why, you asshole!" yelled the second guard, now running over to Paul and the other guard, closing to within arm's reach.

Paul bowed his head slightly, continuing to act drunk. "Looks like you both afraid you might lose at arm wrestling. Maybe the two of you want to share the honor. Here." Paul continued, thrusting out his pelvis. "Both of you grab hold if you can't stand the thought of waiting your turn. Have at it!"

The two men came in close, both with fists low to punch Paul in the crotch. Paul responded to the opportunity presented, and quickly brought both elbows into each man's nose, crushing their noses and sending them to the pavement. He then kicked each man in the head, totally disabling both. With the guards down, he grabbed their guns and used one to break the small window to the office, and then used the handle to clear the ragged glass remaining in the frame. Paul crawled through the window and stepped inside. Even in the dark, he could tell that Sylvie was still alive. He untied her hands, allowing her to free her eyes and mouth, while he freed her ankles. "We're going out the front door. It's safer that way. If there's trouble, we're going into the Red Piano."

They reached the front door and exited. Sylvie could barely walk, and Paul wanted to carry her, but knew that would attract attention. Instead, he put his arm around her and steadied and half carried her to his car. They were in his car and leaving.

"Are you okay? You look like you'll be fine."

"Yes, I'm a mess. He wouldn't let me go. He wouldn't untie me."

"It's okay, you're safe now. I'm taking you somewhere you can get cleaned up. We'll make calls on the way."

Paul's first call was to Chris. "She's fine, but she's not coming back to the villa. Tell everyone to celebrate and we'll be in touch." He hung up the call.

He next called Nico. "She's fine. Be prepared to enact the plan we discussed. Will call you when I know more."

Paul then placed a third call. "She's fine, just shaken up. You and Lauren are about to have company. She will be staying in your room tonight with you and Lauren. We'll be there soon." With that last call completed, Paul focused his thoughts on the next part of his plan.

Lauren heard Paul and could not believe the wonderful news. She was excited to welcome Sylvie home. The early morning news was the new highlight of the trip.

SIXTY-TWO

EVERYONE WAS DANCING for joy at Villa Islandtude. All were exhausted, and the news brought a flood of relief, and also a realization of how tired they were. They knew it would not last long, but they had no choice but to celebrate. They all gathered in the entertainment room, and Chris and Paulie served everyone their favorite drink. There were several toasts, and they all tried to squeeze into one big selfie. The prospect of no sleep had improved to potentially about five hours of sleep.

Tammy searched the Bose music box for Egyptian music, challenging everyone to a belly dancing contest. Without finding appropriate music, they settled on sounds of the 1970s. There was a men's category and a women's category. The women were the judges of the men, and the men the judges of the women. After much laughter and an array of awkward body contortions, Chris was crowned the men's belly dancing champion of Villa Islandtude, with the warning that he would be challenged for the title on their next stay in St. Maarten.

Tammy was the favorite going into the women's competition, primarily based on it being her idea. She gyrated herself into first place for the ladies. Cell phones came out for a short video made of the two belly dancing champions showing off their winning form. The video was quickly uploaded and sent to Sylvie's phone along with their expressions of relief and their plan to see her very soon.

The next competition was to be for the villa limbo championship. They did not have a limbo stick, so tried using a pool float to limbo under. The limbo competition moved to the pool deck. Everyone completed the first round with the float held at shoulder height. The second round saw the float dropped to halfway between the shoulder and waist. That knocked the competition down to just three contestants, Dale, Jeanne and Catherine. Dale started talking limbo smack and said he would go first. "Ladies, watch me dance my way under the float! Enjoy!" With the float held at waist height, "ChippenDale" as he wanted to be called, just made it under the float, rubbing the top of his head on the float as he passed. "Catherine the Great" was next, and cleared her head by a wide margin, with it dropping below her shoulders. Instead of her head being the body part to rub against the underside of the float, it was her breasts. When she cleared the other side of the float, she exclaimed, "If I'd been wearing a bra, I would have never made it!" The third remaining contestant was Jeanne. "I Dream of Jeanne" named Chris her limbo master. She claimed she had emerged in a puff of smoke from the flower vase she gripped in her butt cheeks as she emerged to the other side of the float. Everyone was having a great time, and all three were named as winners of the "Thrilla in the Villa".

Tammy, Chris, Jeanne, Catherine and Dale were the first team All-Americans. It was time to name a Most Valuable Player. The winner of the MVP award would be the person who could carry a plastic plate the length of the pool without touching the plate with one's hands. Chris was the first contestant. He struggled to grip the plate by stepping on its edge, then capturing it between his calves,

It took just over two minutes for him to penguin-walk the plate to the far end of the pool.

Jeanne was next, picking the plate up quickly with her toes, then going down to clasp the plate with her knees. She shaved thirty seconds off Chris's time.

Third up was Catherine. She copied Jeanne's toe technique for her start, but flipped the plate and caught it with her mid-section. She then leaned her body back until her body was supported by her feet in front and her hands behind. She crab-walked the plate across the finish line in a contested time similar to that of Jeanne.

Fourth was ChippenDale. He learned from the prior contestants and was quick to grasp the plate with his toes, flipped it up much as Catherine had done, and caught it on his stomach. He leaned back into the limbo position and danced the plate over the finish line, the first contestant to break the minute mark.

The last contestant, but definitely not the least contestant, was Tammy. She stepped to the starting line full of confidence. When the timer began, she stepped on one edge of the plate to lift one side eight inches off the floor. She then leaned over at the waist, engulfed the plate between her breasts, and used her hands on the outside of her MVP winning assets to easily finish the length of the pool in thirty seconds. The MVP was crowned. The four runners up went to their knees and bowed to Tammy with outstretched hands for the MVP victory photo.

With the conclusion of the poolside Olympics, the proper atmosphere of frivolity had been restored at Villa Islandtude. Now thoroughly fatigued, everyone went to bed and fell quickly asleep after saying prayers of thanks for the safe return of their dear friend.

SIXTY-THREE

....

WHEN PAUL AND Sylvie reached Ben's room, Lauren flung the door open and enveloped Sylvie into her outstretched arms. They stood together in a tight hug for several seconds. Lauren released Sylvie and led her into the bathroom shower. She sat on the edge of the bathtub, keeping her company as the shower washed away the horrible violation of the kidnapping.

Paul hurriedly left, saying he had another errand, and that he would call Ben later. Paul quickly drove to the warehouse where Samuel was immobilized on the concrete floor. He injected another dose of ketamine and released him from the support column. The tape, rope and gag were gathered and thrown into an outside commercial dumpster. Paul scooped the man back onto his shoulders, returned to his car and once again tossed him in the trunk. He returned for the blanket and threw it in the trunk with Samuel. Paul was getting very tired but it was necessary to complete the mission. He drove to Samuel's house, returning Samuel to his bed. Paul put the blanket in the car, and as he drove to his home, tossed the blanket out the window where someone would find it and be able to use it. He arrived back at his home, and within five minutes was sleeping the sleep of the dead.

As Paul was returning Samuel's life back to normal, Sylvie was stepping out of her long, hot shower. She dried and wrapped herself tightly in a towel. She and Lauren walked out into the sitting area of the room. Knowing she had not eaten for hours, Ben made her a sandwich and brought her a bottle of water. Grateful, Sylvie sat at the small table and ate.

"You're staying here tonight. You, Lauren and I will be safe here. Tomorrow we will execute the plan we discussed that will keep you safe. We'll wait for Nico to call to say when it will begin. I'm sure everything will be coordinated with Terri as we get underway."

Sylvie finished her sandwich, then stood looking at Ben and Lauren. Words were not needed, and Ben walked over to her and gave her a huge hug. They stayed like that for an extended time.

Lauren was next and spoke in a comforting tone. "Sylvie, I think we should go to bed now. Are you ready to go to sleep yet?"

"Yes, I'm exhausted. I'm feeling more like my old self. The shower and food were a big help. I think after I get a few hours of sleep, I'll be good as new."

"You girls take the bed. I'll be here on the sofa. Everything is safe here now. The door is locked as is the deadbolt. If you need anything, just let me know. We can all sleep well tonight."

Ben turned out the lights and walked over to the sofa. Sylvie and Lauren snuggled close and sleep finally came.

SIXTY-FOUR

THERE WAS ACTIVITY early at Villa Islandtude. Terri was eager to get in touch with Sylvie. She did not want to risk waking Sylvie with a phone call, but could not resist sending a text message asking Sylvie to call when she was awake.

By now, everyone in the villa was awake and still feeling the excitement from finding out Sylvie was safe. The group congregated poolside, and at seven o'clock they were ready for the ten-minute drive to the Croissanterie in the Marigot Marina Royale. The open-air restaurant had become a favorite of the Florida tourists. They walked up the steps and took a long table along the shaded waterfront. Everyone's appetite had returned after the good news of Sylvie's safety and the hard-fought poolside events from the night before. Tammy was wearing her sun visor with the series of triangles cut from a sheet of paper and inserted in the band to represent her championship crown. Everyone continued to enjoy the silliness that was generated by the group.

Bacon, eggs, pancakes, French toast, and ham, egg and cheese croissants were the primary meals. They were followed with chocolate croissants and raisin bread as lighter dessert items. After breakfast, all ten friends overwhelmed the shop next door, Boutique Ananas, with purchases of scented soaps and pareos for everyone. All ten wrapped a pareo over their clothes and had a fellow shopper snap a picture of their shopping conquests.

They were ready to go back to Villa Islandtude to plan their day. At the villa, they put away their newly acquired purchases and went poolside to relax in the lounge chairs.

At the same time the Islandtude group prepared to eat their breakfast, Ben was already up and showering, getting ready for the day's events. After showering, he stepped over to the bed and gently kissed Lauren on the forehead. She stirred as he continued to pepper her face with small, gentle kisses. Smiling, she murmured, "This is the second time I've had your wake-up service with kisses. What a great way to start the day." She reached up and hugged Ben, who was sitting atop the bed sheet. They stayed like that for a minute before Ben stood to look out the window to the bright morning.

Sylvie began to stir and sitting up, she smiled at Ben standing in the incoming sunlight. "Wow, my Knight in shining sunlight! It's not the same as being awakened by kisses, but I am enjoying the view!" It was obvious that Sylvie had recovered from her ordeal and was exhibiting her normal personality.

"Why thank you, Miss! Flattery will get you a long way with me. How did you sleep?"

"Like a rock. It was perfect. Thank you both for taking me in. As good as it was, I'm guessing I won't be sharing your bed again tonight."

Now that Lauren was fully awake, she was hungry. "Ben, do you think we could all step out to Papatwo for breakfast this morning? Or do you think that would be too risky?"

"I think it's a risk we can take. I don't know that anyone would still be looking for Sylvie at her place, but even if they are, they can't be everywhere. I don't think anyone would specifically be looking for her at breakfast at Papatwo. Let's try to have a normal breakfast as much as a man can in the company of two beautiful women."

Sylvie and Lauren got out of bed. "Sylvie, I have some pareos. Let's each of us wear one to breakfast."

"That sounds great." Sylvie looked through the pareos, chose one, and Lauren helped fashion a dress of it on Sylvie. Lauren chose her pareo and Sylvie secured it on Lauren. Ben took this opportunity to get dressed, grabbing some shorts and a collared shirt. "I thought I'd better step it up beyond a t-shirt this morning if I'm going to be seen with you two! You look great! Let's go."

The three of them walked barefoot the short distance to the Papatwo. They sat at a table and enjoyed the magnificent view of Orient Bay. "This is a beautiful place. I'm so glad I happened to come to St. Martin for my vacation," said Lauren. "This is a great way to start the day!"

"I should call Terri when we get back to the room. I'd like to hear her voice. She's been a great roommate through this ordeal. I'm sure she's awake. But first I just want to breathe this ocean air and enjoy still being a small part of creation here."

Their breakfast order came quickly, and with being in close proximity to Ben's room, they were back in his room in thirty minutes. Sylvie checked her phone and saw she had a message from Terri and called her back.

"Oh Sylvie, it is so good to hear you this morning! I'm so sorry for what you went through. Are you okay?"

"Yes, now I'm fine. It was something of a blur, and I'm putting it in the past. I don't know all the details, but Paul was amazing. I was left tied up, blindfolded and gagged. Somehow, just in time, he found where they had taken me and brought me to Lauren and Ben's place. He was amazing!"

"What would you think of me coming over there this morning? I could bring some toiletries to you and we could hang out there if it's okay with Ben and Lauren."

Sylvie looked at Ben and Lauren for a response. Ben shrugged his shoulders as if he was indifferent, or was not sure if that was a good idea, while Lauren was nodding that it was. "It looks like it would probably be okay, but you have to be very careful and make sure no one is following you. You probably won't be able to have a carefree day like you could staying with everybody at Islandtude. What do you want to do?"

"I'm going to ask somebody to drive me over and I'll see you in thirty minutes!"

Debi agreed to drive Terri over as she planned to go to the Royal Palm after dropping Terri by Ben's room. Debi gathered her belongings and the girls hopped in Debi's car for the drive to Orient Beach.

"It will be great to see them," began Debi. "It's such a great beach. In fact, Orient is by far my favorite beach. Instead of me going back to the Royal Palm, do you think we could hang out on the beach for a while after we visit with Sylvie, or maybe hang out with her at the beach, also? I don't want to do anything crazy, but it would be fun if everybody approves."

"I would love it! I agree. I sure don't want to do anything that might put Sylvie at risk. Let's just see how everything goes once we get there."

Debi drove her fastest and continued to glance in her rear-view mirror as a precautionary measure. They pulled into Orient Beach in record time. They went to Ben's room, knocked on the door, and a hugging celebration immediately followed. They all sat inside, on the bed and couch, and the five had animated discussion.

Debi looked at Ben. "We want to go out on the beach for a while. Do you think it would be okay?"

"I'm expecting Nico to call any time. When he does, we'll need to spring into action for the next stage in keeping Sylvie safe. If you have Sylvie with you at the beach, you definitely should not venture beyond this resort and you need to be low key. It would be crazy to walk down toward La Playa. I wouldn't think anyone would expect Sylvie to break free and then go where they've been waiting for her to return, but I also think it's a good possibility that someone is still watching her room at La Playa."

Debi responded, "That sounds reasonable to me. Girls, do you want to join me on Orient Beach? It's a beautiful morning, and I can't think of a better way to spend it than sunning with friends on Orient."

Terri, Sylvie and Lauren were all wanting to get on the beach, and were not letting Ben's caution dampen their spirits or plans for the sunshine on the beach.

Debi continued to speak for the girls. "Ben, do you have towels we can use?"

"Yes, I'll get you each a towel. I might join you in a bit, because I know that with you staying on the resort grounds, I'll have no trouble finding you," he warned.

"Yes sir, heard loud and clear. You have our full agreement to not walk down the beach."

With that, Ben went to get beach towels. "Here you go. One for you, Lauren. One for you, Debi. One for you Terri, and one for you, Sylvie. Have fun, and remember, stay alert. I wouldn't think anyone would try to do anything crazy like kidnap you off the beach, but let's pay attention and make sure."

"Done. Girls it's time to get ready to hit the beach." Debi began, peeling off her clothes and placing them neatly on the bed. She then wrapped herself in her towel. "Are you girls going to get ready and join me?"

The others shucked their cares and disrobed in like fashion, with four small piles of clothes laid out on the bed. "Let's go," said Lauren. With that, the four girls left the safety of the room and moved to the beach. They came to the opening where no chairs were set out, removed their towels and laid them in the sand. They sat on their towels laughing and talking, and any tension slowly slipped away. For the moment, life on Orient Beach had returned to normal.

SIXTY-FIVE

....

THE GIRLS HAD been on the beach for an hour when Ben got the call from Nico. "Ben, I've heard from Paul. He's recovered from his activities of last night and this morning. Today he'll be working on the financial documents and getting the people needed on the legal documents for Sylvie. While he's working that, it's time for us to get started. Is everybody still on board?"

"Yes, we've been expecting this call. I'll round up Sylvie and Lauren and we'll start next steps in about fifteen minutes." They hung up and Ben walked out to the beach, where the girls were all on their stomachs soaking up the sun. Ben sat in the sand next to Lauren. "I just got the call from Nico. It's time to get this show on the road. I'm sorry to break up the party, but it's time. Terri, do you want to go with Sylvie?"

"Yes, definitely, I'll be ready."

"Okay, let's all go in. Once inside, Debi, you should give your goodbyes to Sylvie and Terri. You're welcome to hang out on the beach if you'd like, I see no risk to you going forward."

"Lauren, as was agreed, you and I will drive to Terri and Sylvie's place, we'll go in and you'll throw their items in their bags. We can put them in the trunk of the car. Next, we'll come back to my room, where you and I will go in to get their items from the safe. Then the four of us will get the heck out of here as fast as we can. Is everybody in agreement?" Nodding in agreement, the girls stood up, shaking the sand out of their towels. Back in Ben's room, Lauren quickly dressed and she and Ben left the others to say their goodbyes.

Ben drove and parked behind La Playa. Running up the stairs and into the room, Lauren quickly threw everything into the carry bags. Ben made one final walk-through of the unit making sure nothing was left behind. Ben carried the bags and placed them in the trunk. They quickly drove back to his room, locked the car, and went inside. Debi was gone and Terri was dressed. Sylvie wanted her bag, so Ben went back and grabbed both bags, not knowing if the items were separated by owner or which bag belonged to whom. The girls opened the bags, Sylvie grabbing an outfit and dressing quickly, while Ben opened the safe. Everything given to Ben from Sylvie and Terri was there. Ben took the items and handed them to the girls to put in their bags. They all huddled for one final hug and hurried out the door to the car, with Ben following behind carrying the bags.

It was a short drive to Simpson Bay Marina. Ben glanced in the rear-view mirror occasionally but did not spot anyone following them. He was not sure if he would recognize a tail if there was one. But to be safe, the plan included the possibility of being followed. Nico was on his boat, ready and waiting. The girls hurried to the dock while Ben was a few steps behind with the bags. Once everyone was on board and seated, Ben untied the lines, and they were off.

The plan was for Nico to go out about sixty miles, or one hundred kilometers. They would attempt to make an at-sea transfer of Sylvie and Terri onto a sailboat. An at-sea transfer was thought to minimize chances of Sylvie and Terri being followed or found. The transfer well off-shore was also to prevent the slower sailboat from being overtaken if leaving from St. Martin. After a successful transfer to the sailboat, that boat would continue the next sixty miles to St. Thomas. With favorable seas they could arrive in St. Thomas before midnight. Customs would be closed but would be open at eight o'clock the next morning. Sylvie and Terri could go through customs in St. Thomas on Monday and fly home from there.

Everyone was hopeful with the plan. They were leaving at noon and expected to be at the designated transfer spot around three o'clock. As Nico drove, Ben, Lauren, Sylvie and Terri had a snack lunch packed earlier by Nico, and washed their lunch down with sodas. They were enjoying the fast speed of the boat as it headed out to sea.

At one o'clock they were making good time and had covered almost half of the designated distance. They should be at the drop-off point early.

"Ben," said Sylvie, "in a little over an hour, Terri and I will be leaving to go home. If I have anything to do with it, I will be seeing you guys again, and hopefully soon. I have everyone's contact information and will be getting in touch. I reached an agreement in principle with Gregorio, and Paul is handling all the details. The papers are to be presented on Monday, and if all goes well, the transfers will be authorized that day. I've worked out a deal with Debi, who through her connection on island, will have money for me in an account that I can then use freely. I plan to share with everyone who has helped me. I will never forget how so many people came to my rescue."

Lauren responded before Ben. "Sylvie, you've become a very close friend, and this adventure of yours will probably make this the most memorable vacation I'll have in my lifetime. I'm not sure when I'll be able to get away from the U.S. again, but hope to see you soon. And to see you again soon, too, Terri. I want to say our goodbyes now, because when it's time for the transfer, I don't want to hold it up."

The three girls hugged, teary-eyed but smiling. Ben sat back quietly, thinking nothing further needed to be said. He was eager to have Sylvie and Terri safely off the boat and head back to St. Martin.

At two-twenty in the afternoon, Nico had reached the meet-up spot. They could see the sailboat, Eclipse, that they were meeting, about five minutes in the distance. Sylvie and Terri secured their life jackets, readying themselves for the transfer. As they came closer, the two handsome men aboard Eclipse waved to those on the power boat. The bumpers were put out on both boats, and instead of each gearing to neutral, Nico's boat throttled down to a slow idle speed to match the speed of Eclipse. The transfer sounded as if it would be easy in the plan, but the movement of the boats and the unsteadiness in the waves was scary. Neither Sylvie nor Terri felt comfortable trying to make the dangerous move to the sailboat. The sailboat's captain shouted out to them. "It's okay, I have a line. I'll secure it at the stern and put the ladder down. I'll toss the line to each of you, you'll secure it under your arms, and we'll pull you on board. The tricky part is going to be when you try to come up the ladder. I'll time the waves and position the boat to minimize any movement, and we'll haul you up when you reach the ladder.

While they were close, Ben tossed the bags over to the two men. Turning to Sylvie and Terri he said, "Okay girls, let's do this."

With Ben's help, Sylvie secured the line under her arms, and as the boats drifted a little further apart, she jumped in. She was quickly hauled aboard. Terri went next, following Sylvie's actions and was brought aboard as well. The leap of faith taken by Sylvie and Terri into a boat with two strange men was now complete.

Sylvie and Terri sat down in the sailboat and removed the line and the life jackets. They turned to wave to Nico, Ben and Lauren as the boat turned to head back to St. Maarten. Now, it was time for the formal introductions. The captain started. "Welcome aboard. We plan to be in St. Thomas before midnight. I'm Brad. The gentleman with me is also an accomplished sailor, when he's not helping people with their smiles. He's a dentist when he can't be out on the water."

"Good to meet you both. I'm Keith. I hope this will be a great sail to St. Thomas."

Sylvie and Terri smiled, and looking at the two handsome sailors was a welcomed distraction from the sadness of having to leave their St. Martin friends. They were confident that they would enjoy the sail into St. Thomas. The distance between them and their former boat mates grew quickly as Eclipse moved further away from St. Martin.

Nico was captaining Lauren and Ben quickly back to the dock at Simpson Bay Marina. Everyone had a long, somewhat stressful day and was sleep deprived.

"Nico, thanks for all you've done this past week. You've been an amazing friend. Could we please take you to dinner tonight to celebrate?"

"That sounds good to me. I have plans to have dinner with Jenny, but I'm sure she would be happy if we could have dinner with you two."

"Great," added Lauren. "I would like to get back, get cleaned up, and then maybe we can meet for dinner around seven-thirty. I'm starving and I think we need a fitting feast."

The boat was back at five-thirty, and Ben helped Nico wash it down and flushed the engine with fresh water. Lauren and Ben left to drive back to Orient. They would quickly get cleaned up to make their seven-thirty dinner date. The decision was made to go to Izi Ristorant Italiano in Simpson Bay. The thought of an inside meal of hearty food was especially appealing.

David, the owner of Izi, had a special table already prepared for his friend Nico, and the four friends were quickly greeted by their food server. It was a fitting meal for the end of such a successful day, starting with bruschetta and Caprese for appetizers. Their entrees were generous portions of homemade pasta dishes and finished with the award-winning tiramisu for dessert. Several bottles of wine were consumed, and the meal was a major success. Ben and Lauren added Izi as one of the restaurants they would highly recommend on St. Maarten.

It was after ten o'clock when Ben and Lauren left Izi. Lauren was falling asleep on the drive back. When they were at the resort, Ben walked Lauren to her room, and went inside to visit for only a few minutes. It was at that point that they decided they were both desperate for sleep. Holding her tight and kissing her goodnight, it was time for Ben to go back to his room. With the long day behind them and their appetite sated, they both slept soundly through the night.

SIXTY-SIX

DEBI DECIDED TO sun on Orient Beach after her friends left for their boat trip. She placed her towel back on the sand and not too long after, she met Kris and Larry. They normally were found at Cupecoy Beach, but the sand had disappeared there and was a beach mostly of rock instead of sand. Kris and Larry set towels down next to Debi and were set for a day of swimming and sunning. Kris was very outgoing, and shared with Debi that when not vacationing, she was a nurse in Michigan. For the most part, Larry was quiet and let Kris do most of the talking. They were an attractive couple who were both animal lovers, and were active on the island with helping feed and care for stray dogs and cats.

"Larry, do you want to dip in with me? After we splash around for a while, maybe we can go get a bite of lunch somewhere. Debi, would you join us for lunch? We'd really enjoy your company."

Debi readily agreed and stepped into the water with them. Debi was eager to hear from Lauren that all had gone well with Sylvie's and Terri's escape. She decided to step out of the water to call Jodi. "Jodi, good morning, what have you got planned for the day?"

"Karen is going to Cupecoy, and Jan and I are driving over to Orient. Where are you?"

321

"That's great! I'm at Orient now. I'm where the old Pedro's used to be. Park in the last lot before Le Galion Beach and come on down."

"Sounds fun. We'll be there in five minutes!"

Debi stood at her towel and waited for her friends. Jodi and Jan spotted her and rushed down to meet her. "I'm so glad you came to Orient. I have so much to tell you. The boat trip around the island yesterday was amazing. We had some great stops, one was at Tintamarre, and another at Cupecoy for lunch. I saw Karen and Rick there. Then when we came back to the villa, a van had partially blocked the driveway. We parked on the road and went inside, but someone called to Sylvie and she stayed down to talk. A little later, we checked on her and she was gone, and so was the van. It was awful. It became the worst night ever, but very late, actually early this morning, we got a call that all was well, and had a huge celebration. I've got a new appreciation for how special every day is."

"What a roller coaster that was," replied Jodi. "We had a quiet day, but it's great to be with you now. Are you planning on being with us the rest of the day? What about tonight? Do you have plans?"

"I have no plans. After the beach today, I'd like to eat with you tonight. Do you know what Karen has planned?"

"We're pretty sure she's going to be with Rick for dinner again tonight. Between the two of you, we're averaging seeing just one of you on the vacation."

"Well, things are going better with Dean. I told Karen, but haven't told you. I'm guessing she told you all about it. I'll be around tonight, but if things go as I hope, I will probably be eating with Dean tomorrow night. We have some catching up to do. I'm thinking we will be doing a lot of celebrating. By Tuesday morning, I think he'll be completely reassured that he made his best decision!"

Jodi and Jan shook their heads and rolled their eyes. "Somehow, I don't doubt you," Jodi responded. "I'm glad you're having such a good time. Whose towels are these?"

"Those are Larry's and Kris's. I met them a little while ago. They're in the water now." She nodded her head to them. "They're nice. Set your towels down. We're thinking of getting some lunch in a bit if you'll join us."

Jodi and Jan set their towels down, removed their coverups, and laid back in the sand. When Kris and Larry came back to their towels, introductions were made, and as typical on Orient Beach, new treasured friendships were started. After lunch, they all traded contact information so they could stay in touch. They talked about different people on the island that the others might know. Debi mentioned Robert Vaughn's name, but withheld that Dean was doing business with him. At the mention of his name, both Kris and Larry had sour looks on their faces.

"He's not a good man. Larry did some work for him once. As he found out more about him, Larry decided he didn't want to work for him any more after the contracted project was finished. My recommendation is you should steer clear of him. Bad stuff happens around him."

Debi took note of the warning. It was especially chilling in that, although she had just met Kris and Larry, she believed that they were two of the most kind and loving people she had ever known. For Kris to say something so negative about Vaughn, Debi believed her and was certain it was not just general complaining, but was intended as a specific warning. She would definitely mention it to Dean. Dean certainly knew Vaughn was not a good person, and knew he should take extra precautions in dealing with him.

The afternoon sunning time was coming to an end at Orient and Kris and Larry packed up to leave the beach. Debi, Jan and Jodi dipped into the refreshing water one

last time, then laid out for the sun to dry them. After
thirty minutes they were packed and driving to the Royal
Palm. When they arrived, they started to get cleaned up
for dinner. Debi's cell phone rang. "Debi, it's Lauren.
Ben and I are back and Sylvie and Terri are safely away. I
want you to know not to expect to hear from them until at
least tomorrow, but I don't want you to worry. Just know
everything is good and I 'm sure Sylvie will reach out to
you when she can."

"Thanks for the update. When I do hear, I'm guessing
Sylvie will have a lot of interesting new stories."

Later that night, Debi, Jodi and Jan had a rare dinner and evening together. Debi welcomed the quiet night
with her friends as she anticipated her meeting with Dean
the next day.

SIXTY-SEVEN

THE AFTERNOON SUN was warm and welcoming aboard Eclipse. Seventy miles from St. Martin, Brad and Keith maintained a formal demeaner. They wanted their guests to have confidence in the safety of their sailing abilities.

"Keith can show you around and get you towels to dry off. Keith, do you want to give them a tour?" Brad called out. "Take a look around and relax. It will be an easy sail into St. Thomas. Make yourselves at home and move about freely. I'm hoping we're there before midnight."

Keith had towels and handed them to Terri and Sylvie. He seemed especially interested in Terri. The girls wrapped the towels around themselves and followed Keith for the tour. It was a beautiful sailboat. Sylvie was thinking she could be happy living on a sailboat, and Brad could be a great captain. She smiled to herself at the thought as they finished the tour.

"Terri, this is great. Let's get changed out of these wet clothes and then we can go back up." Keith left them in the cabin to change.

Keith rejoined Brad at the helm. "Those are two beautiful ladies. We've done some crazy things in our day, but an ocean rescue of two beautiful ladies has to rank up toward the top. Maybe not one of the craziest, but definitely one of the best."

Laughing, Brad agreed. The girls returned in skimpy bikinis. Brad chose to engage the autopilot and released the helm. He joined Keith in greeting the girls.

"This is one spectacular sailboat," marveled Sylvie. "If there's nothing we should do, we're thinking of laying out in the sun for a while until we get closer to sunset."

Brad and Keith sat with the girls as they placed their towels down and laid on their stomachs. Sylvie raised her head to continue talking. "What a beautiful, peaceful day. It's great to feel as if one with the sea." The girls untied their tops to keep their backs tan line free, but remained covered on their stomachs.

"Would you girls like something to drink?" asked Brad.

"That sounds great," responded Sylvie. "Terri, are you thirsty?"

"Something to drink would be great, thanks. I can help or can get it, though. We don't expect you guys to rescue us and then serve us, too."

"It's all part of the deal. We'll get it, so what would you like?" asked Keith.

"Anything is good with me. Surprise me. What about you, Sylvie. Any requests?"

"No, anything is fine. Brad, let me help. I can at least serve the drinks." She sat up and got to her feet. "Show me the way."

Brad grinned a very happy grin. "This way. Keith and Terri, we'll be back in a few minutes." They went inside and Sylvie helped Brad mix up some Painkillers for everyone. They each walked out with two drinks in hand. Terri was already sitting, anxious for the cold drink of rum, pineapple juice, orange juice, cream of coconut and a little nutmeg. They enjoyed drinking the Painkillers and the girls told of their vacation's activities, leaving out all that pertained to Harrington and Sylvie's abduction. They finished their drinks quickly.

"Terri, now that I know where everything is and how to make Painkillers, why don't you and I make the next round?" Sylvie grabbed her bikini top from the deck and stood with top in hand to make the next round. Terri did likewise and followed Sylvie into the galley.

Once inside, the girls compared notes as they prepared the potent drinks. "Terri, it is obvious that Keith is very attracted to you. They both seem like great guys and I feel very safe with them."

"Yes, me too. I'm glad Keith seems to like me. It's interesting that he's a dentist. He can check out my smile anytime. It looks like you and Brad might be exchanging looks for each other as well. This could be a spectacular ending to a special Caribbean vacation."

They laughed and finished making the drinks. "Terri, I guess we can put our tops in our bags before we go back up. I don't think we'll need them until we get much closer to St. Thomas." Sylvie reached for her bag and placed her top just inside. She paused, grinned mischievously, and slipped her bottoms down. She placed the bottoms in her bag with the top. She looked at Terri.

"Well, I can't have you going back out there like that by yourself." She followed Sylvie's lead and stowed her suit in her bag. "Okay, I'm ready. I think we're ready to serve the drinks!"

Each girl carried two drinks. They were greeted with wide-eyed appreciation. Neither Brad nor Keith mentioned the disappearance of the suits. Brad and Keith accepted the drinks and pretended as if they did not notice their lack of clothing. Sylvie and Terri carried the conversation for the next few minutes while Brad and Keith adjusted to the wonderment of sitting with their beautiful and uninhibited guests.

Brad asked Sylvie if she'd like to try her hand at taking the wheel of the sailboat. Sylvie enthusiastically agreed to join Brad at the helm. Once separated as couples, all formality by Brad and Keith ended. They remained respectful of the girls, but were eager to move their new relationships forward. Around five-thirty they gathered in anticipation of viewing the upcoming sunset. Closer to six o'clock the sun began setting, and the temperature was dropping in the breeze on the boat. Sylvie and Terri retreated to select coverups to fend off the slight night chill. They returned to Brad and Keith, and Sylvie greeted Brad with a kiss.

"That was a beautiful sunset and you two have been complete gentlemen. You've made us feel very comfortable with you out here in the ocean." Sylvie stopped talking and again kissed Brad, and he returned the light kiss.

"I'm very glad Nico is a friend and reached out to us." Brad continued, "I don't know the full story of what's been going on, but I'm glad we were asked to help. We were happy to do it. Nico gave no real details or a description of who we'd be taking on as passengers. I never imagined something that started out as a good deed could be such a wonderful thing for me. I hope this does not have to end after we've reached St. Thomas."

Terri and Keith remained silent, but Terri took the pause after the professions of Brad and Sylvie as the perfect time to plant a kiss on Keith. Terri's kiss was enthusiastically received.

The two new couples sailed dreamily to St. Thomas, anchoring approaching midnight. Customs would not open until eight o'clock Monday morning. They would not be able to step foot in St. Thomas until they had been cleared by customs. No one on board the sailboat was displeased with the wait.

SIXTY-EIGHT

IT WAS MONDAY morning and Paul had completed the papers needed to facilitate Sylvie's transaction with Harrington. He had established the company that would be taking possession of DEP. The company would also recognize the immediate sum of six million dollars in revenues. Although it was only seven o'clock, he knew Harrington was an early riser and began work as early as six.

Paul called Harrington. "Good morning, Gregorio. It's Paul. How are you today?"

"I'm fine Paul, how can I help you?"

"First, I'd like to update you following our prior discussion. I am pleased to share that the majority shareholder of the corporation taking possession of DEP has been located and all is well. My client is eager to complete the agreed upon transaction. The papers for your signature are complete. I am sending them to you electronically as we speak."

Paul paused briefly for Harrington to have an opportunity to respond. When he remained silent, Paul continued. "We are expecting the transaction to be completed today. I would appreciate your signature and return of the documents as quickly as possible. It is my understanding that a pressing deadline is in place, and that the business dealings that you and my client expect to continue will be jeopardized gravely if all documents are not in place at the close of business today. I do understand that this is exceedingly quick, and not typical in any way. My understanding, however, is that you have agreed to this incredibly short deadline to prevent any further impact on continuing operations. Do I have your assurance that your review will be completed swiftly and that any minor details of concern will be resolved prior to day's end?"

"There is an agreement, and I am prepared to maintain my obligation. With that said, let me emphasize for you to communicate very clearly with your client. Although this transaction will be completed as agreed, any additional thoughts or attempts to, shall we say, sweeten the deal, will be dealt with swiftly and harshly. Am I making myself clear?"

"Yes, Gregorio, your candor and cooperation are both understood and appreciated. You may rest assured that there will be no discussion with any outside parties. You have the utmost respect from my client, and there will be no actions taken by my client that will create any hardship for you, or for my client."

"Very well, I will look at the papers shortly and this matter will be put in the past."

"On another matter, if I may be so bold as to take up more of your time, there is a group that has questions about someone thought to be an associate of yours. Are you familiar with Robert Vaughn?"

"I am familiar with Mr. Vaughn, but it would be an extraordinary exaggeration for him to be considered as my associate. With that said, how might I be able to help you regarding Mr. Vaughn?"

"Mr. Vaughn has made a very unfavorable impression on a group I represent. His business practices have been extreme and unacceptable. The desire expressed is for Mr. Vaughn to cease all business operations in French St. Martin and Dutch St. Maarten. Are you in a position to reach out to Mr. Vaughn and express the need for his operations on island to be relocated outside of the Netherlands Antilles?"

"I believe I can help you with that. In return for that help, would it be appropriate for your group to direct future business to me? That, along with a recognition that when there is a future opportunity to help me, that I can reach out to you, as representing your, umm, group, and I can expect favorable consideration?"

"You have my personal promise, Gregorio, and if I can be of service on a future matter, you should not hesitate to contact me."

"Thank you, Paul. I am eager to complete the current transaction based upon your assurances."

Harrington ended the call with Paul. He dialed Baldo. "We have a new project. Undoubtedly, Mr. Robert Vaughn has stepped out of line. I believe he was attempting to infiltrate my businesses. That activity cannot be tolerated. My request is for this matter to be resolved before the sun rises tomorrow. Will you be able to take care of that piece of business for me?"

"You can consider it done. You will receive confirmation that the project has been completed tomorrow morning."

"Thank you Baldo, I appreciate your loyalty."

Harrington hung up, the day taking a positive turn. Although he would be losing a small business share to Sylvie, he would be cleared to more than offset that loss. Of greater value, he was assured that he had kept Paul from becoming an enemy.

Harrington opened the attachments and quickly reviewed them. He had several changes that he wanted and marked the minor edits, initialing each of the changes. He signed and returned the executed document via email, with the expectation that the minor changes would be accepted and the deal completed.

He called Paul to inform that he had reviewed the papers. The two discussed the edits, and they reached a compromise. Instead of executing the edited documents, Paul created clean documents incorporating the agreed upon edits. He emailed them back for Harrington's final review and execution. In turn, Harrington reviewed and signed the new documents, and delivered back to Paul. Paul had been given power of attorney to act on behalf of Sylvie, and he was an authorized signer of the new corporation. Paul executed and sent the final documents back to Harrington. All parties now had agreed, executed, and had final documents. Harrington's arrangement with Sylvie had been completed.

It was ten o'clock on Monday morning in St. Thomas. Sylvie had not yet exited Eclipse to go through customs. Her cell phone rang and she reached over to answer, her voice still husky from the late night. "Good morning, Paul. It is great to hear from you. What's going on?"

"Sylvie, I have good news. I have been working with Harrington, and everything is complete. You are now the proud owner of DEP. Your company should continue to generate revenues for many years to come, and significant profits as well. In addition, the payment of the substantial sum is underway. Debi's companion Dean is aware and very appreciative of the opportunity. Because of your friendship with Debi, you are getting an exceptionally good deal. Of the six million dollars, 5.4 million will be available to you later this week."

"Paul, you are amazing! My plans are to share some of the money with various people, including you. Will you be able to handle that for me as well?"

"Absolutely, give some thought as to what you want distributed by name, and I will do the legwork to handle the distributions. I have another piece of good news. I have been assured that as of the end of today, you will have no future interactions with Robert Vaughn. I suggest you maintain a low profile for a few more hours, and then you should be able to resume your life as you see fit."

"I can't believe all this! This is just amazing! Thank you! Thank you! Thank you!"

"Now, if you'll humor me for one more minute. This is a very serious warning. You were very lucky. There are many things that could have gone wrong. Some of them did. And although you came out okay, there were several times that the outcome could have been deadly. My warning to you. Never attempt such a thing again. You won the lottery, enjoy it, but don't play the game ever again. And for your final warning, you are okay with Harrington, but if you give him even a hint that you could be trouble, I will not be able to help you. Do you understand?"

"Absolutely, I understand. I will do nothing to ever cross him again. And I will not dream up any more schemes for quick financial gain. I have as of this morning everything I could want. If it's okay, I'd like to call you back a little later once I've decided on the distribution amounts. I would like the distributions handled as quickly as possible."

"That would be fine. I'm available most of the day." With that, Paul and Sylvie ended their call.

Sylvie looked over at Brad. "Brad, I have reason for some more celebrating. Would you be interested in celebrating with me?"

"I can't think of anything I would like better. Are you about ready to go through customs?"

"I think customs can wait a little while longer. We could check with Keith and Terri, but I think they will tolerate quite well a little extra delay disembarking." The celebration began anew.

SIXTY-NINE

....

BEN WAS AWAKE early on Monday morning. He called Lauren and she immediately answered. "Good morning, Ben. I'm awake and ready for a great day! Are you rested and ready for me?"

"I just woke up but can be ready in no time. Do you have anything special you want to do today?"

"Whatever you want to do is fine with me. Should I come on over?"

"Sure, but only if you promise not to slow me down getting ready," he joked. "If you don't have anything special you'd like to do, I was thinking we could call the group at Islandtude. They would probably like to hear about the day yesterday and know that Sylvie and Terri made it safely on the sailboat out of St. Martin. Maybe we could go by the Croissanterie for breakfast and then visit with them later this morning. I'd like to come back to the beach, and maybe try Orange Fever for lunch like we talked about."

"That all sounds good. I'll come over now, and while you're getting ready, I can call Jeanne and Tammy and see if they'd mind us coming over. When we go by the Croissanterie, maybe we could carry breakfast with us for everybody."

"Sounds good. The door will be unlocked and I'll be in the shower. No peeking!"

They hung up and Lauren gathered her wallet, comb, sunglasses, suntan lotion and beach towel and put them in her beach bag. She went over to Ben's and sat on the bed to call Tammy.

"Good morning, Tammy. It's Lauren. I hope I'm not calling too early."

"No, everyone around here is an early riser. How are you?"

"We're great. Ben and I wanted to know if it would be okay if we invite ourselves over to your place this morning. We could be ready to leave in about fifteen minutes, and want to stop by the Croissanterie and bring breakfast for the group. Do you think that would be all right?"

"Yes, definitely. Everyone here would love for you to come over. Bringing breakfast will be a bonus. Maybe you could just get an assortment of croissants and everybody should be happy."

"Okay, we'll be over soon." Lauren was getting excited about the day. She was rested from finally getting a decent amount of sleep, and wanted to spend the day with Ben. Adding in the fun friends made it even better. She paused and decided she would be smart to make sure she did not disappoint Ben this early in the day. She cracked the bathroom door open and quietly opened it. Ben was in the shower with the towel draped over the glass shower door.

She walked next to the shower. "I talked to Tammy and they're expecting us to bring them breakfast soon. So don't be too long."

"Okay, I'm getting out."

He turned off the shower and looked to step out. Lauren was standing on the bath mat, bath towel in hand. "We don't have long, so I thought I could help out. Your drying service is here."

"This resort provides more services than advertised. If they marketed this, they would never have a vacancy." Ben stepped dutifully onto the mat and raised his hands out to his sides. "I'm not sure how this works, as I've never had a drying service before. So, if I'm doing anything wrong, let me know."

"No, that is perfect. My drying service is very serious about doing a good job. That's great how you have your arms raised to help. Try to relax, we don't have much time, but that won't stop me from being extremely thorough."

After being dried, Ben quickly shaved. He stepped to his suitcase and slipped on a pair of shorts and a t-shirt. He grabbed his wallet and sunglasses, and stuffed a towel into Lauren's beach bag.

"I think I'm ready. Thanks for the special drying service." He kissed her forehead as she beamed at him. "By the way, you look beautiful. Thanks for coming over. This is going to be an awesome day!"

They walked to Ben's car and Ben drove the fifteen minutes to the Croissanterie. About ten minutes later, Ben and Lauren were loaded down with croissants and on their way to Villa Islandtude. When they arrived, they noticed the sign requesting visitors ring the cow bell announcing their arrival. Lauren rang the bell, and Tammy looked over the railing from two stories above. "Come on up, the gate is unlocked."

Lauren and Ben walked up the stairs and were warmly greeted by the group of tiki hut friends. Tammy was first at the top of the stairs. "Welcome back to Villa Islandtude! It's great to see you again. Come on in!"

As everyone gathered around the outside table for breakfast, Ben shared his update. "We wanted to let you know how everything went yesterday for Sylvie and Terri. Lauren and I were with Sylvie and Terri and drove them to Simpson Bay Marina where Nico was waiting on his boat. We went about sixty miles offshore, halfway to St. Thomas, where Nico had arranged for a friend of his to meet us in his sailboat. Sylvie and Terri boarded the sailboat at sea, and were on their way to St. Thomas yesterday afternoon. They were expected to get there some time last night. They should be there now, and I'm hoping we'll hear from them today."

There were a lot of questions and discussion, and Lauren enjoyed reliving that leg of the adventure, as well as providing more details. Everyone finished breakfast and moved to the poolside lounge chairs.

Jeanne, as the president of the Northeast Florida Tiki Hut Association, held court. "I have a few announcements. First, on behalf of the Association, as new but privileged friends of Sylvie and Terri, we extend our thanks to you two for all you've done. Second, we are adding you to the membership list of our association as honorary members. Third, we have a serious request of you, Ben, that we'd like to discuss. But before we do that, as you know, our group is big on documenting events with pictures. We'd like to get a picture of you two poolside for our membership directory." Chris, Jeanne's husband, took the pictures of Ben and Lauren. "Next, we need a picture of the men of Islandtude. The men need to hop in the pool, line up on the far side with the mountain in the background, and face the camera for a picture. Chris, I'll relieve you of photographer duties."

The men, Chris, Mark, Dale, Paulie and Ben, all jumped in the pool and posed for the picture. Jeanne took several from different angles and proclaimed success. "Now, we need a picture of Lauren in the center of her tiki group sisters." Jeanne handed the photography duties back to Chris. Jeanne orchestrated the photo shoot, having them line up with first Catherine, then herself, Lauren in the middle, Tammy and finally Mary. They all submerged in the water, along the same place in the pool as had the men. Chris took what he hoped would be enough pictures to satisfy his wife.

After the photo session was completed, it was time to talk business. Jeanne acted again as the spokesperson. "Okay, as we all are here in this informal setting poolside, it is now time for new business in our meeting. Ben, we understand from our previous talks with Lauren, that you are in investments and have been successful in managing the money of a large insurance company. We don't have a lot of money, but we'd like you to become treasurer of our association and manage the association's money. We would also like you to consider investing for each of us individually. Would you be willing to do that for us?"

"I can certainly try to help you on an informal basis, and would be happy to share information that might be useful for you in managing your money."

"Thanks, we appreciate that. But I'm asking if we can make an official arrangement with you."

"Well, there are filings I'd need to make to become officially a money manager for you and the association. I don't know if I'd be able to do it officially, but am happy to help however I can."

"Ben," Lauren interjected, "when I met you, you said you were tired of your job and didn't know what you would do next. It might take a little time, but maybe this is just what you're looking for. You could do whatever is needed to register as an investment advisor, and begin investing for individuals and companies instead of for the insurance company. I can help by looking into the legal requirements for you to get started. This might be just what you are meant to do."

Ben paused and looked at each of them. "I'll give it some thought. Even if I were to say yes, it would take some time to get everything in order. I'll help as I can, and will let you know if or when I'm able to do more. As the newly elected or appointed treasurer of the association, whichever it may be, I suggest we move from this business portion of the meeting back to having fun!"

"As president of the Association, we will accept Ben's recommendation, noting for the minutes Ben's position as Treasurer, his willingness to manage money, and that we will be looking to hear more soon on his official role. With that, I open the floor for any final comments."

Lauren spoke up again. "Ben and I have a lunch planned today at Orange Fever on Orient Beach. As the newest member of the Association, I suggest we all head over to Orient for the rest of the day, with a leisurely lunch at Orange Fever."

"That sounds great," said Tammy. "If there is no opposition, let's end this meeting and get ready to go to Orient." Everyone acknowledged an end to the pretend meeting by beginning to gather their items needed for a day on Orient. Within fifteen minutes, they were all ready and loading into their cars. It looked to be another beautiful day for fun at Orient Beach.

SEVENTY

IT WAS NEAR lunch time on Monday and Sylvie, Terri, Brad and Keith had all cleared customs in St. Thomas. They arranged for a hotel, and planned to check out on Tuesday. Sylvie and Terri were checking flights to fly home and Brad and Keith were going to continue their sail to Florida. Once they checked in, Sylvie had an opportunity for privacy and decided to call Paul.

"Paul, this is Sylvie. Thank you again for all your help. I'd like to discuss with you distributing some of the $5.4 million. First, what are the charges for everything for you and your team of attorneys or whoever that have been doing work?"

"For all of my consultants, and those who will need a little cash to make certain all records are as needed, so that there will never be any questions, will take about a hundred grand."

"Okay, that seems fair. That leaves me with $5.3 million. I want to share a meaningful amount with you and Ben, another sizable amount with Nico, something for the group who took me in at the villa, a little something for Debi and Lauren, and then a splitting of what's left with my good friend Terri. Any suggestions?"

"That's a lot of gifts you want to make. But please, with the payment of a hundred grand, I will have been appropriately compensated. For the others, I suggest you let your conscience be your guide. Most people, upon receiving a large sum, would be talking themselves out of sharing despite any prior intentions."

"I don't want to fall into that category. No matter what I share with you and Ben, it is arguably too little as I literally owe my life to the two of you. Maybe I can back into the amounts. I'd like to be left with about two million, with Terri to receive a comparable two million. That leaves $1.3 million to still be distributed. If Debi gets a hundred, and Lauren gets a hundred, I still have $1.1 million to distribute. I'd like two hundred thousand to go to the tikiers as a group, and hold a hundred back to pay for an all expenses return for them to St. Martin for a vacation on me. That leaves eight hundred. I'd like for Nico to get two hundred, and you and Ben to each have three hundred. Would you be able to make those distributions for me?"

"That is very generous, and I thank you very much. I'm sure the others will be overwhelmed. I will be happy to make sure the distributions are made. I'll reach out to each and coordinate with them how to best make it happen."

"That is fantastic. If you'll let them know, you can pass along the information on my behalf. You can let them all know that Terri and I are doing great, but that we are trying to make our arrangements home. I'll be reaching out to everybody in a few days." Paul was happy to be the messenger and after assuring her that he would take care of things, ended the call.

Sylvie looked at Terri, who had walked in during the conversation. "Terri, I don't know if you heard, but Paul will be arranging for you and me to each get two million dollars! Can you believe it?"

"Are you serious? That is an amazing amount of money. I can't believe it. Are you sure you want to do that?"

"Absolutely, and tonight the four of us are celebrating on me. I'll be having money come in from a company that I now own, so I should be getting a substantial amount more over time."

Terri squealed, jumped in place, and uttered unintelligible words. She was overwhelmed. She hugged Sylvie, broke the hug, and did it again and again. "This is crazy. I know we were planning on flying home tomorrow, but what about us staying in St. Thomas for a few days? That would be my treat on the money you're giving me."

"That's a deal," Sylvie said without hesitation. "Maybe we can convince the guys to take us sailing for a few days before we fly back."

"I think they'll agree to that. Sylvie, I'm picturing them on the boat and you and me, just like yesterday, serving them drinks! A number of rounds of drinks! This is going to be another vacation that might be life changing! Who knows, you may be living on a sailboat for a lot longer than a few days!"

"I could see myself living on Eclipse with Brad. Let's go talk to them and let them think it's their idea that we stay a few extra days on the sailboat with them."

Brad and Keith had never met anyone like Sylvie and Terri. They were overwhelmed when the girls agreed to stay onboard the sailboat for several more days. It was a great decision Brad and Keith thought they had made.

The foursome continued to enjoy each other's company. They sailed to deserted Caribbean beaches during the day, and went into St. Thomas at night to take advantage of the food and nightlife. They were all living a dream made possible by Sylvie's escape in the islands.

SEVENTY-ONE

....

PAUL BEGAN MAKING calls to each of the beneficiaries, informing of Sylvie's charity. He called Ben and reached him on the beach. "Hey Paul, Lauren and I are at Orient today. If you and Lisa are free, we'd love for you to join us. We're here with the group from Islandtude."

"Thanks, but I'm doing a little work today. I have some good news I'd like to share with you. It might be fine for those around you to overhear, but I suggest you step away a short distance where we can talk. Then, you can share as you see fit."

"Okay, let me call you right back." Ben hung up and turned to the group. "I need to take a call. I'm going to step up away from the water a little further for the call and will be back in a few minutes." He walked away from the group and dialed Paul. "Okay, I'm good now. What's going on?"

"This has to do with Sylvie. Good news this time. She and Terri are safely in St. Thomas. She is receiving a nice sum of money, and is feeling charitable. She's elected to gift you three hundred thousand dollars, and is making an equal gift to me."

"Oh my gosh. Is that something I can accept? I'm in investments, could this possibly get me kicked out of ever working in the investments industry?"

"Not a chance, Ben. I've handled everything. The money you're receiving is one hundred percent clean. There can never be a problem. I think you'll have access to the money by Friday."

"She kept saying she was going to reward me, but I didn't really think I would get anything, especially nothing substantial. Besides, I really didn't want anything."

"Well, you've got it. Do with it as you wish. If you want to be charitable and give it all away, you can certainly do that. While I've got you on the phone, you're making my job easy for me. Sylvie is also giving a hundred thousand to Lauren. You can let her know to be expecting it."

"We've got to be equally careful with her. She's finishing up law school. I don't want her disbarred before she even graduates!"

"Not a problem. It's a gift. Every dollar is clean. There is nothing wrong with her getting the money. I suggest you tell her about it, and it will be easy for you to do so privately, because I'm going to ask you to hand your phone over to Jeanne. Sylvie has made a gift to the group through the Northeast Florida Tiki Hut Association where they can divide the money any way they wish. In addition, Sylvie is offering an all-expense paid vacation for the group if they choose to return to St. Martin. I'm guessing they will be happy to accept that offer."

"Sylvie was very generous. Do you mind telling me any other amounts?"

"The majority is being retained by Sylvie and Terri. They will be splitting four million dollars equally. This is not all of Sylvie's newfound wealth, however. She now has ownership of a small oil company worth about ten million dollars. I plan to recommend that she hire you for financial advice with her money and for the new company.

Think about it and let me know if you would be interested in negotiating a deal."

"This is a lot to take in. Only a couple hours ago I was asked to manage money for their association and for their individual members. Now I could be asked to manage several more million. Today is giving me a lot to think about."

"When opportunity knocks, smart people don't delay for long. I recommend you think quickly."

Ben walked back to the group. "Jeanne, this is Paul for you. I'll leave my phone with you. Lauren, why don't you dip in the water with me while they talk." They edged into the water while Paul delivered the news and congratulated Jeanne on the gift from Sylvie to the Association.

Ben shared with Lauren the news of her windfall.

"You're kidding! She's giving me a large amount of money? Why?"

"It's true, Paul just told me. She's giving money to her friends, including giving me three hundred thousand. She's giving three hundred to Paul also, with the two of us getting larger sums for saving her life. I've quizzed Paul and emphasized to him that neither of us can participate in any illegal transfers of money. He assured me that the money is rightfully Sylvie's to give. You'll need to be comfortable with whatever you decide to do. Now, let's enjoy floating in the Caribbean while we wait for Jeanne to finish talking with Paul."

After Jeanne finished the call with Paul, she held Ben's phone until Lauren and Ben rejoined them on shore. "What a call! It looks like we'll be back for a vacation paid for by Sylvie. We'll be planning our next trip on the flight back!" She told the others about Sylvie's generous gift.

After more excited chatter, the group, wearing swim trunks and coverups, walked to Orange Fever for lunch. The celebratory mood was enhanced by the outstanding food. Jeanne asked the waiter to take a photo of the group. "Just a minute," she said. She then drew two huge dollar signs in the sand in front of their large table. "Okay, now snap the picture." The lunch celebrating the large gifts was officially recorded.

As the afternoon drew to a close, the group staying at Villa Islandtude packed up for the drive back. After the last hugs were done, Lauren and Ben were left alone for the last of the afternoon sun. After the sun had set, Ben and Lauren continued to sit on the beach outside their rooms. "This has been another crazy day," Lauren began. "It's too much for me to process everything. A lot of new friends, a windfall of cash, an amazing tropical setting, and spending another great day with you. It's overwhelming." Although Lauren's words conveyed that she was overjoyed, she instead appeared somewhat wistful.

"It's certainly been an amazing day, and a vacation of a lifetime. I agree, it's a lot to take in. I've got a lot of thinking to do on what comes next for me. I was tired of my job when I left for vacation, but making a job change to a whole new way of life is a huge step. I've complained, but I'm not sure I'm really ready to make such a big change."

The enthusiasm of both Lauren and Ben was tempered. "Lauren, why don't we go in and get ready for a super meal tonight. Where would you like to eat?"

"Why don't we try Chesterfield's? I saw it on Jeff Berger's Everything St. Martin site, and it looked like it would be a great choice with a variety of seafood."

"That's good with me. When you're ready, we can get cleaned up and go to Chesterfield's." They sat quietly on the beach for a bit longer, then went to prepare for dinner.

At seven-thirty, they were seated at Chesterfield's. The mood remained more somber than celebratory. At the conclusion of the meal, Lauren looked at Ben and her eyes reflected that she was troubled. "Lauren, what's wrong? You don't seem to be having as much fun as I would have thought."

"Well, everything is fine, for sure. The food is really good, and the view is beautiful. Today has been an incredible day. But I think, when we got the call and everyone was getting money, instead of being one more unbelievably good thing, it somehow emphasized that none of this is real. It's been an amazing vacation, and I don't know that if I live another hundred years, I could have another vacation to match this one. But it's about to end, and I have to hitch a ride on the pumpkin when this fairy tale ends. I have a real life that I'll be returning to. I'm just starting out and have dreams of a successful career that's not even started. I don't know how living a fantasy life for two weeks fits realistically into whatever happens next. And as much as I've loved our time together, you have a life outside of St. Martin, too. It's a lot that has unfortunately started weighing on me. I'm sorry."

Ben could not think of a comforting response. "I understand. We each have a lot to think about. Let's head back and try to let another day take care of itself. This is a special place and a special time, and you deserve to fully enjoy every minute of it."

They drove back to the resort, both lost in their thoughts.

SEVENTY-TWO

....

IT WAS AFTER noon and Dean was missing Debi. He had not heard from her following the meeting where she introduced Rick. He decided he could not wait any longer for Debi to call him. He dialed her and was relieved when she answered. "Good afternoon, Dean. It's good to hear from you."

"Hey, Debi. I have news that I imagine you've probably already heard from Paul. We are handling six million dollars from your friend, and the retention has been greatly reduced on the friends and family plan to only ten percent. Of that, I instructed Paul to set up an account in your name funded with half a million. It is the first step of my memorializing our new partnership and the continuation of our relationship. I want to celebrate with you at dinner tonight. Would it be okay for me to pick you up at six?"

"I'll be ready. If you don't have too much work this afternoon, you might want to take out time for a short nap. I'm ready to celebrate, and I hope you will be, too. I look forward to seeing you at six."

Dean could not stop smiling. He was addicted to Debi and was desperate for a fix. Just the sound of her voice excited him. She was the perfect combination of business and pleasure.

While Dean resumed his work for the afternoon, Debi went with Jodi and Jan to the beach. They went to a beautiful stretch of beach on Simpson Bay and grabbed some chairs at the Karakter Beach Bar and Restaurant. "Girls, today is on me. I think we each need a beach massage. Jodi, Jan, would you be interested in getting a massage?"

The massage service at Karakter had several masseuses, and all three were able to have relaxing massages at the same time. Jodi and Jan were enjoying glasses of white wine, while Debi resisted and stuck with water. She wanted to be ready for her evening with Dean. They stayed on the beach only until four o'clock, as Debi wanted an early start on getting ready for her evening. They went back to the Royal Palm. Debi selected her dress and shoes, and was confident Dean would not be disappointed. She was ready and waiting for Dean when he arrived.

"Good evening, Debi. You look stunning." Dean greeted Debi with a kiss at the door. "Are you ready for a great evening?"

"I'm ready. Where are we eating tonight?"

"I made reservations at Vesna's for six-thirty. She has some of the best food on the island. It is in Simpson Bay and close to the house. When the meal ends, I don't want the trip to the house to take longer than necessary."

Vesna greeted Dean and Debi warmly when they arrived at her restaurant. She showed them to a prime table tucked away near the wine door. The meal began with a bottle of wine brought to the table. They each ordered salads and entrees of filets with mushroom sauce, but chose not to order dessert and skipped after dinner drinks. They thanked Vesna for the amazing meal as they eagerly stepped out to the car.

Dean drove them the few minutes to Dean's rental house. They walked through the house and sat in poolside chairs. Debi dipped her toes in the pool, and discovered in addition to being beautiful, it was heated. She lifted her dress over her head and draped it on her chair, then made a splashless dive into the pool. When she surfaced, she swam to the pool's edge near Dean, and rested her arms on the pool deck. "Why don't you get us two towels and join me?"

Dean hurried to grab two beach towels and set them at the edge of the pool. He followed her instructions and joined her soon after in the pool. Dean was rewarded for his obedience.

Debi stepped out of the pool and dried on one of the beach towels. "I'll be right back." She stepped into the house, and returned with two glasses, a Canadian whiskey for Dean and a glass of white wine for her. She set them on the edge of the pool, then slipped back into the water. When the glasses were empty, Debi again stepped out of the pool and brought them new drinks. This time she set them at the pool steps, where they enjoyed the drinks and each other's company.

"Dean, why don't we take a short break inside?" They stepped out of the pool, dried, and went inside. They sat together on the couch, and it was time to have a business discussion.

"Debi, thank you for arranging the new business. I hope you're pleased that half a million dollars that you earned is being set up in your account. In addition, I am now expecting business from Gregorio Harrington, which is business you are indirectly responsible for introducing to me. I understand your needs, and I hope you accept my setting up the account for you as my commitment for you to be my partner in every way. I am pursuing dissolution of the marriage. For it to be done quickly, I have already proposed mediation. If we agree, the mediator will file a petition for divorce on behalf of both spouses and the divorce will be granted with little delay. I want to avoid a very ugly and public process that could be damaging. I'm hopeful a settlement will be reached soon for the joint filing, and I will keep you updated. Until it is final, the financial arrangements I've made for your benefit are my commitment to you that it will be done."

Debi liked everything she heard. She was good at reading people, and she knew Dean was telling her the truth. "Dean, I appreciate your willingness for our mutual commitment, and the steps that you've taken." She paused and gave him a passionate kiss. She stood and grabbed one of his hands in hers. "Now, let's go back to the pool."

Tuesday morning at six-thirty Dean was asleep when his phone rang. He saw who the caller was and answered. "Good morning Gregorio. To what do I owe this pleasure?"

Gregorio Harrington was an early riser and had been up for an hour. "I have a proposition for you, Dean. I have been spending time with someone who recently moved to the island. She is interested in meeting others and adjusting to island life. Would you and a lady friend be able to meet at the beach today? Perhaps my friend, Michele, could begin a new friendship while you and I talk about business opportunities."

"Gregorio, thank you for the call. I have a new partner who I think would enjoy meeting Michele, and of course I am interested in discussing mutually beneficial business. Perhaps we can meet around nine o'clock this morning?"

"That would be perfect. We'll be at Orient Beach in the vicinity of where Pedro's was before Hurricane Irma. We'll look to meet you there." They ended the call.

"Debi, my dear, are you up for a day on the beach with me where we meet Gregorio and Michele?"

"Spending the day at the beach is always a great idea. I want to go by the Royal Palm to get a swimsuit and coverup. Maybe I can convince you to take me to breakfast on the way to the Royal Palm?" Dean was easily convinced.

SEVENTY-THREE

....

LAUREN AND BEN were beginning their last full day in St. Martin. They stopped at the Papatwo for a breakfast of croissants and pancakes. The food was good, and they were ready for a walk. They walked past La Playa, reminiscing about their time with Sylvie and Terri. "Ben, I guess Sylvie and Terri are either still enjoying St. Thomas today or on their way home. I'm glad I've got another full day today. I called my friend Deana. She's the one I drove to the airport when we first met, and I shared a little of my adventures with her. Some of what's happened is probably better never mentioned other than with those who already know." Ben agreed.

"So, what will you do on Thursday when you're back in Florida?"

"Well, I guess I'll start by going through a ton of emails. I'll be taking it easy in the market for a few days after being away. I'll make some calls to brokers I do business with, and probably spend Thursday and Friday trying to catch up. I'll recover over the weekend, and guess I'll be ready to hit it hard on Monday." They continued to walk in silence. "I know it's close to time for us to leave the island, but I don't really want to talk about it. Let's make a pact. No more talking about it for the rest of the day." Lauren nodded her agreement.

After their walk, they found two chairs and secured their towels to the chairs. They chose not to bring books, but planned to talk, swim and focus on the beautiful setting. Around eight-thirty Lauren spotted Michele and waved. They walked over to meet her. "Hey, Michele, you're here early today."

"Yes, Gregorio is habitually an early riser, and if I'm spending time with him, I have to be prepared for an early start. Lauren and Ben, I'd like to introduce you to Gregorio. Gregorio, I met Ben and Lauren here and they posed for a number of photos for me. They are two of the first friends I made on the island."

"Good to meet you."

They talked for a few minutes, primarily between Lauren and Michele. All of a sudden, Lauren squealed in delight. "Hey, look Ben, it's Debi." Lauren waved and rushed over to meet Debi as she and Dean continued walking toward Michele and Gregorio. Lauren and Debi greeted each other with a big hug. They continued walking, stopping to set up next to Gregorio and Michele. Introductions were made all around.

"Lauren, we should head back to our chairs." Ben addressed the others. "Come by and see us. Let us know if you'd like to join us for lunch." Ben took Lauren by the hand and led her away. He then began talking just to Lauren. "I believe Gregorio arranged to meet Dean to talk business. I thought it best we came back to our chairs. I was happy they wanted to visit with us, but I don't want to interfere in whatever they may have planned." Lauren squeezed Ben's hand in understanding and agreement. They enjoyed chatting at their chairs, but primarily spent the rest of the morning in the water. At noon, Michele and Debi joined them in the water, and after a few minutes, Ben decided to let them continue talking while he took a walk.

Ben began the normal walk on the beach, but had no plan to walk the full length of the crescent. As he neared Gregorio and Dean, Dean signaled him over. "Ben, the girls are enjoying their time together today. I have heard a lot about you and your financial prowess from Debi. I'm not ready to make an offer, but before I spend a lot of time on the possibility, would you be interested if I have a need for someone to help with financial advice and manage money for me?"

Ben was stunned at the question. He did not know Dean, and was apprehensive to the point of being fearful of Gregorio. He did not know if the question included Gregorio, or was just for Dean.

"Well, as you can probably tell from my reaction, I was not expecting such a question. I fly back to Florida tomorrow. I appreciate even the thought of being considered for such a role, but I am not looking to make a change, and if at some point I did, it would be after much thought. I have a few things to think about on the plane tomorrow. I don't want to intrude on your talks, so I'll finish my walk and be going back to my chair. I'm planning on having lunch with Lauren soon, so anyone interested is invited to join us." Ben walked away and shortly returned to his chair.

Lauren saw Ben had returned and waved him into the water. He eagerly splashed out to her and gave her a big hug. "I've only been gone a few minutes, but I missed you." He planted a big kiss on her lips and hugged her again.

"Wow, maybe you should take more walks. I like it. Are you about ready for lunch?"

"Yes, that would be great. Debi, Michelle, would you like to do lunch with us? Maybe Gregorio and Dean would be willing to join."

"Yes, we would. I'm answering for Dean," replied Debi. If he acts hesitant like a party pooper, I will convince him to think a little more if he wants to make me happy."

She grinned, then gave a look that was convincing of her persuasive skills.

"I don't know if my standing with Gregorio has reached that of Debi with Dean, but I'm trying to get there. When he suggested we come to the beach today, I was encouraged that I'm making headway to getting there. I think he likes Leandra's. Would you guys be okay eating there?" They all agreed, with Lauren and Ben going back to their chairs to await a sign, and Michelle and Debi began sashaying over to Gregorio and Dean. Debi and Michelle waived them over and they all walked together to Leandra's.

Lunch passed quickly with no discussion of business. Debi and Michelle used their natural born skills to work their dates. Ben believed Gregorio and Dean to be ruthless businessmen, but saw Michelle and Debi as poised to exert much influence over them. Lauren recognized it, too, and shared a knowing grin with Ben. The afternoon slipped away with most time spent as couples. At the end of the day, the others left the beach, leaving Ben and Lauren with their last late afternoon and evening there. It had been a great trip, but now it was coming to a close.

SEVENTY-FOUR

WEDNESDAY HAD COME too quickly. Ben and Lauren were at the airport waiting for their flights, Ben to Miami and Lauren to Charlotte. Also at the Princess Juliana Airport was Debi. Rick and Karen wished her a safe flight. They were going back to Cupecoy for one more day before they would be going back to the U.S. Debi promised Dean she would return to St. Maarten in several weeks after tying up loose ends at her home. She was prepared to turn her next visit into permanent residency in St. Maarten, which was also dependent on the complete resolution of Dean's past relationship. The large group from the Northeast Florida Tiki Hut Association was also in the airport. Their flight was scheduled to go through Fort Lauderdale on their way to Jacksonville, Florida. They had made tentative plans to return to St. Maarten in July, accepting Sylvie's charitable offer of funding the trip. Nico called Ben, wishing both Lauren and him safe travels. He looked forward to seeing them both again soon. Lauren then called Sylvie. Sylvie and Terri were spending a few more nights in St. Thomas. They planned to return to St. Martin several more times during the coming year.

"Ben, it's the time I've been dreading. I'm about to board for Charlotte, and you're heading to Miami. I'm feeling sick," she said, tears streaming down her face.

Ben looked at Lauren, his eyes watering, unable to speak. Instead, he gave her his biggest hug. They broke the hug as Ben's group was called for boarding. "I'll call you. We'll work this out. Have a safe trip." He turned to board, his emotions preventing him from saying anything more.

"I love you, Ben," Lauren said after he had left the gate. "I hope it's enough."

CPSIA information can be obtained
at www.ICGtesting.com
Printed in the USA
LVHW100212281121
704648LV00015B/895